Praise for *The Mortsafeman Trilogy*

Book One: Dead Scared
In this gloriously macabre novel—the first installment of a series—
Blake channels Stephen King and 1980s cult films like *Re-Animator*.
Fans should claw at Blake's windows for more graveyard tales after
this delightful series opener. —*Kirkus Reviews*

An intense and brooding tale that delivers . . . plot had me instantly
hooked . . . writing is often lyrically lovely, but this never gets in the
way of the action and horror that this book is steeped in. Most highly
recommended. —*Readers' Favorite*

Book Two: Dead Silent
Quite the gift, complete with a black bow, to horror fans . . . [Dead
Silent] juggles the Gothic New England ambiance, the parade of sleazy
characters, and the occasional supernatural mauling with panache. . . .
A ghoulish gem for those continuing—or new to—this series.
—*Kirkus Reviews*

A monstrously good romp. One of the best horror/dark fantasy series
I've come across in some time. An awesomely dark and mind-expand-
ing piece of thinking man's horror. Most highly recommended.
—*Readers' Favorite*

Ivan Blake excels in crafting enjoyable, seat-of-your-pants, high-oc-
tane tension. Readers who like fast-paced horror with a big dose of history and mystery, and who can't get enough intrigue and deadly
encounters will find *Dead Silent* heady, engrossing, and nearly impossible to put down. —*Midwest Book Review*

Book Three: Dead Reckoning
Blake knows how to build up a story and have readers rocking on the
edge of their seats until the bitter end! . . . I would certainly recommend
Dead Reckoning to fans of the existing series, and to any reader seeking
a psychological, fulfilling, and bone-shaking horror story with com-
plexity and genuine terror.
—Award-winning author, K.C. Finn for *Readers' Favorite*

Books by Ivan Blake

The Mortsafeman Trilogy
Dead Sacred
Dead Silent
Dead Reckoning

Coming Soon!
Earthedge
The Man Who Made an Angel

**For more information
visit:** www.SpeakingVolumes.us

Dead Reckoning

The Mortsafeman
Book Three

SPEAKING VOLUMES, LLC
NAPLES, FLORIDA
2023

Dead Reckoning

ISBN 978-1-64540-921-2

Dead Reckoning

The Mortsafeman
Book Three

Ivan Blake

For my dad, Kenneth William Blake
1921 - 2013

Acknowledgments

Dead Reckoning is a work of fiction. Although I have drawn upon several notable historical figures in concocting the story, the events and principal characters are entirely imaginary. For example, Rabbi Eliyahu ben Aharon Yehudah (Chief Rabbi of Chelm from 1550 to 1583) was in his time a very highly regarded scholar and man of faith. He was also said to have made a golem. Nothing in my description of his actions, however, is based on historical fact. Nor is my account intended in any way to demean his merits as a religious leader.

As for the setting of Dead Reckoning, it is deliberately noir. After all, this is a tale of horror and the supernatural. That said, I feel compelled to apologize to the city of Halifax, Nova Scotia. The grand old seaport is, in fact, richly historic, charming, and endlessly fascinating, and the weather is nowhere near as awful as I've suggested.

I must also say something about Cavendish College. Its physical appearance is based very loosely on a real university in Halifax, but that's where any similarity ends. The actual university is a remarkable institution, centuries old, with innovative programs and affiliations to rival some of the finest schools in the world.

And finally, I want to acknowledge the help of several friends in completing this book. My writing circle, Wendy Patterson, Jason MacDonald, and Monica Furness, have once again provided terrific guidance in rounding out the book's characters and plot. Rachel Eugster provided a wealth of insightful editorial comment and indispensable guidance on the depiction of the Judaic elements. And, of course, I'm so grateful to my wife who continues to support my writing and permit me the time and space to pound out my stories. I absolutely could not do this without her endless patience and invaluable help.

These are the twenty-two letters
with which engraved Ehyeh Yah, YHVH Elohim, YHVH,
YHVH Tzavaot, Elohim Tzavaot, El Shaddai,
YHVH Adonoy,
And with them He made three Books,
and with them He created His Universe,
and He formed with them all that was ever formed,
and all that ever will be formed.
From the *Sefer Yetzirah, The Book of Formation 6:6*[1]

Raba bar Rav Huna said: If the righteous desired it, they could—by living a life of absolute purity—be creators, for so it is written. But for your iniquities, your power would equal God's, and you could create a world....

Raba created a man and sent him to Rav Zeira. Rav Zeira spoke to him, but received no answer. Thereupon he said unto him, 'Thou art a creature of the magicians. Return to thy dust....'
Rav Hanina and Rav Oshaia spent every Sabbath eve in studying the 'Book of Formation', by means of which they created a third-grown calf and ate it.
From the *Babylonian Talmud: Tractate Sanhedrin 65b*[2]

I fear our departed, those whom we purport to have loved and revered, may one day line our own path to Paradise to greet us, not with flowers but with rage. Baying like hawkers at a bazaar, they may scream their anger, their anguish, and their demands for redress. They will shriek like banshees the many ways we wronged them after their passing— our denigration of their lives, our corruption and loss of their memory, and our desecration and destruction of their graves. The most pitiful pleas, the most harrowing tales, the most grievous injuries, all shall be heard and weighed in the balance. And those of us who owe the most appalling debt to our forebears will be turned away from Paradise without pity or recourse.

Dead Reckoning: On the honor, glory, and gratitude we owe our dearly departed
Selected Sermons of the Reverend Michael Ainsley Tiltwhistle, unpublished
Church of Saint Mildred and the Paupers
Parish of Tonnesworth by the Tarn

Prologue

Chelm, Poland 1570

The synagogue door flew open. A gust of raw night air carried several of Rabbi Eliyahu's pages from his worktable and away into the shadows.

"*Rebbe*," the portly chaver gasped as he staggered down the aisle, panting and wheezing from his mad rush across the ghetto, "Rebbe, you must come. Your creature has left the market."

"That's not possible," the rabbi replied as he snatched up several folio sheets from the dust.

"But it has," the chaver said, still struggling to breathe. "It left on its own."

The rabbi's interest in his papers evaporated. "I don't believe it. The creature can only move on my command."

"Rebbe, I swear, the creature has left its place by the meat seller. It's wandering about the quarter. The sexton is following it and bade me fetch you."

Rabbi Eliyahu flew to the cupboard for his cloak, shouting as he ran. "But it's forbidden to move, except to protect those of our faith. Was someone in danger?"

A rhetorical question. Someone in the community was always in danger. After nearly four hundred years of existence, the Jewish congregation of Chelm still numbered fewer than 40 households, and King Sigismund Augustus had only recently granted it the privilege of trading with gentiles along the Uhreka River. Yet the Russian Orthodox locals were already resentful of the community's early successes in this enterprise and never missed an opportunity to vent their bitterness and suspicions.

Despite his youth, Eliyahu ben Aharon Yehudah—"Elijah son of Aaron Judah"—was the spiritual leader of the community. He was also one of the most prominent Talmudic scholars and Kabbalists in Poland's eastern province. Eliyahu had already earned the title *Baëal Shem*, a designation conferred upon especially pious figures possessing secret knowledge of the holy names of God. He'd confirmed the title's aptness when, after a series of bloody attacks on his congregation, the rabbi crafted a creature from the mud of the Uhreka River to protect Jews and intimidate Gentiles who might try to disrupt their market.

Before dawn each market day, the rabbi marched his monstrous creation with an enormous ax in its hand to the square where it stood motionless by the butcher's shop for hours. No one lingered near the giant figure, with its dead eyes and limbs as hard as stone, since it stank of the mud and blood from which Rabbi Eliyahu had formed it. Even dogs shied away from its stench.

At the end of the trading day, when the streets were dark and still and only malingerers might be abroad, the rabbi walked his creature back to the *Beit Hamidrash*, the tiny house next to the new synagogue where the rabbi tended to his congregation. The beast climbed into the attic, there to await the next market day. Sometimes, when the rabbi got wind of an impending attack upon his community, he would lead the creature in a night-long march through the streets of the Jewish quarter. The beast might terrify and intimidate, but it had never before moved of its own volition, never mind strayed from the Jewish quarter. So why now?

"I don't understand," the rabbi muttered as he buttoned his cape. "Surely the hour for its return to the *Hamidrash* is not yet come?"

"It is long past, *Rebbe*," the chaver replied.

Rabbi Eliyahu had been so wrapped up in writing to his teacher, Rabbi Solomon Luria of Lublin, that he'd lost track of time. What a fool he was. He should long since have escorted the creature from the market, but in his selfish preoccupation, the rabbi had forgotten all about his ghastly creation.

The following spring, Rabbi Eliyahu was to host a gathering of prominent rabbis from all over Poland. He and Rabbi Luria planned to propose the passage of the *piske dinim* allowing an *agunah* to remarry. The *piske dinim* would be the crowning achievement of his career, and his correspondence on the topic had so preoccupied him that he'd entirely forgotten his creature.

"God forgive my prideful arrogance," he muttered under his breath. "Did anyone try to stop it?" the rabbi asked as he knotted a scarf around his neck.

"Yes, several of us, but it pushed past like we were nothing and walked on. A poor woman encountered the creature in a narrow alley where she had the misfortune to become trapped between it and the stone wall. The monster stumbled against her and crushed her arm. Her cries have drawn a large crowd into the streets."

The rabbi pulled open the synagogue door. "Is it coming this way?"

"No. It's wandering, sometimes in circles. I fear it may already have left our quarter."

"Get the cart from the shed behind the synagogue," the rabbi shouted as he ran off into the dark, "and . . . and bring a hammer. I'll meet you in the market square. We'll start our search for the creature there."

Rabbi Eliyahu raced through the maze of darkened lanes to the now-empty square. There he stood for a moment, feeling helpless and confused, dread coursing through his veins like ice water. He waved his arms in the air, cursed his negligence, and implored God to end the night without any more bloodshed. Then, from the direction of the river, he heard the cries and shouts of the creature's pursuers echoing through the narrow alleys. He dashed off again and, after a time, caught up to the creature and the dozen people trailing it. They shouted their prayers and supplications to the creature and implored it to stop, but it lurched onward undeterred.

Monstrously tall, the creature was stiff, inflexible, as if in the throes of *rigor mortis*. Its face lacked any features save for two eye sockets and two nostrils. Rocking from side to side as it staggered forward, neither the creature's arms nor its legs appeared to have joints. The monstrosity bore no anatomical detail of any sort, except for a horn-like lump in the center of its forehead.

The rabbi shouted to the creature to stop, but it paid him no mind. His cries did, however, silence the crowd and it dutifully fell in behind him.

The wagon pulled by the chaver rumbled up alongside Rabbi Eli-yahu. The rabbi grabbed the hammer from the cart and worked his way around the creature to stand in its path. He called out, "Aron, Aron, listen to me. I'm sorry I wasn't there at dusk. You must have been so confused. But I'm here now. Can you hear me?"

The creature stopped and looked down at the rabbi. It rocked back and forth as if it might topple at any moment. Behind the thick mask of dried mud that passed for its face, the creature's eyes appeared moist with tears. The ax which it carried in its left hand fell from its grasp. Some of the clay that caked the creature's hands had cracked and crumbled away, and beneath the broken mud, patches of raw muscle and sinew glistened. The creature raised its right hand toward the rabbi in seeming supplication. Mud cracked and fell from its elbow and shoulder. The hand trembled. More shards of clay fell from its fingers. The nightmare beneath bore no flesh, merely tendons, and bone. The creature raised the hand slowly to its face and suddenly struck the space where there should have been a mouth. More clay cracked, bits fell away, and two rows of rotted teeth without lips appeared.

"Going mad, *Rebbe*," the creature muttered in a dry, rasping voice that seemed not to have emitted sound in many months. "Going mad."

"Hush, Aron. You're going to rest now. We're going home."

Rabbi Eliyahu moved cautiously toward the creature, and then, in one sudden movement, he swung the hammer toward the creature's forehead, striking the knob at its center, shattering it.

The creature toppled backward. The crowd screamed and scrambled clear of the monster as it fell, parts of the creature shattering like unfired pottery as it crashed to the cobblestones.

The rabbi leaped on the creature and pulled from the shattered knob on its forehead a folded piece of vellum which he quickly thrust into the pocket of his cape. A thin stream of blood also issued from the hole in the creature's forehead. Rabbi Eliyahu tried to climb from the beast's chest, but before he could struggle clear, the monster's arm struck him across the face, crushing his cheek. He screamed in agony and rolled away, but the arm continued to wave in the air, pieces of dried mud falling away to reveal only tendon and bone beneath.

Even though he was spitting blood from his injured mouth, the rabbi managed to cry out to the sexton and the chaver, "Cover him, for God's sake, cover him."

The chaver grabbed a canvas from the cart and tossed it across the creature as the elderly sexton helped Rabbi Eliyahu to his feet.

The rabbi turned from the crowd of onlookers and whispered to the chaver, "Get him into the cart and take him back to the *Beit Hamidrash*. And if he stirs, you are not to speak to him no matter what he might say. Do you understand? If he speaks, you are to strike him again on the head. Hard! And then you must put him in the attic and bolt the door. Clear? Bolt the door and let no one see him. Bring me the key.

And you must do all this as fast as you can. I will join you at the synagogue presently."

As he watched the cart rumble away down the alley, Rabbi Eliyahu drew the folded vellum from his coat pocket and wiped from it the last of the dried mud and dust. Carefully, so as not to tear it, he unfolded the vellum, read it to himself, refolded it, and pressed it to his heart. He reached inside his shirt and drew forth a medallion from around his neck.

Perhaps two inches across, the medallion was cast in bronze and engraved with *Malachim* or archangels. On one side, it bore Gabriel signifying the tribe of Judah, and on the other, the remaining three archangels Michael, Uriel and Raphael.

For a moment, the rabbi struggled to loosen the two halves, but then he broke their seal and carefully unscrewed the one half from the other. He withdrew a tiny sketch of his beloved mother, which he kissed and slipped into his pocket. Then he placed the folded vellum in the medallion and screwed the two halves together as tightly as he could.

"Never again," he murmured to himself. "The blessed names must never be used again for such a terrible purpose."

****

Mauthausen Labor Camp, Austria, February 1942

The train's brakes screamed as a dozen railcars lurched and shuddered to a halt. Crushed together on the floor, in the dark and the cold, Bruchner's fellow prisoners grumbled and cursed and rolled first this way and then that as their stinking cattle car came to a stop.

The tiny child huddled inside Bruchner's coat trembled but made no sound.

With shrieks and sighs, the doors of the car rolled open on their rusted wheels, and the maniacal bellowing began.

"*Raus*! Everybody out now!" bellowed several *Schutzstaffel* soldiers.

Bruchner squinted against the watery morning light. The scene outside was a frozen hell. The overnight snowfall had already been mashed into a muddy soup beneath a hundred jackboots. Snowbanks were soot-covered. A pall of gray smoke hung motionless in the cold morning air above the many derricks and sheds and service buildings.

The sight was both familiar and strange: the same tang of granite dust in the nostrils and on the tongue that he'd known since childhood; the same familiar thrum of the quarry engines and incessant pounding of the granite cutters that he'd known all his working life. Yet there were so many more people, so many more barracks and barbed wire fences, and towers and searchlights, and guns and screams, and of course, *SS*.

Hundreds of shabby figures were already scrambling from the other rail cars and down onto the dirty snow. By their clothing, Bruchner guessed them to be Russians for the most part, staggering and stumbling like walking skeletons, shrouded in filth and misery. They'd been locked in their cars for days, judging by the way they shielded their eyes from the sunlight, and by the number of frozen corpses the *kapos* pulled from the cars.

Everywhere, the *SS* troops shouted and struck at the prisoners as they tumbled from the train. The guards and their *kapo* lackeys were herding the Russians into ragged lines and marching them away toward a complex of low huts. The guards' shouts grew angrier, their blows from whips and rifle butts more frequent and indiscriminate. As the *SS* men became increasingly frustrated at the slow progress of the

Russians, they fired first into the air, then into the dirt, and then into the limbs of the slowest prisoners.

A woman fell from a cattle car, and others tumbled on top of her, crushing her into the mud.

The guards laughed at her screams as her limbs snapped beneath the avalanche of bodies.

Bruchner's rail car was the last in the long line and filled not with Russians but with the most hardened inmates of Graz-Karlau Prison. They'd been marched from their prison the previous afternoon and put aboard a railcar bound for somewhere far worse. During the night, their carriage had been shunted onto a spur, disconnected from one train, and hitched to another. An express from the Russian front, someone said. Bruchner's traveling companions were murderers and maniacs, rapists and perverts, and he knew them all. They were the hardest, the most brutal of Graz-Karlau's inmates, and he'd been one of them.

At six foot four, Bruchner had survived his nearly four years among the inmates by matching their brutality with brutality of his own. He'd grown up among quarrymen and had been hard as stone even before turning sixteen, so madmen hadn't scared him. Only now, he had a small child clutched to his chest, and he was terrified for her.

More shouting and gunfire erupted directly outside their rail car. "Out, out!" several *SS* men screamed, waving pistols and firing into the air. Bruchner pressed the child closer still to his chest, held his coat tightly closed, and jumped from the car.

The *SS* soldiers were beating the Graz-Karlau prisoners with extraordinary vigor, cracking skulls with rifle butts and shins with clubs as they herded them into lines. The *SS* must have been warned about the men in the last car and were taking no chances. Bruchner too received a random crack across his head from a passing guard. Ever alert, however, he spied the senior *SS* officers overseeing the unloading operation. A foot soldier passed among the officers with a tray of steaming mugs. That's when Bruchner recognized a familiar face, a portly man in a black cashmere coat and homburg carrying a clipboard and chatting with one of the SS officers.

Even at a distance, Bruchner could make out the officer's insignia. Without a doubt, this was the camp's Standartenführer, the colonel in charge. Both the officer and the civilian declined the hot drinks, and after a moment, the SS man marched away. The civilian in the homburg seemed engrossed in his clipboard as he wandered in Bruchner's direction. Bruchner saw his chance.

"Director Leitner," he cried out. "Director Leitner."

The man looked up from his clipboard.

"Director Leitner, it's me, Bruchner."

At first the man hesitated and glanced nervously in the direction of the SS officers but then moved toward Bruchner.

"Director Leitner, please, sir, you must remember me."

The man stopped several feet away from the line of prisoners. "My God, Bruchner, keep your voice down." He quickly walked up to Bruchner and pulled him from the line. "How in God's name . . . ."

"On the train from Graz-Karlau. The SS emptied the prison yesterday. They told us we were to be kapos. But sir, I have my daughter . . . ." He opened his coat an inch.

When Leitner glimpsed the child, he hissed, "Oh Christ, Bruchner."

An *SS* guard must have noticed the encounter because he started toward them. "Follow me," Herr Leitner ordered. "And for heaven's sake, keep the child hidden."

Bruchner did his best to keep up as Director Leitner hurried up the stairs and into the administrative offices of the *Mauthausen Granite Company*. In all Bruchner's years at the quarry, the company had been owned first by private interests and then by the city of Vienna. But in prison, he'd heard that the *SS* had acquired the company for two purposes: first to feed the Führer's insatiable appetite for granite for his gargantuan building projects across the Reich, and second, as a camp where undesirables like Russians, Spanish communists, madmen, and Jews could be worked to death in the tens of thousands.

Leitner marched through the outer secretarial area and straight into his private office. A large older woman was busy arranging the Director's files for the day on his desk when they entered. Bruchner recognized Frau Müller, older of course and heavier still, but the same stalwart office manager he'd known for decades. Despite his being Jewish, Frau Müller had always treated him with respect, even attended his wedding. He had to trust her now. What choice did he have?

At Leitner's arrival, she'd looked up. Her face became a mask of horror at the sight of a filthy prisoner trailing after Leitner. Bruchner hesitated, then opened his coat and lifted out the tiny child. He placed her on a vacant office chair where the child immediately curled up in a ball and pinched her eyes shut.

"*Herr Director*, my God," Frau Müller gasped. "*Herr Director*, they can't. They're Jews. They're not supposed to be . . . ." she blustered.

Director Leitner took Frau Müller by the shoulders and looked into her eyes. "Frau Müller, I need your help. Please, take the child to the women's washhouse, now, as quickly as you can."

"But *Herr Director*, whose child is it . . . and . . . and she's filthy. She's soiled herself."

"She's my child, Frau Müller," whispered Bruchner.

She spun around. "Herr Bruchner! It's you! God in Heaven! How did you get here?"

"They were on the train," Leitner replied. "Bruchner arrived on a car from Graz-Karlau."

Bruchner spoke as calmly as he could. "The *SS* emptied the prison yesterday and brought us here. My old neighbors, Quakers, visited yesterday, and they'd brought my daughter. They'd adopted her when my wife died but would bring her to see me once a month so I'd know she was well. But then an *SS* officer looked at her and me and guessed she was mine and a Jew. He took the child from my friends and ordered me to bring her on the train. He couldn't leave a Jew wandering about, he said, even a tiny one. Then he laughed. When the child screamed, the officer struck her with his pistol. She hasn't made a sound since. She hasn't even opened her eyes."

"But . . . but what good will it do to hide her in the washhouse?"

"Please, Frau Müller, just take her, please," Director Leitner said. "We'll figure out something. Cover her with a blanket as you carry her. If anyone stops you, say the child belongs to one of the quarry engineers, and she's throwing up."

"All right, I . . . I'll do what I can."

"I'll come and get you very soon. I promise," Leitner whispered.

"Thank you, Frau Müller," Bruchner called after the woman as she carried the child from the room, closing the office door behind her.

"God in Heaven, Bruchner, the position you've put us in," the Director said as he paced the room.

"Please, Herr Director, they brought us here to work. Let me work for you. I could be very useful to you. I know more about the quarries than anyone. You know that's true."

"Yes, but you're a Jew. They'll kill us both if they think I'm helping you."

"I'm not asking you to help me. Give me a job. The worst you can imagine. Make me your *kapo*. I'll do everything I can to make you look good, I swear. No limits."

"But what of the child?"

"Back at the prison, it was said that *kapos* get their own rooms, provided they show no mercy in the performance of their duties. If you make me a *kapo* in your office, I will show no mercy in making the quarry a success and in protecting my child."

The door opened suddenly, and in strode the *Standartenführer* that Bruchner had seen earlier in the rail yard.

At the sight of the giant with the yellow star on his filthy coat, the *SS* man immediately drew a pistol and aimed it at Bruchner's head. "Herr Director, what is this Jew doing here?"

"*Standartenführer*, uh, I'm thinking of making him a *kapo* in my office."

"But the man is a Jew."

"Yes, sir, but he's also a murderer and . . . and I know him."

"You what?"

"Yes . . . he . . . he was our manager of works for years . . . until he murdered his wife and her lover. I recognized him when he disembarked from the car from Graz-Karlau. As a murderer, he has been deemed suitable for duty as a *kapo* in the quarries, but I thought he might be more beneficial here in the office."

"If he is a murderer and a Jew, why is he still alive?"

"The two people he killed were Jews as well."

"Ah. So how do you propose to use the Jew?"

"Well . . . to oversee work schedules, set performance quotas and ration levels. He will know which shifts are performing up to requirements and which are not, and which should be, uh, disposed of. He can also tell us where we might economize and find efficiencies. He knows the quarry so well, and he will be so much closer to the uh, the workforce."

"Won't he be inclined to help his fellow prisoners?"

"At the first sign of weakness, he will be gone too."

"Herr Director, we both want this camp to succeed, and so if you think this . . . this person can assist you, let it be on your head."

"Thank you, *Standartenführer*!"

The *SS* man holstered his luger, turned on his heels, and left the office.

"Oh Christ, what have I done?" Director Leitner gasped as he slumped into his chair.

"You will not regret it, I swear," Bruchner whispered.

The Director looked up into Bruchner's eyes. "You realize if you do the job as the *SS* will expect, you will be the most hated man in the camp. And there will be no companions for your child, no escape, no future, nothing. Not even food or drink for her."

"Unless I take what we need from the others," replied Bruchner. His voice was as icy as the nearby Donau River.

Chapter One

Bangor General Hospital

Gillian Willard's collapse had been so sudden. One minute they'd been together in a close embrace on the North Arnot beach. The next, she'd turned pale, pinched her eyes shut, screamed, and fallen to the sand in a dead faint.

The most beautiful and courageous person Chris had ever known, and the woman he loved without limit, Gillian had not stirred since. She remained unconscious, frail, and barely a whisper from oblivion. And, God forgive him, Chris was about to walk away from her forever.

Never again would he hear her voice or see her beautiful face or hold her in his arms. Worse still, he would never know whether she flourished or failed, whether she had embraced a new life or lay rotting away in the tiny Willard Family Cemetery. He would never know because he would never let himself know because if he knew she lived, he was certain to put her in mortal danger all over again.

In the hours following her collapse, doctors at Bangor General had stopped the bleeding in her brain, stabilized her condition, and kept her in an induced coma to await the endovascular surgery which might save her life. A prominent neurosurgeon, flown in from Manhattan at Nigel Harrow's expense, had cautioned, however, that she might not last until the operation. The cerebral vessel had been so severely compromised by the successive blows she'd suffered that it might rupture at any moment. She'd bleed out before anything could be done, and Christopher would be to blame.

If Gillian managed to survive until her operation, the surgeon warned that the likelihood of its success was slight. The damaged vessel might come apart the moment he touched it, she'd bleed out on the operating table, and Christopher would be to blame.

And even if by some miracle Gillian got through the operation, she'd almost certainly insist on rejoining Chris in whatever battles might come. He'd be too weak to prevent her because he loved her beyond all reason. But then, at some point in their struggles, she might suffer yet another head injury and die, and Chris would be to blame.

No, he had no choice. To save Gillian's life, he had to walk away.

Chris had been waiting at her bedside for days for her surgeon to deem her strong enough for surgery. He'd hoped to remain with her until the very last moment, until the nurses wheeled her away to the operating theater. But as days became weeks, Chris felt his resolve weaken. He feared his selfish desire might overwhelm his unselfish intent. But he couldn't let that happen.

He heard staff out in the corridor distributing dinner trays. Gillian's mother would soon arrive to spend the night at her daughter's side. She and Chris usually chatted awkwardly, taking turns holding Gillian's hand and sipping coffee until dawn. If he didn't leave soon, he wouldn't have a final few moments alone with Gillian to say what was in his heart.

"Gillian." He could barely get her name out. "Gillian, you are the most wonderful thing that has ever happened to me." He swallowed hard. "And I wouldn't leave you . . . I wouldn't leave you to save my own life, but . . . but to save yours, I have no choice." He fell silent. After a moment, he squeezed her hand, bent over the bed and kissed her lips. His tears moistened her cheeks. "I . . . I will love you forever," he whispered and then left the room.

From the hospital, Chris took the Number 87 bus heading uptown to Riverfront Park. There he walked head down past families and joggers enjoying the late afternoon, past a play structure and through a copse of trees, to an isolated spot by the river's edge. He dropped his backpack and suitcase and sat down on the concrete embankment to watch the shadows lengthen.

"Oh God, Gillian, all the pain I've caused you," he muttered. Then he pulled from his shirt the pendant that Rose DuCalice had crafted for him. He studied the tiny fragment of bone and said, "For dragging you into my nightmare, I deserve so much more pain than this." Then he lifted the pendant from around his neck and shoved it into his jeans pocket.

Mallory Dahlman was on him in a flash. Her face burst through a sudden blaze of sparks and fire. Her maddened eyes, ringed with ash and embers, glared at Chris. Her mouth opened in a scream of rage. With her first strike, she knocked Chris backward onto the jogging path. She then dragged him face first through the gravel before whipping him against the concrete embankment like laundry against river rocks. Mallory's grasp burned Chris's legs, his left shoulder popped as it struck the concrete, and his eardrum burst as Mallory vented her rage in one crazed scream. She then tossed him over the embankment and into the murky river where its current carried him out toward the mainstream.

The sounds of Mallory's attack drew onlookers to the embankment. Someone spotted Chris in the water, tossed a Parks Department life preserver, and hauled him up onto the bank. There, on his knees, Chris pulled Rose's amulet from his pocket and slipped it over his head once again, then flopped down on the grass, retching and heaving up filthy water.

"Ambulance is on its way, kid," said a Parks cop who'd arrived with the crowd of onlookers.

"No. Please, no ambulance," gasped Chris. "I'll be all right."

"But your shoulder looks bad," said someone in the crowd.

"I'm sure it's just twisted or bruised or something," Chris replied as he struggled to his feet.

"What happened? You didn't jump, did you?" asked the cop.

"No, no, absolutely not, sir, no," Chris said as he backed away from the crowd.

"It sounded like lightning," someone shouted, "Like he was hit by lightning."

"Okay, thanks," said Chris, "but I'm okay now." He turned, picked up his pack and suitcase from the grass, and hobbled away. "Besides, I've really got to be somewhere."

"At least wait for the paramedics to check you out," the cop shouted after him.

Chris shook his head, and in spite of the pain, waved his injured arm as he headed out of the park in the direction of the Highway 9 intersection. As Chris exited the park, he glanced back to the embankment. The crowd had already dispersed.

Highway 9, nicknamed the Airline Trail, meandered a hundred miles or so to the Canadian border through forest and farmland and over hill and dale like a nauseating roller coaster. There are few houses and even fewer businesses along the Trail. It was improbable anyone was going to recognize him as he hitchhiked through the Maine wilderness, and that's just how Chris Chandler wanted it.

****

Cavendish College, Halifax, Nova Scotia

Ignatius Greyson waited beneath the towering columns of Sinclair Hall, Cavendish College's administration building, for the worst of the sudden downpour to pass. "That American kid had better get here soon, or else," he muttered. Greyson had managed to buy more time, but the bastards were closing in. The Prague amulet was the only answer, and the boy from Maine was the key to finding it.

He drew a deep breath and tried to calm himself, but the whole damned college turned his stomach. How he hated every bloody stone in this quadrangle; from the admin building behind him to the men's residences—called Bays for some stupid reason—to the crumbling old library opposite. He hated every inch of its *faux* Gothic architecture, the smog-stained filth of its stonework, the pretension of its leaded windows, the ludicrous busts everywhere of thinkers and scholars no one knew or cared about anymore, and the chapel no one attended. A goddamned dump the place might be, but there was no way they were ever going to force him out of here, no way in hell.

During a break in the downpour, Greyson dashed down the wide granite stairs and across the quadrangle toward the college chapel. He headed, not for the processional steps up to the chapel's main entrance, but for the narrow stairwell at the side of the building. It led deep below ground. The sign on the wrought iron railing at the top of the stairs read *The Mildred Harper Chair in Faith Studies, Ignatius Greyson, Ph.D. Incumbent.* Greyson splashed down the steps and banged on the heavy wooden door at the bottom.

"Who is it?" asked a voice from behind the door.

"It's me, you idiot."

The door opened a crack, and a young man's face appeared. Michael Ashworth, Greyson's principal research assistant, said, "I . . . I was afraid it might be the campus police or maybe even the movers."

"Not today," Greyson muttered as he pushed past the boy and stepped inside.

The doorway opened onto a narrow landing at the top of another very long set of concrete steps, which descended a further twenty feet below ground into a cavernous chamber. The cellar beneath the chapel was one large room, the size of a tennis court, with concrete walls and a concrete floor. The air in the chamber was damp and smelled of incense and mold and adolescence. Coatracks, ropes, and blankets divided the space into sitting areas, study spots, and even a laboratory of sorts with monitors, light standards, and measuring devices. Several students were sprawled on couches smoking and playing guitars in a shared area at the chamber's center. The far corner of the cellar was the only portion of the space completely walled off from the rest.

It even had a rude plywood ceiling. More like a child's fort than a real office, its door bore a roughly painted sign which read, *The Altar*.

Greyson pulled off his raincoat, threw it over the railing, and clumped down the two dozen stone steps.

Ashworth called after him, "So how did it go?"

"Better than expected."

"And Lilith?"

"I believe . . . she helped."

Greyson navigated through the maze of curtained spaces to his makeshift office.

"So are we staying?" the boy called.

"Yes, for now. But we still have work to do." Greyson slammed his door behind him. Oh yes, they had lots of work to do. He drew a long breath and dropped down onto his couch.

He had indeed been expecting the meeting with the college president to go badly, what with all the threats of changed locks, forced eviction, and a lawsuit arising from an earlier confrontation. But no, this time, all the doltish president had tried were more empty threats. Would the weasel never learn? Idle threats accomplished nothing. If one threatens pain, one must deliver pain.

Greyson's battle with the college had been going on for years, in fact through three presidencies, five academic vice presidents, and two chancellors. None had driven Greyson out, and this latest patsy wasn't going to be any more successful.

****

Greyson had arrived on the campus of Cavendish College to splashy fanfare back in the sixties. A *wunderkind* of sorts, his career had started well enough. He'd received a tenure-track appointment in psychology at the University of Toronto right out of grad school in Michigan when he was just 22. But then his esoteric interests rankled colleagues, and the Department of Religious Studies denied him tenure. Any hope of an academic career might have ended then and there but for the help of his novelist mother. At her urging, he'd penned a pop-psych study of near-death experiences, and his mother's agent had helped him find a publisher.

The book was a bestseller, and he'd attracted a bevy of admirers. Indeed, his book had so reassured an elderly widow she'd soon see her beloved husband that she desired to fund Greyson's ongoing research. The woman offered to endow an academic chair for him at any school that would immediately tenure him. The sole condition of the endow-ment was that he be permitted to continue his research into life beyond death no matter where it might take him. Only one institution at the time had been desperate enough for the cash and the public attention to agree to such an outrageous condition, Cavendish College.

Founded as a seminary by the Anglican Church two centuries ear-lier in a picturesque town many miles from the port city of Halifax, the original Cavendish College had burned to the ground in 1893. Its staff and faculty had relocated to land donated by a much larger university in Halifax. The small college eventually severed its association with the Anglican Church and then struggled for years to find a new purpose and identity.

The college might have thought it had found in Ignatius Greyson the first of a new generation of creative young scholars. The Board might have hoped Cavendish College could rebuild around Greyson's notoriety, but that wasn't how things turned out. A reviewer for the *Edinburgh Literary Supplement* had revealed that Greyson faked much of the research behind his bestseller, and overnight, Greyson became a pariah. The publisher canceled an international lecture tour and quickly withdrew the book from print. An avalanche of hate mail overwhelmed the college mailroom. Fortunately for Greyson, the elderly widow who'd endowed his Chair hadn't lived long enough to learn how she'd wasted her money.

Soon after, Greyson's colleagues began complaining that his presence on campus was an embarrassment and a sea anchor on their own efforts to reinvent the college as a credible institution. Greyson's once-robust classes fast dwindled as his crackpot interests and outrageous conduct offended nearly everyone.

In the late sixties, he experimented with LSD as a portal to religious revelation. In the early seventies, he decided sexual expression was a form of religious worship. In the late seventies, he drew laughter from nearly everyone when he espoused the notion that early Christians consumed hallucinogenic mushrooms and had been, in fact, followers of an ancient fungus-worshipping cult. And in the early eighties, he discovered Kabbalah and the ancient belief in the mystical power of Hebraic letters to reveal emanations of the Divine[3]. One especially hungover morning, Greyson confessed to his class that he'd developed his new research interest while sitting on the can reading an article about Madonna.

Successive college administrations had been trying to break Greyson's tenure ever since his publishing debacle. Still, for all their revulsion at his antics, his faculty colleagues were such a weak and embarrassing lot that none was willing to jeopardize the sacrosanct convention of tenure for fear of what the precedent might mean for their own security. Hence, without a legal means to sever Greyson's endowment or a faculty willing to break his tenure, there wasn't much the college could do beyond threaten and bluster.

The latest effort to drive him from campus, however, was not going to be quite so easy for Greyson to dismiss. To cut its post-secondary costs, the Government of Nova Scotia was in the throes of consolidating the province's many small academic institutions. One of the Government's proposals was to create a single college of divinity to be known as Birch Hill Divinity School. Since Greyson's chair was ostensibly in religious studies, his position was slated for transfer. But Ignatius Greyson wasn't going to leave Cavendish without a fight, no goddamned way.

For more than two decades, he'd had unfettered use of his 'lab' beneath the college chapel where he claimed to be researching the psychology of faith and the religious experience. It was also a hangout for the small gaggle of doting students whom he'd gathered to do his bidding. Greyson's greylings, they were called by the rest of the student body.

Over the years, the greylings had been associated with several sordid incidents. Early in Greyson's tenure, he'd married, then divorced, a girl half his age. Then he'd moved in with two other girls when he'd had to vacate his seaside cottage for a time after a lady friend tried to burn it down. Three years back, one of his greylings under the influence of a hallucinogen had jumped to her death from the Halifax harbor bridge. And then, quite suddenly last term, a young member of his circle died of complications associated with an abortion. Despite the campus outrage and several faculty ethics inquiries, nothing directly linked Greyson and his so-called research with the two deaths. And nothing would ever be found because after decades of on-again-off-again research, Greyson's recent discoveries were finally about to bear stunning fruit.

In the past three years, he'd made such progress that it took his breath away to imagine the power he might soon possess. His first breakthrough came at a monastery in Russia. He'd been sent there to undergo an inane withdrawal treatment. But in the monastery library, he'd made an extraordinary and entirely unforeseen link between certain holy letters and the hallucinogenic properties of an ancient pharmaceutical. A whole new world had opened to him, a world of mystical revelation, incredible power, and nightmarish pain. And then, at a near-derelict monastery near Prague, he'd made an even more stunning find. With these discoveries, he was confident he'd be able to wield almost limitless power with impunity . . . if only he could bring together the necessary instruments. That's why he needed more time to refine the drug, clarify the ceremony, locate the grave, and most important of all, retrieve the amulet. And to do all that, he couldn't afford any more interference from idiots like the new college president.

When he'd received this latest summons to the president's office, he'd expected to be told the moving trucks were on their way and the locks were about to be changed. But as it turned out, all the president wanted was to tell him the move would happen later in the fall. Furthermore, the college had no intention of honoring the offer of a full scholarship which Greyson had made to some young American publicity seeker named Christopher Chandler.

Greyson rocked the president back in his chair when he leaped to his feet and bellowed at the diminutive sociologist. The college would damn well honor Greyson's commitment to Chandler, he shouted. The terms of Greyson's endowment gave him the absolute right to nominate a scholarship student to assist him, and that's what he'd done. No way was the college going to change that.

"Try to move me or cancel the kid's scholarship, and I'll sue this dump for so much, even your chalk dust will belong to me," he'd shouted as he stormed out of the president's office, slamming the door behind him.

Greyson's screaming fit also masked his sleight of hand. While leaning across the desk to shout in the president's face, Greyson had dropped a slip of parchment into the poor man's wastebasket. בואי לילית אהובתי ותעני, it read in scarlet. *Come, beloved Lilith, and punish my enemy.*

The president's secretary stared at him in horror as he marched across her office. "I think President Milling may need a few minutes to himself before his next appointment," Greyson said with a smile.

He was halfway across the quadrangle when he heard the unearthly scream from inside the admin building. No, Greyson wasn't going anywhere. And when the Chandler boy arrived, he'd have the final tool he needed, the means to identify the Prague cantor's grave.

****

There was a gentle tap on his office door. "I have some herbal tea for you," a girl said softly.

"Come," Greyson shouted. The sirens and the screech of tires as the firetrucks and ambulance roared into the quadrangle overhead echoed through Greyson's lair as he accepted the tea from his latest lady friend, a nubile student in first-year named, what? Virginia? Vanessa? who claimed she could read auras.

Chapter Two

Monday, September 7

Airline Trail Motel

Route 9, between Bangor and Calais Maine

After old lady Landry popped Chris's dislocated shoulder back into place, and Chris had slapped on a goodly dollop of Rose Ducalice's salve, the swelling took less than a day to go down. Ten days on, however, the gashes on his wrists and ankle and the abrasions on his face were still scarlet and continuing to weep.

In the past eighteen months, he'd been tried, jailed, and released, battled a gang of grave-robbing goths, been parted from his family, and buried two dear friends. And now, hiding here in the middle of nowhere, in this crappy old motel—its only guest in a week—he'd had more time than was wise to reflect on all he'd endured since his encounter with Dr. Meath. Alone in this seedy room, Chris had come to realize two gut-wrenching truths. First, the heartache of those partings would never go away. And second, the pain and guilt of abandoning Gillian Willard would torture him to the end of his days.

Chris rolled from his bed, pulled on jeans and a sweatshirt, and headed outside. Not another car in the motel parking lot; indeed, he couldn't see another soul in any direction. He walked to the back of Unit 4 and on down to the water's edge.

Passameque Bay. What a grim stretch of Maine's north coast the Bay was at that time of year. The trees had been prematurely stripped of their autumn foliage by an unseasonably early Nor'easter the previous week. The morning sky was the color of slate. The tide was out, and the slick, dark rocks were draped in greasy seaweed. Greenish seawater like filthy motor oil shifted listlessly against the rocky shore. To the north, lights of an oil refinery twinkled weakly through the morning mist. Moving silently, a dozen fishing vessels, their dark shapes silhouetted against the ashen sky, were making their way to sea. The only hint of color in the coastal palette of stone and sea was a first hint of rose on the horizon away to the east.

Chris's last hours in Maine; there'd been a time when he'd longed for this day. But now? With Gillian back in Bangor, awaiting the surgery which would either save her or . . .?

"Oh Christ, what am I doing," he muttered.

He rubbed the crust from the corners of his eyes and realized he'd been weeping as he'd slept.

He tossed a pebble or two into the sea, then wandered back to the parking lot and across to the motel office. Old Lady Landry was already seated behind the cluttered counter. She'd probably been there since 4 a.m. when her husband left for his shift at the refinery. Mrs. Landry perched on a stool with her enormous backside turned to the door. In her bright pink and yellow housedress with its many brown stains, and the waxy flesh of her bare arms, she brought to mind a giant potted begonia. Sipping a coffee, Mrs. Landry was engrossed in Bangor's morning TV news show. Because she was hard of hearing and had the volume on her ancient black and white Philco cranked way up, she didn't register Chris's presence.

All week Mrs. Landry had been a sweet old dear to Chris. Patched him up that first night, made him a decent breakfast each morning, and never pressed him for details on his sorry state. And because her eyesight was about as shaky as her hearing, she had no clue a celebrity was staying at the Airline Motel. Besides, Chris had registered under the name Nigel Harrow.

Through the crackle and the snow on the 17-inch screen, Tiffany Dawn, Bangor's answer to Barbara Walters, said, "and so the cats are now in the care of the Portland ASPCA." She chuckled and turned to her co-anchor, Robert Bellworthy. He joined her in their strained moment of levity. But then her partner, slope-shouldered and unnaturally tanned, turned very serious and said, "Our next story grows more bizarre by the moment." Over Bellworthy's shoulder appeared a photo of Bemishstock's main street.

"Here we go," muttered Chris.

"Governor Jenkins called a press conference late yesterday to present the recommendations of the State's Special Panel on recent events in Bemishstock. Who can forget the horrific details? Dozens of bodies stolen from a local funeral parlor by a discredited doctor, bodies he'd used in gruesome experiments. And the doctor's violent confrontation with a local teenager, which led to the doctor's fiery death. The Governor had tasked the Panel to investigate conditions in the State's judicial system, which allowed the doctor to get away with his crimes for years and made an innocent young man the scapegoat for the system's many failures. So we go now to our *Maine Morning* reporter at the State House, Phil LaBelle. Good morning, Phil."

The picture switched to a murky shot of a stocky, balding reporter on the steps of the State House in Augusta.

"Morning, Bob," Phil LaBelle replied. "Yes, the Governor held his press conference over the dinner hour yesterday to formally announce the Panel's proposals. There were few surprises. Tighter regulations on funeral homes, improved training standards for personnel in the funeral industry, dissolution of the Bemishstock Police Department, and the assumption of its duties by the Maine State Police. But when the Governor invited questions from the packed press theater, the session fell to pieces. The first question came from the journalist with the *Bangor Daily News* who initially broke the Bemishstock story. She asked whether the State planned to compensate the boy, Chris Chandler, for his time in detention. That's when the yelling began.

"A large contingent of Bemishstock townspeople and former drivers from the now-defunct *Balzer Trucking Company* filled the back of the pressroom. All leaped to their feet and began screaming, 'What about compensation for us?' and 'What about our torment?' One ex-trucker grabbed a press mike and screamed, 'If Chandler hadn't stuck his nose in where it didn't belong, we'd all still have our jobs.' "

Tiffany Dawn asked, "Phil, why do you think folks in Bemishstock aren't more grateful to Chandler for exposing that doctor's crimes?"

"Well, Tiffany, I put that question to one of the townspeople present."

A shaky video clip began.

"Oh sure, it's sad and all what Meath did to people's like . . . their dead family members, but hell, they was dead anyway, and they don't care where they are now, do they? And like family can still go visit their gravestones, can't they? But we, we gotta live, and if that goddamn kid hadn't started pokin' around, we might still have our jobs. We can't stay in Bemishstock 'cause there's no work, and we can't leave 'cause we can't sell our homes. We're the ones bein' tormented. So to start talkin' about givin' that kid cash and not us? That's nuts!"

"Meanwhile," said Tiffany, "Chandler's friend, Gillian Willard, is awaiting surgery for the brain aneurism she suffered . . . ."

Okay, Chris had seen enough. He tapped Old Lady Landry on the shoulder. She spun about and swore, "Christ Jesus, boy, you scared the piss out of me!" She reached over to the old set and turned down the volume. "So you be hearin' what them state fellers be talkin' about? They be thinking of payin' that Chandler kid for diggin' up bodies!"

"I don't think the Chandler kid did the digging up, Mrs. Landry," Chris shouted.

"Next, they'll be settin' up committees to be decidin' who gets buried and who gets burned."

"I think it was the other guy, the doctor who was digging up the bodies," Chris tried to explain.

"Sonny, I knows what I heard. Damned governments do the stupidest things. Why some peoples be callin' that kid a hero is beyond me." As Mrs. Landry spoke, she shifted papers and pop cans and paper plates off the counter and then asked, "So lad, what can I do you fer? Some breakfast, maybe?"

"No, Mrs. Landry, I'm afraid I'm gonna be checking out."

"Oh dear, Mr. Harrow. Sorry to hear that. It's been a pleasure having you stay with us."

"And you've been very good to me, Mrs. Landry."

"Well, you looks to be a lot better today than you was the night you limped in here."

"I was grateful for the job you did, bandaging me up and all." Chris had to bellow each response.

Old Lady Landry tallied Chris's meals and nights and video rentals, and he settled in cash.

"So I s'pose you'll be headin' on to that college up in Canada, now, that right?"

"Yes, ma'am, classes begin in a few days."

"You gonna hitchhike to Calais and the border? My boy Jimmy's comin' over from Beagles Pond to run errands for me. He be going into Calais for some lumber and nails and stuff, so if you be likin' a ride?"

"That would be great."

Chris headed back to Unit 4 to collect his things and await Mrs. Landry's boy.

From St. Stephen, the Canadian town right across the border from Calais, Chris planned to catch a bus to Halifax.

Of course, he couldn't leave without Mallory's bones. Somewhere out there, someone would know how to lay her spirit to rest, and when that day arrived, he'd need her skull at least. But how was he to get a suitcase full of bones past a Canadian border guard? That's when it had hit him. He'd make her into a lamp, or at least what looked like a lamp. He'd swathed her bones with plaster of Paris and packed them in a cheap suitcase along with the wiring from an old lamp. If anyone at the border asked, 'It's my lucky desk lamp,' he'd explain. 'Made it at summer camp; been with me ever since.'

As he waited in the parking lot for Mrs. Landry's son, the horizon in the east turned from watery gray to blood-red. What's that old saying? Sailors take warning?

****

Cavendish College, Halifax

In Detective Sergeant Bain's view, the fire marshal's report was just plain crap. How could anyone self-combust, never mind the president of a goddamn college? What did that even mean? Like he just burst into flames? No, the fire marshal had to have missed something. Maybe the prez had spilled booze and a cigarette in his lap, or he'd dozed off smoking a pipe or his, what the hell, his electric pen or his supersecret spy ink had exploded or something! Nobody just self-combusts! And yet, that's what the report said: *no combustible material detected; no apparent cause of ignition.*

Al Bain had been handed the case five days after the incident. How stupid was that? You get squat if you don't talk to the persons involved in the first twenty-four hours. And all the excuses for the delay were goddamn lame: they had to wait for the fire marshal; the prez was still in a coma; his secretary had been traumatized! All bullshit! And now it was Bain's mess to clean up.

Okay, so it was the first day back at work for the prez's secretary and Bain's first opportunity to speak with her, along with the prez's temporary replacement. God, he hated being on these campuses, and the city was littered with them, all with their stuck-up academics looking down their noses at him because he only had a high school education. Well, one of them had set fire to the prez, and Bain was going to nail the bastard responsible, Ph.D. or not.

"So, Miss Longmire, you were the first to hear your boss's scream, right?" Bain asked, not looking up from his notebook as he paced around the president's restored office. The new bookshelves were still empty and the newly painted walls still bare, but there were once again carpets on the floor and a few pieces of furniture about the room.

"That's right," replied the middle-aged lady in tweeds.

"And you ran into his office."

"Yes."

"And he was lit up like a tiki torch."

"Detective!" said the elderly acting president seated beside the secretary. He patted her hand. "Have a little compassion."

"Sure, right. So had the president been drinking? Did you see a glass or a bottle on his desk?"

"No. Nothing like that."

"And he wasn't smoking?"

"No. The president never smoked."

"And no one else was in the room. You weren't, were you, sir, uh . . . ." Bain checked his notepad. "Uh, Dr. Crawdad?"

"It's Croudeit, like Crew Deet, Dr. Emile Croudeit."

"Is that Polish or something?"

"Armenian."

"Okay then," Bain muttered as he scribbled *army man i*n his note book. "So, Doc, you weren't in the room at the time?"

The old gentleman looked like a deer caught in the headlights. Acting prez, bullshit, the guy had probably wanted the job for years.

There you have it. Motive.

The secretary piped in. "No one was in his office, not when President Milling started screaming."

"Wait, so are you saying someone *had* been in his office right before he screamed?"

"Yes, Professor Greyson."

"Greyson? Okay, so this Professor Greyson, how long before?"

"Ten minutes, maybe?"

"But the president was okay when Greyson left?"

"Well, the president might have been upset. But I don't think he was on fire when Greyson left if that's what you mean."

"What do *you* mean, 'the prez might have been upset'?"

"Well, because they'd been arguing, Professor Greyson and the president."

"Huh, and do you know why they were arguing?"

She looked at her hands. Bain could see the sheen of sweat.

"Because they'd been shouting, and . . . and because the president had wanted to . . . ."

The old gentleman, the acting president, suddenly interrupted the secretary. "Because the president was supposed to dismiss Greyson!" The old geezer paused to catch his breath before he shouted. "Because he was supposed to send Greyson packing, once and for all!"

The vitriol in the old guy's voice caught Bain off guard. He couldn't believe Crawdad could muster that kind of energy. Holy shit, this case had suddenly taken a bizarre turn.

"So you're telling me that right after the president fired this guy Greyson, the president burst into flames?"

The acting prez drew a long breath. He looked at the secretary and shook his head. "No. It turns out the president didn't fire Greyson. He caved. He merely warned Greyson, like we haven't done that before." The disgust in the old man's voice was unmistakable.

"So why was this prof . . . what's his name?"

"Greyson."

"So why was this Greyson supposed to have been fired?"

Once again, the old man replied. "Because he's a charlatan and an embarrassment to the college."

"What, like he dresses funny or has bad breath or something?"

The old man looked like he was about to explode. This time, however, it was the secretary who spoke. "No. He was being dismissed for cause. Professor Greyson has a history of questionable academic conduct, but he recently crossed a line. He invited a young American to campus."

"And inviting an American is a bad thing?"

"No, of course not. But Professor Greyson offered him a full scholarship without the college's approval, even though the American has been in jail for the past year. You see, this young man, this boy actually since he's only nineteen, well, I gather he has a reputation."

"Reputation for what?"

Calm once again, the acting president replied, "For being a trouble-maker. For attracting attention."

"What's this kid called?"

"Christopher Chandler."

"And where's he from?"

"From Maine."

"So what kind of trouble has he caused?"

"At the president's request, I collected a lot of newspaper clippings on the boy," replied the secretary. "About his trial and imprisonment, and strange events in Vermont, and the Governor of Maine's inquiry, a whole lot of stuff. Some papers say he was a hero, others that he destroyed a whole town. And one paper in Vermont even called him 'the defender of the dead.' But I can get you the file if that would be helpful."

Bain needed a moment to take all this in. "Okay, let me see if I've got this right. So you're saying the prez and the prof fought because the college wants to fire this Greyson guy and because Greyson has recruited a kid who 'defends the dead.' And right after their fight, with no apparent cause, the prez burst into flames. Is that what you're telling me?"

"Yes," old man Crawdad and the secretary said in unison.

"Oh sweet jeez . . . ." Bain muttered.

****

Duncan's Cove outside Halifax

A still, damp day. Fog enshrouded the cove. Gulls glided out of the mist and then slipped away again. Waves washed languidly around the pilings beneath the weather-beaten cottage. How the hell could anyone ever think living by the sea might be inspirational or romantic or whatever? It was never anything but cold and wet.

Greyson clambered down the ladder from his sleeping loft and collapsed onto a ladder-back chair at the kitchen table. He looked out through the floor-to-ceiling window making up the entire east side of the building. But then the motion of the water made him nauseous, and he had to turn away. In the living room, a naked girl was sprawled unconscious on the couch. "Oh Hell," he muttered.

His head still rang with his mother's screams. "Liar, you god-damned liar!" she'd bellowed through the phone lines. One o'clock in the morning, she'd called. One in the goddamn morning! And right in the middle of his . . . his dalliance with the girl. His mother was out of her mind!

"Where's the money?" she'd screamed. "You promised the money. They're going to throw me out of here if I don't make this month's payment. Is that what you want? To see me out on the street?

"You promised! You promised I'd have the money in time! If you knew you wouldn't be able to make the payment, why didn't you just say you couldn't pay? You're such a goddamned liar!"

Where did his mother get off calling him a liar? Her! She lied about everything, her age, her work, her husbands. He hadn't been more than seven when he'd overheard her tell one of his teachers that her second husband had abused her poor dear child. Where had she got that idea? And why was she telling such stories to his teachers anyway?

"You told a lie," he'd said at the time.

"It's not a lie if you'd like it to be true," she'd replied. If you'd like it to be true? So that's how you tell the truth from the lie? If you wanted what you said to be true, then it was true?

It wasn't long after that he'd started lying to his mother. Lies made life so much simpler. Mother was only ever satisfied with good news, so that's all he gave her. He'd never dared tell her the truth—not about the bullying or the failures he suffered or the petty crimes he commit-ted—for fear she'd beat the crap out of him. She didn't want to know what a lonely, disappointing freak he was. And for years, his lies had done the trick until the scandal over his bestselling book blew every-thing to shit.

Okay, so maybe he'd cooked the data in his book, perhaps he'd faked a few interviews with folks who claimed to have returned from

Heaven, but so what? The book's message was essentially true, that the near-death experience includes visions of Heaven. And besides, the claim that his exhaustive research had proven the existence of Heaven was what people wanted to hear, so what was so wrong with giving them what they wanted? Greyson never understood why people made such a fuss over a few faked interviews. He'd done no one any harm.

Anyway, when the accusations that he'd cooked his data first surfaced, his mother had tried to save his reputation, and her own by extension. On his absolute assurance that the charges of fraud against him were baseless, she'd paid for the very costly court case against his publishers and the magazine that had broken the story. But he'd lost, and his mother had compromised her own reputation in the process and burned through most of her savings, and now lived on what he was able to send her. Most months, he'd been able to send something, just not this month. Okay, so maybe he had said he'd pay, but how could she say he'd lied if his intentions had been good?

The trouble was, with the years, as lying to his mother became easier, lying to others became easier still. He'd grown accustomed to telling people what they wanted to hear. The trick had been to make sure each lie contained a grain of truth, some hint of what people wanted to hear because that way, they were predisposed to believe the lie even before he told it. As for the doubters, the fact-checkers, they were few and far between. Most people took him at his word on just about everything. They rarely ever bothered to fact-check his claims because they wanted to believe him.

For example, he'd promised—absolutely guaranteed—the wealthy old lady who'd endowed his Research Chair that she'd soon see her husband. He'd crafted test results with squiggly lines and fake recordings and even handwriting on the wall of her home to prove her husband was nearby in the Realm of Shades, anxiously awaiting their reunion. She'd eaten it up. That was how he'd convinced her to lock in his funding. None of the crap he faked had really been a lie, not really. It had been what she wanted, no, what she'd begged to hear, and giving it to her brought her great joy until the day she died. Besides, he hadn't been after her money for his own sake. He had intended to use it for science. And if he could only keep the college and his creditors and his mother off his back long enough, he still intended to use the old lady's remaining funds to accomplish something extraordinary. And the amulet from Prague would be the key, the amulet and the American kid, that is.

But first, he had to deal with the girl on the couch. Veronica? Vanessa? Okay, so last night, maybe he had said how much he respected her and longed for their physical intimacy to seal their intellectual partnership. It had been true at the time, sort of anyway. And besides, she'd wanted him, that had also been obvious, the way she'd hung around the lab after everyone else had left. Thinking back now, she'd practically begged for it, and he'd only slipped the Rohypnol into her drink to help her relax.

But now he had a problem. Hours later, the girl was still out cold, and her breathing strangely shallow. He had to get to the lab soon, and he couldn't waste any more time on her, so what was he going to do with her? Okay, so first he'd get her dressed and back to the lab. If anyone asked, he'd say they'd gone to a diner for a late meal, and she'd got food poisoning. And if she claimed any different, he'd accuse her of abusing lab drugs without his approval. And as for the bruises on her thighs? Nope, he knew nothing about them. Besides, who would believe a flake like her with purple hair and piercings in her navel? And anyway, Henry and James could always take care of the girl, as they had before.

Right then, a quick shower, get the girl back into her clothes, and head for the college.

****

Freddy's Diner, Halifax, Nova Scotia

Freddy Gothall of *Freddy's Diner - All-day breakfast* owned the L-shaped building at the corner of Duke and Hollis Streets, all five crumbling floors of it. Freddy no longer took much interest in his property, however, because he was fighting his final rounds with lung cancer. He'd long ago leased the diner fronting Hollis Street and apartment above it to a married couple of Pakistani extraction, Rashid and Dolly Minhas, while he left tenants who rented single rooms in the portion of the building facing Duke Street to pretty much fend for themselves.

Sammy Brook had never met Freddy. Good thing, too, because if given the chance, he'd have smashed the bastard's nose for the crappy condition of his building. The place was a deathtrap, with its cracked windows, dark hallways, bare wires, and broken stairs, not to mention the single stinking toilet on each floor that tenants had to share. Someone should have complained long ago to the city or the province, or God knows who—if, that is, the tenants weren't more concerned about their anonymity than the stench of the bathrooms.

Sammy had hauled the broken armchair all the way from a dumpster behind the *Nova Scotian Hotel* to the rooming house. At eighty-four, he was exhausted and soaked with sweat. But the chair was a great find, and it might make him as much as twenty dollars' profit with the right fabric. Yes, a good find. He left the chair leaning against the brick wall outside and entered *Freddy's Diner*.

"Good evening, Mr. Brook, sir," said Mr. Minhas. "Your toasted lettuce and tomato sandwich is ready, sir." Minhas stood proudly with his hand on the shoulder of his daughter Basalah, who held the paper sack out to the old man.

"Just as you like it, Mr. Brook," said the little girl.

Sammy took the paper bag from the girl with a grunt and the slightest hint of a smile.

"Will there be anything else?" asked Minhas. "Can we tempt you with a slice of the pie my wife just made?"

Goddamn Pakki asked the same goddamned question every night, and every night Sammy's answer was the same. "No, this is good. *Danke*." He handed a dollar to the child. "Bassy Lassie," he muttered, patted her head, and turned to leave.

"Good night then, Mr. Brook, and come again."

Was the man dense? Of course he'd come again. He'd been coming to *Freddy's* every day for a couple of years, ever since his previous lodgings had been condemned. And tomorrow would be no different. He'd buy his egg and toast in the morning and his lettuce and tomato sandwich in the evening, and he'd do the same the next day and the day after. Every goddamn Sunday morning, he'd buy his sticky bun and sweet coffee till he was pushing up daisies.

So why *Freddy's*? Because he had no choice. He couldn't cook in his firetrap of a room upstairs, and he couldn't afford any of the stupid bistros and fancy cafés popping up on the harbor front. Goddamn Bistros! Goddamn yuppies.

Sammy pulled the keys from his pocket as he exited the diner, turned immediately to his left, and unlocked the chipped and dented metal door. It bore the number 31 along with a scrap of cardboard taped to it that read "Room for Rent" in pencil.

He held the door open with his right arm as he wrestled the broken chair into the tiny foyer with his left, then let the door close behind him.

"Wait a fuckin' minute!" someone shouted from outside as a hand grabbed the door just before it latched. "Shit! Ain't you got no manners?"

"I didn't see you," Sammy muttered.

"You fuckin' blind?" the young man shouted. Sammy didn't answer. "Deaf too?"

The guy, little more than a kid, was wiry and tall, almost as tall as Sammy, although the kid probably thought he towered over Sammy. Sammy topped six foot four but shuffled about as stooped as a shepherd's crook. He preferred that others underestimate him.

The kid, on the other hand, was an open book. He was dressed all in black, which only accentuated the gray pallor and hollow eyes of an addict. Despite the hood and long coat the kid wore, his dirty brown hair was plastered to his scalp with sweat, and he was shivering and as jumpy as a cat. His friend, who barged into the foyer next, was in even worse shape.

The second fellow leaned against the wall, closed his eyes, wrung his hands, and danced from foot to foot like he had to piss. The fellas were followed into the building by two ladies of indeterminate age, both bundled against the cold drizzle from the waist up but almost naked from the waist down. They wore ridiculous heels for the slippery conditions outside, skirts that barely covered their asses, and fishnet stockings that were so tattered they'd let porpoises escape.

Sammy pushed the broken chair against the wall to make way for the foursome, but not soon enough for the first young tough.

"Get the fuck out of the way, old man." He bent over to have a look at Sammy's chair. "Why the fuck are you bringing more trash into the building? What the fuck do you do with all the shit you're always dragging in?"

"I will fix and sell it. It's how I live."

"You're shittin' me! That's one god-awful way to live. Now, if you got yourself some ladies . . . ." and he grabbed the ass of one of his companions, who winced and then giggled.

"Come on, Jeremy, leave him," said the second young man. "Oh shit, I gotta get upstairs. I really need a hit. I think I'm gonna barf." But the first kid wasn't done with Sammy.

"Must be some old ladies round here you could pimp out to your war buddies. Whole new market, eh?"

Sammy straightened up somewhat and stared the punk in the face. "Toilet's plugged again," he said.

"What's that to me?"

"You and your friend and the young ladies, you are responsible."

"How the fuck could you know that?"

"Because I clean the traps in the cellar. They are full of condoms, capsules, needles, and bottle caps."

"And no one else in the building has our tastes?"

"You know the answer."

"Okay, so you keep on cleaning them out."

"I do not get paid to do that. I only do it for other tenants who don't know how. So I wish you'd stop clogging our toilets, okay?"

"No, not okay, you goddamned dried-up old clown." Without taking his eyes from Sammy, he kicked the chair aside and grabbed the front of Sammy's jacket. "You old fool, you go right on cleaning out the toilets, and I'll go right on flushing whatever I wanna. And if any time the toilets are clogged, and I have to piss out the window, I'm coming for you, get it?" He spotted a glint of silver around Sammy's neck and pulled a chain from the old man's shirt. "What the fuck is this? One of them stars like Jews wear? You a Jew?"

"Yes," Sammy replied, in a voice that should have scared the crap out of the kid if he hadn't been too thick to hear the menace in it.

"No fuckin' way any Jew is ever gonna lecture me on how I take a crap. You will always, always, clean my shit, get it? And you won't ever again tell me what I can and cannot do. Do I make myself clear?" He released Sammy's shirt and stepped away. "So glad we had this little talk." He turned and started up the stairs. His friend and the two ladies followed.

"Ah, but we are not done," Sammy whispered. The tension in his face smoothed away some of the wrinkles around his eyes. His icy gaze at the departing thugs only hinted at the murderous strength that Sammy could muster when roused.

****

Greyson's Laboratory, Cavendish College

"Eleven in the morning and still not here," Ashworth muttered.

The bastard had called an hour earlier to cancel his tutorial. No surprise in that. Greyson canceled classes practically every week. And no sign of his latest groupie either, Vanessa what's-her-name. Nope. No surprise in that either.

It was a mystery to Ashworth why so many sluts threw themselves at a wreck of a professor like Greyson. But so what? Greyson could have all the fun with his girlfriends that he wanted, so long as none of his bimbos came between the greylings and their work. Their work was everything, and Greyson's biological needs were a mere irritation. The greylings had come so far in recent months. They were on a quest to uncover ancient secrets so profound they'd stand the academic world on its ear. Ashworth wasn't going to let Greyson's weaknesses get in their way. Not tears, not tits, and not the prospect of Greyson getting canned—nothing would stop the greylings' work. For Christ's sake, it was his work! Michael Harper Ashworth's work! He'd done all the real thinking, all the planning. No one else. The rest of the greylings, they all just did what he told them to do. And so long as Greyson didn't screw things up, Ashworth would eventually get his just reward.

"We gonna have to move?" Ryan, the kid with the guitar, called from the common room sofa.

"Apparently not. Not yet, anyway," Ashworth replied.

"Great, I got a new batch of salvi cooking, and it needs at least a week."

"Everyone, listen up," Ashworth shouted. The half dozen greylings scattered around the chamber paused in whatever they were doing. "When the boss gets here, he wants to discuss next steps. Maybe in an hour or so? Okay? Good."

Ashworth headed into the testing area, picked up a clipboard, studied the columns of figures, and made a few notes. Then he switched on an oscilloscope and an ultraviolet light and placed a page from an illuminated manuscript in their path.

"Hey Ryan, could you give me a hand?" he called to the kid in the common room. "I want to run this series before Greyson gets here."

"Yeah, sure." The kid rolled off the couch and joined Ashworth. Bonnie, or Angel Girl as Ashworth called her, tagged along as well. "So what do you need?" asked Ryan.

"Okay we've tested the electro-resonance of the manuscript at cycles below 50 hertz. We've already established that observers under the influence of *salvinorin banisteriopsis* see the demons described in the text. But we haven't tested the manuscript's resonance between 50 and 60 cycles, and I think the images might become even more vivid at the higher frequencies. The demons, well, they might even . . . let's say . . . become more autonomous."

"Isn't there a risk we might, you know, like release something dangerous from the manuscript?" cautioned Bonnie. "That's what Greyson said anyway."

"Oh, that's crap," replied Ashworth. "We won't be releasing anything. But maybe we can make the figures more responsive to our . . . our manipulation."

"To, like, control them? That would be so cool," Bonnie exclaimed. "I've already missed my classes today anyway so can I watch?"

"Okay, so let's have some fun," said Ashworth.

"You drinking the salvi or me?" asked Ryan.

"Can I?" interjected Bonnie. "You guys keep talking about this demon thing, but I haven't seen it yet. If we're a team, then it's got to be my turn sometime, no?"

"I guess" said Ashworth, "if you think you'll be okay."

"Yeah, no problem," she said with a tentative smile.

"All right then. So you drink this," Ryan said as he took a flask of blue liquid from a minifridge and poured a hundred milliliters into a flask. "You don't need to worry. It's nothing poisonous. Just a kind of tea we brew from salvia. It's a kind of mint, and from ayahuasca, this Peruvian plant. It's supposed to be good for regularity. Anyway, when the brew starts to work, you'll first feel a tingling in your arms and legs, then you'll see auras around the lights, and finally, you'll see crimson everywhere. The whole room will be bathed in crimson."

"Like blood?" the girl asked, then sipped the salvi tea.

"Okay, sure, like blood," Ryan replied.

"It's not so bad," she said after a tentative sip, and then drained the flask.

"When you tell us the world is crimson," said Ashworth, "that's when I'll turn on the UV light, and you'll look at the manuscript and tell us what you see. We'll also have a camera rolling."

"What does the light do?" she asked.

"It's kind of like our magic wand," said Ashworth.

"A while back, Dr. Greyson discovered that the inks used by the monks of the All Martyrs Monastery in Slatrastya, Russa contained some really bizarre stuff," explained Ryan. "It had unusual levels of zinc cadmium sulfide and zinc sulfide and silver silicates of manganese and a bunch of other rare earth metals. That's when Greyson realized the sulfides were the same phosphors as those in black and white television screens. And that gave him the idea of exciting the manuscript with a high-intensity electric field to see what would happen."

Bonnie looked puzzled. "Exciting the manuscript?"

Ashworth broke in. "He means we pass an electrical field over the phosphors, the stuff in the inks, and they glow, like the inside of a TV screen."

"But those Russian monks wouldn't have had any electrical field," said Bonnie.

"Well, maybe they did. Like from natural magnets or maybe during electrical storms," explained Ashworth.

"Okay, so at first Greyson got nothing," Ryan continued. "But then he smoked up, and just like that, he discovered that exciting a manuscript while under the influence of some hallucinogen got all these figures moving around on the page. And then, when he started reading some cabbalistic texts aloud at the same time, well, he got some incredible results."

"And we've been perfecting the combination of herbs, energy levels, and cabbalistic phrases ever since," Ashworth said proudly.

"Okay, got it," Bonnie said. From the weird grin on the girl's face, it was apparent the tea was beginning to take effect.

"You might want to sit," said Ryan as he helped her to a chair.

"Oh wow. You look, you . . . Christ!"

"Now remember, when the room turns crim—"

"It is! It's red!" she cried out.

"So now you have to look at the text, and I'll turn on the lamp." Ashworth flipped a switch. Lights in the cellar dimmed for an instant.

"There's blood! I . . . I see blood. It's everywhere," muttered Bonnie. The nervousness in her voice was obvious.

"You read Hebrew, right? Okay, so can you read this text?"

"Okay, so, uh . . . *Then the light shall dim all over the land and the earth shall be shaken* . . . . No wait, there's these guys everywhere. Christ, they see me! Oh no, they see me! And they . . . they're angry."

"Just keep reading, please," coaxed Ryan.

"They're climbing off the page." Bonnie pressed herself to the back of the chair. "And the blood, they're splashing me with blood. No, please, get them away. I don't like this. Make them stop. There are so many of them! Please, make them stop!" Bonnie screamed. She screamed so loudly the plywood door to Greyson's office rattled on its hinges.

At that moment, the cellar door opened, and Greyson appeared, his arm around a bedraggled and barely conscious Vanessa. "What the hell is going on?" he shouted.

"It's Bonnie," Ashworth started to explain.

"What's happened to her?" he said as he rushed down the stairs, leaving Vanessa slumped on the landing.

"She's helping us with tests between 50 and 60 hertz, and she's having a bad reaction to the salvi."

Bonnie continued to scream and then fell to the floor where she rolled about and then curled up in the fetal position, whimpering and muttering to herself all the while.

"Shit, can someone take her to the washroom and make her throw up?" ordered Greyson. "Now, goddamn it! Before she has a stroke or something. And you, Ashworth, what the hell were you thinking, running tests without my approval?"

"You weren't here, sir."

"You never run tests without my approval." Greyson marched up to Ashworth and roared in his face. "You're not in charge here. You may think you are, but you're just a lab assistant. You're nothing more than a lab rat, goddamn it!"

Ashworth was breathless with humiliation. He'd carried Greyson for months. He led the team when Greyson was busy with his slags, which was like every day. And now? Shit! All the authority he'd cultivated over the team, it might now be gone, shot, spent as a result of Greyson's outburst.

Ryan tried to interject. "Sir, we have to complete the test cycle if we're—"

"Why? Why?" shouted Greyson. "Those tests! They're not worth shit!"

"But what we've discovered, sir," Ashworth said, "it's incredible. "We . . . no, I mean you sir, you discovered something no one else ever suspected, that monks used narcotics in combination with incantations to intensify their faith. When we've finished the tests, the article you'll be able to write! It'll blow peoples' minds."

"Shit, don't you get it?" snarled Greyson, "I'm not interested in writing an article, not anymore. I'm so sick and tired of watching devils dance on a page. Where's the power in that? Besides, no scholarly article is going to save this lab."

Ashworth couldn't believe what Greyson was saying. After all they'd done, all they'd accomplished, it was so . . . so infuriating!

An article won't save you, Greyson, you freak, but it might save the rest of us.

"Okay, sir," Ashworth said aloud, "but can some of us at least continue the work on the manuscript?" Around the cellar, Ashworth saw heads bobbing in agreement with this request. "On our own time, maybe?" Surely Greyson would see the merit in this proposal. But no.

"On your own time? Idiots! You don't have your own time. This is my research center, and you're only here to do my bidding, and as of tonight, my bidding is that you forget the bloody manuscripts. Don't you get it? We've already found everything in the manuscripts that we need. We have confirmed the hallucinogens they used, and we have the range of light frequencies they somehow rigged. So now all we need are the right words, the most holy goddamn words. That's it! Nothing else! With the right words we won't just make demons dance on a page. We'll have the power to create life! But there's only one fucking way we'll ever find those words, and that's to find the goddamned Prague amulet. Got it?"

Ashworth turned away, muttering, "Oh Hell, that bloody amulet again." If it even exists, the damned thing was only supposed to serve one purpose, to wake up some ludicrous creature made of mud and blood. Like that was ever going to happen. What a total waste of time when there was a whole encyclopedia of Kabbalistic phrases out there to be tested.

"Look, sir, I understand you think the amulet is important," said Ryan. "But it's not like we haven't tried to find it. The odds it's even here in Halifax are like so—"

"It is here," screamed Greyson, "I'm sure it is. The documents I found in Prague, they confirm it."

"The documents are vague, sir," said Ashworth in a voice barely above a whisper.

"Vague? Did you say vague! To someone without imagination, maybe they're vague." Greyson strode about the cellar, waving his arms in the air like a madman. "That's why I recruited the Chandler kid from Maine, because you're all dimwits. You're not in his league. He's got imagination. He's what we need to complete our quest, and from now on, all of you, you do nothing except pull together your stuff on the amulet and prep them for Chris Chandler. When he gets here, he'll tell you what to do. Until then, you do nothing."

Still sprawled on the concrete landing by the cellar door, Vanessa chose that moment to throw up. Her vomitus dripped from the landing down onto a desk twenty feet below. James ran up the stairs to catch the girl before she rolled down the steps.

"Christ, someone clean up that mess, and put Virginia—"

"Vanessa," said Ryan, "What happened to her?"

"Virginia, Vanessa, whatever," Greyson shouted. "Henry, could you and your brother get her out of here before she barfs again?" He walked over to Henry, whispered something in his ear, and then retreated to his office, slamming the door behind him.

The greylings looked at one another and then at Ashworth.

Get ready for Chandler? That's all Greyson wants?

Ashworth drew a deep breath. Okay, then that was what they'd do. They'd prepare a welcome for the American, a welcome he'd never forget.

****

Jensen's Storage Ltd., Unit 27, Halifax

"There can't be any connection to me," Greyson had whispered to Henry as his brother carried the unconscious Vanessa out into the fresh air. "So maybe you could use the same trick as last time, okay? No reason it shouldn't work again, right?"

It wasn't much trouble repeating Greyson's trick once they'd hauled Vanessa to their storage locker. *Ditch the bitch*, they called the trick.

Henry pulled the blindfold from Vanessa's eyes, shone a flashlight directly into her face, and smiled.

"Hi Vanessa," he whispered through his mask. The boys couldn't let her identify them. The masks also helped distort their voices. "Feeling a little better?"

She raised her head from her chest and squinted into the darkness. In a dry and painful voice, she whispered, "What's happened? Where . . . where am I?" But then she realized her hands were bound by duct tape to the arms of a wooden chair, and she started screaming. Over and over again, she screamed.

"Not helping. Please stop," said Henry, but then James charged out of the shadows, shoved his masked face right up against hers, shouted, "Shut the fuck up, bitch!" and swung his fist at her with all his might. Instead of hitting the girl, however, he misjudged his swing and struck the back of the chair.

"Shit!" James screamed, then grumbled, "Fuck, fuck, fuck!" as he retreated back into the shadows.

Stunned, Vanessa gasped, gagged, and then started to sob. She could barely catch her breath as she wept.

"Better. Thank you," said Henry. "Now we can talk, okay?"

Still sobbing, Venessa nevertheless managed to look around the room. Her captors were entirely concealed by the darkness, however.

"Who are you? What do you want?" she muttered between sobs.

"We'll ask our questions first, okay?" said Henry, "and then perhaps we'll answer some of yours."

"Oh . . . okay," she whimpered.

"Right then. So, first question, what do you remember about last night?" asked Henry.

"I . . . uh . . . I was at Professor Greyson's cottage."

"I'm sorry, but you're going to have to be more precise."

"Well, we'd been going over my term paper in his office when he said it was getting late, and he asked if I'd like to continue our work at his cottage? I said sure because he was being so nice. We have so much in common. He said so."

"Good, go on."

"Well anyway, so later the lights were off, and we were looking at the stars through his window. He was being a real gentleman. He got me a blanket and opened a box of chocolates as we chatted. I . . . I remember . . . when he put a chocolate in my mouth, I kissed his fingers, but he said he didn't want to take advantage of me, and I said, oh, he'd never do that. And then he opened a bottle of wine, and I remember I took a sip, and that's when things got kind of swirly. And I . . . I don't remember anything after that."

"Yeah, some people just can't handle their booze," muttered James still cradling his injured fist.

"Well, we can remember a great deal, young lady," said Henry. "We remember how you decided to dance for us."

"Us?" asked Vanessa.

"Dr. Greyson's neighbors, five of us, I think. Five, right?" he asked his brother. "You don't remember Dr. Greyson inviting us in when you first arrived at the cove?"

"No . . . no, I don't."

"Must have been when he was parking the car. Anyway, you did this dance, and oh my, how . . . how uninhibited you were."

"I was? No, I wouldn't. You drugged me. Dr. Greyson must have put something in my drink."

"We have five people who say he didn't. Anyway, after you were done dancing, then you pulled us out of our chairs and did the most outrageous things to each of us in turn."

"No! No, you're making this up." Vanessa was sobbing and thrashing about. "I would never."

"Ah, but we have pictures," said Henry. There was a slight chuckle in his voice. Of course, there were no neighbors, no dancing, and no pictures, but what did this bitch know?

"Pictures?"

"Of course, pictures. We couldn't let a performance like that go to waste."

"No . . . no, please, why are you lying?" Vanessa sobbed quietly now. She must have finally realized how utterly helpless she was. Her head had fallen forward onto her chest again. A line of drool ran down across her sweatshirt. But then she rallied slightly, looked up, and asked, "So why am I here? Is this Dr. Greyson's cottage? Is he behind this?"

"Oh, no. Dr. Greyson was appalled by your conduct. In fact, he asked us to remove you from his cottage and return you to Halifax. So here we are, in my storage locker."

"What do you want from me?"

"Well, two things. First, that you will say nothing to anyone about last night or our pictures will make their way to your parents."

"You wouldn't do that, would you?"

"Of course we would. Don't your parents have a right to know what kind of a daughter you are?"

Vanessa began sobbing again.

"And second, you will never show your face on campus again, and certainly not in Dr. Greyson's class. He was simply so mortified by your conduct and so embarrassed in front of his friends and neighbors that he could not abide another moment in your presence."

Vanessa could only shake her head in horror.

"And with that, we'll set you free."

Chapter Three

Tuesday, September 8

Gothall's Rooming House, Halifax

The bus from St. Stephen arrived at 8 a.m. after a twelve-hour meander through every backwater hamlet in Atlantic Canada. Entry into Halifax was an uninspiring drive alongside an endless line of shipping containers on railcars. Somewhere out there, beyond the wall of rusted metal boxes, was Bedford Basin, the largest port on the Atlantic seaboard, where once, mighty convoys formed up for their perilous crossings through U-boat-infested waters to embattled Great Britain. But you wouldn't know the Basin was even there from where Chris sat, pressed against the bus window to escape his slouched and snoring seatmate.

Once in the city proper, the bus wound its way through colorless streets of drab wooden houses. Then it circled around the eighteenth-century hilltop citadel that had been a bastion of British might in North America, before descending toward the harbor front. The town below the fort was a jumble of gray stone buildings blackened by decades of coal smoke and car exhaust, wooden clapboard buildings faded from their former colorful glory, and office buildings of indifferent architectural style. In the watery light of the fogbound morning, the city looked mournful and unnaturally still.

"Barrington Street," the driver called out as the bus rolled to a stop in front of a sandwich shop.

Cramped and stiff, with a throbbing headache and red-raw grazes across his face and hands, Chris wanted to push forward and fling himself from the bus into the fresh air. He might go mad if he didn't soon find coffee, aspirin, and a toilet that didn't singe the hairs in his nostrils.

But he didn't. He waited for all the other passengers to disembark before making his way forward and out into the chill, dismal morning.

A heavy mist that smelled of a tidal shore had draped itself across the city like a shroud on a corpse.

"So wet, it might as well be raining," someone remarked as the passengers waited on the sidewalk for their luggage.

"Some cold for September, eh?" another said. "The damp, it cuts to the bone."

From where Chris stood at the back of the group, he could see both up and down the length of George Street, up to the town clock and the Citadel and down toward the harbor. George Street about summed up Chris's first impression of Halifax, all ups and downs, much like its fortunes. In the reading he'd done over the summer, the story of the old port seemed painfully clear. Time and again since its founding in 1749, the city had appeared on the cusp of prominence and great fortune only to then tumble back into lassitude and obscurity.

At last, the driver hauled Chris's backpack and suitcase from the locker beneath the bus. "Should get them cuts seen to," he said as he handed Chris the bags.

"Yeah, sure," Chris muttered. "Thanks."

Not gonna happen.

Chris headed east along Barrington Street. Barrington might once have been a stylish shopping area, judging by its many elegant stone buildings. Now it was a sad mix of tattoo parlors, ethnic grocers, and fast-food outlets. He turned down toward the harbor at Duke Street, walking past several gracious buildings all for lease, and zigzagging back and forth across Duke to avoid stretches of torn-up sidewalk. Somewhere amid the jumble of featureless office towers was the Provincial Legislature which Alexis de Tocqueville had once described as the most beautiful building in North America. Now it was virtually lost amid the mediocrity of modern-day Halifax.

Chris was to meet Freddy Gothall of *Freddy's Diner* at nine. He got to the intersection of Duke and Hollis Streets with twenty minutes to spare. Hopefully, he'd have time for some breakfast before his appointment.

The diner occupied most of the ground floor of the five-story brick building on the northwest corner of the intersection, its doorway transecting the two streets. Freddy'd said the place wouldn't be hard to spot, and he was right. Its exterior brickwork up to the second floor had once been painted lavender but was now quite faded. Even so, the garish color was still striking.

Above the diner on the Hollis side of the building were three floors of large windows, their casements freshly painted, with curtains and potted plants visible inside. On the Duke Street side of the building, all the windows above the ground floor were dark, small, single-hung, and filthy. Those on the top floor were even boarded over, save for one window whose covering now dangled from a single nail, partially obscuring the window below. Directly above the café door was an enormous sign in the shape of a lighthouse. It hung with an ominous tilt to the left. As Chris waited to cross the intersection, he tried to glimpse Freddy inside the diner. Condensation and the luncheon specials hand-painted on the large windows, however, made it impossible to see more than shapes inside. Besides, he had no idea what Freddy looked like.

Chris had come across a Halifax newspaper in the Bangor public library, and among its classifieds, he'd found an ad for a single room for rent in Halifax's charming downtown. He'd already decided not to live on campus. He wanted anonymity and some way to shield others from Mallory's attacks.

A single room in a brick building some distance from campus seemed a sensible solution. Besides, money would be very tight, and anything Chris could save on accommodation he could spend on food. He had phoned Freddy, who, through myriad hacks and coughs, confirmed a room was still available, and said he'd conduct a showing on Chris's arrival in town.

A bell tinkled above the café door as Chris entered. The place was doing a brisk business. A dozen patrons seated at tables and the small counter ate eggs and toast and chatted quietly over coffee. A slender Indian gentleman with a broad smile and crisp white shirt carried plates to and from the grill where a petite woman in a sari tended eggs and sausages. The aroma was heavenly.

Chris waited in the line at the cash register. When his turn came, a little girl who was barely visible above the countertop asked, "May I take your order, please?"

"Bassy!" the Indian gentleman called out, "please dear, go now. You're going to be late for school. The rush is over. Your mother and I can cope."

"But Papa!"

"I said go." The gentleman came to the cash register, shooed the small girl who exited the café through a curtain at the end of the counter. "I'm sorry, sir. Now, may I take your order, please? Oh, gracious, what happened to you?"

"Accident," Chris muttered. "Can I get some breakfast?"

"Of course, and coffee? And juice?"

"The works, sure."

"That'll be $3.50 for the Bounty Breakfast. Pay when you've eaten."

"I'm supposed to meet somebody here at nine. A Mr. Freddy something. I think this is his place?" "It was once but now it's mine," the

57

gentleman said. There was a note of pride in his voice. "Mr. Freddy owns the building. However, I doubt you'll be seeing him today. He's—"

"Rashid," the lady at the grill called out, "Rashid, it's the guy Freddy phoned about."

"Oh, of course, yes. You're the American."

"Yeah."

"And you want a room."

"Right."

"Well, why don't you eat your breakfast and let my wife and me clean up from the morning rush. Then I'll show you the room. Mr. Freddy gives us a break on garbage collection for doing him the odd favor. So today, you're that favor!" The proprietor led Chris across the diner. "Here," he said, "eat by the window. Let me wipe the steam so you can see the view."

The view was indifferent but the breakfast was magnificent. The lady from the grill delivered it to Chris and smiled a golden smile as she placed the plate before him.

As Chris settled his bill, the gentleman said, "So my name is Rashid Minhas. Freddy calls me Rich. It's his idea of a joke, but I don't mind."

"I'm Chris, Chris Chandler."

"Welcome, Mr. Chandler. And that's my wife Dolly, and you met our daughter Basalah. Our other daughter is in physics at McGill University in Montreal. I understand you're a student, yourself."

"I . . . I'm just getting started."

Mr. Minhas headed for the door with Chris trailing behind. He pulled a bundle of keys from his pocket as they left the café. "Let me carry that," Minhas said as he took Chris's suitcase, the one containing Mallory's bones.

"Never too late for a good education. That's what I tell my children." Minhas chattered on as he walked several steps along the sidewalk to a gray metal door just beyond the café windows. "I was a teacher before we came to this country. I taught hydrology at the University of Jaipur." He unlocked and opened the door onto a dark foyer at the foot of a narrow staircase. "But enough about me," he said as he started up the stairs.

His voice was now barely above a whisper. "There are two rooms on each floor and a shared toilet. Two young men and their . . . their lady friends occupy the second floor. They're probably asleep at this hour because they, well, I think they work at night. I suggest you try not to disturb them. They can be somewhat unpleasant, if you get my meaning."

Mr. Minhas continued up the stairs to the third floor. An icy draft flowed down the staircase like a mountain stream. "There's a tiny problem on the fifth floor," explained Minhas. "A window, it keeps popping open."

"And the tenant doesn't mind?"

"Oh, no one lives on the fifth floor, not anymore. Just storage." Suddenly the crash of a window slamming shut echoed through the building. The draft died. Momentarily speechless, Minhas looked up the stairs, but then his smile returned. "There, you see? Problem solved." And on he climbed.

"On this floor, we have Mrs. Norris and Mr. Brook. Mrs. Norris is a dear. Not quite right in the head, but a dear all the same. Her husband owned this building many years ago, and in her mind, he still does."

They next passed a room with an open door. Inside, an old gentleman was seated on the floor, sanding a wooden chair.

"Good morning, Mr. Brook, said Minhas. "This is our new tenant. Would you care to meet him?"

59

The old gentleman looked up, scowled, and returned to his sanding.

"All right then. Have a good day, Mr. Brook." Mr. Minhas then whispered, "I gather he had a bad time during the war. Quiet though. Keeps to himself. So let's see your room, shall we?"

As they climbed to the fourth floor, Mr. Minhas set out the rules of tenancy. Rent must be paid in cash each Monday. You can pay me if Mr. Freddy doesn't make it in. No pets. There is to be no cooking in the building. You may have a kettle but no other kitchen appliances of any kind. For the moment, you have no other neighbor on this floor so you won't have to negotiate a bathroom schedule. But I have to tell you, the toilets can be temperamental so you might want to chat with your neighbors on the third floor about . . . alternate arrangements should the need arise. There is to be no noise after ten at night. And if you must smoke, please lean out your window when you do."

The hallway on the fourth floor was especially dim since the hoarding dangling from above obscured the only window.

"So here we are. The room's last occupant left us recently after falling out with the two fellows on the second floor. I . . . I don't mean to worry you, but please, Mr. Chandler, avoid them at all costs."

"I'm sure I'll be fine," Chris said.

"Very good then."

Minhas unlocked the door. The room smelled musty. It had a single bed and bedside table, a desk, an armchair, and an old armoire. Mr. Minhas crossed to the small window and, after a struggle, managed to raise it an inch or two. The tang of the harbor crept quickly into the room.

"Sticks sometimes in the damp," he explained.

"Is it noisy here?" Chris asked.

"There is traffic noise during the day, and it can be a bit noisy when the bars close. But otherwise . . . ."

"So, noisy then. But that's okay. I'll be at school most of the time anyway."

Mr. Minhas put Chris's suitcase on the bed and said, "I hope you will be comfortable here, Mr. Chandler."

Chris wanted nothing more than to stretch out and sleep for a few hours before he went out to explore this new town. But Mr. Minhas wasn't done.

"May I ask where you'll be studying?"

"Cavendish College."

"Long walk from here. But the buses aren't bad. Have you been to the campus yet?"

"No, I came directly here. I want to settle in first. I've got a free day before registration."

And I really need sleep.

"Can I tell Mr. Freddy you're taking the room?"

"I'll stay a week, and then we'll talk again. Will that be all right?"

"I'm sure. Now remember, no cooking in the room, but we'll give you a discount at our café." Minhas opened the hallway door to leave.

"Mr. Minhas," Chris called after him. "My money is going to be tight. I need to find a part-time job. Would you have any suggestions?"

Minhas was pensive for a moment, then smiled and said, "I suppose I could use a late-night cleanup man."

"That would be great," replied Chris.

Suddenly, from somewhere overhead, a loud creak like the yowl of a cat in heat ripped through their conversation.

"It's . . . it's nothing," said Minhas. "Old building, that's all." Then the icy draft returned.

****

Duncan's Cove

Greyson pushed his breakfast plate away and peered out over the steel-gray sea. As waves sloshed about the pilings beneath his cottage, he shut his eyes, rubbed his temples to alleviate the throbbing, and for the umpteenth time, ran over the plan in his mind.

He had the chemistry sorted: the drug to knock the guy out, the bath to strip his flesh, and the composition of the mud shell to be applied. He'd soon have the ritual mapped out; the formation, the words, and the activation. And he'd finished his task list: find clay, lye, animal glue, and both a transgressor from whom to extract the required amount of blood and a soulless person. All he needed now was to find the Prague amulet. And that task would fall to the American.

His revenge was so close he could almost taste it. But getting to this point had been such an arduous journey.

Before their lawsuit against Greyson's publisher went to court, his mother had insisted he enter rehab. On the advice of her literary agent, she'd paid his way to a monastery in Russia famed for its grueling method of treating Russia's drug-addicted Afghan veterans. At the All Martyrs Monastery, Greyson first stumbled upon the entangled power of pharmaceuticals, illuminated manuscripts, and sacred language. At first, he'd been overjoyed. Revealing to the world this heretofore unknown entanglement would very possibly stand the academic world on its ear and redeem his career. But then he realized how little he actually had to report. Given his reputation, no scholarly journal was likely to publish anything from him, never mind a story about hopped-up monks seeing demons. Greyson's stint in rehab failed, his disillusion with academe darkened, and he fell ever deeper into despondency and delusion.

Thereafter he'd flirted with one ludicrous idea after another, one relationship after another, and one pharmaceutical dependency after another until even he was disgusted with himself. During an especially nasty inquiry into the suicide of a co-ed with whom he'd been involved, Greyson fled to Europe again, this time for the Christmas break. He chose Prague for no other reason than he'd recently seen the silent film, *The Golem*. But despite the holiday season, Prague was a depressingly gray and dismal city suffering under the grip of its communist masters. And so when he read an ad in a local paper for another monastic retreat some seventy miles south of Prague, he set off for the Upper Palatine Forest.

High in the Bohemian Massif, the Monastery to the Annunciation of the Virgin Mary advertised rest and relaxation away from the rigors of urban life. It turned out to be an almost derelict cluster of gothic buildings at the end of a dirt track high above the tiny town of Piron.

Portions of the monastery's buildings had crumbled away. The wall around the commissary garden had collapsed, and the onion dome atop its tower tilted ominously to the right. Where once there might have been lawns, now matted yellow grass beneath a crust of dirty snow snaked among unkempt and desiccated shrubs. Tree roots pushed up through gravel pathways. Twisted creepers crawled along interior corridors, leaving a trail of dry leaves. Clouds of dust danced across bare stone floors in icy drafts which probed every chamber. Meltwater from the snow-covered roofs dripped down the commissary walls. And the monks' infernal, mind-numbing plainsong—not the soaring clarity of young voices but the damp and crumbling voices of old men—drove Greyson practically round the bend. Too old to be of much use to anyone anymore, the dozen monks still in residence clearly had little to do. Once, they might have illustrated manuscripts or made beer, or played volleyball between their bouts of singing. Now they watched the grainy black and white television in the scriptorium for hours on end and chatted about Dynamo Kyiv and the battle for the European Cup.

Greyson's cell had a rude iron bed with stained sheets, a threadbare blanket, a wobbly wooden table, a chair with missing rungs, and an oil lamp perched on an orange crate alongside his cot. Nothing more; there was not even a cupboard or bench for his backpack. During the days, Greyson walked the snowy hills around the monastery, smoking and muttering to himself in the vain hope he might come across a lovely young shepherdess. At night, when the monastery was as still as the grave, Greyson shivered interminably, not just from the cold but from want of certain pharmaceuticals.

In desperation on the third night, he wrapped himself in his blanket, left the cell, and set out to prowl the halls until dawn. At the far end of a long, vaulted corridor, its walls once decorated with vivid paintings which were now faded to a memory, he spied a flickering light beneath a heavy oaken door. He knocked . . . nothing, knocked a second time . . . and again nothing, so then he heaved open the massive door.

On the far side of the octagonal-shaped room, an old monk sat snoring loudly beside an enormous stone fireplace. By the flickering light from the last embers of the small fire, Greyson could tell he'd found the monastery library. Timber shelves on every wall disappeared into the shadows overhead. Folio tables ran off from the center of the room like the spokes of a wheel. Every surface, including much of the floor, was cluttered with scrolls and leather-bound tomes, all covered in dust. Apparently, no one had put a book away properly in decades.

Greyson prowled about the room for some time before the old monk stirred, loudly cleared his throat, and then muttered, "Found what you're looking for?" in perfect English.

"You're American?" Greyson asked.

"No," he replied. "German, but I like your TV shows."

"Are you on guard duty?" asked Greyson. "Anything worth stealing?"

"Doubt it. Just a lot of record books. Our monastery was once the repository for penitentials from across Bohemia, but we lost that function in the thirteenth century. They can make for entertaining reading . . . if you read Latin and have many long nights to kill."

"So that's it? That's all you have?"

"There are the manuscripts our brethren illuminated over the centuries, but we must have been a boring lot because our work is very pedestrian. We do have a collection of medieval medical texts with some quite wonderful and, might I say, arousing illustrations. There's a copy of *Lilium medicinae* from 1303 by the medieval physician Bernard de Gordon. However, the mold is starting to eat its pages."

"Hmm."

"Oh, and there's a heap of Hebrew documents in that corner."

"Hebrew? Why Hebrew?"

"Our order has always had a mandate to convert the Jews. Not surprisingly, we weren't very successful at that. But then, in the eighteenth century, the Bishop in Prague assigned our monastery the task of more aggressively troubling the Jews. Jews had always enjoyed significant Royal support in Bohemia. Throughout the eighteenth century, they flourished to the point where there were six hundred Jewish communities across this land. But then state policy began to change. In December 1744, Maria Theresa expelled Prague's Jews and only allowed their return upon payment of a massive increase in their Tolerance Tax. And that's when my brethren did their worst. They'd attacked and burned synagogues all over Bohemia for decades, but in 1754 they attacked Prague's Jews directly. To this day, our Abbot brags that our brethren in a single day set fires across the Jewish town that destroyed 190 houses and 6 synagogues. And during that raid, they seized wagonloads of books and documents from Prague's grandest synagogue, which our brethren hoped might reveal the Jews' evil blood rituals. Of course, they didn't, and the stolen trove has been rotting away in that corner ever since."

"By their grandest synagogue, you mean . . . ."

"The *Altneuschul*, yes."

"May I have a look?"

"You're Jewish?"

"No, but I do read Hebrew."

"Go ahead. You'll be the first to use this library for any purpose in years. Besides me, that is, and I'm only here for the fireplace."

Greyson spent an hour or two sifting through the documents. Much of the rag paper was still intact. The heap contained a bit of everything, old prayer books, religious texts, records of meetings, accounts, and dozens and dozens of essays and analyses stretching back centuries. There were also medical texts, and judgments, and correspondence, so much, in fact, he was barely glancing at each item as he quickly leafed through the stacks. Until that is, he came across the name Judah Loew ben Bezalel.

Greyson knew the name immediately. Talmudic scholar, Jewish mystic, and philosopher who lived in Prague in the latter half of the 16th century, Rabbi Loew was known to scholars of Judaism as the Maharal of Prague or simply The Maharal. And, of course, his name was also associated with the legend of the Prague golem.

Greyson wasn't sure why his heart raced when he came across Judah Loew's name, but it did. And when he realized just how much material in the heap dated from Loew's tenure at the *Altneuschul*, he almost passed out. The collection might change Judaic scholarship fundamentally. And it would attract a shitload of cash if the collection ever came to market.

It was almost dawn now. Greyson turned from the books and documents to find the old monk had departed, but not before he'd placed a candle on the folio table over Greyson's shoulder. Its flame guttered in a pool of wax and went out. By the watery morning light coming through the filthy windows high overhead, Greyson left the library and returned to his cell for a few hours of sleep before the midday meal.

Later, in the commissary, he approached the old monk and asked if he'd be allowed to revisit the library that afternoon.

"Move in there if you wish. No one will disturb you," the old monk replied through a mouthful of cheese.

The Judah Loew material was overwhelming. There were rough drafts and notes on every one of his works, from his first book, *Gur Aryeh*, to his essays on the various festivals. Although Loew never called himself a Kabbalist, reams and reams of his notes demonstrated his belief that the ideas of Kabbalah were the most deeply true of all the Torah. The notes also revealed just how interested Loew had been in scientific research, so long as the research did not contradict the final authority of divine revelation, however. Greyson had no doubt; no matter what else there might be in the pile of material, the Loew collection alone would be worth a fortune. Universities and Jewish scholars the world over, not to mention the state of Israel, would bid big money for the material.

Greyson's excitement grew as he sifted through Judah Loew's letters on topics as diverse as chemical properties, medical practices, astronomy, and alchemy. And then he came across the document that changed his world.

At first, Greyson thought it merely described some sort of medical treatment. But it quickly became apparent the single sheet was far more than that. Greyson had shaken the document from a wooden tube scorched at one end. He was familiar with such tubes. They'd often been used to protect important documents from the elements during long journeys. The page appeared to be the sole remaining portion of a far longer letter, but from whence the letter originated, there was no indication.

The first thing Greyson realized was that the page was not written in Judah Loew's hand, nor was it written on Loew's customary fine white rag paper. Even so, the hair on Greyson's arms stood up the moment he began picking his way through the Hebrew text.

Each day, our community faced simmering hatred and looming danger from our neighbors.

Raba bar Rav Hunan said: If the righteous desired it, they could—by living a life of absolute purity—be creators, for so it is written.

I contemplated creating a guardian for our people, a golem, but I knew in my heart that I had not lived a pure enough life to be a creator. But what was I to do? If I mustered our brethren to fight back in defense of our community, I doubted we would survive their overwhelming numbers and the torrent of violence that would rain down upon us.

But then, in a dream, it came to me. I must create not a golem but a golem-like creature. If our enemies already believe we engage in dark arts and blood rituals, then why not give them a taste of what they already fear? And so I began.

After days of cleansing and purifying my flesh, I went in search of a man without a soul. Aron was the spawn of a prostitute and a gentile. He was known to our community by his dead eyes, his pale and clammy skin, the weakness of his grip, his bluish lips and fingernails, and his disinterest in all things immediate. I thus knew him to be without a soul.

I administered a medicinal purgative to cleanse his organs and then a tonic to induce a waking sleep.

When he became insensitive to pain, I laid him in a bath of water and lye that I'd leached from wood ash. By our sand horologe, he lay in the bath no more than a quarter of the hour. Horrible though the procedure was, I deemed it necessary to replace his sinful and disobedient flesh with new flesh amenable to my will.

I lifted him from the lye. All his flesh had been removed, exposing sinew and muscle, but the soulless one felt no pain. I dried him, being careful not to rupture any vessels or displace any organs.

I had previously ground a quantity of comfrey root and lobelia in a mortar and pestle and mixed them with a sufficiency of honey. It is a formula the Turcomans employ to replace the destroyed skin of their burned warriors.

I circled the corpus reciting the words, "The Lord G-d formed a man from the dust of the earth, and He blew into his nostrils the breath of life, and the man became a living being." As I spoke, the chaver applied the mixture in the manner of an artificial flesh. He was instructed to seal every part of Aron's exposed organs. We then wrapped him in strips of clean linen inscribed with homilies from the Zohar.

Our chaver and I had previously mixed ground chalk with milk and glue boiled from animal hides. We then blended the mix with clay taken from the riverbank and linseed oil to form a thick, malleable paste resembling bread dough. I applied it to Aron's body, leaving holes for his eyes and nostrils. I then applied a final layer of river clay and the blood of a transgressor obtained from a corpse hanged at the gates of our city.

The mixture dried to a thick flexible coating like heavy leather. It remained flexible for many days, after which some cracking did appear. I then patched the cracks with the remaining mixture.

Then came the section that nearly stopped Greyson's heart.

I could no longer conceive of this monster as poor Aron. I circled my creature seven times, reciting the most secret and holy names of G-d. In my dream, the exact pronunciation of the names was made very clear to me, and I repeated them very carefully since a single slip in pronunciation would likely result in Aron's death as well as my own. And then I also pressed into the creature's forehead the secret names of G-d, which I had previously inscribed on a piece of vellum. And with this gift of G-d's most holy names, the creature stirred. It rose from the table whereon I had assembled him and accepted my commands as one without sense or impulse of its own.

Rabbi Loew's golem! This was Loew's actual account of creating his monster. But, holy Hell, he hadn't turned mud into living flesh! Instead, he'd wrapped living flesh in mud. And then he'd used the holy names, not to breathe life into the creature of mud, but merely to command the madman within! What Greyson had discovered would turn the entire Golem legend on its head. And if Greyson could repeat the process, he might actually prove the tale to be a historical fact!

Greyson rushed from the library in search of the old German monk and found him in the commissary watching an American western. He beckoned the old man outside, and when they were seated out of the icy breeze on a low garden wall, Greyson put the question to him.

"Can I buy the Jewish material?"

"Why?"

"Well, for one thing, scholars of Judaica would be quite interested in it." Greyson didn't want to show too much excitement. He couldn't afford to get into a bidding war. He couldn't even afford the cost of shipping the crap back to Canada if it came to that. But one bridge at a time. "And for another, you guys might be able to afford a new television with your take."

"Most of us can't actually see the TV we already have, and we'll all be dead soon enough anyway."

"But the material in that pile could be invaluable to scholars."

The old man shook his head. "I guarantee, the moment our Abbot hears the material from the *Altneuschul* might be of interest to Jews today, it will go up in smoke."

"Why?"

"It's been the mission of our Order for a thousand years to hate the Jews. I'm now too old to hate anybody, and we're probably the most useless monastery on the planet. But I can assure you, our Abbot would take it as vindication for our purposeless existence if he could deny Jews the pleasure of discovering their lost treasures."

"Okay," said Greyson, "but can I remove any of the material at all?"

"The less, the better," replied the old man, "but I must warn you. If the Abbot discovers what you've done, you'll be scourged. And we may look a decrepit lot, but Brother Gregos is still capable of administering a ferocious scourge."

"Okay, so one page at most," Greyson said, and he knew precisely what page that would be.

Greyson flew home as agitated as an addict in withdrawal. Back in Halifax, he spent months studying Rabbi Loew and the golem. Legend had it that Rabbi Loew had been forced to disable his creation when it ran amok. He was said to have locked it away in the attic of the *Altneuschul*, where some believe it remains to this day. As for the secret names of God, the holy words with which Rabbi Loew commanded his creature, those he was believed to have locked away in an amulet that he wore until his death.

So what became of the amulet?

During the first decades of the twentieth century, Prague's Jewish community, the largest in Europe, was thrown into turmoil, not by external forces but by forces from within. There were calls from across the Jewish community for modernization, of relations, of business practices, and above all, of religious worship. Many older synagogues were

71

leveled, and even the *Altneuschul* feared it might be destroyed. Rumors circulated that reformists wanted to seize the *Altneuschul's* treasures. Others believed the *Altneuschul's* elders intended to send away the synagogue's treasures before anyone could get their hands on them.

In the course of his research, Greyson became obsessed with two questions. Could Rabbi Loew's amulet have been among the treasures dispatched from Prague? And if it was, where had it gone?

The questions ate at Greyson, and so the following March during the college reading week he'd returned to Prague. He'd received permission to examine the synagogue's public records on the pretext that he was exploring links between the Prague Jewish community and Jews in Atlantic Canada.

Among the synagogue's records, he'd stumbled across three tantalizing documents. The first was a portion of a letter written in March 1912 to a New York synagogue. It mentioned that the Prague cantor would be visiting America bearing a special gift for his hosts. The gift was referred to as *one of the most treasured possessions of our venerable Jewish community*. The second was a brief summary in the rabbi's diary of a meeting in February of 1912 between the synagogue's rabbi and its cantor. During the meeting, the rabbi apparently instructed the cantor to make his way to Southampton and secure passage to New York. And the third document was the carbon copy of a letter written in the autumn of 1912 to the New York synagogue inquiring whether the Prague cantor had ever arrived.

At first glance, the documents were relatively innocuous, but Greyson convinced himself he'd discovered a link all other investigators had missed. The gift carried by the cantor had sailed from Southampton for America and never been seen again.

That was when Greyson made his most audacious connection. The missing gift must have been Rabbi Loew's secret names. What more priceless or coveted or fearsome treasure could the synagogue have possessed? Furthermore, the cantor had never made it to the New York synagogue. Could that have been because the cantor's ship never completed its crossing? In 1912, only one ship famously failed to complete its Atlantic crossing—the *Titanic*. To Greyson, the conclusion was obvious. Rabbi Loew's secret names of God had vanished with the *Titanic*.

The amulet was almost certainly at the bottom of the sea. That said, three hundred corpses had been pulled from the icy Atlantic following the *Titanic's* sinking, and one hundred fifty of them had been interred in Halifax. Was it too much to hope the cantor might have been among *them*? Greyson had almost fallen to his knees at the thought. It was as though the gods of scholarship had ordained his resurrection. Fate or fortune might have placed within his grasp the most potent words imaginable. Judah Loew's amulet containing the secret names of God, the names with which he'd commanded his terrifying creature, those very words might be out there, in a *Titanic* grave not five miles from Greyson's office.

"Of course it will be," Greyson had muttered to himself over and over again. "It has to be."

Greyson opened his eyes, but the sight of the dried egg yolk and ketchup smeared across his plate immediately nauseated him. He took several deep breaths to calm his nerves and downed another whisky. Oh, Christ, his head was killing him. Maybe he had a touch of the flu or something. But there was no way he could make it to the college today. He'd have to cancel his class and get a few more hours of sleep. He'd let the greylings have more time to pull together their crap on the amulet. Knowing them, they'd find nothing of value, but he'd give them one last chance anyway.

Soon, very soon, the American would arrive. With the kid's curious powers over the dead, he was sure to find the right grave, and Greyson would have the final piece in the puzzle, the last stroke in his master-piece, his crowning achievement! And then, what pleasure it would give him to rub the noses of his tormentors in his triumph!

****

Greyson's Lab

Just after 8 a.m., Ashworth surveyed the group gathered around the common room table. Ryan, angel girl or Bonnie, Sheila, brothers Henry and James, and Jeffy. Not bad, especially since they'd worked through the night to prepare for this meeting.

"Any news of Vanessa?" Ashworth asked.

"She was just so embarrassed after throwing up like that," said Henry, "she wasn't sure she'd be able to face us again. I tried to tell her it was okay, but, you know . . ."

"Okay. So anyway," continued Ashworth, "Bonnie bought coffee and muffins, and we each owe her like two bucks."

There followed a few minutes of shuffling and chatter as people forked over change and started in on their meager breakfast.

Okay, good start.

Ashworth didn't want to get caught grinning, even if his first move to reassert influence over the group after Greyson's outburst was off to a pretty good beginning. Get a jump on Greyson's new priority; that was Michael's plan. Of course, finding Greyson's stupid amulet was going to be almost impossible, and the whole project was complete crap, but its failure would not be the greylings' fault. After they'd been able to lay out the facts, Greyson would finally be forced to admit his scheme was nuts. Until then, however, they'd carry out Greyson's orders to the letter.

"So, Mike," Ryan called from the far end of the table.

Christ, how many times did he have to tell people? "It's Michael!"

"Okay, sure, so you really think this is a good idea, meeting like this without Greyson?"

"Absolutely. You heard him. He wants us to pull our notes together on the *Titanic*. That's what we're doing."

"But he also said to wait for the new guy."

Michael gave Ryan an icy glare. "You really think we need a new guy? Anybody here think we need a new guy? Do we really need someone who knows nothing about our work? We'd lose days, weeks even, explaining our stuff. And Greyson said himself he's worried the college might move against us, like today even!"

"It's just so sad," Sheila said. "We were doing some really cool stuff with the manuscripts."

"I know, but Greyson's idea about the amulet might be cool too," Michael replied. He didn't actually believe that, not for a minute. The amulet was complete crap, but Greyson was the boss, so what the hell. "And it's not like we're starting from scratch. We've been playing around with this *Titanic* idea for a year now, and it looks like there might be something to it."

No chance in Hell, but whatever keeps the group together, that's all that matters.

"Yeah, but even if we did believe this Prague medal thing had some kind of message about the names of God in it, finding one particular Jewish guy with a medal who died on the *Titanic* and is buried in Halifax? Give me a break," Ryan muttered. "We don't know what name the guy used as a passenger. We don't know he actually had this medal. We don't even know for sure he died. It's crazy."

Jeez! Why couldn't they all just shut up and do what he asked? "If he didn't die, then why did the *Altneuschul* and the New York synagogue both try to find him? We know they did. We've got the letters." Michael was almost shouting.

Ryan shook his head and slumped back in his chair.

"So anyway, as I explained last night, I thought we should meet this morning to review what we do know so we can lay it all out for Greyson when he's back tomorrow. After that, we'll give him our ideas on next steps. That way, he'll see we don't need this new guy. Right? Ryan, why don't you start? I asked you and Bonnie to pull together what we already know about the *Titanic* victims."

Ryan heaved a melodramatic sigh and moved forward in his chair. "Okay, so I think we can save everyone a lot of time with what we found. To make it simple, if there's any chance this pendant thing is in Halifax, we think we already know where. Right, Bonnie?"

Bonnie nodded her head.

"Hold on. Let's not get ahead of ourselves," Michael said. "So you did investigate the Jews on board, right?"

"Oh yeah," sighed Ryan. "Okay, Bonnie, you explain."

"Well, yes, and right off, it was clear there was a lot of confusion about how many Jews were aboard and how many Jewish bodies were recovered. We know there were 2228 people on the *Titanic* and somewhere between 1503 and 1517 were lost. We know something like 328 bodies were recovered, 119 were reburied at sea, and 209 dead were returned to Halifax, where they were laid out in the Mayflower Rink. 59 bodies were eventually claimed by families, and the remaining 150 are buried in three cemeteries here in Halifax, of which more than 40 are still unidentified."

"But what about Jewish passengers?"

Ryan took over. "That's what I wanted to tell you. It was thought there were 100 to 200 Jews aboard the *Titanic*, but someone checked the passenger list and found only 89 Hebrew surnames. The best guess was that 100 Jews were lost. On Thursday, May second, Halifax Rabbi Jacob Walter was asked to identify Jews among the dead, so they could be buried before the Sabbath began. But that's when things went crazy. He thought 44 of the bodies might be Jewish. But then there was this fight. Coffins were pried open and bodies stolen from the rink, then seized by the police. In the end, only ten were ever buried in the Baron de Hirsch Jewish cemetery. It later turned out the rabbi's techniques for identifying Jews weren't reliable anyway. Even the Jewish community later condemned him. But we do have copies of his notes anyway. And that's where Bonnie found something cool."

Bonnie drew a thick stack of pages from her bookbag, flipped through them, held up one sheet, and pointed to an entry. "Here," she said. "Rabbi Walter describes one of the ten buried in the Jewish cemetery as a large man in his fifties. And get this, he writes that the guy was wearing a chain and medallion."

"That's great," Michael said.

"So then, job's done. Let's get out of here," Ryan replied as he pushed away from the table.

"No, wait," said Michael. "That won't satisfy Greyson. He wants all our notes. On Prague, and Southampton, and New York. All of it."

"Why?"

"Well, if it turns out the guy you found isn't the Prague cantor, he'll want to examine the whole picture again to figure out what we do next."

Ryan said, "Look, I don't for a minute think the guy we found is the cantor that Greyson wants, but we found a fat guy with a medallion, and that's good enough."

"But shouldn't we review everything we've got before we talk about your guy?" Michael looked at the others. "Everyone's worked hard, and we're here now, so why not review what we've got, okay?"

There were several muttered 'all rights' from around the table.

"Good. So first, I want to go over what happened in Prague."

He passed around a photocopied picture of the *Altneuschul* in Prague and of the fragmentary notes Greyson had found in its archive.

"You know the legend of Rabbi Judah Loew ben Bezalel and his golem. And that the creature, along with Loew's secret names of God, were hidden either at the synagogue or somewhere outside Prague. We also know that Jews by the end of the nineteenth century were modernizing their quarter. The rabbi of the *Altneuschul* in 1912, Rabbi Nathan Ehrenfeld, was concerned about the destruction by his own people of the old Jewish way of life in Prague. He suspected some of the leaders of the modernization movement had ulterior motives. They wanted to find the ancient knowledge concealed in the *Altneuschul*. Rabbi Ehrenfeld's diary records that he feared for the old knowledge concealed in the synagogue and the graveyard. He doesn't say whether he did anything about it, however. The records of the *Altneuschul* are skimpy since it has suffered several fires over its long history. However, Greyson found a reference in the rabbi's diary to a meeting in which he instructs the synagogue's cantor to carry one of the *Altneuschul's* greatest treasures to New York."

"There's no mention of the *Titanic* in the letter," Ryan interjected.

"No."

"And ships made the crossing every week back then."

"But only one ship was lost that spring, and only one cantor went missing. So connect the dots for Christ's sake, Ryan."

Michael looked around the room. Right, good, he'd finally shut Ryan up.

"We also know the rabbi wrote to a New York City synagogue asking that they receive a visitor, but we can find no evidence the visit ever happened."

Sheila piped up. "Okay, so I tried to find out everything I could about the Prague cantor. There's not much, but we do know this. He was a large man in his fifties named Gruber. He was said to have been very good, but all mention of him in Prague ends in April of 1912. His disappearance could be a coincidence, but it's intriguing. One last bit of information. Dr. Greyson also found in the *Altneuschul* archive a clipping from an American newspaper that covered the *Titanic* funerals in Halifax. In the margin, he noticed a handwritten note likely by Rabbi Ehrenfeld. It read, "Our beloved friend was buried in Halifax today." No idea who the friend may have been, but it could have been Gruber. Oh, and Ehrenfeld died right after he wrote that note."

"Thank you, Sheila. So now, let's consider what happened in Southampton, since the rabbi's letter suggests the cantor was traveling in that direction. Henry and James, that was your job."

"Right," began Henry, "well, the Southampton synagogue was bombed during the war, and not many records survived. But we do have the transcript of an interview with some old lady from the 1950s. It was made as part of a local history project. She'd been the synagogue's secretary back at the time of the *Titanic* sinking, and she was asked if the synagogue lost anybody aboard. Her answer was weird. She knew one victim well, some guy named Kennel. But she also thought maybe a second member of the synagogue might have been lost.

"I guess she saw a note in the rabbi's diary that two friends of the Southampton synagogue were gonna be buried in Halifax, not one. Since Kennel was the only guy she knew, it's possible the other reference was to the visitor from Prague. The secretary later reported that the rabbi was upset about the misidentification of one of the bodies in Halifax, but then he too died before he could fix it.

"Anyway, one of the first jobs of the new rabbi was to host some guy from America. He was sent very quickly by a New York synagogue to find out about Jews aboard *Titanic*."

"Great, okay finally, so what happened in New York City? That's you, Jeffy and Sheila."

Jeffy began. "Right, well the American Henry's talking about was named Ed Rubin, and he was from the 35th Street Synagogue in New York that the Prague cantor was supposed to have contacted. We know for sure Rubin had hurried to Southampton and arranged a meeting with the rabbi because Rubin telegraphed his boss back in New York to say that he'd arrived. No account of the meeting has ever been published, however, not in Southampton, not at the 35th Street synagogue in New York, and not in Prague."

"So maybe the meeting never happened, or maybe this Rubin guy wasn't even looking for the Prague cantor," Ryan said.

Michael was quick to respond. "Or maybe the search for the cantor was hushed up. To reveal their frantic search for the cantor might reveal the importance of the treasure he'd been carrying. The Prague rabbi in 1912 was afraid someone was after the synagogue's treasure, so maybe he didn't want anyone to know where the cantor had gone or why."

Everyone sat in silence for a moment, trying to absorb the significance of what they'd learned.

This was the moment Michael had been hoping for, a chance to get everyone on the same page. "But this is what we think is important." And he quickly summarized.

"The cantor, a large man, was dispatched by Rabbi Ehrenfeld because he was concerned for the fate of the *Altneuschul's* treasures. In the first week of April, the cantor left Prague for Paris and Southampton carrying one of the synagogue's most treasured possessions. The treasure may have been the secret names of God, since legend had it they'd been in the possession of the *Altneuschul* for centuries. The secret names were probably inscribed on or in an amulet because amulets were often used to conserve beloved texts. The cantor visited Southampton, where the local rabbi helped him book passage to New York. The cantor almost certainly sailed aboard the *Titanic* since he was never heard from again. The only ship lost that spring was the *Titanic*. Among the recovered corpses, one was described as being a large man wearing a medallion, and since his corpse was never claimed, he's buried here."

"And that's what we have," Michael concluded.

"And we have his grave number," Bonnie piped in.

Ryan lurched forward, clearly frustrated. "Yeah, sure, so the guy has a medallion, but I say again, the odds of him being the Prague cantor are incredibly remote!"

"But we have to check it out, right?" Michael looked around the table.

Sheila shook her head. "It's such a shame. We were making so much progress. Why are we wasting time on this? Like Ryan said, the odds are ridiculous. 1500 lost, and only 150 buried here, and we have no real idea who was Jewish."

Michael practically lost it. "Because if Greyson is right," he shouted, "nothing will provide more proof of the power of Holy incantations than that damned medallion!"

Jeffy, wimpy Jeffy from Rhode Island, chose that moment to speak up.

"I think Michael's right. If we show the college admin our work with the manuscripts, they'll only say it's the drugs. We know what happens with the manuscripts isn't the drugs. It's the power of the words themselves, the power of Kabbalah. But they're not going to believe us without more proof. So maybe we do need this medallion thing. We report to the press we've found the first tangible proof that the rabbi of Prague really did make a golem, and the whole world will go crazy."

Holy crap, Michael was going to have to reward Jeffy somehow.

"And if he's wrong, which he almost certainly is?" Ryan asked.

Henry spoke. "Then we go back to the manuscripts and hope we have enough evidence in them to persuade the college to let us keep going with our research."

Michael said, "Look, I think we have no choice. I think we should open this Gruber guy's grave tonight before this goddamned American arrives."

The meeting erupted.

"What?"

"You're crazy!"

"Us? Open a grave ourselves?"

"We can't do that!"

"Quiet, quiet," shouted Ryan. The table fell silent for a moment. Ryan then yelled, "Michael, are you out of your gourd? We'd end up in prison!"

"Not if we're careful," Michael said calmly. "Look, if Greyson comes in today, okay, we're ready to hand him all our stuff. But if he doesn't, then why not check out the grave ourselves?"

"Because," shouted Ryan, "a bunch of kids climbing into a Jewish cemetery in the middle of the night, we'll probably be shot!"

"How else did you think we were going to get that amulet?"

"Well, for one thing, I thought we might leave the job to this American guy. Let him get shot!"

"And let him have the glory? No goddamned way!" said Ashworth.

"If you're so hungry for glory, then you dig up the fat guy's grave yourself," Ryan said and pushed away from the table.

Michael grinned. The momentum was shifting his way. He spoke with icy resolve. "If you're all such cowards, then fuck yes, I will do it myself."

After a moment of silence, Sheila said. "I don't know, maybe we should try. I mean, this grave does have a big guy in it, and he has an amulet."

"We don't even know where the grave is!" exclaimed Bonnie. "Have you ever been to the Fairview Cemetery? I sure haven't."

Michael was delighted. If they were debating the location of the grave then the meeting was his! "Okay, one of us has to go there this afternoon and find the grave in daylight so we can go straight to it in the dark."

"This is insane!" grumbled Ryan. "I swear we're gonna get killed!"

****

Bemishstock, Maine

Ricky Pike taped shut the last carton of Chief Boucher's personal crap, kicked the carton across the office, then slumped down onto the floor, and sobbed like an infant.

It was just past 7 p.m. Ricky had less than an hour before his shift at the *Piggly Wiggly* began, and he was alone in the former police station. Every other constable had only been given five minutes to clear the building when the State Police arrived to impound the department's files and take over its responsibilities. Ricky was the sole Bemishstock police officer who'd been permitted to retain a key to the old building, at least until the place was emptied.

Of course, the State Police wouldn't be seen doing business out of the ex-pizza joint that had served as Bemishstock Police Headquarters for more than a decade. No, they had to have fancy new digs in city hall. So here Ricky sat, carrying out his final assignment before his career in law enforcement came to an ignominious end.

How the hell had everything gone so wrong? One day he had a good job—he'd been an actual civil servant with real benefits and the promise of a pension—and the next, he was shit. One day he was working for a man the town—Hell, the whole State—respected, and the next day that man was dead and branded a corrupt cop and a pervert. And all the police department's work over the years—every arrest, conviction, and investigation—was now suspect, and Chief Boucher's legacy was a huge heaping pile of crap. One day Ricky was himself the acting Chief of Police. The next, he was a jeezly night security guard for the *Piggly Wiggly Supermarket*. And on top of everything else, one day this was his office, and the next, he had to clean the place out by himself like he was the goddamned janitor.

Probably what bugged Ricky the most, however—what absolutely ate him up inside—was the fact that he hadn't seen any of this coming, especially the Chief's goddamned body slam. Why hadn't the Chief trusted him enough to talk about his pain or his secrets? Ricky had once thought they were, well, sort of friends, maybe. He'd worshipped the Chief, considered him a hero and a great man. Not for one second had he ever suspected the Chief led any kind of secret life. So to discover his hero was some kind of, you know, homo . . . or gay guy . . . or whatever. You could have blown Ricky over with a fart!

But, then again, if the Chief had ever actually opened up to Ricky, what would he have done? Would Ricky have understood, or would he have been appalled to learn his hero was a . . . a fag? Ricky's emotions were raw. And anyway, it was too late to do anything now. Everybody in town already assumed Ricky had known about the Chief. Most folks probably believed Ricky'd been party to the Chief's . . . private interests. Oh Christ, what a total disaster this was.

Ricky's heart almost stopped when the old black phone on the Chief's desk rang. The first time it had done so in weeks. It took him a moment to gather his wits, wipe the tears from his cheeks, and pick up the phone. From force of habit, he said, "Bemishstock Police Department."

"Good evening. I'm calling from Canada. Could I talk to your Chief, please?"

"Uh, sure." What the hell, this might be the last time he'd ever get to play Chief. "That's me. Chief Ricky Pike."

"You're putting in some long hours, Chief Pike."

"Oh yeah, and got a full night ahead of me as well. So who are you?"

"Name's Detective Sergeant Bain with the Halifax Police Service up here in Nova Scotia. I could use your help, Chief Pike."

"All right. What's up?"

"Well, the name of a young American came up in connection with an investigation here, and I'm told he's from your town. He's called Christopher Chandler and I'm wondering if you're familiar with him?"

Bugs crawled across Ricky's skin.

"You still there, Chief Pike?"

"Yeah. I'm here. Why would you want to know about Chandler?"

"There's been a violent incident, and this Chandler fellow might have been indirectly involved. So I thought I should do a little background check."

Ricky felt his face burn. His hands trembled. Where to start? What could he say? That the Chandler kid had cost Ricky everything, his job, his future, his reputation? Christ, that Chandler had destroyed the whole goddamned town of Bemishstock?

"I . . . I can't tell you much, Sergeant Bain. The uh, the matter is now in the hands of the State Police."

That wasn't strictly true since the State had already ruled on the matter of Chandler, the stolen bodies, and the Bemishstock police. And the State had totally screwed Chief Boucher, and Ricky, and the whole department and everything good they'd ever tried to do. But Ricky wasn't about to tell some Canuck that.

"But I guess I can say the kid is bad news, Sergeant Bain, he's so goddamned dangerous he makes my guts ache. But that's just a personal opinion."

Bain took a moment to respond. "Okay. But could you be a bit more specific? Like what did he do that was so bad?"

Ricky knew he was on dangerous ground. He had no official standing, no right to say anything about the Chandler case, especially not to another police force. If the State Police found out he'd said anything at all, they'd probably have his guts for garters. Then he remembered Vermont.

"Look. I think the best thing for you to do, Sergeant Bain, is to call the police department down in Lewis, Vermont. Chandler was mixed up in some big case down there a short while back. Those records are still in the hands of the local department. Our files have been taken by the State Police. I better shut up."

It gutted Ricky that he couldn't unleash every emotion he'd ever felt about the Chandler kid, but he just didn't dare. Ricky had always known he wasn't the sharpest tack in the box, but in this one situation, he knew silence was probably his best course.

"Another thing I can say though, watch your ass. You have no idea how dangerous the Chandler kid can be."

"Is that right? Okay, well, thanks for your time, Chief Pike."

"No problem," and he hung up.

Ricky sat on the floor with the phone between his legs, his hands still shaking and his skin moist. If he never heard the name Chris Chandler again, it would be too soon.

"Hello?" someone called from the reception area out front.

Crap, he'd forgotten to lock the outer door when he'd come in earlier to clean out the Chief's office. Ricky tried to compose himself and then scrabbled to his feet. "In here," he shouted and sat down at the Chief's desk.

A moment later, a slim, darkly tanned, silver-haired man entered the office. He wore jeans and a stylish leather bomber jacket embroidered with a company logo Ricky did not recognize. "Is this the Police Department?" the stranger asked.

"Sorry," Ricky said. "Not anymore."

"But it used to be, right?"

"Who's asking?"

The stranger held out his hand to Ricky as he approached the desk. "Dahlman, Captain Dahlman. I think you know, or rather you knew my family."

The last hint of color drained from Ricky's face. "Holy fuck! Oh, sorry, so sorry. It's just . . . I never expected to ever meet you, sir."

Ricky's stomach heaved. Captain Dahlman. Here! All the nightmarish images associated with that name came rushing back to him. The girl Mallory, blue, frozen stiff in the back of that car in her gas-filled garage. The old lady, the color of clay, covered in hardened vomit, surrounded by soiled diapers and rotting food. The boy's body shipped back from Vermont, broken, misshapen, and that horrid face! Ricky thought he was going to puke.

"No I expect not," said the captain.

Ricky took the man's hand. "What . . . what can I do for you, Captain Dahlman? I used to be the police chief, well acting Chief. I . . . I found your wife, sir. Christ, I'm so sorry for your losses."

"Good of you to say, Captain Pike." There wasn't a hint of emotion in the man's face.

"Why are you here?"

"I'm in town to dispose of our house. It'll be knocked down."

"Good thing. It sure did stink. Oh sorry."

"No, I expect you're right. I also have paperwork to settle up. But I wanted to see you, to thank you personally. You tried your very best to bring that boy, the one responsible for my Mallory's death, to justice and I'm very grateful for that."

"We tried, sir."

"What you did was good, even if others didn't see it that way. I'm so sorry you and your fellow officers have been made the scapegoats in all this. I'd like to make things up to you somehow. Perhaps a small financial reward? For you as their leader, I mean?" The man smiled. His expression seemed warm, genuine.

"Oh no, sir, that's not really . . . ."

Like money? Is he going to give me money?

Ricky's pulse quickened.

"Of course, I understand you were only doing your duty. For that, I want to do something to help you, and in return, perhaps you could do something for me?" Captain Dahlman's look darkened.

"Sure, certainly. I'll do whatever I can."

"I'd like to have a chat with the Chandler boy, and I thought you might help me find him."

****

Gothall's Rooming House

Sammy Brook opened his mailbox in the foyer and pulled out the official-looking letter. Ice water coursed through his veins the moment he glimpsed the postmark. Israel. He then read the return address carefully. *Nahum Dobrin Law Office, 2 Medinat HaYehudim, Herzliya, Israel.*

Oh God, help me!

He raced up the stairs to his room as quickly as he could. There he tossed his dinner sandwich on the chair, dropped onto the bed, and ripped open the letter.

Mr. Bruchner,

This is to advise you that Miss Tirza Bruchner has retained our law firm to initiate legal proceedings against you. We have been instructed to take all necessary steps to ensure you never again contact Ms. Bruchner by post, telephone, or telegraph, either in person or through an intermediary. Your campaign of emotional harassment has caused our client indescribable pain. If it continues, we shall be forced to initiate criminal proceedings against you in the Canadian court system. Your recent correspondence indicated that you intend to travel to Israel to speak with our client. I can assure you that will not happen. Any attempt on your part to enter this country will result in your immediate arrest under the Nazis and Nazi Collaborators Punishment Law of the State of Israel of 1950. You have our assurance your relationship with Miss Bruchner is now absolutely at an end.

Sammy crumpled the letter, threw it aside, and then moaned like a wounded animal. His head fell forward, and he slid from the bed to the floor, where he curled up in the fetal position. There he sobbed pitifully for the child he'd now lost forever, and for the soul he'd sold to save her.

****

Gothall's Rooming House

Chris napped for much of his first day in Halifax, had a burger for supper at the diner, then put in a long evening helping Mr. Minhas scrub out the kitchen. They cleaned grease traps, scoured counters, mopped floors, removed several crates of spoiled lettuce from the cold room, and crushed cardboard boxes for pick up the following day. Shortly before midnight, Mr. Minhas paid Chris in cash and thanked him for a solid night's work. "Anytime you want to earn more pocket money, I'd be glad of your help," said Minhas.

"That's great, sir."

"No problem," he replied. "My older daughter had a job when she was an undergraduate. I think having to earn at least part of your keep teaches a person to manage one's time and take one's studies seriously."

"Your daughter doesn't have to work now?"

"No. She has a scholarship to McGill, a big one. We're very proud of her."

"Must be nice."

"I'm sure your time will come."

"Maybe."

"So what are you studying?"

"Just doing an Arts degree at the moment," replied Chris. He didn't mean to sound ashamed of his choice, but it probably came out that way.

"In?"

"Well, in Comparative Religions."

90

"Oh, now that is a brave choice," said Minhas with a chuckle.

"Yeah, not much demand for its graduates these days."

"No, perhaps not, but maybe it'll turn out to be a brilliant first degree," said Minhas with a pat on Chris's shoulder. "Good preparation for business or law or some other sort of professional studies for your next degree."

"I guess, but at this stage, I just want to find out if I have the guts to do this."

"You should meet Mr. Brook. He survived a Nazi labor camp. Terrible thing. I expect he can tell you a few things about having guts."

"And the elderly lady on the same floor? You mentioned her family once owned this building. Are she and the old gentleman together?"

"Oh no. She's . . . well, it's sad. You see, Mrs. Norris's father once owned most of the buildings in this part of the city. She grew up in an elegant stone house down the street. Wealthy they were. But her father lost his shipping business, and then her husband ran off with what little money she had, and I guess you might say she lost her mind. She thinks she still owns this building and we're her staff. She believes Mr. Brook is her butler, and me, I guess I'm her house boy. But it doesn't hurt to humor her."

"That's very kind of you, Mr. Minhas."

"Never hurts to be kind. But one thing you should know. Mrs. Norris thinks her son is still living on the fifth floor. But he's not. He killed himself some time ago. Anyway, if she says something about him, perhaps you could play along?"

"I . . . I guess."

Chris left the diner and headed for his room. At midnight, the light above the outside door and all the building's hall lights switched off automatically. As Chris crept upstairs in darkness, he heard someone, probably one of the young thugs, retching his guts out in the toilet on

91

the second floor. The third floor was completely dark. There was no hint of light from beneath either of the two doors. But from the old gentleman's room, he heard weeping.

****

Chris had one last chore to perform before sleep. He slid the suitcase containing Mallory's bones as far under the bed's sagging springs as he could manage. Then he folded back the bed covers and climbed in. The sheets felt damp, and fingers of a chill draft worked their way beneath his door. He was asleep in minutes all the same.

****

Across the casket, Mrs. Willard said, "Now? You show up now? After she's dead?" She dabbed the corner of her eyes, snuffled, and lowered her gaze to the corpse in the open casket. "You should have been here when she came out of surgery!"

Her remarks echoed through the funeral parlor's cavernous receiving room.

"She asked for you! Not for me, not her grandfather, you! And we had to tell her you were gone! That you'd run away!"

"I was afraid she wouldn't make it," Chris whimpered.

He stepped up to the casket, tears streaming down his face. As white as alabaster, Gillian lay on a bed of crisp, cream-colored silk in the powder-blue crocheted dress she'd worn on her first visit to the Portland Correction Center.

"Your cowardice killed her," Mrs. Willard said with such malice. "My darling Gillian, after we told her you'd run off, she sighed, whispered that you'd betrayed her, closed her eyes, and . . . and then she just slipped away. The doctors said she died of a broken heart. The surgery was a success, but her disappointment at your selfishness was too much for her heart to bear."

"No," Chris cried out. "Gillian was stronger than that. She wouldn't die of a broken heart. She'd fight, maybe even punish me, but she wouldn't just give up."

"But I did," said Gillian as she sat up in her coffin. "I couldn't believe you'd leave me like that."

Mrs. Willard wiped a frozen tear from Gillian's icy cheek as her daughter spoke.

"I got this protecting you," she said as she lifted her hair away from the massive bloody hole in her right temple. "And how did you repay me? You ran. Twice I forgave you for your weakness. I guess my heart wasn't strong enough to forgive you a third time. And so I died . . . ."

****

Chris choked on his grief and awoke with a gag and a gasp. As he lay there in the cold and empty night, in a strange and darkened city, he tried to feel Gillian's presence in the world, to sense her spirit somewhere out there, to know she still lived. But he sensed nothing. Merely the echo of his guilt.

He wiped away tears and pulled the bedsheet over his face against the hateful images that rose in the dark to shame him.

****

Greyson's lab

They'd spent the evening drinking coffee and Kahlua and playing *CastleVania* on Jeffy's new *Commodore Amiga 500*. It was well past 2 a.m. when Michael called their impromptu party to a halt. "I think we can probably go now," he said.

"This could be the dumbest thing we've ever tried," muttered Ryan.

"And that's why we need you to come," sneered Michael. "You're so spooked already, you'll make a great lookout."

"I'll dig too," Ryan grumbled. "I just don't know why we're doing it. There's no way we're actually going to find anything. It's too cold, too wet, and we're just a bunch of friggin' nerds, for God's sake."

But then, to everyone's amazement, Ryan got up from the couch and pulled on his coat.

"Good man," said Michael. Right, that was Ryan sorted, so who was next? "Henry, we'll need you too."

In their fourth or fifth or maybe even sixth year of a general arts degree, Henry and his brother James were from a farming family in the Annapolis Valley. As such, they were probably the only ones among the greylings who had ever actually dug up anything. Unfortunately, James wasn't coming because he'd somehow injured his wrist. How the two brothers had ever become involved with Greyson was a mystery to Michael. When Michael, in his first year, had first registered for Greyson's *Intro Religions* course, the brothers were already fixtures in Greyson's orbit. They kept to themselves, rarely spoke, and did whatever Greyson asked of them. The rumor was Greyson had something on them, or they had something on him, but no matter. They provided the muscle none of the rest of the greylings possessed.

Bonnie piped up and insisted she was also coming. "It's my kind of night," she said, by which she meant she probably hoped to see one of her angels in the mist. Angel girl was becoming pushy. Michael didn't like that.

"Okay, but you can't get all scared and whingey in the cemetery, and you can't scream or anything if you do spot one of your stupid ghosts," said Michael.

"They're not ghosts, and they're not stupid," she muttered.

"And Jeffy, of course, since you know where the grave is, and besides, we need your car."

"I figured," replied Jeffy as he shoved gloves and a flashlight into his backpack.

Jeffy, the sweet but stupid Classics major from a ritzy Rhode Island family, had volunteered to visit the cemetery earlier that day to locate Herr Gruber's grave. And he also had a really nice car, a dark blue '87 Pontiac Bonneville SE big enough for the entire raiding party. If Jeffy hadn't been scared of his own shadow, he could probably have had practically any girl on campus because of his car. "My dad chose it," Jeffy would say, staring at his feet anytime anybody complimented his car, like he found its pretense humiliating. Jeffy had once let it drop that he'd tried to join the priesthood, but his parents had overruled him and threatened to sue any religious order that might accept him. So he'd decided to hide himself away in Nova Scotia, where he'd somehow got swept up in Greyson's circle of zealots.

"If we're gonna do this, let's get it over with," Ryan said as he grabbed one of their sacks of gear and headed for the stairs.

****

The many lights of the Fairview Cove Container Terminal shimmered through the drizzle like some kind of crystal city in a fantasy film. Even at that late hour, its monstrous cranes and carriers moved back and forth, up and down, like hulking alien beasts. Away from the

Terminal, however, most of the roads that crisscrossed the cove were empty and dark.

Jeffy parked the Bonneville on Strawberry Hill in an unlit yard behind a small sheet metal shop. The raiding party piled out of the car, grabbed their flashlights and shovels, and headed down the slope to Windsor Street. There they paused in the shadows at the side of Connaught Avenue until they were sure the divided road was silent. Then they dashed across the brightly lit thoroughfare, splashed through the many puddles, and darted back into the shadows once again. They then crossed the sodden grassy margin, clambered over a low stone wall, and dropped down into the Fairview Lawn Cemetery.

"Okay, Jeffy," Michael whispered, "Where to?"

"This way," Jeffy replied and ran off into the darkness.

The group avoided the gravel track that wound past the graves, remaining concealed among the trees and out of the spill light from the highway. After a hundred yards or so, they came to a large elevated walled section to their left and a small fenced area to their right.

"That's the Jewish graveyard, up there inside that wall," whispered Jeffy. "And over here are the Jewish *Titanic* graves."

He climbed up onto the wrought iron fence. Inside the fenced area was a cluster of stones in two rows of five. "I think that's Gruber," he said, pointing to the second marker from the left end of the first rank.

Michael tossed his shovel and flashlight over the fence, and said, "Here, somebody give me a boost."

Once inside, Ryan asked, "So who's gonna start?"

"I am," replied Michael, as he drove his shovel into the turf.

"And me," said Henry.

"We'll take turns," Michael said, already winded after three shovelsful. "You only need to dig near the, you know, the head."

"And there won't be much to find anyway. Jewish tradition is to bury the dead in a plain wooden box so I doubt there'll be much to see," said Ryan.

"Small mercies," whispered Bonnie.

"Wood. That's wood!" cried Sheila as she sifted through Ryan's latest shovelful.

"Quiet! For God's sake!" Michael hissed, then jumped into the pit beside Ryan and turned on his flashlight. There, in its beam, they saw fragments of splintered wood and scraps of rotten winding cloth. Michael crouched down, pulled several pieces of the wood from the hole, and pushed aside loose earth. Then he lifted a piece of cloth, gasped, and fell back on his rump.

"Oh God," whispered Bonnie.

A skull peered upward from the wet earth. Its crown was crisscrossed with matted hair. The eyes were nothing more than dark holes. The gaping mouth was filled to its crooked teeth with worms and soil. And in the weak light from the tiny flashlight, the skull appeared about to scream.

"Mr. Gruber," muttered Ryan.

No one moved for several seconds, then Jeffy said, "I think we better hurry. There's more traffic up on Connaught Avenue."

"Right, yes," replied Michael, and he moved forward to kneel over the skull. "So we have to, like move his . . . his head, and we should find the guy's chain."

"Let me help," said Henry. He knelt down beside Michael and began digging through the dirt and mud with his hands.

"Got something. I've got something," Henry said excitedly. Slowly, he pulled a portion of chain from the soil and then stopped. "It won't come. It's stuck in the guy's neck."

"Gimme the shovel," Michael said to Sheila. He stood over the skull for a moment, staring down into its empty eye sockets. No way was Michael going to be stopped at this point. In one motion, he drove the blade of the shovel down through the spine of the corpse.

"God, what have we done?" murmured Bonnie.

"What we had to," replied Michael. He bent down, shifted the skull to one side, and tugged on the chain. From among the splinters of bone and wood and a tangle of winding cloth emerged a large round disc.

"That's it!" said Ryan. "God, we've done it!"

Jeffy, Sheila and Bonnie all hugged, Michael and Henry shook hands, and Ryan pumped his fist.

In the distance a siren was approaching. Everyone froze. The police car roared down Connaught Avenue, past the cemetery, and continued on toward Rockingham.

"I nearly wet myself," whispered Sheila.

"You and me both," said Jeffy.

"We gotta get out of here," said Ryan. "Start filling this in." He tossed a shovelful of earth at Michael's feet.

"We don't have time for that," Michael replied as he shoved the medallion in his jeans pocket and climbed from the pit.

"We can't just leave the grave like this. Everyone will know we were digging here."

"But they won't suspect college students, not if we make it look like some crazies did it." He pulled a can of spray paint from his coat pocket and sprayed a large swastika in orange on the grass alongside the grave.

"You can't do that!" Ryan said angrily. "That's . . . that's evil."

"And digging someone up isn't? Besides, don't we want people to think this pit is the work of Nazis and Jew-haters anyway? Here Henry, while we gather up our stuff, you go write some hate crap up there on the wall around the Jewish cemetery."

"This is so screwed up," muttered Ryan.

In the car on the way back to the college, Michael pulled the medallion from his pocket, and with a wad of tissue, began wiping away dirt and discoloration from its two sides.

"Can you open it?" Ryan asked.

"No, not yet." Michael continued to rub and twist the disc, then gasped, "Holy shit," as an image emerged from the dirt and corrosion.

"What? What is it?" everyone asked.

"There's this engraving on it, some guy standing over a body. I bet it's Rabbi Loew and his golem!"

"Professor Greyson's gonna be so pleased," Henry said.

"It's incredible," murmured Ryan with a shake of his head.

"And there's writing! I can't make out the words, but oh God, I think it's KBLH. This word! I bet it's Kabbala! Hell yeah! This is a Kabbala medallion!"

"We are the champions!" Henry sang out.

And everybody joined in, "We are the champions, we are the champions of the world!"

****

Back in the cellar, after everyone'd had a wash and a beer, they gathered around the common room table as Michael rinsed the medallion in a small bowl of cleaning fluid he'd found under the utility sink in the janitor's cupboard.

"See, there," he said as the image and the words became clearer on the blackened surface of the disc. "The guy over the body."

"But the body, it doesn't look like a man, does it?" said Sheila.

"Looks more like . . . like a bull or something," said Henry.

"But the words. That's *Kabbala* for sure," said Michael as he polished the inscription around the perimeter of the medallion. "See? Some other word and then *Kabbala*. Right?"

"That looks like a k, and that's definitely *t*, and I think the little squiggly thing under it gives you the vowel a. It's *Katav Kabbala*," said Ryan.

"What does that mean?" asked Bonnie.

"There's a Hebrew dictionary in Greyson's office." Michael ran off as Ryan turned the disc over and continued wiping away dirt and corrosion.

"The guy's in a circle of knives. Why knives?" muttered Henry.

Michael came rushing back. "Got it," he said as he flipped through the dictionary. "*Ktav . . . writing . . . written or script.*"

"Okay, so check *Kabbala*," said Ryan.

"We know what that means. It means tradition or wisdom," replied Michael.

"Christ! Check anyway," said Ryan.

"*Kabbala*. There, see? *Wisdom*," said Michael, his impatience rising. This was not going well. Ryan was really getting on his nerves. And yet, he couldn't deny something felt wrong, especially with all the knives on the medallion. What were they all about?

"Or," and Ryan pointed to a second meaning, "*Kabbala* means mysterious art or doctrine."

"So?" asked Bonnie.

"So then *Ktav Kabbala* means what? Like maybe . . ." muttered Ryan, clearly thinking out loud, ". . . maybe it means some kind of script or a permit to practice some mysterious art?"

"A mysterious art involving a lot of knives," said Henry.

"You think maybe this guy was, like, licensed to kill?" asked James.

"Like some kind of James Bond, or maybe it's a license for a golem to kill gentiles," said Michael, his pulse quickening.

"Oh shit, no!" exclaimed Ryan. "I know what it is. It's like a license for a man to kill animals!" he practically shouted.

"What?" Bonnie gasped.

"Look at that body. Yes, damn it. That's a cow. And the other side, those are the guy's butcher knives." Ryan took the medallion from Michael and held it very close to his face. Then he shook his head and muttered, "Oh yeah sure, if you look really close, you'll see there's another word. *Shechitah*. Right there."

"Look it up," ordered Michael.

"Don't bother," said Ryan. "My stepdad's Jewish. He owns a couple of kosher grocery stores. I know the word."

"So? What is it?" asked two or three greylings simultaneously.

"It means the laws of slaughter, which also means the guy's a *shochet*, and this medallion is his license."

"So not a cantor then," murmured Jeffy.

"No, the guy's a butcher. We just dug up the *Titanic's* kosher butcher."

"I've seen that *shochet* word," said Bonnie.

"Where?" asked Michael angrily.

"In Rabbi Walter's notes, scribbled beside Gruber's name."

"So Rabbi Walter's notes told us that Gruber was a butcher? And you already knew that?" screamed Michael.

"I didn't know what it meant. I thought maybe it was just a description of the condition of his body."

"Well, now we're the dead meat," muttered Ryan.

Chapter Four

Wednesday, September 9, 1987

Gothall's Rooming House

At the change of tide, the stink from the harbor put an early end to Chris's troubled night. He rolled from the narrow, lumpy bed, pulled on jeans and a sweatshirt, and headed downstairs to pick up coffee and a Danish from *Freddy's Diner*. He'd eat and then head out to get a few things. He needed clothes and college supplies. Damn. He'd never imagined there would come a day when he'd need supplies for college.

On the third-floor landing, Chris passed Mr. Brook's open door. Without intending to, he glanced inside. The old man was seated on a wooden chair weeping, his face in his hands and his shoulders heaving up and down with his sobs. Mrs. Norris stood alongside whispering softly, her hand resting gently on his back. For an instant, Chris considered stopping to offer assistance but then thought better of it and continued down the stairs. Just as he reached the foyer, he glimpsed blue flashes near the ceiling and smelled sulfur. "Oh crap, Mallory," he muttered. Breakfast would have to wait.

The streets were filling with cars on their way to work and trucks heading for the container port. The sidewalks were becoming busy too. While Chris wore the Magdalene pendant, he was in no immediate danger. Still, he didn't want to explain to strangers Mallory's murderous rage. A short distance up Duke Street was an alley that ran behind the diner. He entered the alley just as swirling winds lifted dust and litter from its every corner.

A dumpster near the diner's back door almost completely blocked Chris's passage to the end of the alley. Chris squeezed past its stinking mass. Beyond, the alley ended at a rusting barbed wire fence. The space between the dumpster and the fence was crammed with wooden produce crates, a dozen overloaded garbage cans, broken sheets of sodden drywall, and at least a dozen discarded tires. There were also a couple of makeshift shelters of cardboard, plastic sheeting, and blankets. The alley stank of rotten vegetables, urine, and worse.

Concealed behind the dumpster, the air around Chris crackled and whirled in a mad dance of dirt and debris. Garbage cans, chunks of drywall, tires and splintered cartons all joined in the merry dance. Can lids clattered against walls. The dumpster bounced and rocked, then tipped from side to side, spilling bags of rotting food. With his eyes pinched against the cloud of detritus, Chris barely glimpsed Mallory's malicious glare. He sure heard her bloodthirsty howl, however. And then she was gone.

Chris wiped what grime he could from his face with a tissue from his pocket, and ran fingers through his filthy and tangled hair before starting back to the street.

At the sound of the maelstrom in the alley, several passersby had stopped on the sidewalk to peer as best they could into the whirling cloud of filth. No one had dared enter the alley, however.

When Chris emerged, people peppered him with questions. "What happened? Are you all right? What was that howl?"

"Uh, dog fight," he said as he squeezed through the crowd, "but it's okay. They're gone."

Then he heard Mr. Minhas shout from the back door of the diner. "Get out of there, you hippies! I've told you before, I'll call the police!"

Chris fled the alley as fast as he could.

Freddy's was doing a brisk business. Its signature breakfast special, the two-egg, two-sausage with curried hash browns platter, had attracted a dozen or more customers. The smell was so tantalizing.

"They're gone," said Mr. Minhas in a deep and menacing voice when he returned to the diner, "but the mess they made. I've told Freddy a thousand times, I won't pay for garbage pickup out of my own pocket! That's the building owner's responsibility, but does he listen?"

"Ah Mr. Chandler, here you are," Mrs. Minhas said warmly as Chris entered the diner. "Some breakfast, maybe?" she asked.

Mr. Minhas brightened at the sight of Chris and once again became the solicitous host. "Mr. Chandler. Did the noise in the alley disturb you? I'm so sorry. It's squatters, you see. They make such a mess of the garbage left there, and sometimes, when they're . . . you know . . . on something, they can go crazy. But enough about that, what can we get you?"

****

Returning to his room with his coffee and pastry, Chris encountered Sammy Brook coming out of the elderly lady's room.

"*Danke*, Jessica, for listening to me," the old man said as he closed her door. "And bless you," he muttered. Then he spotted Chris and his face darkened. He wiped the tears from his cheek and growled, "What are you looking at?"

"Nothing, sorry," Chris replied, "but I couldn't help noticing—"

The old man pushed past Chris. "Get out of my way."

"It's just that I'm your new neigh—"

The old man spun about. "*Drecksau*, I know who you are."

"Well, if there's anything I can do."

"For me?" he snarled, "Ha!" Then he moved toward Chris. "Was that you in the alley? Making all that noise?"

"No."

"Are you going to be trouble? Well, I'll tell you, *ben-zonah*. You will not give me trouble. You and those two *manyaks* downstairs, you think you can give me the trouble? *Nah geh!* I have broken men two times your size, so leave me be." He spun about, entered his own room, and slammed the door.

****

Bangor General Hospital

Everything worked! Everything! Fingers, toes. Heavens, she could even wiggle her ears! And despite the dull throb in the side of her head where the surgeons from New York had drilled through her skull, she actually felt okay. The nurses said she had good color and bright eyes. Of course, no one remarked on her shaved head, no one except her best friend Madelyn who said she looked cool, like the angel of the dead she'd been dubbed by the Bangor newspaper. So a successful surgery, favorable prognosis from her doctors, and the promise of a rapid recovery, all in all, a pretty good outcome. And yet . . . .

And yet, she'd been weeping for hours. "Damn Christopher Chandler," she muttered through her tears. "Damn him." He'd run away just as she'd suspected he might. Left her without so much as a goodbye, the coward. Okay, so maybe he'd remained at her bedside for days. The nurses said he hadn't left her alone from the moment she'd collapsed on the beach right up until the evening before her surgery. Yes that was nice but she'd been unconscious the whole time, for God's sake! And now that she was awake, now when she could actually have enjoyed his company, where was he? Gone!

Gillian's hospital room door opened a crack, and her mother peeped in. From the puffy redness of her mother's eyes, it was apparent she'd been crying too, but the moment her mother realized Gillian was weeping, she rushed to her daughter's bedside.

"Oh Gillian, what is it, darling? Are you in pain?"

"No, Mother, I'm fine. Just a little uncomfortable, that's all. But you, what's happened? Why are *you* crying?"

"You first, you tell me what's wrong, then I'll tell you my news."

"Okay, it's Chris. I miss him, I really do."

Her mother pulled away, looked stone-faced, and then spoke ever so softly. "I'm sorry, dear, but you know how I feel about Chris Chandler. All the suffering he's brought you."

"Mother, don't start. He didn't bring me any suffering. All he's ever tried to do is protect me. That's why he isn't here now. That's why he's gone. In his own stupid way, he's still trying to protect me. You know that's true."

"Perhaps, yes, but—"

"Did he say where he was going?"

"No, he never said a word to me about leaving."

"Mother, please, you have to tell me."

"Darling, I swear. He said nothing about leaving. He did say a couple of times that he'd never put you in danger again. But beyond that . . . ."

"The idiot! What a chauvinist! When I find him—"

"Whoa! Wait a minute, young lady, you're going nowhere, not for a long time. You need to take care of yourself."

"The doctor says I'm okay, better than ever, in fact. He'll be releasing me very soon so I can get my school year under way."

"I know exactly what he said. He said you need at least ten more days in here and then lots of rest and care at home before you can think about returning to school."

Gillian glowered at her mother but didn't pursue the matter of her release any further. There was no point upsetting Mother with her plans. She would learn them soon enough.

Dabbing her own tears, her mother asked, "So now can I tell you my news?"

Gillian reached out and took her mother's hand. "Absolutely! Are you okay?"

Her mother grinned like an excited child and said, "Nigel Harrow has asked me to marry him."

Gillian gasped, then smiled broadly, and almost shouted, "Well, it's about time! That's so wonderful!" She held out her arms to her mother, and they embraced and giggled like children.

"Tell me everything! How far along is the planning? Have you picked a date? Can I give you away? Where will you live? Does Grandpa know?"

"Grandpa knows. He says he's happy for me."

"You're going to set up house together somewhere, aren't you? Not out at the farm, surely?"

"No. Farming's not really Nigel's thing. No, we're getting an apartment in New York City. He thinks his current place would be a little small for the two of us, so we're house hunting."

"That's so incredible. From working like a dog on an apple farm in Maine to living the glamorous life in the world's greatest city! That's so amazing!"

"I don't think where we live will change us that much. We still plan to keep the farm, and we'll come back from time to time. But Nigel insists we do some renovating, like, turning it back into a single-family home."

"And Grandpa? Where will he live? With you?"

"No, although we tried to persuade him. No, he wants to go into a home. And he's already picked one out."

"Here in Maine?"

"In Manhattan. It'll cost Nigel a fortune, but he says he's delighted to pay, and Grandpa loves the place. He's visited it twice already. Amazing physiotherapy services, all sorts of activities, and so many lovely single ladies. He says he can't wait."

There was a knock, and two faces appeared around the door. Madelyn and Jackie, both grinning like naughty children. "May we come in?"

"Sure, certainly," replied Gillian's mom. "We're just chatting."

"Mother's engaged!" exclaimed Gillian.

The two girls smiled warmly and embraced Mrs. Willard.

"And she's moving to Manhattan. Do you believe it?"

"Oh, we're so happy for you. Can we be bridesmaids? Oh, please?"

"Hold on a sec, you two," said Gillian. "I'll be planning this affair, so back off."

"And you wait too, young lady," said her mother. "You have a lot of healing to do before we start planning anything. Look, I'm going now, leave you three to chat, but it's wonderful to see my daughter looking so well and chatting like old times with her two best friends."

The three girls glanced at each other and grinned.

Jackie and Madelyn had become quite close following the Lewis disaster. Jackie, almost a decade older than Madelyn, nevertheless treated her like a comrade in arms, on a mission to win vengeance for their dearest friend.

"Okay, to business," said Gillian patting the bed cover beside her. "What have you found out?"

Madelyn plonked herself on the bed while Jackie slid a chair alongside and then tugged a stack of notes from her satchel. "Okay, so Chris told no one his plans," began Jackie, "but Bernard Monsegur in Lewis says he did mention that he'd been accepted by a college."

"Really? A college? Where?"

"No idea, not yet. But we're going to check out the bus lines first," said Madelyn.

"I managed to track his bus to Lewis after he left the reform school, so that's what we're trying to do now."

"And when we find him?" asked Madelyn. "What then?"

"We go after him, of course!" answered Gillian. "I'm going to teach that numbskull a lesson. He thinks by running away, he's protecting me, but that's not his job. I can protect myself, well once I'm better anyway."

****

Duncan's Cove

Greyson worked his way down the ladder from the sleeping loft and dropped onto a kitchen chair near the sea-facing window. He sat there transfixed by the languid waves lapping about the rocks and pilings at the water's edge until their motion made him feel even more nauseated than his hangover already did. He turned away from the window, switched on the tiny transistor radio in the middle of the kitchen table, and buried his throbbing head in his hands as the radio warmed.

The moment Greyson heard the lead story on the 8 a.m. news, he knew the dimwits in his lab were to blame.

"Overnight there was a despicable attack on the Baron de Hirsch Cemetery and a Titanic grave was desecrated," said the announcer.

Greyson had already been about to vomit from the smorgasbord of drugs he'd consumed the previous evening. Details of the cemetery attack—the splintered coffin, a skull hacked from the spine, mud splashed across other graves—made his nausea so much worse. Oh shit, what had those fools been thinking?

He'd had enough! They were gone! Okay, maybe not Bonnie, not yet anyway. But the rest, absolutely! The moment he got to the college he'd order them out of his lab once and for all.

****

Greyson had been in no shape to drive, and yet somehow he managed to negotiate the twists and turns of the narrow coastal road from Duncan's Cove without hitting anything or flying off the highway. His tires squealed as he roared into the college quadrangle and parked diagonally across several spaces.

From the top of the cellar stairs, Greyson bellowed, "What were you assholes thinking? You're such total screwups!" He continued screaming as he descended the steps. "You've ruined everything! We'll never be able to get anywhere near that cemetery now!"

The greylings, who were all seated at the common room table when Greyson burst in, turned toward him, pale, sheepish, but surprisingly unmoved by his display. The table was littered with fast-food containers and coffee cups. They'd obviously been sitting there for some time.

"We think we've deflected attention," Michael said softly.

"How?"

"We painted a lot of Nazi stuff around the cemetery, made it look like skinheads had done it."

"You what? That wasn't in the news."

"They probably don't want people getting too upset."

"How are they going to keep swastikas secret? Oh shit, every Jew in town is going to be on the phone to the Mayor."

"But I don't think anyone will connect us with the damage," replied Michael.

"I don't give a crap what you screw-ups think. I want you out of here, now. All of you!"

Michael stood up. A diminutive five foot six, he had to look up into Greyson's face. "No, sir, I don't think we're leaving."

For an instant, it appeared Greyson might lunge at Michael. "You'll leave if I tell you to leave. You are my lab assistants. You get paid if I say you get paid. You get in this lab if I let you in. And you'll leave when I tell you to leave!"

"All that may have been true once," said Michael, "but we've been talking, and well, we see things a little different now."

"Oh? How? How do you see things different?"

"Professor Greyson, we've all been working with you." Michael's tone was condescending, even patronizing.

"*For* me! You work *for* me!"

"No, *with* you. We've been working *with* you for at least two years. Henry and James longer than that. And we've seen things."

Greyson's stomach heaved again. "What things?"

"Well, there was the girl who jumped off the bridge. We all saw you with her that night, even though we denied it at the faculty inquiry . . . as you asked us to."

Greyson, who'd already been the color of chalk, became paler still. "You little shit," he muttered.

"And there's your drugs. We know where you keep them and who you buy them from."

Greyson's stomach rolled and churned like maggots on a corpse.

"And there's also all that garbage in your accounts, about lab equipment, and overtime and travel, the accounts you have to submit each semester to the old lady's Foundation. Hell, I wrote most of that crap myself because, as we all know, you couldn't keep track of a freight train on a short siding. So you see, sir, we aren't going anywhere."

Greyson marched up to Ashworth, and towering over him, he murmured, "You're threatening me?"

"No, absolutely not," said Michael with a look of apparent contrition. "We just want to continue with our work." Several other greylings nodded.

"After the mess you made last night? You think we'll get to continue working on anything?" boomed Greyson.

"No one is going to connect us with what happened last night. Only we know you're interested in the *Titanic* graves. And okay, so maybe we screwed up once, but we can fix it."

"I'm guessing you found nothing?" Greyson rolled his eyes in disgust.

"We found the *Titanic*'s kosher butcher, but—"

"You found the butcher?" Greyson roared with laughter.

"But," Michael continued, "we had a lead, and we thought it worth a shot since the guy fit the description of the Prague cantor, and he was said to be wearing a medallion."

Greyson felt physically ill. He couldn't continue this discussion much longer without vomiting. He rubbed his eyes, wiped the sweat from his face, and took a deep breath.

He stared at the greylings, first in disgust and then resignation. "All right. So," he started slowly, "if you're going to continue working in this lab, then you have to work on something other than the *Titanic* project."

"No problem," said Ashworth.

Bonnie and Sheila smiled. Ryan even pumped his fist.

"The American kid will take care of the *Titanic* project. You lot can go back to the manuscripts. I don't give a shit what you do with them.

But if you want to remain here, then you must never freelance again, got it?"

Greyson mustered the most hateful glare he could, given his pounding head and roiling stomach. "And while you're screwing about with the manuscripts, I'm going to be looking for the perfect opportunity to crucify each and every one of you little turds for defying me."

No one seemed the least bit rattled by the malice in Greyson's voice, which only made him angrier still. He bellowed his next remark.

"The American kid arrives tomorrow, and when he does, I don't want you fuck-ups saying a goddamned word to him. Not one goddamned word! Got it?"

Greyson went into his office and slammed the door. The gesture might have been more dramatic had the door not been crafted from a single sheet of quarter-inch plywood.

****

Bemishstock, Maine

Clyde Breeble of *Adamson, Goulding, and Breeble Attorneys at Law* pulled his fifteen-year-old Mercedes off the highway and into the Dahlmans' long drive. Something rattled loudly from the rear of the car. "Meaning to get that fixed," said the skeletal lawyer in the ill-fitting suit. Apparently, there wasn't much money to be made in a dying town, even for lawyers picking over the bones of the town's many ruined lives.

"I hope this won't be too painful for you, sir," Breedle said.

Captain Dahlman found Breedle's feigned sympathy nauseating. He snorted. "I'm here to find documents and items of value, not memories, so let's just get this over with." Besides, any reminders of his wife would be too sickening by half.

"It's a fine-looking property," said the agent from *North Coast Realty* seated in the back. "I've always admired—"

"The house is an eyesore, and the sooner it's torn down and the land sold, the happier I'll be," muttered Dahlman.

"You understand, sir, the house, well, it's a bit of a mess," said the lawyer. "Your son Rudy, well, he seems to have had some sort of fit before he fled because, well, he sort of trashed—"

"I'm aware of what the boy did," Dahlman replied. "The police told me." The gargoyle, weasel-faced Rudy had finally snapped. No surprise in that, what with that mother of his.

As Breedle fumbled with the door key, Dahlman said, "I thought you were going to have someone unlock and air out the house before we got here."

"Uh, my nephew, yes. Well, he . . . he came . . . and got . . . well, he got sick at the smell and left before . . . . Ah, that's got it."

Dahlman pushed the door wide. The stench—a fetid stew of feces, urine, rotting food, and death—overwhelmed the three men. They fell back from the door, gagging, nostrils burning, eyes watering.

The lawyer muttered, "Oh Christ, we can't go in there."

"Stay here then," said Dahlman, and with a handkerchief to his face, he stepped inside.

A thought struck him, and he giggled. The stink was grotesquely appropriate; after all, the house had always sickened him. The fetor only made manifest Dahlman's utter hatred for the place. A fitting end for this parody of a home, now so sunken in its misery. He'd revel in watching the place wiped away.

Time and again, he'd said how much he hated Maine. Time and again, he'd told his witch of a wife he'd only married her for a green card. She wasn't a dunce; she must have realized how ill-suited they were. She, a stick insect of a woman with cartoonish features, and he a decade younger, muscular, with a full head of blond hair. But would she let him leave gracefully? "Oh no," she'd screamed, "not like that." She'd never let him humiliate her. He would have to remain with her until she decided the time was right for him to go. Until then, she expected him to put on a show for family and neighbors. If eventually she relented, she would only do so if he continued to support her handsomely. But if he left a moment too soon, she swore to have Immigration on him, "so fast your blond curls will be burned to a crisp."

He'd stayed, returning to this hole after every voyage, for years on end. When the child came along, his wife had probably thought she'd have an unbreakable hold over him. But he'd had the last laugh because the child had been just what he needed to break free from the shrew. He'd won the child to his side, made her an ally and more than that. He'd done whatever was required to frighten and disgust his wife. All the gifts, the clothes, the cuddling, the private time with the girl, they'd worked a charm. Soon his wife was only too pleased for him to stay away. And when her gargoyle of a son came along, sired apparently by some other patsy, he knew he was free.

Now here he was, sorting through the wreckage of his wife's pathetic life, stink rising from every corner. Her body had been removed, but virtually every other stain in her life remained. Wreckage was strewn everywhere. Broken furniture, filthy clothes, dirty dishes, spoiled food, and soiled adult diapers, dozens of them tossed about, their excrement left to crust wherever they'd landed.

He picked his way carefully through the filth to his study, gathered up files on investments and holdings and deeds, then moved on to his daughter Mallory's room. What a stupid twit she'd been. So anxious to please. How willingly she'd done anything he'd asked of her. From the moment of her birth, he'd stoked his daughter's resentment of her mother, prompted the girl's outbursts, fueled her bitterness.

Oh, she did have her merits. Her fascination with Torajan lore gave him some satisfaction, and he'd fed that fascination as best he could. And daughter or not, she was one good-looking bitch. It hadn't been a trial, tormenting his wife, what with the 'cuddly times' he'd spent alone with Mallory, the whispering, the secret notes. The utterly pathetic aspect had been how seriously his dimwitted daughter seemed to welcome his attentions. Ah well, the price one had to pay.

Dahlman smiled to see all the Torajan artifacts decorating Mallory's room, much of which he'd sent her. And on her desk, he found the many letters he'd written, now ripped to pieces by Rudy, no doubt. Dahlman continued sifting through the debris on Mallory's desk and came across an odd little toy car with two dolls seated in it. One doll was clearly intended to represent Mallory and the other . . . .

Well now, here we go, so this must be the boy who broke my daughter's heart.

She'd apparently attempted to cast a spell in her last hours, obviously without success, but she'd tried all the same. And so now the boy lived, and Mallory was dead . . . or not quite, perhaps.

That drunken night with the priest Rahmet back in Tana Toraja, the idea that Mallory's spirit still walked the earth had seemed entirely plausible. All Rahmet's talk of Mallory's cleansing death had seemed so convincing at the time. And on the chance Rahmet's spell had worked, when they'd sobered up, Captain Dahlman had sent his wife a message and instructions imploring her to undo Rahmet's spell. He'd received a fax in reply indicating his wife would do as he'd asked, but the fax had been so poorly written, it had to have been the work of rat-faced Rudy. And if Rudy had indeed interfered then Captain Dahlman couldn't be sure Mallory's spirit had been released from her corpse. Dahlman had to find out before he returned to Tana Toraja. He couldn't simply abandon his daughter's spirit to stumble about, struggling mindlessly to find her way to Tana Toraja until the last of her rotting flesh fell from her bones.

Or perhaps her spirit had never made its way back into her corpse. Maybe it was now adrift, wandering the world without end or purpose. Whatever Rahmet's spell might have done to his daughter, Dahlman had to find out. And while he was at it, he'd teach the ex-boyfriend responsible for her death a terrible lesson. His grandmother always said an offense unavenged is like an earwig tunneling inside your brain; it will eventually drive you mad. Dahlman recalled her saying that the night she returned to their mountain hideaway carrying the heads of the Japanese guards who'd murdered her husband and son. This boyfriend, Chandler, had offended Captain Dahlman. It followed the lesson had to be as unimaginably brutal as a father could conjure to avenge his darling daughter, pathetically stupid though she may have been.

Chapter Five

Thursday, September 10

Cavendish College

Chris's first day as a college student began with a long hike across the city in a steady drizzle and chill autumn breeze and went downhill from there.

He tried to begin the registration process in the registrar's office. Every staff member greeted him with icy indifference. He was kept waiting for an hour as other registrants came and went. Secretaries wandered about with his file, sifting through its contents, whispering and making numerous phone calls before someone finally gave him a student ID and registration package. The finance office manager muttered something about Professor Greyson being made to pay Chris's fees from his own resources. When Chris asked her to repeat the remark, she merely stamped his registration *Paid* and walked away. He had no idea why he was being treated with such disdain. Still, it was pretty obvious his presence on campus was not appreciated. Only at midafternoon, when he visited the counselling office for guidance on course selection, did he finally get at least a partial explanation.

"It isn't you," the counselor said, "not really. Okay, so a few people do know you had some trouble in the States, but I don't think anyone holds that against you."

"A few people?"

"The president, the registrar, the admissions officer, me, but no one else. I don't think so anyway."

"That's a lot."

"You don't need to worry about that. No, the reason you're getting grief from my colleagues is your association with Professor Greyson. They see you as another of his greylings."

"His what?"

"Greylings. Professor Greyson has this small group of students who think he's something special, kind of like his groupies. Anyway, the college wants Greyson gone . . . so as his latest recruit, you're getting hassled too."

"Gone? Why?" Chris's felt an icy chill raise goosebumps across his flesh.

"It's a complicated story."

"I think I should hear it. I've come a long way at Greyson's invitation and given up a lot. And now you're telling me, the college wants to get rid of him and me as well?"

"Not you. Not necessarily. I think you'll be okay. Just do your work. And have as little to do with Dr. Greyson as you can."

"But my scholarship requires that I help him with his research."

"Yes, well, that's true, but . . . but be careful. Don't do any more than you have to. And when Professor Greyson is dismissed—"

"Wait, when he's dismissed, will his funding end as well? And along with it, my scholarship?"

"I . . . I'm not sure, but we'll probably be able to help you anyway, at least with your tuition."

"But I'll have no money for rent or food, and you're not sure I'll even have tuition when Greyson's gone, is that the bottom line?" Chris waited for some expression of reassurance, but the counselor simply sat there with a look of sympathy on her face.

"Okay, so that sucks," said Chris. "Seems like I'm starting a program I may not be able to complete. And I have to work for someone

119

the college wants to get rid of. And when the professor eventually does go, the college isn't sure it will want me to stay either."

"I'm so sorry."

For an instant, Chris's temper flared.

Why wasn't I warned about this mess? Why didn't I check out this Greyson guy before I accepted his offer? What kind of an idiot am I?

He drew a deep breath, wrung his hands, and stared at his feet.

Then again, what difference would a warning have made? Would I have gone somewhere else? It wasn't like many other schools were interested in me. No, the hard truth is I didn't have much choice.

"There's nothing you can give me in writing to say my place here is safe?" Chris asked.

"I . . . I don't think so. At least not until the president returns to work," the counselor replied.

Chris shook his head. All right, if anything was to be salvaged from this situation, he'd have to focus on the things he could control and put aside the things he could not. "So basically, I have to do well in my courses and keep Greyson happy for the time being. After that, I guess, I just wait and see."

"That's about right. And be careful. Greyson, he has a . . . ."

"A what?"

"Never mind."

"Please, a what?"

"A reputation for using people and then . . . casting them aside."

Just great. But I've got to get something out of this mess.

"Okay, good to know," Chris replied. "But for now, could you help me figure out my courses? As for the rest, I'll just have to deal with matters as they come."

****

Greyson's Lab

The morning drizzle had become a steady rain. The cobblestoned quadrangle was now one enormous ankle-deep puddle. In the minute it took Chris to run from the admin building to the Department of Faith Studies, or "Greyson's lair," as the academic advisor called it, he'd been drenched. So now, chilled to the bone, dripping wet, and sickened by his predicament in this strange new world of academe, he was about to meet the man who'd enticed him into this mess, Ignatius Greyson, Ph.D.

Along the side of the college chapel was a set of concrete steps that descended some twenty feet into the earth to a door cut into the chapel's foundation. At the top of the steps, a rusted iron railing bore a peeling sign which read *The Mildred Harper Chair in Faith Studies, Ignatius Greyson, Ph.D. Incumbent.* Also tied to the railing was a piece of plywood bearing a hand-scrawled arrow pointing down the steps. Despite the rain, Chris paused for a moment to gather his thoughts. How could he have let this happen? How could some stranger have suckered him so easily? What an idiot he'd been! After several deep, calming breaths, he started down the slippery staircase.

At the bottom, standing in a veritable waterfall from the chapel's overflowing gutters high above, he hammered on the heavy black door. Standing there, waiting for someone to answer his knocks, he tried to imagine how he could possibly extract something positive from this first meeting with Greyson.

The door opened. A skinny young man in a filthy lab coat opened the door and asked, "Yes?"

"I'm here to see Professor Greyson. My name is Chandler."

"Ah," replied the skinny kid, looking Chris up and down. "Come in."

Chris stepped through the door onto a small stone landing overlooking a cavernous chamber the size of a gymnasium. The room was one huge space, without windows or beams or paneling, divided like a rat's maze by shelves, curtains, and even bedsheets into seven or eight makeshift workspaces. At the approximate center of the chamber were two larger open areas partitioned one from the other by bookshelves and a projector screen. One of the spaces contained laboratory equipment and worktables cluttered with beakers, Bunsen burners, and bell jars. The other, judging by its threadbare armchairs, sofas, and rickety end tables, served as a common room, a space for relaxation. An enormous meeting table and an assortment of mismatched dining chairs occupied the very center of the common room. Every surface in the space was littered with pop cans and coffee cups, pizza boxes, and takeout food containers.

Several young people were sprawled about the common room chatting, reading, sorting through papers, and in one case, even strumming a guitar. Greyson's greylings, Chris presumed. As soon as he stepped through the door, every head turned in his direction.

"People," the skinny kid called out as he started down the narrow stone steps, "this is Chandler. Chandler, this is us."

"The greylings," said Chris aloud as he followed the boy downstairs.

The boy stopped on the bottom step, turned, and glared at Chris for several seconds before saying in a quiet, icy voice, "That is not how we refer to ourselves."

"Oh, sorry. So what do you call yourselves?"

"Researchers, of course."

"Of course."

The boy turned on his heels and continued across the chamber. "Greyson wanted to see you as soon as you arrived."

Every eye in the room followed Chris. He smiled and nodded to folks as he passed, but no one acknowledged the effort.

Okay, so they're not happy to see me either.

Greyson's office was little more than a windowless box in the back corner of the cavernous chamber. Skinny-kid knocked on the unsanded plywood door. "Professor Greyson? Chandler's here."

The door flew open. "Ah. Good. Come in."

Greyson was a shambles of a man. His filthy salt-and-pepper hair was pulled back in a greasy ponytail. He bore several days of stubble and more wrinkles than his gaunt face could accommodate. His pants were stained, and his Led Zeppelin tee-shirt faded and torn. And despite Greyson's emaciated physique, his prominent belly protruded in all its pallid glory from below his shirt and overhung his belt like an avalanche about to let go.

Greyson's office was every bit as chaotic as the man. A chipped and stained dining table seemed to serve as Greyson's desk. It was hard to conceive Greyson ever did any work at his desk since its surface was entirely covered in dog-eared files. Takeout food containers occupied every other flat surface in the room. Apparently, Greyson slept in his office from time to time because an old sofa against the far wall was almost hidden beneath a heap of rumpled blankets and stained pillows. Abandoned paper cups, many with solidifying dregs in them, along with several partially emptied wine bottles topped the several stacks of leather-bound tomes scattered about the large and badly-soiled oriental rug. The damp, musty smell which filled the rest of the chamber was absolutely oppressive in the office.

Greyson pushed books from a wooden chair, pulled it up to his desk, and gestured for Chris to sit. He then shoved files aside and sat on the corner of the desk.

"Well now, how do you like Halifax?" Greyson asked with a smile.

"Uh, I really don't have an opinion yet. I guess maybe, historic?"

"Now that's a coward's way of saying, old, decrepit, crumbling. I'll tell you what. Halifax reminds me of an old lady sitting alone in the sunroom of some ungodly retirement home. She may have been interesting once, perhaps even beautiful, but now she's far too foul-tempered to talk to and much too smelly to sit near. We can only hope that when her time does come, someone realizes she's dead before she really starts to stink."

Greyson smiled, proud of his metaphor and probably waiting for Chris to acknowledge his eloquence. But Chris merely stared at the wreck of a man before him.

"But then again," Greyson continued, "perhaps you'll turn out to be one of those folk who takes to the fog and the gales and the mystery and the noir atmosphere of an old seaport."

"Perhaps I will."

"Mmm," said Greyson. He fell silent and stared back at Chris. His face hardened. Chris was beginning to find the silence awkward, but then Greyson tried again. "And your courses? I'm guessing you've registered?"

"Yes."

"No trouble then?"

Now we're getting to it.

"Yes, actually."

"Oh?" Greyson got up from his perch on the corner of the table, walked around it, cleared debris from a desk chair, and sat down.

Trying to put a margin of safety between an irate Chris and himself, was he?

Chris drew a breath and began. "First, I was treated like some kind of pariah by staff in the registrar's office and the finance office. Then I learned from my academic advisor that my continuing presence at the college is very much in doubt, as I gather is yours."

Greyson chuckled and waved his hand dismissively. "Nonsense. I'll be here long after the academic advisor and the rest of the bastards in Sinclair Hall are gone."

"But she told me the college is determined to get rid of you, and because you're sponsoring me, I will likely have to go too."

"Look, son, it's simple." Greyson began moving files about as he spoke, ostensibly to restore some order to his desktop. "It's a question of academic freedom, and I can assure you, the principle is on my side. The college doesn't like my work, so the administration wants me gone. But they have no grasp of my work's significance. And besides, I have an iron-clad contract and a very generous endowment that are untouchable. No, we're not going anywhere." He sat back in his chair and grinned.

Chris was almost reassured by Greyson's confidence.

"Let me worry about the administration, all right? You, Mr. Chandler, need only focus on your studies and, of course, on the work we're going to do together."

"And what is that?"

"Ah. Well, here in the Department of Faith Studies, we're looking at a range of extraordinary phenomena arising from the confluence of spirituality and pharmaceuticals."

Pharmaceuticals? Like drugs? Oh crap, is this aging hippy some kind of Timothy Leary wannabe?

"When you say pharmaceuticals, do you mean like hallucinogens?" asked Chris somewhat tentatively. "Like LSD and spiritual visions? I thought that stuff went out with the sixties?"

"No. No, we're way past LSD," replied Greyson with a smirk. "For example, one of our projects has examined how monks used ergot, a kind of mold, to animate the demons in their illustrated manuscripts. I mean, it's like film strips, like watching demons dancing and cavorting across the pages! And now we're conducting experiments to determine the levels of hallucinogen and photoelectric stimulation required to manipulate the demons imprisoned in the manuscripts."

"You believe you can control demons?"

"Not like sending demons out to do our bidding, no. But in the reading and interpretation of the manuscripts, yes. In the same way some people can control the content of their dreams through meditation and consuming certain foods and drink."

"Okay."

"You're skeptical, I get that. But when we have a moment, we'll give you a demonstration."

"I'll look forward to it."

Greyson stretched his arms out, then clasped them behind his head, and rocked back in his desk chair. "Let me step back a moment. What unites all our projects is not the mere use of pharmaceuticals but, more fundamentally, the power of words. Belief in the power of holy language is as old as organized religion. In every faith the world over, certain words and texts are deemed to have profound significance. Today, most people assume these special words are merely ceremonial, hollow phrases, anachronisms, and wishful thinking."

There appeared an excited twinkle in the eyes of this decrepit hippy. He was now hunched forward in his chair and leaning excitedly across his cluttered desk.

"But here in our lab we have discovered that, in fact, many of these extraordinary words, when spoken in combination with certain ancient concoctions, can unleash remarkable spiritual phenomena. That's our mission, to unleash and explore the power of religious words and texts. We want to understand how to augment and properly use these holy words." He fell back in his chair with a look of self-satisfaction. "And there's no better place for you to begin your own journey of discovery than with the many ancient texts which make up Kabbalah."

"I've heard of that. Jewish mysticism, right?"

"Yes and no. Kabbalah is not mysticism. Today, it's considered a way of viewing the world and living one's life, a way of understanding how God works through his creation and through each of us. But Kabbalah hasn't always been viewed that way. For many centuries Kabbalah represented the search for the holiest, the most powerful language imaginable, language that could unveil the deepest mysteries of creation, and even the power to create . . . just as God himself created."

"So how could you possibly need me in this search of yours? You already have a full team out there, and they already understand this stuff."

"No. None of the children out there know what you know."

"And what is that?"

"You're the Mortsafeman; you tell me," said Greyson with a stern glare.

"I'm not a Mortsafeman."

"Perhaps not in name, but in practice. According to press accounts I've read, you have interceded at least twice to restore the dead to their rightful reward. Isn't that true? And to do what you have done, I'm guessing you have actually seen and spoken with the dead. You may even have influenced their behavior."

Chris did not reply, but his skin had begun to crawl.

"If we are to uncover the ancient secrets of Kabbalah, then we need your talent," Greyson said ever so slowly.

What talents was he talking about? But again, Chris made no reply.

"All right, putting aside your special ability for the moment, I want you to get familiar with Kabbalah. Go to the library, put together your own reading list, and plunge right in. I propose we meet in a week's time. Once you have a grounding in Kabbalah, I'm going to throw you right into the deep end. I shall have an urgent assignment for you which will be vital to our work and a real test of your talent."

"And if I'm not comfortable with your work?"

"Ah, well," Greyson said with a smile, entirely out of keeping with the cold gaze he'd been giving Chris. "I'm sorry to say you don't have a choice." Greyson rocked forward in his chair once again and scowled across his desk. "I believe the paperwork I sent you made very clear that your assistance in my research is the single-most essential condition of your financial support. Your financial support is not coming from the college but from my endowment fund, and I have absolute control over your funding. Do we understand each other?"

Chris did not reply.

"You've had a bit of a rocky start and I'm sorry for that, but I'm confident you'll enjoy our work once you're more deeply involved."

Greyson stood up and moved toward the door. Apparently the interview was over. But with his hand on the door latch, Greyson hesitated. "Before you go, however, I do have a question for you. What is that charm around your neck?"

Chris covered the Magdalene pendant with his hand. "Nothing. A gift from a friend."

"Ahh, secrets. Well, all right then. So we'll meet again in a week. You'll be up to speed on Kabbalah by then, and I'll fill you in on your first assignment. Clear?"

"What about the students working outside? Shouldn't I get to know them?"

"Hmm," replied Greyson. He appeared to think about the question. "Well, let's say that it's best if you don't. I don't want to cross-contaminate anybody's work. They have their assignments, and very soon, you will have yours."

****

Greyson's lab

Ashworth steamed the entire time Chandler was alone with Greyson. Goddamn it, just like high school. The same disrespect all over again. Shut out when he was the only one with any real clue what was going on!

Back in grade twelve, he'd clearly been the best and brightest in the graduating class, but was he chosen to be valedictorian? No! And only because some jock who'd almost certainly used family connections to win a scholarship to Oxford got the nod. Then, because of his goddamned guidance teacher who'd always had it out for him, he'd been rejected by every one of his preferred schools in the States. So to escape his parents' constant harping about not getting into Harvard, he'd opted for a Canadian school, but here too he'd been confronted by the same mediocrity as high school, and it nearly drove him nuts.

In first-year, he'd been ignored at every turn. He'd worked his butt off, preparing questions for every class, offering observations on each significant point, and suggesting avenues for further inquiry which no one else could possibly have conceived. And what did it get him? Nada. Profs treated him like a nuisance, ignored him when he raised his hand, took their sweet time returning his assignments, and made only the most meager comments on his work. He could only conclude his profs found his intellect intimidating. Utterly disappointing. He'd expected so much more from university. He'd anticipated rigor from his teachers, stimulating conversation from his fellow students, and challenge from other intellectuals. Instead, he got nothing. Everyone else seemed content to coast. But not him. He would never be content to coast. Never.

Then in second year, he'd signed up for a course with Dr. Greyson, and what a surprise it had been. Greyson actually appeared grateful for Ashworth's interjections. Later, of course, Ashworth realized what everyone else already knew, that Greyson appreciated anyone and anything that ate up class time since it meant he'd have less time to fill with his lecture. Even so, Ashworth volunteered to help Greyson with marking a couple of tests, then with marking term papers, and finally with actually writing a couple of academic treatises under Greyson's name. None was ever published, but Greyson was grateful enough to begin treating Ashworth like an actual research assistant, like a colleague even.

Ashworth moved much of his personal crap into Greyson's laboratory. He crammed clothes in a box beneath his desk, appropriated a file cabinet for his own notes, and dragged a cot from a dumpster so he could sleep over in the lab if his work required.

Two other students, Henry and James, predated Ashworth's arrival, but Greyson showed no interest in their academic abilities. He only ever employed them in tasks requiring muscle, like moving furniture, equipment, and unconscious females. And as others joined Greyson's circle, it wasn't hard for them to see that Ashworth was the real brains of the group.

He loved the work they were doing. Their research would soon make Greyson's—and by extension Ashworth's—reputation for years to come. No one else had ever recognized the part played by naturally occurring hallucinogens in the monastic illuminations of holy manuscripts. No one had even broached the idea.

It was as if the dedication and holy intent of the monks had given them a hall pass to indulge in their unholy pastime. And yet Greyson's team had found hallucinogens in large quantities in the parchments and inks that the monks of All Martyrs Monastery in Russia had used. The same hallucinogens had likely been present in the food they consumed and the air they breathed. The hallucinogens originated in the ergot mold on their grain, but the mold had probably morphed into other hallucinogenic compounds in the close, damp air of the monastery and the musty, smoky confines of the scriptorium. Ashworth had already isolated the residue of seven different hallucinogens in the monastery's manuscripts. The monks there seemed to have lived in a soup of mind-altering drugs. No wonder they'd had a reputation for ecstatic visions and angelic visitations.

With all his distractions, Greyson didn't contribute much to the research. To his credit, however, he was the one who'd first suggested the monks might not have been the passive victims of their drug-laden environment. They might, in fact, have learned how to manipulate their visions and even influence some of the creatures they concocted. Greyson's insight stemmed from the realization the monastery had a curious connection with Jewish Kabbalah.

One of the monastery's brothers had journeyed to the Holy Land in 1262. In Accra he'd met the great Catalan rabbi, Rabbi Moses ben Nachman, also known as Nachmanides or Ramban, and had studied Kabbalah with his circle. From Nachmanides, the Russian monk might have learned about the creative power of the Hebrew alphabet. Kabbalists believed that various mystical combinations of Hebrew letters could influence crops and reveal the future. Greyson suggested the monk could have used the power of Hebrew letters to control the monastery's illuminations and manipulate the scenes they depicted.

The greylings' breakthrough had occurred when they found in one illuminated page an account of the trial and punishment of a woman from Stamatz. Accused of cursing a neighbor's cattle, she'd been purged and burned, but not before the monastery's abbot had pronounced upon her a curse in Hebrew. Why the abbot had used Hebrew at the woman's execution was unclear, but Greyson speculated he might have been trying to create some kind of bond with the woman, a bond which could possibly survive her death. Greyson suggested the Hebrew phrase the abbot had used might have come from the Kabbalistic *Book of Creation*, the *Sefer Yetzirah*. Lo and behold, in the *Sefer Yetzirah* they found the abbot's exact words. With that discovery, they had the key they required. It had been like finding the Rosetta Stone. So in the *Sefer Yetzirah* and other Kabbalistic works, they went looking for more such invocations and they'd turned up a treasure trove.

At first, Ashworth had thought Greyson was out of his mind to attribute power to mere words, but then, hey, he thought, why couldn't words have power? After all, the world is filled with examples of people attributing extraordinary power to words, mantras, blessings, curses, and prayers of all kinds. Christians the world over believe that words spoken over a wafer bring about its transubstantiation into the body of Christ. We bless one another when we sneeze. For that matter, what does the *Book of Genesis* say? *In the beginning was the word . . . .* So if the universe really is made up of quanta or vibrating strings or quantum gravity or whatever, then maybe the vibrations of our words do have an effect at some quantum level. Maybe Greyson and the Kabbalists weren't so crazy after all.

Sure enough, by experimenting with different dosages of hallucinogens and combinations of the Hebrew letters culled from the words used by the Russian abbot, Ashworth and the others had managed to animate at will the images of saints and demons on the folio pages of the illuminated manuscripts from the All Martyrs Monastery.

Then came the most extraordinary breakthrough of all, when they first succeeded in summoning the burned woman's presence, lifting her image from the vellum. For an instant, she'd spun and whirled about in the air like a fiery dust devil. She'd writhed as though still in flames, her face twisted in agony before she'd suddenly been sucked back onto the page.

For a while Greyson was fully engaged in their work. He conducted the second summoning when they'd managed to direct her crazed dance from one part of the lab to another. And when Greyson succeeded in having her fiery form ignite the trash in a garbage can, he'd been so excited he'd paid for everyone's Chinese dinner. After that, Greyson had used her manifestation twice to do harm—to terrorize a girl who could have caused him embarrassment, and recently, to punish the college president. Of late, however, Greyson's interest in the manuscripts had waned.

Ashworth loved everything about Greyson's laboratory. The only thing he hated was Greyson himself. The bastard was forever getting involved with girls half his age. But with every one of Greyson's catastrophic entanglements, Ashworth believed his hold over Greyson grew stronger. He only hoped the outcome of their work would eventually offset the damage Greyson himself was doing to their credibility. Ashworth's intention was to complete his degree, do grad work here, and eventually earn a paid position with Greyson's endowment. After all, there was no way Greyson could ever deny him, not with everything Ashworth had on Greyson. Ashworth's pathway forward was clear, or at least it had been until this bastard Chandler showed up. Who was this Chandler creep anyway?

Ivan Blake

****

Cavendish College cafeteria

Chris left Greyson's office and headed for the staircase and fresh air. His footsteps echoed as he crossed the chamber; but no one paid him the slightest attention. He was already back up at ground level when he heard the cellar door open and someone call, "Chandler!"

Chris looked back down into the stairwell and saw the skinny kid who'd shown him to Greyson's office.

"Hey, Chandler, we, I mean the gang, we're gonna take a coffee break, maybe get something to eat at the cafeteria. You want to come along, meet everyone?"

What's this about?

"Okay, sure."

"Good, right. So how's about we meet you there? You know where the cafeteria is?"

"Yeah." It had been a stop on the compulsory campus tour for new students that morning.

"Okay, great, then we'll see you there," he said and went back inside,

Interesting development.

How would Greyson react to the news that he'd agreed to meet with other members of Greyson's circle? He hadn't been enrolled at college for more than a morning, and already he was defying his professors.

****

The cafeteria was a large featureless room filled with long wooden tables and metal chairs. It had a high ceiling, off-white walls, and gray flooring with no discernable pattern. Tended by four older ladies in white, steam tables and freezer cabinets stretched the width of the room. A few students were eyeing the food display. Chris took a tray and cutlery on the chance something might appeal. Since it was not yet dinnertime, the cabinets contained little more than dried-out slices of pizza, day-old sandwiches in plastic wrap, and muffins of indeterminate vintage. He abandoned the tray, purchased a black coffee, and found a vacant table against the far wall.

He'd figured the greylings might take a few minutes to grab coats and cross the quad. Nearly twenty minutes passed before the skinny guy and his henchmen drifted into the room, drifted in the sense that they straggled some ways behind their leader. Apparently, they were none too keen to meet Chris.

One at a time, they bought their coffees and muffins and wandered over to join Chris. "Hey," each said in turn, and to each, Chris replied with a "hey" of his own. Skinny guy, who'd spent a few minutes bickering by the coffee urn with one of his colleagues, was the last to arrive. He was carrying a paper bag.

"Like, sorry, man," he said. "Getting this group to agree to anything is like herding cats." He smiled, sat down, and poured creamers into his coffee. "Anyway, so everyone, this is Chandler, Greyson's new project."

"Chandler what?" asked one of the girls.

"Actually, it's Chris, Chris Chandler."

"Okay, so introductions," said the skinny guy. "That's Sheila. She's clairvoyant. That's Jeffy. He's American too, like you and me, and he has an incredible set of wheels. That's Bonnie. She sees angels whenever it rains. The brothers, Henry and James, over there. And finally, that's Ryan, our resident nihilist."

"Screw you, Ashworth," replied Ryan.

"And I'm Ashworth, from Connecticut. I'm kind of Greyson's right-hand man."

"Like hell you are," muttered Ryan.

Ashworth shot Ryan an angry glare. "Like I said, I've been working with Professor Greyson the longest. I'd like to think I've managed to keep him focused on our work since he has a habit of taking on more new projects than we can manage."

"And women," said Ryan.

"Yeah, like every day," said Bonnie.

"So we try to keep our work moving forward despite Greyson's dubious work habits."

Chris hesitated, then asked, "It's Greyson's research lab, is that not so?"

"Sure, yes," replied Ashworth. "As you'll soon discover, however, Greyson's interests are all over the map."

Without meaning to sound too confrontational, Chris had to ask, "So why are you telling me this?"

"Well, some of us are concerned—"

Ryan interrupted. "That you might be another whim."

"Huh," said Chris. "You mean like another distraction?"

"Okay, yeah," said Ashworth.

The girl, Bonnie, chimed in. "You see, we're doing this incredible stuff with religious texts. We have extracted not just new meanings but actual images, animated images of the sins and the demons that haunted the monks who illuminated the texts. We're exploring the real power behind the images on the vellum."

"And we don't want Greyson chucking all the progress we've made just because he's taken a fancy to a new line of inquiry," added the clairvoyant, Sheila.

"You're afraid I'll encourage his new whim. That I'll be working in opposition to your interests."

"Something like that," said the guy named Ryan.

"He's given us some idea what you're going to be working on," said Ashworth.

"More than me, I bet," replied Chris.

"Has he got you studying Kabbalah?" asked Ashworth, pulling a book from his paper bag. "I figured you might need this," he said and slid a book across the table.

"*The Handy College Guide to Kabbalah*," Chris read aloud. "Thanks. But the one thing Greyson did tell me was that I'm not to interfere with your work."

"You mean we're not to interfere with yours, right?" asked the Ryan fellow.

"He kind of implied that."

"I'm guessing you don't even know what Kabbalah is," continued Ashworth.

"No," replied Chris.

Ashworth slumped back in his chair. "So Greyson tells us to stay out of his new project because he has some superstar coming in to help, and it turns out his superstar doesn't know the first thing about Kabbalah."

"Maybe it isn't my knowledge of Kabbalah he needs."

"So, like, what is it he needs from you?" Ryan asked.

"I'm not really comfortable talking about this."

"Because Greyson told you not to talk to us?" said Ashworth.

"He didn't want us cross-contaminating our research."

"What a load of crap," muttered Ryan.

"So did he tell you that you'd be working on golems and *Titanic* victims and hunting for amulets?" asked Ashworth.

"No." Chris suddenly felt very ill at ease. This group seemed far more intense than he'd expected any ordinary bunch of undergrads to be, and the subject matter far weirder than he'd anticipated. Golems? The *Titanic*? What the hell?

"Did he tell you anything about our work," asked the blond girl, Bonnie, "because it's very exciting."

"Not much."

"What did he say you were to do first?" Sheila asked.

"Familiarize myself with Kabbalah."

"Christ, this is so nuts," said Ryan, shaking his head.

"What's nuts?" asked Chris, surprised by how angry this Ryan guy appeared to be. In fact they all seemed quite steamed about something.

"Greyson. You. The whole goddamned situation," Ashworth grumbled. "We're doing this really great stuff, and Greyson, the space cadet, can't see what's right in front of him."

"What's that?" asked Chris, not sure he really cared to know.

"A path to survival for his job and our lab, that's what!" Ashworth was getting very upset, and Chris had no idea why. "If Greyson would only let us publish what we already have, we'd make him a star again. But no, the idiot has to go chasing off on another of his quests, with you as his new Sancho Panza."

Chris slumped back in his chair, took a deep breath, and looked around the table. "Well, it's good to know how you feel. Thanks for that. But hey, I think I'm done with my coffee. Anyway, it's been interesting." He started to get up.

"Okay, right, sorry, so I got a little excited," said Ashworth, "but a word to the wise, Chandler." He paused, then leaned forward across the table, and said softly, "Stay out of our fucking way."

"Excuse me?"

"We've worked very hard to carve out a research area that's so bloody significant we don't think even Greyson gets it."

"Look," interjected Ryan who'd apparently calmed down a little, "I know Ashworth can be kinda dramatic, but he's only trying to tell you what we all feel. You gotta know how scared we are that the crackpot project Greyson's brought you in to push is going to end up bringing us all down."

Ashworth was still leaning across the table, his eyes glued to Chris. He nodded. "Chandler, take my word for it. If Greyson becomes a danger to us, we have so much crap on him we'll throw him to the wolves in a heartbeat. And you too if it comes to that."

Chris sat back in his chair, crossed his arms, sighed, then grabbed his bookbag and got up slowly. "Well, nice meeting you all," he said, shoved the Kabbalah book from Ashworth in his bag, and left.

****

Camphill Cemetery

Chris felt nauseous. Greyson, his greylings, the college administration, the whole damned situation, it all made him ill. And who was to blame? He was. He'd made one reckless, impulsive decision after another with no thought of the consequences. Leaving Maine, leaving friends, leaving Gillian, rushing headlong into this train wreck of an academic predicament. He'd been so stupid.

Okay, so what should he do now? Break his deal with Greyson and simply walk away? But walk away where? He had to face facts; he'd had no better offers and no other options. Or should he suck it up and stay? He knew he could put up with hostile officials and students; after all, he'd been doing that for years. And he could probably deal with Greyson; he'd managed other nutcases before. No, the real question wasn't whether he could endure this place but whether he could endure Gillian's absence? If anything was going to break him, it was going to be the void in his heart where Gillian used to be.

Outside, the rain had stopped. The air felt clean and crisp. Just what Chris needed to clear his head and calm his nerves after the crapfest of a day he'd had, a good long walk in the fresh air back across town to his room.

The route took him east along Coburg Road to Robie Street, then north to the Camp Hill Cemetery gate. There, he set off through the burial grounds in the direction of the Citadel, the city's hilltop fortress.

Graves in the cemetery dated all the way back to the founding of Halifax in 1749. Their stones were tipped and tilted in every direction. The grass was deeply rutted as each grave's occupant in their turn had crumbled away.

Leaves scudded across the paths and among the gravestones. With the late afternoon change of tide, a fog was also beginning to rise. Walkers emerged from its shroud only to drift away into its clutches again.

Amid the fog and the droplets from the trees, a sudden burst of sparks flickered and twinkled like a swarm of angry fireflies. The moisture-laden air muffled the crackle and sputter of the myriad tiny electrical flashes.

Mallory! Had it really been two days since her last attack? But there was no avoiding her now. She had to have her moment.

Just then, a nasal voice behind him said, "Hey."

Turning back, Chris replied, "Sorry?"

"You heard me. I said, 'Hey.' "

"Okay, hey," replied Chris as he watched a heavyset, unshaven young man with a harelip step from behind a great oak.

"Now you gettin' smart mouthed?" the young man asked. He swayed from side to side, perhaps in an attempt to look menacing. It wasn't working. "You some kind of a perve?"

Apparently, the fellow had been waiting outside for some time because his thin cloth jacket and torn sneakers were sodden, and he was visibly shivering.

"Just walking home," replied Chris.

The guy's pallid skin, the twitch of his lip, and the shake in his hands all suggested he was in some sort of distress, withdrawal perhaps. "I don't think you walkin' home. I think you in this park 'cause you lookin' for somethin'. Other perves maybe, eh?"

"Nope, not looking for anything."

This guy might actually be having a worse day than me.

"Well, you found somethin' anyways. You found a shitload of trouble, bein' out here lookin' for other perves. Somebody's gotta teach you a lesson."

Chris smiled. "Maybe, but sorry, that's not going to be you, and sure as shit, not today. I'm having a bad day too."

"What you say?" The young man clearly took angry offense at Chris's nonchalance. "Fuckin' asshole, but only one of us got this," and he pulled a kitchen knife from his coat pocket. "Only one of us gonna be doin' the teachin'."

"Wrong again, friend," replied Chris, shaking his head. "And I have to warn you, you don't want to try teaching me anything. You'll be the one learning a very painful lesson."

For a moment, the kid appeared shaken by Chris's self-assurance; but then he puffed out his chest and shouted, "What? So you wanna try me? I done knifed guys twice your size."

Chris smiled and said, "And I've ripped guys three times your size into tiny pieces."

The kid was clearly rattled now. This encounter had obviously gone on too long. "Look, just gimme that backpack of yours, and I'll let you leave with your balls."

"No. You give me that knife, and I'll let you leave with your face," replied Chris.

"Christ, you nuts, man!" the young man shouted and took a step toward Chris. Before he could take a second, however, Chris was on him.

He dove forward and embraced the kid, pinning the knife hand against the guy's leg. "Sorry," said Chris, then kissed him on the cheek and stepped away.

"What the fuck!" the young man yelled as he wiped his cheek with his sleeve. "You really are a perve!"

The air exploded.

Flashes and sparks flew in all directions. Flames and smoke burst from a ball of golden light, and a face emerged in its midst, the eyes afire, rage twisting the mouth. Mallory. Her face howled, rose into the air, and then fell upon the kid. The young man swung his blade frantically, but his arm was suddenly jerked up into the air. There he dangled inches above the ground. First his wrist twisted, and then he whirled about like a circus performer, his arm bending, cracking, and eventually snapping. The boy screamed in agony, then dropped to the ground, where he writhed in pain and disappeared in the swirling cloud of dirt and smoke.

Protruding from the cloud, the boy's legs kicked frantically. Screams echoed across the cemetery. Seconds later, amid the dust and smoke, Mallory's maniacal face rose from the boy to reveal his twisted form. The arms were distorted, misshapen, shattered, and the face was a bloody pulp. Bits of flesh—nose, ear, and finger—were strewn about the path. Mallory hovered over the whimpering figure, grinning with satisfaction, then turned to Chris and screamed before vanishing into the receding swirl of smoke and sparks.

"So sorry, kid. That was probably worse than you deserved," said Chris as he turned away and continued on his way. "I did warn you."

Sometimes it felt wrong, turning Mallory's wrath on others like that. Inured by now to such brutality, it disturbed Chris to think what he was becoming. Then again, after the day he'd had, watching Mallory kick the crap out of some creep felt damned satisfying.

"Did you hear something?" asked a passerby approaching out of the fog, "Like screaming?"

"Dog maybe," replied Chris, "over that way, I think. Hope it's not hurt."

He walked into the fog. "Going to need a warmer coat," he muttered. The raw damp cut to the bone.

Back at his building, he bought the diner's pot roast special for supper and turned in early. He slept so well he barely registered the crackling light and whirling presence that appeared up near the ceiling around ten. "No, Mallory, not twice in a day," he muttered, rolled over, and drifted off again.

Chapter Six

Captain Dahlman had said he'd be staying at the *Tidewater Motel*. Ricky parked the police car by the motel office. For one more week, he had the use of the only remaining cop car still painted in its original Bemishstock colors of black and green. All the rest of the fleet had been repainted and put up for sale. State Police wouldn't be caught dead patrolling in cars that once belonged to some crap local force.

The radio in the motel office was playing *How I Know I'm Saved* on the local Christian rock station.

"Hey June," he called to the thin woman behind the desk.

"Oh hey Ricky, what can I do you fer?"

"I'm looking for one of your guests, a Captain Dahlman?"

"Oh yeah," she said with a big lascivious smile. "Christ, that man's a looker. Saw him goin' into the restaurant ten, fifteen minutes ago. You still doing police business?"

"Sorry, June, confidential." He waved and left the office. Okay, so the last couple of days, Ricky'd been working up his story. No point telling Captain Dahlman right off he'd had a call from Canada telling him the Chandler kid was up in Halifax. It's gotta sound like he's done some good investigating and shit.

A large lunch crowd had the motel restaurant hopping.

"Hey Ricky!" the hostess called from across the room. "Need a table?"

"No thanks, Becky. Meeting someone."

"Okay, I'll send a waitress right over when you find him."

Ricky spotted Dahlman seated in a booth beneath a large framed print of Elvis at his last concert. Jeez, that man got fat. Dahlman was occupied with a small garden salad.

"Captain Dahlman, how's she goin'? Ricky said. "The motel office said I'd find you here."

"Acting Chief Pike, well, good to see you again. Please, will you join me?"

"Uh, sure." He squeezed into the booth opposite Dahlman.

"I've ordered today's special," said Dahlman, "a hot hamburger sandwich and something called Maine Sugar Pie."

A waitress came to the table. "Hey Ricky, can I get you something to eat?"

"Sure, Jenny, I'll have the special."

"Okay. Be right back with your salad. Comes free."

"No, forget the salad. Just a glass of coke and the ketchup?"

After the waitress left, Captain Dahlman spoke. "I imagine you're here because of our little conversation the other evening?"

Ricky was still watching the waitress. "You know, she used to be a friend of your daughter's. Nice ass, eh?"

"My daughter?"

"No. No, shit, I'm sorry," Ricky blurted out. "No, I meant Jenny, not that your daughter didn't have a nice ass too. Oh Christ."

"Just tell me what you've learned."

"Okay sure. Well, so like I tried calling the State Police about Chandler, but those pricks wouldn't give me nothin'. So then I figured if he ain't in town no more, maybe he's back down in Lewis, Vermont. That's the last place where he got in trouble big time. So I called their cops. Nothing. So then I figured maybe he's gone to New York to be with his buddy, this Nigel Harrow guy, but then I figured how the fuck am I gonna find him in New York? So then I figured maybe he left the

country on a plane or something for like London or England or someplace like that, but then I couldn't see how I'd find that out either."

"You're telling me you haven't learned a damn thing, is that it?"

Ricky clued into Dahlman's impatience. "No, I got real good stuff."

"Well then, please, spit it out."

"All right, so when I figured out Chandler had probably left the
country, I thought I'd call a buddy with the bus lines about tickets
'cause, you know, the buses are right here, so maybe that's all he could
afford. Anyway, this guy I know, he says, okay, I'll have a look. But at
first, he finds nothing, but then he says, well, maybe he bought a ticket
on one of our partner companies. I guess these bus companies, they
work together kinda. Anyway, bam, he finds the kid's name. Seems
Chandler bought a ticket from the company they own across the border.
Chandler bought a ticket across from Calais, a Canuck town called St
Somethin'. He got it for Halifax, Nova Scotia. It's like up north of us,
well east kinda, it sorta sticks out from us."

"I know where Nova Scotia is."

"Okay, so anyway, it seems Chandler left four days ago. But then,
like, I think, maybe this Halifax might be sorta large, so I figured we
needed to know why he was going to Nova Scotia so we could figure
out where in Halifax you could find him. So then I remembered this
girl used to be in my class. We was kinda sweet on each other. Face
like a cow but boobs out to here. Anyway, I called her mother, and I
says, hey, is Louise gonna be back in town any time soon 'cause some
of the old gang want to have a reunion, and I was wonderin' if she
might like to go with me? Her mother was always kinda nice to me.
Shit, she even grabbed my ass one time. Anyway, she tells me Louise
is with the Federal Health Department or maybe Fisheries, and she
gives me her number. She's like down in Portland, so I calls her. So she
says she wouldn't be able to find out anything about a suspect traveling

out of the country, but she says she knows this girl with the State De-partment at their branch office in Boston, and she'd call if I'd like that. Sure, fucking hell, I would like! Well, if maybe we could go to the movies when she comes home on the weekend, she says, then maybe she'd make the call for me. That'd be great, I said. So now I gotta take this girl out."

"But was she helpful?"

"Oh yeah. So this girl, she calls me back the next day and says her friend found out that Chandler's got some kinda visa to study in Can-ada. Some school called Cavendish College. That bastard's gonna be a student, do you believe that?"

"Excellent."

"Okay, so I'm on this roll, see? So I thinks maybe I should call the cops up there in Halifax. Just see if they know anything about this Chandler kid. And bingo. I gets this sergeant on the line, and he tells me, get this, he's already investigating Chandler. Holy crap, I thinks."

"Anything serious?"

"Not sure. Guess Chandler's name has come up in a couple of dif-ferent investigations, and the kid's only been up there a couple of days!" Ricky's starved. He starts looking around for their orders.

"Did you tell this Canadian cop anything about my interest in Chan-dler?"

"Uh, no. Should I?"

"No, certainly not, no. You did very well, Captain Pike. Lunch is on me."

Jennifer arrived just then with their food.

"This is nice," said Ricky as he took the bottle of ketchup from Jenny's tray.

But all that crap I just' fed you has got to be worth more than one friggin' lunch. Ain't that right?

Ivan Blake

****

Bangor General Hospital

Gillian was racked with doubt. Her Grandpa always said, 'Doubt is the Devil's theme song.' It's like Bob Hope's *Thanks for the Memories* or Jack Benny's *Love in Bloom*. Wherever the Devil goes, he sows doubt.

'Lovely day,' says the Devil in one breath.

'Yes,' you reply.

'Ah, but is it?' he says in his next.

It's no surprise so many hospital patients die in the wee hours of the night, hooked up to some machine, alone. That's when the Devil stalks the corridors, playing his tune.

"You really feel better? Have you seen yourself lately?"

"Is all this pain really worth it? You don't actually think you can beat this, do you?"

"With the burden you've become, do you really believe your family wants you home again?"

Beyond the door to her private room, Gillian could hear . . . nothing, silence, emptiness, as the Devil made his rounds. He slipped into her room, crept up to her bed, and whispered into her soul.

You don't actually believe Chris Chandler ran away to protect you, do you? Isn't it possible he fled because you've become a burden?

You're always getting hurt. Constantly worrying about you must have distracted Chris terribly.

Besides, what have you ever actually done to help him? Nothing. No, perhaps it is best if you let him go, the way he's let you go.

The tears rolled down her cheeks. She wiped them away with the back of her hand and then ran her palm over her scalp, feeling its new bristles, like the fuzz on a filthy horse blanket. What a wreck she was.

Thank goodness Chris couldn't see her. He'd be gone like a shot. Her blackened eyes, the massive weeping incision across the side of her head, her sunken cheeks. But, of course, he was already gone. He'd fled even before she'd looked like this. So why should she try to get him back?

Maybe it was for the best, this new start. She'd already begun physio. It wasn't going badly, and her hand-eye coordination was pretty good already. Even her balance was coming back. If she worked hard enough, she'd be well in time for her mother's wedding, maybe even to walk her down the aisle. And New York! How exciting would that be?

Maybe she could transfer from U Maine to a New York City school like Columbia. She could live with her mom and new dad, study writing, go to galleries and restaurants and museums, and one day get a big city job like at *Time* or CBS. She might meet some investment banker, have an apartment on the Upper East Side overlooking Central Park, and write books. They might even get a place in the Hamptons for the weekends, send the kids away to some swank school in Connecticut . . .

Or maybe she could head off to heaven knows where, to chase after a guy who sees ghosts and tries to protect the dead. An ex-con, hated by half of Maine, with a bad back and a demon for a sidekick. A guy with straggly blond hair and icy blue eyes, a guy who made her tingle to her toes when they made love and who inspired her to rise to any challenge they might encounter. A guy who . . . who wanted her safe, who loved her so much he would break his own heart to save hers.

No, she didn't doubt for a second he'd fled to protect her. The only question was what she could do about it.

Gillian thought of a dozen reasons for remaining in Maine; her studies and scholarship, her mother, the wedding, and her grandfather. By contrast, she could come up with only one reason for leaving, but that one reason trumped all others. Chris Chandler, the idiot, had to be taught a lesson. Even if she had to beat it into that thick skull of his, she had to make him see they were meant to be together. There were many things in life about which Gillian was uncertain: her abilities, looks, dreams, and desires. Still, she was absolutely sure of one thing: Chris was hers, and she was his. And she so wanted to tear a strip off his stupid hide for doubting it.

The first rays of sunlight probed around the edges of her curtains. The sounds of the morning echoed through the hospital corridors. Nurses with paper cups of pills, clean bandages, wash cloths, breakfast, and ice water bustled in and out of Gillian's room. Several doctors visited to probe and chatter and scribble notes on her chart.

"You must be feeling better, young lady. You're looking lovely."

"It's wonderful how strong you are."

"You'll beat this, and you'll be better than ever."

"How happy your family will be to have you home again!"

"You'll see, all the pain and the effort will be so worthwhile."

So the Devil had been banished for another day.

And then her friends arrived. "We've found him!" they shouted in unison, and that's when Gillian knew with utter certainty what she had to do.

****

Greyson's Lab

Greyson wasn't coming in to work today. Ashworth, always the first in the lab each morning, had taken the call. Greyson mumbled something about an awful headache, which meant he was probably at home with some new bimbo. So they'd have the lab to themselves.

Ashworth quickly put out the word he wanted to meet right after lunch to discuss the Chandler situation.

It was now just past one, and the greylings were seated around the common room table with pizza boxes and sandwich wrappers battling for space with class notes and textbooks.

"I'm sorry, but I don't get it," said Bonnie. "What Chandler situation? He seemed like he was nice."

"And you're a good judge, are you?" replied Ashworth. "We all saw you ogling him yesterday."

"That's not fair," protested Sheila, but Ashworth had always reckoned Sheila had a thing for Bonnie.

"Why are you so bent out of shape about this guy, anyway?" asked Ryan. "He has his project, and we've got ours, so what's the big deal with him being here?"

"I would have thought the risk was obvious, even to you. The American is displacing us."

At Ashworth's insult, Ryan shifted forward in his chair and shouted, "Displacing *you*, you mean. You've been Greyson's lapdog since before most of us got here. So now it looks like Greyson has a new favorite, and you're scared."

"I've never been Greyson's lapdog." For a moment Ashworth was rattled by Ryan's attack. "You heard me after the medallion screwup. I was the one who stood up to Greyson. You didn't. None of you did." He calmed somewhat when no one else challenged him. "But Greyson isn't the issue. I'm worried when the college dumps him, we'll all get dumped too. Don't we want this lab to survive? We'll want some new guy appointed in his place, right? Some prof we can manage? No, when I say this guy Chandler is displacing us, I mean he's putting all of us at risk. If Chandler encourages Greyson in his crazy obsession with the

Titanic amulet, then the two of them could destroy everything we worked for."

"But we just told Greyson that we don't want to be involved in his *Titanic* stuff," said Jeffy. "Now are you saying we do?"

"No, I don't want to be involved in it, but I do want to know what crazy things Greyson is planning. I'm saying we need to know what he's up to, what risks he's running. We've always been able to handle Greyson, sort of anyway, but this Chandler could tip the balance."

"How could we possibly control Chandler and Greyson at the same time?" asked Jeffy.

"First, we gotta get something on Chandler, some way to weaken his influence over Greyson, and failing that, we have to drive Chandler off campus altogether."

At first, no one spoke. A few glances were exchanged, then a couple of nods, and finally, two or three grudging okays.

"We're agreed then?" asked Ashworth.

"Yeah, okay," replied Ryan.

"What do you propose we do?" asked Bonnie.

"I think we start by finding out who Chandler is. I already learned from one of the admin secretaries that he had some kind of trouble with the law back in Maine. In fact, the guy was in prison for something. And now I guess he's sort of a local hero to some and a real villain to others. We need to find out what that's all about and fast. Then I think we'll know better how to proceed."

****

Duncan's Cove

"Would a been a lot simpler to call this guy into the station, Sarg," muttered Constable Publicover as he took the next curve in the coastal road a little too fast. The old police car yawed across the pavement, caught the gravel shoulder, and rocked violently before Publicover got it back under control.

"Christ, slow down!" shouted Sergeant Bain. "Anyway, yeah, well, from everything we've learned about this guy Greyson, it seemed like a good idea to catch him off guard. Seems he's made a career of beating one rap after another. No point giving him any more advantage than we have to. Besides, what's so bad about a nice ride in the country?"

"You call this a nice ride, Sarg?"

The police car had seen better days; its shocks were nearly shot and sway bar already cracked. Constable Publicover had to slow the vehicle to a crawl to negotiate each bend in the narrow road and prevent them both from losing their lunch.

The Chebucto Head Road to Ketch Harbor wove and twisted its way along the rocky south shore like a length of tangled rope on a wind-swept beach. Autumn and salt spray had stripped away what little color the landscape might have had. Everywhere, enormous granite boulders rose above the dark, tangled groundcover of blighted spruce, bayberry bushes, and gorse like great gray whales cresting in a storm-tossed sea.

"There," said Bain. "That's his turnoff."

Up ahead, on the crest of a rise, a gravel lane on the left exited the highway in the direction of the sea. Publicover pulled onto the dirt track, and steering carefully to avoid potholes and ruts, drove down the slope into tiny Duncan's Cove. There, a half dozen rude, unpainted clapboard cottages dotted the rocky shore. Two were even perched on tall stilts above the lapping waves. All had silvered with age, and most were bedecked with glass floats, lobster pots, and faded plywood butterflies.

"Don't suppose there's many fishermen left in this cove," said Constable Publicover.

"Hmm, all artists and crap," said Bain. "There, that's Greyson. Number 9."

Publicover pulled in behind one of the cottages perched over the tidewater and parked alongside a mud-encrusted and battered '68 Porsche 911.

Bain paused to have a glance in the driver-side window. "Hmm, criminal to treat a classic that way," he muttered as he stepped onto the small porch. There he knocked loudly on the weather-beaten door, once, twice, a third time.

"He's here," Publicover muttered. "The college said he'd canceled his classes today because he isn't well."

Bain hammered on the door yet again and shouted, "Professor Greyson, it's the Halifax Police, sir. We want to have a chat with you, sir."

Curtains parted in several other cottages. Faces peered in their direction across the muddy, rutted parking area.

"We're investigating an assault, Professor Greyson, sir," Bain called out. Let the locals know we're here. The embarrassment factor always helped.

The door flew open. "Fuck, you don't have to let the whole world know!" snarled Greyson.

"Oh, sorry, sir. Weren't sure you were at home. Apologies, sir."

"Come in, come in, if you must."

Bain and Publicover stepped inside.

Greyson rubbed his eyes and knotted his robe. "Why are you here at this hour?"

"It's two in the afternoon, sir."

"Oh, hmm. Okay, so I've not been well."

Bain glanced around the cottage. Dusty curtains were drawn across its sea-facing windows. Countertops, tables, chairs, all were littered with bottles, glasses, paper plates, and pill containers. "No, so I understand, sir."

"What do you want, officer?" Greyson went into the kitchen at the back of the cottage and ran himself a glass of water.

"Sergeant, Sergeant Bain, sir. We're investigating the assault on your boss."

"The college president? My boss!" Greyson sneered. "The man's an ass. But what assault? No one was with the guy when he caught fire. How can you call it an assault?"

"Nobody just catches fire, sir."

"Well, I didn't put a match to the president." Greyson downed the glass of water. "I was long gone when he lit up. Probably spilled his pipe or something."

"But you'd had a nasty fight with him, hadn't you?"

"One of many. The man doesn't understand my work."

"Wasn't just about your work though, was it, sir? You've recruited some American kid who has a reputation for, let's say, causing trouble. Could he have had something to do with the fire?"

"What? How? He wasn't even in the city then."

"Do you know that for sure, sir? Works for you, doesn't he?"

"He'll be doing research for me. But he won't be setting anyone on fire for me."

"What sort of research will he be doing for you, sir?"

"You really think you'll understand my answer, officer?"

"That's Sergeant, sir. Try me."

"Well, he'll be doing research on ancient Judaica in order to ascertain the most authentic versions of certain ceremonies and the possible locations of various lost ceremonial implements."

"Okay, so right. And this is the same kid who got his high school diploma by correspondence and spent a year in prison for his part in the death of some old chiropractor."

"Everyone deserves a second chance, Offic . . . Sergeant."

"Certainly. And thank you for your time, sir. I hope you'll feel better soon." Bain turned and headed for the door but then asked, "Oh, while I think of it, you wouldn't know anything about a recent raid on the Jewish cemetery in the city's north end, would you? I've been told you have an interest in the *Titanic* and certain Jewish passengers who may have been aboard."

Greyson visibly blanched. "I . . . I do, but only . . . only as a kind of a hobby . . . like many people. Especially if you live here, where so many *Titanic* dead are buried. But beyond that . . . I certainly don't have an interest in their actual graves. I don't know anyone who does. And as for all that Nazi graffiti, that was horrible! Crazies."

"Most definitely, sir. Only there was no mention of any Nazi graffiti in the press. I'm wondering how you knew about it?"

"I . . . I guess I must have heard it somewhere, from Jewish friends perhaps."

"Oh, perhaps," replied Sergeant Bain. "And do you recall the names of those friends?"

"Uh, not off hand."

"Any of them? No? Well, thank you for your help anyway. And if you do recall which friends might have told you about the graffiti, maybe you'd give me a call, because I would like to know how they found out."

As Constable Publicover attempted to turn the car in the tight little gravel parking area, Bain mused aloud, "Never expected that. It seems our Professor Greyson was somehow involved in the attack on the Jewish cemetery."

****

Gothall's Rooming House

To describe the old woman as thin would have been a kindness; emaciated, skeletal, cadaverous more like. Wearing a torn plastic raincoat and yellow sou'wester and clutching a sopping wet paper bag to her chest, the old lady pulled herself up the stairs using the filthy wooden handrail. She might have topped five feet had she been able to unbend her cruelly twisted spine. Her moist, gray eyes were clouded by cataracts. A few shanks of wet hair were plastered to her hollow cheeks. Her chalky brow was deeply furrowed, her flesh as fragile as onion skin, and her lips, despite a generous slash of scarlet, were pinched and pencil-thin. She muttered tearfully to herself about neglectful servants and selfish housemaids as she struggled upwards.

Chris came up the stairs behind her. "Good afternoon," he said softly.

"Is that you, Samuel?" she asked.

"No ma'am, I'm Chris, Christopher Chandler."

"Oh, a new boy. That's nice. You must be a school chum of my son."

"Uh, no."

"Did my husband hire you?"

"No, Mrs. Norris," said a gravelly voice from the stairwell below Chris. The elderly tenant, Samuel Brook, pushed past Chris and took the old lady by the arm.

"Ah, Samuel, I'm glad you're here. I've had such a terrible day," she said as she handed over her sodden paper bag.

"Then we must get you a nice cup of hot tea."

"And this young man, we should make him a cup too."

"I . . . I not sure," said the old man.

"Thank you. I'd love a cup of tea, ma'am," Chris said.

"He's a school friend of our Stanley."

"Is he?" said the old man, eyeing Chris suspiciously.

"No," protested Chris. "No, I just moved—"

"He's gonna be doing work for me," Brook said to the old woman.

"Ah, well then," she replied. "But we should still make him a cup of tea. It's such a nasty day outside."

"*Aber ja*, but first we must get you warmed up," Brook replied.

Chris followed the old man as he gently guided Mrs. Norris to her room.

The air in the woman's room was heavy with age and stale perfume, and the place was crammed with dark and dusty furnishings. Stacked against one wall were several heavy wooden dining chairs, end tables of varying styles and sizes, and cabinets filled with figurines, cups, and saucers. There were three or four threadbare oriental rugs piled one upon the other on the floor. Under the room's only window was a faded scarlet chaise lounge with threads hanging from every seam. And at the center of the room stood a child's canopy bed painted pink with twinkle lights and a fairy mobile fastened to its cracked and peeling headboard. Across the bed and its ripped and wrinkled sheets was draped a pink and purple afghan with more holes than pattern.

Every available surface in the room was cluttered with framed and fading photos of two proud and smiling young parents and their chubby gleeful infant. In a quick glance around the room, Chris noted a few pictures of an older lad, but none of the proud father in his later years or of the man the child might by now have become.

Mr. Brook helped the old lady to her bedside and slipped the sodden shoes from her cracked and twisted feet. "There," he said as he draped an old bathrobe around her shoulders. "you're warmer now?"

"Yes, thank you, Samuel."

"I'll get your tea from the kitchen in just a minute."

Chris was touched by the gentleness with which Brook treated the woman. But then, as the old guy crossed to a cluttered table, he glowered at Chris.

He really doesn't want me here. What's he pulling on the old dear? Some sort of scam?

"Let me get her tea," said Chris.

"No," replied the old man.

"Please, Samuel, come and sit by me," whispered the old lady.

"All right. So, kid, you go get her dinner. Mr. Minhas will have it ready."

Chris ran downstairs to the diner and returned with three bowls of stew and potatoes. It was a risky presumption to purchase two additional servings for the old man and himself, but Chris felt he had to find out what kind of hold the old man had on Mrs. Norris. He'd never forgive himself if he learned one day the old guy had been ripping her off.

Brook glared as Chris handed him his plate and sat down with his own dinner to join them as they ate. The woman continued her effort to make conversation. "Young man," she said, "so how long have you known my son?"

"I don't, ma'am. I'm a—"

"He is a student, Mrs. Norris," Brook interjected. "You remember I was telling you before. And he is helping me and Minhas with jobs."

"Oh yes. And do you know Samuel from the war? He had a horrible time in the war, didn't you, Samuel. Samuel, show the boy your tattoo."

"I don't think—" replied Brook.

"Of course. Go on, show him."

As Samuel slowly rolled up his sleeve to reveal a long line of tattooed numbers, he shot Chris an angry glance. He obviously resented this intrusion on his privacy.

"The Germans did that, didn't they, Samuel," said the old woman.

"Yes," he replied as he rolled down his sleeve.

"And did the Germans do that to you too?" she asked.

"Oh no, I wasn't born then."

"No, of course not. But you do know my son."

Samuel was becoming agitated. "I have told you, this boy is a student," Brook said aloud. He then turned to Chris and said very softly. "Her son—"

"I know, he died," whispered Chris in reply. "Mr. Minhas told me."

"Did he tell you about Mrs. Norris, that she was once very wealthy?"

"A little."

"The Norris family, they had lots of ships, freighters. The Norris family had been building ships and sailing them all over the world since before Canada is born. But Mrs. Norris's husband lost the company. He owed too many people. And after a couple of bad storms and some sort of insurance crime, the company was finished. The son then drank away rest of the family money and killed himself upstairs. Mrs. Norris may once have understood what happened to her family, but no more. Now *sie ist verrückt,* she is nuts. I don't want her to have any further sadness in her life. She still thinks this is her home, and everybody here, we are her servants. So if you don't want trouble from me, you will play along."

"Forgive me for asking but why do you care?"

"None of your goddamn business," the old man muttered as he wiped his plate with the last of the bread.

****

Gothall's Rooming House

Chris closed the window against the damp and the reek of the harbor, switched on the bedside lamp, and slid beneath the rough sheets and thin blanket of his small bed. There he lay gazing at a stain on the ceiling.

Water leak perhaps? Probably not, judging by the size of the oblong mark. Water damage would have brought the old plaster down by now. More likely the stain is from something spilled on the floor above, some kind of liquid. Instead of evaporating quickly, it must have seeped between the floorboards and then leached into the plaster. So okay, maybe bodily fluids? Maybe from a dead animal trapped between the floors . . . or worse. Fluids from a corpse, oh God, from the old woman's son? Minhas did say the boy killed himself up there.

Whatever had brought that nightmare to mind? Well, obviously an entire evening spent with the boy's devastated mother. Chris shuddered and rolled onto his side.

Enough of that.

He leaned from the bed and pulled several books from his bookbag, books on Kabbalah from the library along with the book Ashworth had given him. *The Handy College Guide to Kabbalah* by Amos Jenkins, Ph.D., from someplace called Mount Amblin Divinity School.

Chris was quite familiar with the publisher, *Handy College Guides of Baltimore*. The company produced cheat sheets and short summaries of the classics. Chris had used their guides to good effect in completing his high school studies in the Portland Juvenile Detention facility. He propped himself against the wooden headboard, opened the well-worn paperback, and began to read.

Introduction

I'm not going to rush this. Kabbalah isn't an easy subject to grasp quickly. The simple truth is Kabbalah presents several conflicting faces to the world and incorporates many competing concepts. Now hold on. We'll begin by setting out a couple of basic facts: first, Judaism regards God as utterly unknowable; second, Judaism categorically prohibits magic; and third, Kabbalah's practitioners today see it as a way of living in the real world rather than as some form of other-worldly mysticism. That said, Kabbalah also makes a couple of assumptions which, on their face, appear to contradict the facts we've just stated. First, Kabbalists believe that an unknowable God can nevertheless be studied through His interactions with His Creation. Second, while Judaism may have prohibited black magic, it deemed acceptable a form of white magic derived from certain statements in early Jewish texts. And third, while Kabbalah itself cannot be described as mysticism, it nonetheless embodies a long mystic tradition.

Where does all this leave us? Well, at the foot of a very steep mountain, to put it bluntly.

Kabbalah draws together a rich set of teachings stretching back two millennia. Furthermore, these teachings all shared one objective, to explain the relationship between God—the unchanging, eternal Ein Sof, *the name used for God's pure essence in Kabbalah—and the mortal and finite universe which the* Ein Sof *created. The assumption was that while* Ein Sof *might be unknowable, it does reveal something of itself through its ongoing interactions with its Creation. Very early in the history of Kabbalah, adherents agreed that these interactions—or emanations, as they called them—could be grouped in ten categories. Together these ten categories of interaction were called the* Sefirot *or* Tree of Life. *The* Sefirot *describes the way these emanations are connected. Kabbalah is, at its heart, the study of the* Sefirot *as a key to understanding how* Ein Sof *interacts with the world.*

Okay, that wasn't so bad, but hang on. It turns out the study of the Sefirot *over the centuries took several very different forms.*

One form with its origins in the Renaissance was a theological or theoretical approach. Adherents sought to understand and describe the divine realm through both a direct and an allegorical interpretation of religious texts. As scholars have done for centuries, they studied and analyzed texts, checked sources, and compared variations.

Then there was the meditative approach. This approach involved the ecstatic contemplation of ancient texts to achieve some sort of mystical union with Ein Sof. *Practitioners employed visions and dreams in an effort to uncover hidden realities within early writings.*

And lastly, a third and far older approach arose from an ancient magical tradition. The practitioners of this art, called Practical Kabbalah, sought to manipulate and alter both the Divine Realm and the natural world through spells, divination, incantations, and the use of amulets.

As early as the 1st century BCE, Jews believed that the Torah and other canonical texts contained encoded messages and hidden meanings. Behind this conviction was the notion that God enacted Creation through the power of the Hebrew language. "In the beginning was the word . . . ." To early Kabbalists, it followed that every Hebrew letter, word, number, and even the accents placed on certain words in the Tanach (the complete Hebrew Bible, including the Pentateuch, Prophets, and Writings) all conveyed exotic meanings. It was believed these hidden messages described a complex spiritual dimension behind the Torah's more unambiguous ideas.

The Names of God, in particular, were given special prominence in this search for hidden meaning. Indeed, one Catalonian Kabbalist in the 13th century contended that the entire Torah was one long Holy name for God. Another maintained that if a person were pure enough in spirit and knew how to correctly articulate all the secret names of

God, he would possess the same powers as God himself, even to the extent of being able to create life.

Chris's eyes opened wide and he gasped. "Oh crap," he murmured. Was this what Greyson had in mind? Was he on some sort of quest to create life? No wonder the college wanted to dump him. "Oh jeez, I haven't got myself mixed up with another nutcase like Dr. Meach, have I?" he whispered.

Chris returned to the book.

The prospect of such power in the hands of rabbis was frightening enough and far too dangerous to be allowed to fall into the hands of the unwise. For this reason, practical Kabbalah was banned in the 15th century, and all study of Kabbalah was restricted to men over forty. Today, practical Kabbalah represents the seamy underbelly of Jewish religious scholarship. It is considered by many to be a minor, shunned tradition within the Jewish faith.

Okay, so maybe things weren't so bad. Maybe Greyson wasn't some kind of nut after all, and he really did have a genuine scholarly interest in Kabbalah. After all, even nonsense can be studied by scholars, right?

Practical Kabbalah did not go quietly, however. On the contrary. For one thing, practical Kabbalah had a profound impact on Christian mysticism. As early as the 14th century, it was transposed into a category of Christian hermeneutics (the study of religious texts) called Christian Cabbalah. Initially, the objective of Christian Cabbalists was to turn the Sefirot *into a weapon to be used against the Jews. In a Europe-wide campaign to convert Jews, Cabbalists argued the* Sefirot, *rather than revealing God's emanations, actually foretold the coming of Jesus. But then the Christian study of Cabbalah took a more sinister turn.*

Kabbalah proved a rich hunting ground for mystics of all sorts. Many believed that early Jewish texts concealed a trove of ancient wisdom. One Greek Orthodox mystic twisted the Kabbalistic concept of Ein Sof's *emanations into the 'energies of God.' Another interpreted the ten categories of the* Sefirot *as the ten levels of power among angels in Paradise. The Hebrew names for the ten categories of emanations in the* Sefirot *were turned into curses and spells and incantations by an undercurrent of cabbalistic sorcery, which has lasted into the present. Mystics from the Rosicrucians to Alistair Crowley believed that when eventually decoded, the* Sefirot *would provide the key to unlocking unimaginable ancient wisdom and power.*

Chris's eyes drooped, and his last thought before drifting off, was, *Not another madman . . . .*

****

The motion of the light flickering and dancing about the walls wakened Chris. He glanced at the glowing numbers on his alarm clock.

Just ten?

Probably an emergency vehicle in the street outside or maybe the lights on a cop car picking up a drunk.

But then, as he rolled over and looked up into the darkness, he realized the light wasn't outside. It was directly above him, up by the ceiling, a tiny point of light, there one second and gone the next. But when the light disappeared, the air near the ceiling still glowed, shifting and rippling like the reflection of moonlight on a dark pool.

He'd seen the air behave this way before, back in the Monsegur cemetery when he'd first seen heartbroken specters hovering by their desecrated graves. They'd been mere points of light at first . . . until Rose DuCalice taught him how to see the dead.

165

"What is it? What do you want?" Chris whispered into the darkness.

The point of light reappeared. Chris squinted, turned his head to the side, and waited. And sure enough, there in the inky darkness, an image began to resolve. Several shades of green—lime, moss, pine—all shifting, rolling, and bleeding into one another.

"See beyond the light, see beyond the light," Chris whispered to himself, as Rose had taught him that night by her family graves.

Chris squinted through the moving palette, looked beyond the darkness, and waited. "I want to meet you," he whispered. And then, amid the rippling shades, there he was. A young man, a mere sketch of a figure, outlined in shimmering green, eyes filled with tears, face anguished, tortured, and although there was no sound, the young man appeared to be screaming.

The face descended from the ceiling to within inches of Chris's own. In fear, Chris squirmed to the top of his bed, and pressed his spine against the headboard. The specter, his eyes filled with grief, his lips moving, pleading, begging, drew nearer still until his face filled Chris's vision.

Begging? Pleading? But for what? And why? What had Chris to do with this apparition? Then he realized the eyes were not fixed on him at all. No, they were looking right through him. Chris slid to one side of the bed. The eyes did not follow. The young man was pleading with someone else, someone who had at some time in the past occupied the bed in which Chris now slept. Chris rolled off the bed and watched as the young man sobbed, begged, and pleaded with the bed's unseen occupant. Suddenly the specter swung about and vanished through Chris's door. Chris hesitated, still aghast at the specter's sudden appearance. But then he threw open his door in time to see the figure sweep up the stairs to the fifth floor and disappear into the room once occupied by Mrs. Norris's dead son!

Without thinking, Chris galloped after the figure. The fifth-floor door was locked, but Chris forced it open. The room was filled with cartons of paper plates, sleeves of plastic cups, and bags of sugar packets. But it hadn't always been a storeroom for the diner's supplies. Once a young man had lived . . . and died in this room. And he was about to die again.

Chris watched as the specter's greenish outline—crackling, flashing, pulsing—kicked away a chair from beneath its feet. For a moment, the iridescent figure dangled in the middle of the room, kicking and writhing. But then the fine wire, from which the boy had apparently crafted the noose about his throat, sliced through flesh, then cartilage, and finally, bone. The headless corpse tumbled to the floor. There it flopped about for a moment before falling still and then fading away. The head, its sinews and arteries still tangled in the wire, dangled for some moments, turning slowly this way and that and dripping gore until it too fell to the floor and vanished.

As a suicide, the boy was trapped here to reenact his death for eternity. If only he'd known the fate of every suicide: to suffer forever the terrible emotions that had driven them to seek escape and to endure their pointless death over and over again till the end of time.

Chris managed to wedge the door shut with some of the splintered wood he'd earlier broken from the frame. That's when he realized how cold the building had become. He ran back to his room in nothing more than boxers and dove beneath his bedcovers.

Why does this keep happening to me? I don't want this, none of it. No more nutcases. No more graveyards. No more tortured souls. And yet . . . .

The old lady's son, the poor kid. Who had he been screaming at? And why was he in such pain? Maybe his mother knew the answers. But maybe not. Would Mrs. Norris want to know that her son's spirit was still here? Should he tell her? Or would knowing that her boy was fated to suffer the agony of his suicide forever push her over the edge completely?

Chapter Seven

Monday, September 14

Cavendish College

Ashworth couldn't have been more satisfied. In fact, he was as happy as a pig in shit, as his idiot father liked to say.

The headline blared across the front page of the college newspaper. YANK EX-CON GETS SWEETHEART DEAL. And then beneath in a smaller font, 'I OWE NO ONE AN EXPLANATION,' SAYS CONTROVERSIAL PROF. Ashworth skimmed the entire article. *College gives full scholarship to notorious Yankee ex-con . . . many unanswered questions about propriety, worthiness, due process . . . embattled professor struggles to defend his unilateral decision . . . opaque, 'unaccountable process' says college admin . . . shadowy American served years in prison . . . horrific stories of death and destruction in both Maine and Vermont,* and on and on it went.

The greylings had taken all the previous afternoon and most of the night to collect information on Chandler and then spoon-feed it to the paper's writers. At first, the paper's young journalists had been reluctant to set aside the front-page story they'd already prepared on hygiene issues in the college cafeteria. But when Ashworth laid out Chandler's whole gory tale of body snatching and death, the writers succumbed to Ashworth's entreaties.

As he crossed campus on his way to class, Ashworth could see students everywhere engrossed in Chandler's story. Okay, so maybe making Chandler's story public was a gamble since the State of Maine had, in fact, adjudged him a hero. But Ashworth figured there was enough uncertainty and grisly confusion in Chandler's run-ins with the law to provide the latitude Ashworth needed to cast the Yank in a very dark light. And the student journalists had seen it that way too. In time perhaps, public opinion might swing in Chandler's favor, but that might take months. If the broader scheme worked as it should, Chandler wouldn't be around long enough to experience the turnabout.

"Michael," he heard someone call. He looked about and spotted Angel Girl Bonnie running toward him. "Shit, what does she want?" he muttered to himself.

"Michael, the administration is furious about the story, and they want to talk to us."

"Us?"

"Yes, or at least someone from the lab. The dean of students sent a note across first thing this morning."

"Why would the dean be upset? I thought the college would be happy to see Greyson criticized in the paper? They want to get rid of him, don't they?"

"Sure, but I guess they don't want the college's dirty laundry aired in public. The story makes the whole college look bad."

"Damn!" said Ashworth. "Anyway, I'll go, and I'll say we knew nothing about the story, and what motive would we have to embarrass Dr. Greyson anyway?"

"But what if the guys at the paper tell?"

"Journalists are supposed to protect their sources," Ashworth replied.

"I think this story was a big mistake," Bonnie said as she walked away.

"What do you know, bitch?" Ashworth murmured to himself as he headed for Sinclair Hall. Just another dimwit questioning his judgment. Did none of them appreciate what he was trying to do? Did none of them understand?

Dead Reckoning

****

Gothall's Rooming House

Why Samuel insisted she lock her bedroom door when she went out to morning mass was a mystery to Mrs. Norris. After all, Mr. Norris was somewhere about the building. No doubt he was taking care of the company accounts or the shipping register or the weather forecasts or the—what had her father called them?—the lads a' sea. But Samuel was so kind to her; why shouldn't she humor the poor dear? It was the least she could do after everything he'd been through.

She started down the stairs. Her loose left heel was giving her trouble, but she had to wear her satin shoes since they went so nicely with her purse and purple gown. When she removed her coat at church, there were always murmurs of appreciation for her attire. Given her husband's standing in the community, she had a responsibility to look her best.

She dropped the key into her purse, the one with all the pearls, the purse Mr. Norris had given her on their anniversary. She liked to carry her best purse on the first Mass of the month because there was always the chance the bishop might attend, and it was such a long time since she'd seen him. She beamed with pride to recall how the bishop had been a regular at their dinner parties all those years ago. If the bishop attended mass today, she would invite him to another dinner. No doubt he'd remember how elegant the Norris dinners had been. There hadn't been a special dinner in this house for some time, but the staff under Samuel's direction would be up to the challenge.

Voices on the stairs below. Those louts. Hanging about again. Whatever had possessed her husband to hire such toughs as these? But then again, that was the shipping business. Filthy ships, ghastly cargo,

171

even more horrid crews. Her father had always joked his crews would sooner sink their owner than leave the dock.

"So she'd shoved this fuckin' wad of tens in her bra like that was gonna stop me findin' it," said the kid seated on the stairs tying his sneaker.

"Warned ya. Fuckin' bitch. D'in I say there had to be a reason Mickey Dick dumped her?" replied the other between draws on his cigarette.

"So why she still walkin' around? Why didn't he just do her? Would a saved me a lot o' trouble."

Mrs. Norris stepped in front of the lout with the cigarette and said firmly to the boy on the stair, "May I get by, please?"

The boy looked up at the old woman. "What's your hurry, bitch? Can't ya see I'm busy here?"

"You're going to make me late for Mass, so would you please move to one side?"

"Look, lady, you're just going to have to wait."

She turned to the other lad. "If he needs help tying his shoes, I'll gladly show him how."

The boy jumped up. "You sayin' I'm too stupid to tie my own shoes?"

She twisted her face away. The boy's breath was appalling. "I merely offered to help, if you're not yet accustomed to tying your own shoes."

"Oh Christ, I'm gonna rip your—"

"Hold on, Fred. Look, lady, you gotta stop. So just say you're sorry and get on your way."

"All right, I'm sorry. But I don't understand. I was just trying to say that I realize deficient children the world over deserve our help."

"Christ, now she's saying I'm deficient? And she's the one dressed up like a clown in that purple sack and those goddamn slippers." He turned from his friend. "Bitch, what you got in that bag, eh?"

He snatched the pearl purse from Mrs. Norris's hand. She tried to grab it back, but the other lout caught her arm. "Fuck, she's as thin as a stick."

The lout with her purse ripped it open, breaking the stitching, and releasing a shower of white beads which cascaded away down the stairs.

"My purse," she screamed, "my purse." She dropped to her knees, crying.

"Your own damn fault, bitch," said the first lout as he stomped away down the stairs. "And clean up these fuckin' beads," he said as he yanked the foyer door open. "Someone could get killed stepping on all your crap," he shouted as he left the building.

Mrs. Norris remained on the floor for some time weeping quietly. When she had no more tears to spill, she gathered up the remnants of her purse, struggled to her feet, and hobbled back to her room.

****

Duncan's Cove

What with the waves and the wind, and the rattling window and the week-old Chinese food he'd eaten for dinner, and the scotch and the wine and the Percocet at bedtime, Greyson had had an especially rough night. And it had been made much worse by the news he'd received from his lawyer earlier that afternoon. The province was planning to introduce legislation annulling the charter of the college's theology program and enacting a new charter for the proposed new divinity school across town. The new charter would supersede the terms of the bequest under which Greyson's endowed chair and institute had been created. The cash remaining in his endowment would be returned to the old woman's family, something they'd been demanding for years. In other words, if the charter was enacted, Greyson would be toast. Oh, and his lawyer had made pointed mention of the fact that Greyson's account was long overdue.

Of course, the proposed charter required legislation which might take some time to draft, pass, and enact. But the province and the college were clearly in cahoots, and the handwriting was now on the wall. He'd be out on his ear unless his scheme to once again capture the scholarly world's attention actually worked. And work it would, so long as the cretins in his lab didn't totally screw things up.

The handful of students who showed up for his morning class on comparative religions—few ever bothered since he tended to cancel more classes than he gave—were all absorbed in the latest edition of the college newspaper. It didn't take long for Greyson to discover why. The paper's headline told the whole tale. EX-CON GETS SWEETHEART DEAL.

He stumbled through thirty minutes of the class. Of course, he knew what everyone else in the room knew very well, that he was just going through the motions. In fact, he'd told the class the first day, "Read the textbook, and you'll pass." His lectures added little beyond what was in the textbook. Besides, he hadn't changed the final exam in a decade, so the questions were public knowledge. Consequently, the only students who came to class were the kind of sickening brown-nosers who couldn't help themselves. There were always a few; like flies around trash cans, they came with the territory.

After blustering on about the universality of belief and brushing off some ridiculous question about Abelard's proof of God's presence, he finally called the charade to a halt and rushed off to confront the asses in his lab.

"What the hell are you idiots playing at?" he bellowed from the top of the cellar stairs.

"Don't know what you're referring to, sir," replied Ashworth from the common room sofa.

"This, this," Greyson screamed, waving the college paper about.

"Oh that, sir," replied Ashworth with a smirk. "We are as shocked as you are, sir. We thought you must have been interviewed by the paper and approved the story."

"I knew nothing about this!"

"Well, that's very unfortunate. How unfair. We should protest immediately, sir. I'm sure the damage can be undone." Ashworth turned to the other greylings, and they all nodded sheepishly.

"So you're saying this isn't your work?"

"What could we possibly gain from torpedoing your new apprentice, sir?"

"If I find out that you did—"

"But sir, you must tell us, is any of this horrible information about Chandler true, sir? Is he an ex-con, sir? Are we safe with him around, sir?"

"Shit, I want you gone! The lot of you! Gone!"

"Not happening, sir, not while this ex-con might endanger you and jeopardize our work, sir. We owe you far too much to allow that to happen, sir. We're here for you, sir."

"Oh, for fuck's sake! And stop with all the 'sir' crap." Greyson turned and left the lab, slamming the cellar door behind him.

****

Greyson's Lab

"Well, that went quite well," muttered Ashworth.

"God, Michael, now you've got Greyson *and* the admin mad at us," said Ryan.

"Forget the admin. They believed me when I said we knew nothing about the story. Besides, we have no choice if we're going to get rid of Chandler and protect our work. But hey, I'm wondering, do you suppose we could also implicate Chandler in our raid on the *Titanic* cemetery?"

"How could we do that?" asked Bonnie.

"Maybe we could plant a little evidence, maybe one of you ladies could manage that?"

****

Cavendish College Administration

In the wake of the college paper's story, Chris wasn't surprised to be summoned to the admin building. His sociology professor read aloud a brief note at the beginning of the mid-morning class. "Would Chris Chandler please stop by academic counseling at his earliest convenience?"

More than a hundred students were enrolled in the class. But the instant his name was mentioned, every eye in the lecture hall turned in Chris's direction, thanks no doubt to his Bemishstock arrest photo in the student paper.

As he climbed the broad granite steps to Sinclair Hall, Chris fully expected the college administration to use the press story to pressure him into leaving the school immediately. Embarrassment, they'd probably say, damage to the school's reputation, parents' concern over the presence of a former convict on campus, and so on.

But instead, the sympathetic counselor Chris had met that first day on campus actually apologized to him. The story was grotesquely misleading, she said. It distorted even the most basic facts about Chris's conviction. It ignored his vindication by the State of Maine and the gratitude expressed by the town of Lewis Vermont for his actions. Chris was especially surprised by the counselor's familiarity with his history.

"After our first meeting," she explained, "I felt bad about your situation, so I . . . I thought I should learn more about you. And, well, I'm quite impressed. It seems you are indeed a hero, Mr. Chandler, and I will do what I can to help you complete your studies here. To that end, I've already spoken with the newspaper's editor and straightened him out. I made it clear to him that if he fancies himself a journalist, then he will have to do a better job of examining all sides of a story before he runs it."

"I'm . . . I'm grateful. But did he give you any idea of why he ran the story in the first place?"

"It seems a source delivered a stack of American news clippings and a precooked story line that seemed too sensational to ignore. But the editor wouldn't say who."

"Will the paper run any sort of correction?"

"I'm not sure. I can't dictate what the paper will do, but I do think its editor has found the experience . . . edifying."

Chris was feeling quite buoyed as he left Sinclair Hall.

Well, that's a gratifying turn of events.

And it didn't hurt that a group of attractive females chatting on the steps giggled and grinned at him as he walked by.

But then Chris spied Professor Greyson. He'd emerged from the cellar steps, slammed the wrought-iron gate, and was standing there, seemingly in a rage, waving his arms about and talking to himself.

Greyson spotted Chris across the quadrangle and bellowed at him, "Chandler, here, come here now!"

The eyes of every student present were upon Chris as he crossed the quadrangle. He took his time, stopped midway to adjust the contents of his bookbag, pulled out an apple, and ate it casually as he sauntered up to Greyson. There was no point in looking like a total eunuch.

Greyson was obviously having a bad day. His hair was more tangled than usual, clothes filthy, and his skin glistened with an oily sheen. "Follow me," he barked as he spun about and descended the steps to the chapel cellar once again. Chris took a moment to look about the quadrangle before he too started down the stairs. Everyone was watching; no one had moved.

Okay, so the soap opera continues.

No sooner had Greyson unlocked the cellar door than he screamed at the greylings, "Out! Out now. Come back in an hour if you must, but get out now."

The greylings looked at one another, several shrugged, a few muttered, "but I'm in the middle of something," or "now? really?" One or two did gather up their books and stuff.

Then Chris appeared behind Greyson, and Ashworth called out. "Ah, I see, the professor needs a moment with his convict. Let's give them some privacy. We'll get a coffee." He picked up his coat from the sofa and started up the stairs. The others followed in no great hurry. As Ashworth slid past Greyson on the narrow steps, it occurred to Chris that Greyson might actually push the boy over the railing, but he didn't.

When they were alone, Greyson walked to the common room table, wiped the sweat from his face with a stained tea towel, and sat down. He drew several breaths to calm himself and gestured for Chris to join him.

"I do apologize for the story in the paper today," he said matter-of-factly. "All bullshit, I know."

"Not a problem," replied Chris.

"Of course, that's right. You've probably had a lot worse written about you."

Chris didn't reply.

"Well, so how are your classes going?"

"I've only had a couple. They're good."

"And your reading for me?"

"I've made a start. But let me ask you a question."

"Yes?" replied Greyson with a look of mild surprise.

"What's your goal with all this Kabbalah stuff? Are you trying to create life?" Chris's tone was surprisingly confrontational. Even he was surprised by the edge in his voice. "Because that would be nuts, and I won't have anything to do with such garbage."

At first, Greyson didn't respond, but then he smirked, chuckled, and said, "Heavens, boy, we're doing real scientific research here, not magic."

"But you do believe that certain words have a special power, is that right?"

"I don't believe words have a special power. I *know* they do," replied Greyson unapologetically. "And I can prove it. I promised you a demonstration before, so maybe now's the time." He went to the small bar fridge and began rooting about for something.

"No, that won't be necessary," said Chris. "Your . . . your lab assistants have told me how you've been animating images from illuminated manuscripts."

"So you have been speaking with them," Greyson said as he returned to the table.

"Briefly, over coffee." Chris saw the displeasure in Greyson's face.

"Well, there is a gulf between what they can do and what I'm capable of. Would you believe me if I told you I can summon demons whenever and wherever I wish?" Greyson sat back with a look of bemusement on his face. "I suspect you might believe me because I think you can too. I'm guessing that charm you wear gives you such power. Or perhaps it protects you from demons when they do appear. Probably the latter, since I did glimpse *of Magdala* inscribed on your pendant. It's an invocation to the Magdalene to protect the wearer, is it not?"

Chris didn't respond, but the fact Greyson recognized that Chris's charm was somehow linked to the Magdalene was unsettling.

Greyson grinned, leaned forward, and continued. He spoke almost conspiratorially. "I truly believe the work I'm doing is scientific. You already know we've identified sympathetic associations between certain religious texts and various pharmaceuticals. Okay, so perhaps you've heard of quantum entanglement, the mysterious ability of separated objects like electrons to share a condition or state over great distances, even light-years? Albert Einstein described quantum entanglement as 'spooky action at a distance.' Well, that's what I'm studying, this same entanglement between religious invocations, illustrated texts, and naturally occurring drugs. I've proven that otherworldly forces can be summoned by using certain words and drugs simultaneously. Furthermore, I believe the ancients had mastered this form of entanglement."

"And how does Kabbalah fit into this entanglement?" Chris asked.

"Because Kabbalah is *all* about the Creator's entanglement with his Creation, what the Kabbalists call his emanations. And to uncover the Creator's holy names is to reveal the many levels of his entanglement with the real world. That's Kabbalah. And if we succeed in identifying the holiest, the most powerful names of the Creator, we may even grasp the Creator's greatest power of all, the power to create life itself. And that's what I'm trying to do. Find the Creator's most holy names."

"So then you *are* trying to create life."

"I'm trying to understand what the ancients claimed *they* could do. Their lore is filled with tales of wise men who made living creatures out of nothing. In cyclotrons today, scientists create elements that exist nowhere in nature. So why do we doubt the claims of the ancients who claimed they could create life out of words and earth?"

Greyson sat back in his chair and stared at Chris in silence for a moment. But then he suddenly slammed his fist on the table, leaped from his chair, and charged at Chris. "You ungrateful little shit," he screamed as he towered over Chris, "that's the garbage I'm into. And if you ever insult me or my work again or refuse to assist me, I will have my demons on you."

Greyson grabbed Chris by his coat front and hauled him out of the chair. "You hear me, boy?"

The air split open. Sparks flew in every direction. A green mist burst into the chamber, and Mallory appeared.

"Ah, here she is," was all Greyson had time to say before Mallory seized him by the hair and threw him across the room. He crashed to the ground amid shattered glass and broken furniture. Mallory's face, a frenzy of fire and sparks, whirled about and flew to the spot where Greyson landed. Twisted and bleeding, Greyson managed to peer up into Mallory's eyes with a look of satisfaction. Mallory roared and was just about to crush Greyson when Chris threw himself across the professor and shouted, "No, you will not have him!"

Mallory flew around and around like some crazed raptor, lashing out at the parts of Greyson's body Chris could not conceal. Greyson's legs were scorched, his arms shredded, and the top of his head lacerated. Greyson's screams echoed through the chamber until Mallory turned from the two men in apparent frustration. She then toppled furniture and tossed papers, smashed dishes, and shattered lab equipment until, at last, she shrieked and faded from view.

Chris scrambled from atop Greyson and helped him into a sitting position. "I would have warned you," he said. "She hates me, but she hates anyone who touches me even more."

"I had to provoke your demon," Greyson murmured through his pain. "From all the stories I found about you in American newspapers, I knew you had to have one, but I had to see for myself. And she's Torajan, isn't she?"

"How would you know that?" asked Chris.

"You must have done some sort of Torajan ritual to summon her, right?"

"No, her father did, all the way from Tana Toraja."

"There, you see? Just as I said, spooky action at a distance. Was it a walking dead ritual?"

"A cleansing second death, but the ritual was interrupted. We need to finish it somehow."

"I've only ever read about Torajan spells," muttered Greyson.

"Then how did you recognize it as Torajan?"

"Her anger. The dead detest being summoned by the living. It's heartbreaking for most of them, but for Torajan dead, it's enraging and only tolerable if the summons helps them get home."

"So if you know Torajan ritual, can you help me lay her spirit to rest?"

"Perhaps," said Greyson as he got up. Shards of broken glass fell from his clothing. Blood dripped from his many cuts. "I suppose I could. But not unless you help me first. And no more insolence, got it?"

****

Cavendish College Library

Following his run-in with Greyson, Chris pushed his way through the greylings milling about at the top of the stairs. "What happened down there?" "What was all that racket?" they called after him, but Chris did not reply.

At the cafeteria he gulped down a coffee, stuffed a packaged sandwich and a Coke in his bookbag, and set off for the library. He found an empty study carrel among the stacks and settled in for a thrilling evening of Kabbalah. But ya just gotta do what ya gotta do; Greyson had made that crystal clear.

Jewish mysticism is an umbrella term covering a range of theories about the Godhead. Kabbalah refers to a particular variety of Jewish mysticism that first emerged in the 12th century CE in Provence and Catalonia. It was about understanding and influencing structures and processes inside the divine realm.

Kabbalah was distinct from an older mystical tradition of Ashkenazic origin. The older tradition involved applying rigorous piety and interpretive techniques to official Jewish texts in an effort to reveal their hidden meaning. Kabbalah was also distinct from magical traditions that focused primarily on harnessing supernatural powers in order to bring about changes in the physical world. What these different strands of secret Jewish lore do share, however, is a belief in the extraordinary power of language.

According to Jewish tradition, the Hebrew language has a divine origin. Every name or noun and the object to which it refers are linked so that the name reflects the God-ordained nature of the object.

Okay, so was this Kabbalist link between an object and its name what Greyson described as their quantum entanglement?

And God is no exception. Kabbalah regards the highest form of knowledge to be a command of all the names of the Divine. Indeed, in the view of Nachmanides, a Catalan Kabbalist of the 13th century CE, the whole Torah is a string of names for God.

But if the entire Torah is the universe of names for God, then Greyson's quest to find the holiest names of all was even crazier than Chris had first thought.

In Genesis 1, God creates the world by pronouncing his will; hence language was taken to have the ultimate creative potential. The Sefer Yetsirah, a manuscript thought to have originated sometime between the 2nd and 7th centuries CE, describes the process of Creation as having taken place through the 22 letters of the Hebrew language and ten cardinal numbers. The Sefer Yetsirah purportedly explained how the process of Creation worked through manipulating the letters of the Hebrew alphabet and how one might repeat it, which is to say, how one might create a living creature. The creature would not possess a soul but would otherwise be a living being. Giving a name to the creature would animate and control it, and conversely, erasing the name would annihilate it.

Hebrew letters swam before Chris's eyes as a soulless creature dangled from the limbs of the tree of life, and turned slowly in the breeze from a choir of rabbis . . . .

Falling asleep while reading about Kabbalah was becoming something of a habit. Chris only awoke when he heard an announcement over the public address system that the library would be closing in five minutes. Glancing at his watch, he gasped to discover he'd lost nearly three hours of study time. Chris gathered up his books and headed out into the chill and moonlit night. He raced across the quadrangle just in time to catch the bus downtown.

****

Gothall's Rooming House

At Duke and Barrington, Chris got off the bus and headed down Duke. Half past nine now, businesses were all closed, and the streets empty. Except, however, for a group of figures on the sidewalk outside his rooming house. In the dim light from the rusted lamp over the rooming house door, Chris could just make out the two thugs from the second floor, their lady friends, and the old man, Sammy Brook. They were having a very animated discussion and Mr. Brook was brandishing the leg of a wooden chair.

"So we told the old bag to get the fuck out of our way," shouted one of the thugs, "so what? What's it to you? And don't you be threatening me with that stick, or I'm gonna snap you like a twig, old man."

Chris approached Mr. Brook and asked, "Can I help you, sir?"

Brook glanced at Chris and replied, "No, I won't need no help." He turned back to the two thugs and snarled, *"Bist du deppert*? Are you an idiot? Did you not hear me tell you to get into the alley?"

"I'm not goin' down no fuckin' alley with you, you old fag," replied the second thug.

"Let's go inside, Billy. I'm real cold," whined one of their lady friends.

"Shut the fuck up. We gotta deal with this piece of shit before we're goin' anywhere," shouted the first thug. "You hear me, Jew boy?"

"Zum Teufel! Dammit! Do as you're told!" Mr. Brook yelled. Then he suddenly swung the chair leg and caught the first thug across the knee cap. The sound was ghastly.

"Ahhhrg! Fuckin' hell! You bastard!" the kid shrieked as his leg gave way, and he crumpled to the ground.

185

"Oh shit, man, you broke his knee!" shouted the other lout, who pulled a large knife from his pocket. But before he could open the blade, Brook cracked the kid across the arm with the chair leg. The thug's arm snapped and the knife fell to the ground.

The girls began shrieking like gulls behind a fishing boat.

"*Halt die Fresse!* Shut the hell up," Brook shouted at the women before he turned back to the thug with the broken arm and said, "Now pick up your friend and get into the alley."

"You're fuckin' dead. Dead! You hear me?" the guy replied as he helped his friend to his feet, and the two stumbled into the alley.

Midway into the alley, Brook said, "Good enough."

The two toughs turned to face the old man. The shock of Brook's initial blows was abating, and their fury was returning. "Okay, fucker, so you got in the first hit. Well even with this buggered knee, I'm still going to kick your ass." With his weight on his good leg the tough raised his fist and readied to dive forward.

The second thug joined in with, "You're dead, old man." Still holding the broken arm to his chest, he bellowed, "We still got you outnumbered."

Brook shook his head and muttered, "You two are always talking *Scheiss*. No one should have to put up with your *Scheiss*, especially not a harmless old lady." With that, Brook moved far faster than his years suggested he could. He savagely laid into the two thugs. One he cracked across the head with the chair leg and the other he kicked in the groin. The first stumbled backward, his eyes rolling backward in their sockets, while the other tumbled to the ground in a writhing, moaning heap. Brook caught the first before he could fall to the ground, grasped him in a bear hug, and squeezed. The boy moaned as his ribs snapped and pink foam oozed from his mouth. Brook then dropped him to the asphalt and turned on the second thug who was still rolling about on the ground clutching his groin. First Brook booted the kid in the face, then in the kidneys, and finally stepped away from the two as if to admire his handiwork.

"I suppose you think I've been hard on you, *Miststück*. Well, let me tell you, if I hear you've been giving Mrs. Norris any more trouble, or any other tenant for that matter, I guarantee it, you will wind up at the bottom of the harbor. Get me?"

It was unlikely either heard a word Brook spoke since both were in shock from their appalling injuries.

The old man turned to the ladies, cowering against the alley wall, gasping and shrieking. Brook advanced with his chair leg raised but then stopped and said in a voice so menacing that it made the cold night feel balmy, "You ladies, you're gonna say nothing, got it? Not to the cops, not to friends, or johns, or anyone else, or I will beat the shit out of you both as well. And your boyfriends, you warn them to shut the fuck up or I'll grind them into dogfood. So are we good? Good. *Servus*. Good night." And Brook walked away.

Chris had been horrified by the old man's brutality. Surely breaking one guy's arm and the other's kneecap would have sufficed. But no, the old man had hammered and kicked them into a pulp. They'd be laid up for days . . . if they even survived.

Without thinking, Chris muttered as the old man emerged from the alley, "Did . . . did you have to be so . . . cruel?"

"Cruel? *Blödsinn*" he grunted, "I learned very early, if you hit a mad dog, you gotta hit him so hard he can't ever come after you again." But then the old man spun away and headed off. "Now I need to help Mrs. Norris."

"Is there anything I can do?" Chris called after him and was surprised when Brook turned back to him.

Ivan Blake

"*Aber ja*, you come too. I'm afraid for Mrs. Norris. She's not good, not good at all."

They raced upstairs together.

****

Gothall's Rooming House

Tucked in her bed, Mrs. Norris was as pale as a dead jellyfish. Her eyes were closed, and her breathing shallow.

"She won't eat anything, she can't go to the toilet, and she says her chest hurts. I'm afraid she's not . . . she's not going to make it till morning. Those boys, they broke her."

"Mrs. Norris," Chris whispered, "Mrs. Norris, is there anything we can get you, some food perhaps or something to drink or maybe someone you'd like us to call?"

Her eyes opened, and a tiny smile cracked the corners of her mouth. "Porter?" she whimpered. But then the smile disappeared. "No, you're not Porter, are you? My dear boy. He's not coming, is he, my Porter?" And she turned her head away.

"Porter was her son," Brook whispered, "the one who killed himself upstairs."

"Do you know why?" asked Chris.

"*Aber ja*. The girl he loved, she was pregnant but she ended the pregnancy and announced she was leaving when Porter admitted he had no more money."

Chris glanced at his watch and then looked Brook directly in the face. "Mr. Brook, sir, will you trust me?"

"Why? What are you going to do?"

"Mrs. Norris, she's not going to make it, is she?" Chris asked as respectfully as he could. "But we can help her, help her to go, I mean."

188

"What are you going to do?" replied Brook with a look of suspicion.

"Lift her, please. We're taking her to my room," said Chris urgently. "We have to hurry."

"Why?"

"We don't have much time."

"I . . . I don't think—"

"Trust me, it will make all the difference," Chris said quietly as he patted Brook's hand.

"Mrs. Norris, please let me," said Sammy as he slipped his arms beneath her tiny frame, lifted her into his powerful arms, and started up the stairs.

Chris pushed books and clothes from his bed, and Sammy laid Mrs. Norris down as gently as dandelion silk landing on a blade of grass.

Chris turned out the light and closed his curtain.

"Now, Mrs. Norris, can you hear me?" he whispered.

By the light from the street below, he saw her nod.

"Good, so now I have a question for you. Your son Porter, when he was a small child, did you sing to him? A lullaby perhaps?"

She didn't open her eyes. She barely stirred. A moment passed before her lips moved. "A lullaby for my Porter? Yes I sang to him."

"Do you remember what you sang?"

"It was so long ago," she whispered. "But perhaps."

"Please sing it for me. It's important. Please sing."

Sammy poked Chris in the back. "*Bist du deppert*? Are you crazy? Why are you doing this?" he whispered. "Why are you torturing the poor woman?"

Chris didn't answer. Instead, he pressed the old lady, "Please sing, Mrs. Norris."

Another moment passed, but then her lips parted, and a tiny, fragile voice emerged, dry and crackling like the first flame among kindling.

"Hush-a-bye, birdie, croon, croon

"Hush-a-bye, birdie, croon."

But then the melody smoothed her tone.

"The sheep are gone to the silver wood,

"And the cows are gone to the broom, broom."

"That's wonderful, Mrs. Norris," Chris said ever so softly. And that's when the tiny spark first appeared up near the ceiling. "Keep singing, Mrs. Norris, please."

"And it's nice milking the cattle, cattle,

"It's nice milking the cattle."

"Now, Mrs. Norris, you must do as I tell you, please. As you sing, I want you to open your eyes. Open your eyes. Good. Now look up, up at that tiny light. Do you see it? Like a firefly? Yes, now I want you to squint, just so you can still see the spark. And now, this is the hard part. I want you to look past the spark, look at the colors beyond it, shimmering and shifting behind the spark. Do you see them?"

"I . . . I think I do," Mrs. Norris murmured in reply.

"Okay, so that's great. And so now I want you to continue singing your lullaby and don't stop. Sing it over and over. And don't stop singing until I tell you."

Her voice brought forth a most perfect sound, music like a meadow in summer, like songbirds bathing in a brook.

"The birds are singing, the bells are ringing,

"And the wild deer come galloping by.

"Hush-a-bye, birdie, croon, croon

"Hush-a-bye, birdie, croon."

The merest outline of the face appeared, full of grief, full of pain, shrieking. It descended from the ceiling. It filled the old woman's vision. She gasped. "It's . . . it's my Porter."

"Please, Mrs. Norris, you must keep singing."

"The goats are gone to the mountain high,

"And they'll not be home till noon.

"Hush-a-bye, birdie, croon, croon

"Hush-a-bye, birdie, croon."

The anguish gradually disappeared from the boy's face. His tears ceased and his face edged nearer to the old woman's. She sang with a tender smile on her lips as her son drew closer still.

"The sheep are gone to the silver wood,

"And the cows are gone to the broom, broom."

The boy's upper body appeared. He dropped to her bedside and slipped his arms beneath his mother. Mrs. Norris rose slightly from the bed in order to nestle deeply in her son's embrace. A warm smile broke across the boy's lips.

"*Mein Gott,*" whispered Sammy Brook.

"And they'll not be . . . not be . . . home until . . . noon."

As the old woman's eyes closed for the last time, her head slipped to the side, she sighed, and her voice faded away. And, with that gentle smile still on his lips, the outline of her son faded also.

Sirens in the street below hailed the arrival of an ambulance and a police car to collect the two thugs. There was no need to hurry for Mrs. Norris.

****

Greyson's Lab

Ashworth and the rest of the greylings worked past midnight sweeping, sifting, and sorting the calamitous mess Greyson and Chandler had made of their lair. After the encounter, both Chandler and Greyson had left the chamber without explaining to anyone what had happened. Was Chandler now history? Had he and Greyson fought? Or did Greyson have some kind of fit brought on by his addictions?

Whatever had happened, the two idiots had done a ton of damage. They'd broken chairs and tables and beakers and flasks, smashed the spectroscope and the laser, spilled several weeks' worth of salvi, damaged two priceless illuminated manuscripts, and destroyed Jeffy's Italian espresso maker.

But now that the worst of the mess had been cleaned up, Ashworth was concerned about next steps. He'd hoped the newspaper story might provoke Chandler's departure, but after the phone call from the paper's editor, he knew otherwise. The editor had been livid. He'd been humiliated by Ashworth's stunt and reprimanded by the Academic Counseling Office for his one-sided reporting. To atone for the blunder, the editor intended to print a formal apology to Chandler in the next edition. Dammit all to hell! Chandler had somehow emerged from Ashworth's trap smelling like goddamned roses. Okay, so the greylings would just have to make a better job of it next time.

Henry and James were finishing up the cleaning while Jeffy, Bonnie, Sheila, and Ryan were flaked out on the sofa, eating the last of the pizza before they headed home for the night.

"I was thinking," said Ashworth, "since we don't actually know what happened between Greyson and Chandler, we gotta get some intelligence."

"Intelligence, that would be a nice change," muttered Ryan.

"Shut up, Ryan," snapped Ashworth. "Look, I mean, we have to know what Chandler is up to. Is he still working with Greyson or isn't he? So I was thinking, Bonnie, we all saw how you were ogling Chandler over coffee the other day."

"I wasn't ogling anybody," angel girl protested.

"Okay, maybe not," said Ashworth, "but let's just say you liked him and gave him some signals. So, maybe you could get close to him, friendly-like?"

"Wait! Are you trying to pimp out Bonnie?" shouted Ryan. "Because that's really sick."

"I'm not asking her to do much, just have another coffee with Chandler. And if she happens to like him, then . . . ."

"Geez, you're an evil bastard," said Ryan.

"No, it's okay, Ryan," said Bonnie. "Maybe I'll try to talk to him, just for coffee."

"Good girl," said Ashworth.

****

Gothall's Rooming House

Chris, Sammy Brook, and Mr. Minhas were outside on the sidewalk listening to the two young ladies explain to the cops what had happened to their pimps.

"I'm sure they was sailors, freaky bearded guys. They didn't spoke no English, hopped up on their A-rab dope and stuff, I bet. They just jumped our boyfriends. They didn't want nothing, just to fight."

"Well, actually, they wanted me," said the second girl, "but I got my standards."

"Standards, yeah right, bitch, you got the standards of a garbage truck," sneered the first girl.

"Oh, and you got taste? You forgotten them four Frenchies?"

"Ladies, please," interjected the cop, "so these attackers?"

"Well, I think they was Germans, you know, with them swastikas all over," said the second girl.

"Swastikas?" The cop was becoming frustrated. "But your friend here just said they were Arabs."

"No, I didn't mean Arabs. They was Russians maybe," clarified the first girl.

And so it went until the ambulance departed with the two thugs, and the cop drove the women to a shelter. They'd refused to return to their own rooms, whimpering that the crazy Arab-German-Russians might return, while never for a second taking their terrified gaze off Sammy.

Minhas muttered that Freddy was going to be upset to learn he'd lost three, maybe even five, paying tenants in one night, then added, "But I'm only sad to lose one of them." He turned and put a hand on Brook's shoulder. "Mrs. Norris was a real lady, Mr. Brook."

Brook simply nodded and lowered his eyes. Minhas went back inside his diner.

Chris told one of the police officers dealing with the thugs that an old lady had just passed away upstairs, and he'd radioed in the death. A short while later, a coroner's panel truck arrived. The attending technician certified Mrs. Norris's death and took away her remains. Chris and Sammy Brook agreed to come to the coroner's office the following day to complete the paperwork and instruct on the disposition of her remains.

As they watched the coroner's truck pull away, Brook said, "You did good, kid."

Chris realized he'd been nervous about how the old man might have regarded his intervention, so the praise came as a huge relief.

"I've got chocolates. You like chocolates?" Brook asked.

"Sure, thanks," he replied, and so they returned to Sammy Brook's room.

"How did you do that, see a ghost, I mean?" asked the old man.

"It's nothin, Mr. Brook. A friend taught me," Chris replied.

"Sammy, please, call me Sammy," said Brook as he opened a tin of Ganong's chocolates and passed it across to Chris.

"Sammy, all right. You were very kind to her, Sammy. That was good of you."

"She was sad. I was sad. So we were sad together. But you, you made her happy, and I'm very grateful for that. So if you need my help with anything, I will give it."

"Forgive me for saying it, Sammy, but you are one very tough old man," said Chris with something of a smile. The image of Sammy wielding the chair leg was hard to forget.

"I was once a quarryman," said Sammy. His eyes were fixed on the floor.

"And then you were in a concentration camp?"

"It wasn't so much a concentration camp as a labor camp. But many people died there. The Germans worked people to death, mainly Russians and Poles, but also Spanish communists and some Jews."

"Where was this labor camp?"

"Austria, Mauthausen, near Vienna, but I don't like to talk about." A few moments passed as they both enjoyed their chocolates. Then the old man asked, "You are a student?"

"Yes, just an undergraduate."

"You have chosen a special course?"

"My major? It's religious studies."

"Hmm, since you see ghosts, I'm not surprised," the old man said with a slight smile. "I noticed you carrying a book on Kabbalah. I know Kabbalah."

"You do?"

"Well, Christian Kabbalah."

"Not Jewish Kabbalah?" Chris said with surprise. "Forgive me, but I thought you were Jewish."

"Yes, maybe, once. But I learned Kabbalah from a Russian monk in Mauthausen."

"What's the difference between Jewish Kabbalah and Christian Cabbalah?"

"Jews want to see God's work in world, his emanations. It's all about understanding how God influences his creation."

"Yeah, I read that."

"Yes, well Christians want God's power. Christian Cabbalah is about uncovering spells and incantations."

"To do what?" asked Chris.

"Maybe save crops, make illness, defeat armies, kill enemies."

"And make monsters?"

"All kinds of people make monsters," whispered Sammy.

Chapter Eight

Bain picked up the phone and said, "Captain Dahlman, I understand you want to speak to me? Do I know you? Are you in the military?"

"Merchant marine. I captain an oil tanker. But thank you for taking my call. I'm phoning from Bangor. I got your name from a former police chief here in Maine. He tells me you're investigating Christopher Chandler."

There was a moment of silence on the line before Bain spoke. "To tell the truth, I'm kinda surprised a police officer would share that sort of information with a civilian, sir. Not something we'd do."

"I appreciate that, Sergeant Bain, and I have no intention of asking any questions regarding your investigations. I just wanted to let you know that I, too, am interested in this Chris Chandler and will be trying to see him in Halifax when I get there. I just wanted you to know."

Sound reasonable, keep it friendly. Don't raise the cop's suspicions.

Again, Bain's brief silence denoted hesitancy, a measure of confusion. "Actually, I'm not investigating this Chandler fella. I was only interested in Chandler because his name came up in connection with a couple of incidents. I was just trying to get the full picture. Background crap, that's all. You can talk to the kid all you want."

"Well, thank you, Sergeant, for clearing that up. But just for your information, I want to speak to Chandler because he was among the last to see my daughter alive."

Play the sympathy card. Seed suspicion.

"Wait, are you saying Chandler had something to do with your daughter's death?"

"No, no, she committed suicide."

Okay, so tug at the cop's heartstrings.

"Jeez, I'm sorry to hear that."

Cue the violins.

"I'm trying to find out what might have prompted our darling daughter to do such a terrible thing. Her mother and I are heartbroken, and we need to know what might have pushed her over the edge."

"But you don't intend this Chandler kid any harm, do you?"

Okay, that was an astute question.

"Oh heavens no. I'm driving to Halifax tomorrow just to chat with him."

"But if Chandler doesn't want to talk to you, you'll respect that, right?"

Not as dumb as I expected.

"Of course."

"Well, as it happens, I'm just on my way to have my own chat with Chandler because his name came up in connection with yet another incident last evening. He might have been a witness to a violent assault."

"Huh. It's curious, isn't it, that Chandler is often nearby when someone else gets hurt."

Good, so nurture his suspicions.

"Mmm. Okay, so anyway, I'll mention to Chandler that you're hoping to see him."

No, no, Christ, don't warn the kid.

"No, Sergeant Bain, I'd rather you didn't do that. It might not happen. My wife, you see, she's still very broken up about our daughter and, well, I might not even be able to get away. So don't mention me to the boy. I'd rather he not worry if we don't speak."

"Whatever you say, Captain Dahlman."

****

Duncan's Cove

Greyson had been in agony most of the night. He should probably have had his lacerations sutured at the emergency department, but he didn't want to go anywhere near a hospital. With all his injuries—the torn scalp, the gashed arm, the burned legs—they'd almost certainly have insisted on admitting him. But he couldn't afford the time. He couldn't be lounging about on a hospital gurney eating hospital crap when the clock was ticking. The college administration, the provincial government, his damned greylings, they were all circling like birds of prey. He had to stay ahead of them, stay focused. He absolutely had to locate the cantor's grave and find that damned amulet! Then, and only then, would he be able to show the world what he was truly capable of. After that, just let anyone try to rob him of his endowment or force him out of his lair.

Greyson finished a second coffee and a third cigarette, and picked up the unopened mail that had accumulated on his kitchen table over the past few days. He tossed flyers, notices, and anything with the college logo on it straight into the trash can. Then he noticed the return address on one particular piece of mail. His mother's fucking lawyer. He felt the weight of the envelope. He'd long since learned that the weightier a lawyer's correspondence, the darker its contents.

He ripped open the letter and began to read.

Retained by your mother, Mrs. bah, blah, blah. She seeks the return forthwith of the $197,000 loaned to you for purposes of pursuing legal action against sundry journalists and publishers.

Loaned to him? For Christ's sake, she was his mother! Surely she'd given it to him as a motherly gift. That's what mothers do. He might have said something about repaying her when he'd first asked for help, but that was just talk. He'd he needed to sue the bastards who'd slandered him, and she'd agreed. Of course, she'd supported his court case as much to protect her own reputation as to help him. She'd willingly covered his legal fees, and there'd never been any further mention of him repaying the money, at least not that he could recall. Okay, so he'd lost his case, but that hadn't been his fault. It was the crap court system, so biased against shit-disturbers and rule-breakers like him. And then there were the crap lawyers his mother had recommended. The guys couldn't have won a case of slander if they'd been fighting for Mother Theresa.

He read on.

Blah, blah, blah, receive in our offices a banker's draft in the amount of $197,000 no later than October 15 blah, blah, blah or will ask the Court to order your premises and vehicle be seized, bank accounts frozen and wages garnished . . . .

Good luck taking control of his bank accounts. There wasn't a nickel to be had in any of them. He'd been living off his credit cards for weeks now. But if that was the good news, the bad news was that he now had less than three weeks to teach his enemies, every goddamned one of them, the lesson of a lifetime. He might once have hoped that a demonstration of the power of Kabbalah, and a display of the artifacts he'd found like Rabbi Loew's letter and the cantor's amulet would earn him international acclaim. But not now. If the debt collectors were already on their way, then Greyson was going to require a hell of a lot more than a show and tell. He was going to have to blow fucking heads off!

But was there nothing he could do to buy just a little more time? Could he countersue his mother? She'd recommended the lawyer who'd blown his case. Maybe he could sue her for damages, or alienation of affection, or maybe even mental abuse? He speed-dialed his Halifax lawyer.

"Horsfall and Childerhouse, Attorneys at Law," answered Marnie, the sweet little thing at reception.

"Marnie, it's Dr. Greyson. I need to speak to Childerhouse."

"I . . . I'm sorry, Dr. Greyson, Mr. Childerhouse is not available at the moment. He's . . . he's in conference."

"Then Horsfall, get Horsfall on the line."

"I can't do that, Dr. Greyson. I'm very sorry."

"Why the hell not? Are they refusing to speak to me now?"

"Actually . . . ."

"Actually, what?"

"Actually, they've instructed me not to put you through to anyone until you respond to our invoices for previous services. We've sent you many but had no reply."

"I must have missed them. My damned secretary is useless. But I'll get on it right away. In the meantime, put me through to one of the bastards."

"I'm sorry, Dr. Greyson."

"Fuck!" he screamed into the phone and slammed it down.

****

Freddy's Diner

The diner was bustling. Mr. and Mrs. Minhas had earned their business an enviable reputation for its ample breakfast. Bain and Minhas couldn't speak over the chatter and clatter of dishes, so they stepped outside.

"I understand from the officers who responded to the incident last evening," said Bain, "that you didn't actually see the fight in your alley."

"Too busy in the diner. And it isn't my alley, Sergeant Bain," replied Minhas. "It's Freddy's, and it drives me to distraction. Bums, they sleep there. Druggies, they shoot up there. Pimps, they sell their women there."

"But you did tell the officer what you thought had happened. You thought some john wasn't happy with the ladies the two lads had procured for him."

"Sure, because that's what those boys do. They sell their ladies. But I saw nothing, only that the two boys were out cold on the ground and their ladies were screaming. What a mess they were, the boys, I mean."

"And you saw no one running away? No one with blood on them or injuries? Just the few folks who'd arrived after the fight."

"In fact, I only knew something had happened when I saw people gathered outside. Mr. Brook and Mr. Chandler, Jeremy the late-night paperboy, and Frank from the bar across the road. I guess Frank had been taking bottles out back of his bar when he heard the women screaming and he came across to see what was going on."

"Yeah, I've already spoken to the bartender and the paperboy, but do you know why Mr. Chandler and the other guy—"

"Mr. Brook."

"Yeah, Brook. Do you know why they happened to be present?"

"Of course, they both live here. Mr. Brook, he often goes for walks at night. He likes to be alone. And Mr. Chandler was just getting home from college. But we chatted, and they didn't see anything either. Only . . . ."

"Only what, Mr. Minhas?"

"Only, like me, they're pleased to see those two boys gone. So whoever beat the boys, we're glad it happened." For a moment, the genteel Minhas vanished and a far harder, unforgiving Minhas appeared.

"You don't suppose either Chandler or Brook could have beaten the two boys?" asked Bain.

And the gracious Minhas was back. "Mr. Brook? Heavens no, he's far too old, nearly ninety. And Mr. Chandler? Well, maybe I suppose, but when I saw him, he wasn't winded or bloodied or anything, so I very much doubt he had anything to do with the beatings."

"No, I suppose not. Anyway, thanks for your time. I'll be back. I need to chat with Brook and Chandler before I can close the books on this one. And of course, if either of the two boys dies, then I'll be all over this area like butter on toast."

****

Cavendish College Library

Chris spent the day cloistered in his study carrel, trying to make sense of Kabbalistic ideas about the names of God. The deeper he dug into the subject, the more confused he became.

Early Jewish texts were filled with lists of the secret names of God. Rabbinic tradition had it that divine names could be derived from ancient texts in all sorts of ways. For example, the 22-letter divine name was derived from the first five words of the priestly blessing in the Book of Numbers. Similarly, the 72-letter divine name was derived from the words in the Book of Exodus that Moses spoke to an angel during the parting of the Red Sea. And the 42-letter Divine name was drawn from a collection of kabbalistic works in the British Library.

Okay, so how many of these Divine names were there? Clearly a lot, and a lot more than Chris was going to be able to find. So what chance did he have of completing Greyson's assignment? Nada, none, zilch. Not unless Greyson gave him some way to narrow the task. Searching for the holiest names of God was going to be a wild goose chase, totally crazy, and a colossal waste of his time. Or . . . perhaps Sammy Brook might be able to help him.

Sammy Brook struck Chris as an interesting fellow. Alone, bitter, broken-hearted, but of course, none of that should have been a surprise. The man was a holocaust survivor from a camp called Mauthausen. And so, out of curiosity and as a break from Kabbalah, Chris went looking for books on Mauthausen. Sometime later, he returned to his carrel with a couple of books and a few magazine articles that touched on the Austrian labor camp.

Mauthausen had been a large, privately owned granite quarry for more than a century before it was purchased by the city of Vienna in 1916. With the *Anschluss* however, Mauthausen had been seized by the Nazis to feed Hitler's voracious appetite for grandiose construction projects. Under the *SS*, Mauthausen performed a double function, as a supplier of granite to the Third Reich and as a forced labor camp where hundreds of thousands of Russians and Spaniards and Romani and Jews could be worked to death. Austrian prisons were emptied of their most hardened criminals to fill out the ranks of the Mauthausen's guards. Murderers, rapists, and sadists were ideally suited to working their fellow prisoners to death. In exchange, *kapos,* as they were called, received better rations, warmer clothes, and carte blanche to inflict on others whatever pain their hearts desired.

That was when Chris came across the name Samuel Bruchner in an article from *Canadian Weekly Magazine* published in 1956. The article entitled, 'Safe Haven: War Criminals Hiding in Plain Sight in Canada' examined the histories of half a dozen villainous characters, from *SS* commanders to death camp guards who now lived and worked in

Canada. Several were businessmen, some laborers, two were teachers, and one was an antiques dealer, or more precisely an antiques conservator named Bruchner.

Samuel Bruchner, an Austrian Jew, had been serving two life sentences for the murders of his wife and her lover when the *SS* shipped him off to Mauthausen in 1942. *Herr* Bruchner found himself a *kapo*. Worse still, since he'd been a manager at the Mauthausen quarry before his conviction, Bruchner was given the extraordinary job of managing Mauthausen's entire slave labor force, a job he prosecuted with ruthless efficiency. Bruchner appropriated food from the most vulnerable and sent the weakest to the worst jobs to hasten their demise so as to stretch food supplies and sustain the more productive. He even pressed one or two inmates into his own private service, but what tasks he had them perform was never determined because they disappeared just before Mauthausen was liberated.

"Oh Hell," whispered Chris as he finished reading the article. Could it be that Brook and Bruchner were one and the same? And if so then Chris was living above a murderous beast . . . and could do nothing about it.

****

Walking to Gothall's

It was past nine when Chris left the library. The rain had stopped but the fog now enveloped the city, and with it, the tang of a changing tide. Chris buttoned his coat to the collar, pulled his hands up inside his sleeves, and headed home.

He didn't mind the walk. Something about the city spoke to him. Perhaps it was the poverty, the disappointment, the sadness, or maybe it was the city's turbulent past, its scars, its character. Halifax was cagey, secretive, complicated, like a kind old man with an explosive temper and a brutal past.

"Chris? Chris Chandler," someone called.

He turned around and peered into the fog. A young woman was crossing the quadrangle's shimmering cobblestones in his direction. "Can I walk with you?" she asked.

He recognized her from his coffee with the greylings; Bonnie, the girl who saw angels.

"I'm heading downtown, down to Hollis Street," he replied.

"Sure, okay," she said as she came alongside.

"Do you live downtown, too?" he asked.

"No. Here in residence, but I wanted a walk, just not alone at this hour. Then I saw you coming out of the library, and I thought you might not mind some company."

"All right," he replied, and off they went. "So how will you get home when we get downtown?"

"Cab, I suppose."

They walked without speaking for some time until Bonnie eventually broke the silence. "Mind my asking why you're here? I mean, you're an American. Why are you here in Canada?"

Chris had no desire to share his story with this stranger. "I wanted to see the world."

"Halifax is not the world. It's not even remotely the world," muttered the girl. "In fact, sometimes I think it's the butt end of the world."

"Am I right in thinking you're from Halifax?" Chris asked with a slight chuckle.

"Is it that obvious? Yeah, sort of. I grew up in a village down the south shore. Dad was a fisherman until he drowned, and then Mom drank herself to death, and my brothers and sisters, they all just drifted out of province, off to Ontario or out to Alberta."

"But you stayed."

"Too scared to leave, maybe, and besides, I got a scholarship, can you believe it?" They fell silent as they waited at an intersection for the light to change. A car drove past, throwing up a fine spray from the wet street.

Underway again, Bonnie continued her tale. "Then I got the crazy idea of studying religion. Why would I ever do that?"

"Have anything to do with your friends calling you angel girl?" Chris asked.

"You caught that, did you? Yeah, well, ever since my dad died, I've been seeing, like, these angels. Nuts, huh?"

"You see them any place special?"

"Kinda," she replied. "It started near my home. We lived next to a church, and from my bedroom window, I could see the churchyard, and that's where I first saw, you know, angels."

They were nearing the intersection of Coburg, Robie, and Spring Garden Roads. The Camp Hill cemetery was off to their left. It was probably best to stay on the lighted roadway at that hour. But then Bonnie said, "I read somewhere that you can see the dead."

"You read that?" Chris asked as they stopped beneath a streetlamp. The girl's golden hair was sodden now and glowed like a helmet of gold. She lowered her gaze.

"Yes, when we were checking you out," she confessed.

"For that story in the school paper," muttered Chris.

"Uh huh."

"And are we taking this walk together so you can find out more about me? Like what happened between Greyson and me in his lab today."

"Yes."

"Well, I'm sorry to disappoint you," said Chris as the light changed and he headed off across the street in the direction of the cemetery. "It's a private matter between Greyson and me."

"That's okay," said the girl as she trotted up alongside. "It's just nice to walk."

They were approaching the cemetery's south gate. Usually, the gate was locked at this hour. But for some reason, it was wide open. The caretaker probably couldn't be bothered coming out in this drizzle. Cast-iron lamp standards lined the path through the cemetery, their lights struggling to penetrate the dank fog.

Bonnie hesitated to enter, but Chris was already disappearing into the mist when he turned back to call out, "Coming?"

No one else was about at that time of night. Nothing moved, only the droplets falling from the trees. Leaves which might otherwise have scudded across the path lay in sodden drifts.

"Does the cemetery bother you?" Chris asked. "Are you seeing your angels?"

"No," she replied, her voice barely above a whisper.

"They're not angels, by the way. What you see, I mean."

"How would you know?" snapped Bonnie with a note of irritation in her voice.

"I'll show you."

Chris stepped from the path onto the wet grass and carefully picked his way among the ancient gravestones. He stopped beneath a giant oak and waited for Bonnie to join him. She followed carefully, shaking the wet from her shoes with each step.

Pointing into the gloom ahead, he said, "Tell me when you see them . . . your angels."

At first, Bonnie was silent, but then she whispered, "I . . . I think I see something over there."

"Mmm, okay. So describe to me what you do see."

"Well, it's like a bunch of scratches in glass. They're catching the light, sparkly-like, only they're moving about, and the air around the scratches is kind of wavey like it's watery."

"Can you make out any sort of shape among all these sparkly lines?"

"No, just the squiggles."

"Okay, squiggles. And you figure you're seeing an angel."

"Well, I figure we're in a cemetery. What else could it be?"

"Actually, the figure you're seeing," said Chris, "she's the mother, and she's mourning her child."

"What?" Bonnie looked at Chris like he'd lost his mind. "How can you possibly know that?"

"I want you to pinch your eyes and squint. Right, now be patient, and try to look beyond the squiggles, look through them."

A breeze rose, the fog swirled. Leaves lifted from the path and danced away into the darkness.

"I . . . I see an outline," Bonnie whispered.

"Okay, so now the air, is it moving like a colored liquid?" asked Chris. "And can you see a form in the liquid, contours within the color?"

"Oh God, yes! It's a woman! She's kneeling. She's crying. Yes, it's a woman. How, how did you know?"

"I look around this cemetery and I see others. Have a look. Over there, do you see? A soldier lost in his grief. And there, by that oak, a child is whimpering in confusion."

"They're *all* weeping. Every one of them. It's so sad. Who are they?" Bonnie whispered.

"The betrayed. The plundered. The defiled."

"Huh?" said Bonnie. "What's that even mean?"

"It means their graves have been disturbed, desecrated. That woman? Perhaps an enraged lover dug her up and tore the babe from her womb. And the soldier's skull might have been stolen by a drunken comrade. And the child . . . ."

"Stop, please," exclaimed Bonnie. "It's all so heartbreaking."

"But that's what happens to the departed when their resting place is desecrated. They're dragged back from Paradise to suffer for eternity by their violated graves."

Bonnie fell silent, staring away into the dismal night as if deep in thought. But then she turned to Chris and asked, "So . . . so the man we dug up in the *Titanic* graveyard, he's now suffering by his grave?"

"That was you? You and the other greylings? You desecrated the Titanic grave? Why in hell would you do that?"

Bonnie shoved her hands in her coat pockets and shook her head. "Because we were idiots. Because Greyson wants this amulet, a cantor's amulet, and we thought we'd found it."

"But you hadn't."

"No. So now Greyson says we're to butt out of his Titanic project entirely because you'll dig it up instead."

"Greyson said that?" Chris was horrified, not just by the greylings' actions, but even more by Greyson's plans for *him*. There was no way Chris would ever consent to defile a grave, no matter what kind of hold Greyson might have over him. No goddamned way!

"Look, I think you'd better head back to campus," Chris said as he turned away and set off into the mist. "You can probably flag down a cab back at the gate. I . . . I don't want . . . I'd rather not have your company anymore."

****

Greyson's Lab

Bonnie's sudden appearance at the top of the cellar steps caught a flustered Ashworth entirely off guard. "What . . . what are you doing here?" he shouted as he struggled to push a couple of old *Playboys* back into his desk drawer.

"Sorry," Bonnie said with a smirk, "I didn't realize you had company."

Her tone of voice only added to Ashworth's humiliation. He was really starting to hate this bitch.

Bonnie made no move to descend the steps. Instead, she unzipped her bookbag, took out her glasses, and dropped the bag on the steps by her feet. "Anyway, the light outside was on, so I wondered who was here. But I'll leave you . . . to your work." And again she chuckled softly.

But she didn't leave. She remained there, at the top of the steps, looking down on Ashworth like she was judging him.

"So leave already," Ashworth muttered. "I've got more work to do. Greyson and Chandler really messed up my notes and stuff. But, hey, I thought you were seeing Chandler tonight, you know, to get it on with the Yank."

"Don't be gross. I said I'd try to find out what happened between Chandler and Greyson, and I tried. That's all."

"Okay, what did you learn?"

"Not much. Chandler wouldn't say anything about Greyson."

"I guess your attributes were wasted on him," he said. Her look of dismissive disgust irked him even more. "Can't seem to do anything right, can you," Ashworth sneered. "Did you learn anything at all?"

"Yes," she snapped back.

"Okay, what?"

"Well, for one thing, he thinks we're total idiots for digging up the Jewish cemetery."

Ashworth gasped. He couldn't believe his ears. "How the Hell does Chandler know we did that?"

"I guess maybe I told him," Bonnie said sheepishly.

Ashworth exploded. "Why would you do that? What were you thinking? We were going to try to pin that on him."

"It just sort of came up."

The stupid bitch was clearly embarrassed, but what good was that? Okay, so now maybe Ashworth had the upper hand, in this conversation at least.

"Fuck, Bonnie, what a useless bimbo you are. So instead of getting stuff on him like we asked, you tell him all our shit." Ashworth shook his head in disgust. "Chandler's the enemy, Bonnie. He wants to destroy everything we've accomplished, and you just handed him a stick of dynamite. You're a goddamned traitor."

Bonnie drew herself up, glared, and shrieked in reply, "And you're an ass!" She took a deep breath to calm herself and continued, "Always giving everybody orders like you run this place. But the truth is you know nothing. Chandler might think we're idiots, you especially, but he's actually kind of a nice guy. And he's right. We are idiots for taking orders from you."

"Oh great, so he's sucked you in now too. I suppose he sees your stupid angels as well."

"No, not my angels because he showed me they're not actually angels. They're dead people mourning their desecrated graves."

"They're doing what?" Ashworth almost laughed out loud. "Are you fucking kidding me?"

"They're mourning over their graves because someone disturbed their rest. And besides, you only make fun of my . . . my ability because you don't have any. You're just a bookworm. You have no special abilities of any kind. Hah! All you can do is read about the supernatural and look at girls' pictures. That's all you will ever do. Look at pictures."

Ashworth's face burned. Had she not been standing twenty feet above him, he might have beaten the crap out of her. Instead, he grabbed his coffee cup and threw it at her with all his might.

The mug flew upwards, spraying cold coffee in every direction. It shattered against the concrete wall right beside Bonnie's face. She flinched instinctively, pinched her eyes shut, and tried to cover her face with her hands against the many flying fragments. Several shards gashed her hands and face. As she twisted away in pain, her glasses flew off, and her feet became tangled in the shoulder strap of the bookbag she'd dropped on the steps beside her. Bloody and confused, she fought the restraint around her ankles and lost her balance. She staggered forward, stumbled against the iron banister, and toppled over the railing. She plunged twenty feet and landed back-first across a wooden chair. The crack of her spine was audible even over her scream. Then she rolled from the chair and down onto the ground, her forehead catching the corner of a low metal filing cabinet in the process.

"Oh shit," shouted Ashworth as he ran to her side. "Bonnie! Bonnie, are you okay? Oh, please be okay."

But of course she wasn't okay. She was out cold, her breathing was shallow, and blood was trickling from the corner of her mouth. Ashworth gagged at the sight of the jagged hole in her forehead.

"Oh, Christ, that's her brain!" he murmured. "I can see her brain!"

He drew back. "Call someone. I've got to call someone." But who? Who could he call? Greyson? Shit, no! Besides, he'd never meant to hurt her, not really. She just fell. He'd never even touched her.

"But then what about the cuts?" he whispered. And, oh shit, nobody was going to see this as an accident. It'd be one more Greyson scandal. This was going to be the end of the lab for sure. And even if the college didn't shut it down, sure as shit, the cops would. A crime scene they'd call it.

Okay, so what if he could get her out of the lab? What if he could make it look like the accident never happened at the college at all? Then the Administration couldn't do anything, could they? Okay, so if he cleaned up the mess and then waited until really late, he could move her somewhere else, right? The others thought she was going to meet Chandler anyway. So maybe he'd dump her on some road off campus. But what if she wasn't dead?

"With those injuries?" he murmured. "It's just a matter of time."

She'd probably have passed before the time came to move her anyway.

"Besides, there's nothing anyone could do for her, not with a cracked spine like that. Probably best for everyone, her included, if she does just die."

Hours passed. Ashworth cleaned up the splashed coffee, the shards of broken mug, and the blood. He pulled the fragments from her face and hands, and then waited. The silence of the cellar was broken only by the rattle of Bonnie's labored breathing.

Past two in the morning, Ashworth crept upstairs, turned off the cellar lights, and peeped outside. Save for a couple of lights still on in the men's bays and the women's residence, the quadrangle was dark and still. He propped open the cellar door and hauled Bonnie up the steps to ground level, then set off into the night. Ashworth wasn't strong enough to lift her, so he had to pull Bonnie by the arms across the cobblestones. Staying in deep shadow alongside the walls, he dragged her clear of the college grounds. Beneath an elm at the side of

Coburg Road, he paused to catch his breath. Bonnie's raspy breathing was really getting on his nerves. "Christ, would you just fucking die?" he muttered. Coburg Road was empty and silent at that hour. One or two homes up and down the block still had a porch light, but there was no movement anywhere. A dog suddenly came running out of the darkness. Ashworth was terrified the mutt might start barking or growling, but with its tail wagging vigorously, it merely sniffed Bonnie before romping away into the dark.

He waited a moment to make sure no cars were approaching, then hauled Bonnie across the street and along the sidewalk in the direction of downtown. He noticed that between the pools of light from each street lamp, there was a pool of darkness, and so he dragged Bonnie into one such pool. There he hauled her to the curb and draped her body in such a way as to appear she'd been struck by a car and thrown to the curb as she'd crossed the road.

Ashworth murmured a few words of apology over her body and then dashed back to the cellar.

Later, bedded down on his camp cot, he rehearsed his lines. "I've been here the whole time. No, Bonnie was never here. No, I didn't see her at all last night. Hit by a car? Really? That's awful. I thought she was going out with Chandler? Maybe you should speak to him."

****

Bangor General Hospital

In the days before she fled, Gillian peppered her nurses with all sorts of questions. How frequently should her dressings be changed? What types of painkillers could she handle? What signs of distress were her nurses looking for, like loss of sensation or dizziness or nausea? And what exercises was she supposed to do to regain full function of her limbs? In the course of grilling her nurses, Gillian became convinced she was perfectly capable of managing her own recovery.

Jackie and Madelyn had agreed to take turns driving to Halifax. They'd bought clothes and everything else Gillian might require for the trip so they wouldn't need to go by the Willards' house for anything.

Beyond a destination, the girls had no real plan. In Halifax, they'd ask around the various campuses. Someone was bound to have heard of Chris. Cute guy, tall, blond, blue-eyed, plagued by a vengeful demon. He shouldn't be too difficult to find. But then what?

This recklessness was so unlike Gillian. But if the days following surgery had taught her anything, it was how important Chris was to her. Sure, she wanted a career, independence, and perhaps a family one day. But as free and independent as she was determined to remain, she also wanted Chris by her side. She especially wanted to be with him when he was eventually free of that damnable creature, Mallory Dahlman.

Oh, Chris was going to get the shock of his life when she showed up, buzz cut and all. She'd probably find him squirreled away in some library, starving, little more than a monk. But if by some happenstance, there happened to be a new person in his life, some Canadian slag, then she'd tear them both apart, Mallory be damned.

As evening visiting hours were coming to an end, Gillian slipped into her private washroom. There she pulled on baggy pants, a shapeless sweater, and rubber boots. She fitted a ratty brown wig Madelyn had pinched from her mother's collection over the stubble on her bandaged scalp. Meanwhile, Jackie and Madelyn arranged pillows beneath her bedsheet. They were out into the hospital parking lot before they dared breathe. But then they burst into laughter and raced away to Jackie's car.

Earlier they might have imagined this trip would be fun, but as Jackie's car wound through Bangor's suburbs in the direction of Route

9 and the Canadian border, the doubts set in. They couldn't foresee Chris's reaction when they caught up with him, couldn't conceive what steps thereafter might be required, and couldn't even envisage what a good outcome to this whole affair might actually look like. There were simply too many obstacles to be overcome—Gillian's fragile health, Chris's determination to spare Gillian his perilous vocation, their diverging prospects, and of course Mallory—before they'd be able to think about a good ending to their quest.

After several hours of driving through the dark and fogbound wilderness, the lights of Calais and the border crossing to Canada came as such a relief. Their initial excitement had long since given way to overwhelming fatigue. They needed sleep, and Gillian needed painkillers and a new dressing.

"You girls are out late," said the Canadian border guard.

"Couldn't leave until after work," they explained. "Meeting up with friends off the *USS Roosevelt* tomorrow. It's docked in Halifax before it's deployed to the Middle East. We had to get as far as we could tonight if we're going to catch them before they sail."

"Well, don't drive too tired. Couple 'a nice motels up the road. The *Bayshore's* good. Ten minutes maybe."

Gillian had lived all her life not two hundred miles from the Canadian border but had never before crossed it. "They're all socialists up there," her grandfather would sometimes say. Atheists, communists, and monarchists, his buddies would add. "Who knows what them Canucks is plotting up there in their igloos."

That's why St. Stephen came as such a shock. Even at this late hour, its misty streets empty, it looked just like Maine, tidier in fact, maybe even more prosperous, and for sure there were more churches.

After a night at the *Bayshore Motel* and a hearty breakfast at *Olive's Café*, the three young women were once again pumped for adventure.

The drive along the coast was breathtakingly lovely in the autumn sunlight. The Loyalist City of St. John was nice enough, except that is, for the stink of its paper mills. Then again, back home in Maine, towns were often blanketed by the same sulfurous stench.

The next urban center on their route was French-speaking Moncton. How could there be a French-speaking city so close to Maine? It was like discovering Europe was just down the street. They stopped for a lunch of grilled sandwiches and milkshakes, and as they were walking back to the car, Jackie asked, "We'll be in Halifax tonight. What's the first thing you're going to say to Chris when you see him?"

Gillian thought for a moment, and then said, "Chris Chandler, don't you ever again presume to decide what's best for me. That's not your place. I'll decide what's best for me . . . and it's you."

Chapter Nine

Wednesday, September 16

Freddy's Diner

"Good morning, Mr. Chandler, sir," said Minhas with his customary smile. "Will you have the Bluenose Breakfast today, sir?" he asked as he led Chris through the busy diner to a table for two by the back wall.

"Why not? Spoil me, Mr. Minhas," replied Chris.

"Oh, and will you be available to assist me this evening? I could use the help."

"That would be great, at nine?"

"See you then," said Minhas as he clipped Chris's order to the lazy Susan dangling in the kitchen pass-through. "Ah, and here's Mr. Brook. Good morning to you, sir."

"*Servus*. Coffee, toast, thank you," Sammy muttered as he walked directly to Chris's table. He sat down without a word of invitation or greeting. Chris wasn't sure how he felt about consorting with Brook after learning of the old man's reprehensible past. He glanced across the table as Sammy sat down but said nothing to the old man.

Sammy didn't seem to register Chris's discomfort. Wringing his hands, the old man grumbled, "I'm not good at saying thank you but I'm grateful to you for doing a nice thing for Mrs. Norris. I'm so pleased she passed happily."

"It wasn't much," muttered Chris without lifting his gaze from the remnants of the morning paper abandoned by a previous customer.

"*Aber ja*, it was amazing. How did you know that a lullaby might tell the son that his mama needed him? And seeing spirits, how did you know how to do this?"

"Learned it from friends. I'm just glad I could help." With that, Chris's attention returned to the newspaper.

"Well, I want to help you too. I know you are studying Kabbalah. I know Kabbalah. I can teach you."

"You did the other evening."

"No, I'll teach you more. I know lots."

Chris folded the paper, put it to one side, and then looked Brook directly in the eye. "How is that? You said you learned Kabbalah from a Russian priest. Why would he do that? I thought the Russian Orthodox Church studied Kabbalah in an attempt to convert Jews to Christianity and justify pogroms."

"That is true. The priest said his monastery was proud of how many Jews it had killed."

"So why would this priest help you?"

Sammy reacted to the question with a moment's silence and a curious look. Then he said very quietly, "We were—how you say—up to our eyeballs in evil. I guess it was natural that we talked about all the shit around us. We talked about murder, death, guilt, punishment, maybe even Hell. We even played a game. What is greater evil? Murder the mother or murder the child? Make the father choose which child is to die, or the child choose which parent will die? We argued for hours like that. Then the next day we would see the real thing."

"I bet you did," said Chris.

Minhas arrived with their food. "Here we are, gentlemen."

"Thank you, Mr. Minhas," said Chris. "And please thank your wife."

"Ah, yes, of course. Oh, and have you gentlemen spoken to the police yet?"

"About what?" Chris asked.

"The two thugs. A Sergeant Bain was here the other afternoon, trying to clear up details of the fight. He's talking to everyone who might have seen something."

"Okay, I'll give him a call," said Chris. And with that, the two men fell into eating their breakfasts in silence.

"Well, have a good day, Mr. Brook," said Chris as he rose to leave. He then turned away and started for the door.

"So will I teach you this evening?" Brook called after Chris. "Will that be a good time for you?"

"No, sorry, not tonight." Chris turned back toward Sammy but didn't lift his eyes from the floor. "I'm helping Mr. Minhas tonight."

"Okay, so another time."

"Yes, another time." Surely the old man had sensed Chris's snub.

****

Outside Freddy's Diner

Greyson's stomach was killing him. Perhaps it was the weeks-old pizza he'd found at the back of his fridge the previous evening. Maybe it was the cocktail of pharmaceuticals he'd had at bedtime, or the Provincial government's plan to shutter his lab. Of course, Mother's latest demand for money certainly hadn't helped. How the hell was he going to find two hundred thousand dollars in a few days? If it was only his mother he'd had to deal with, he could probably have talked her into waiting, but now that she had lawyers involved, the blood-sucking bastards were going to nail his ass if he violated their timeline by seconds. After all, that's what lawyers do; they crucify by the clock.

The pain in his gut shot through him like a knife. After he'd talked to Chandler, he'd have to get something, antacid or something, or

221

maybe just a couple of good stiff drinks. But first, he had to see Chandler.

He'd gotten Chandler's campus address from his student file. A sweet young thing hired for the registration period had obliged.

Greyson's sea-green Porsche 911 Targa might once have impressed, but now with all the rust and dents outside and the fast-food debris and crumpled parking tickets inside, it merely depressed. He found the corner of Duke and Hollis Street and parked on Hollis alongside *Freddy's Diner*. Through the diner's steamy windows, he spotted Chandler chatting with some old man. The smell of frying bacon wafting from the diner turned his stomach. He nearly gagged as bile rose in his throat. Greyson was tempted to barge in on Chandler's chat until he realized getting out of his car without throwing up wasn't going to be possible. He'd just have to wait. Eventually, Chandler got up from the table, paid at the register, and started for the door.

As soon as Chandler stepped outside, Greyson shouted at him and waved an arm through the passenger window.

"Professor Greyson, what are you doing here?"

"Get in," ordered Greyson.

"I've got classes. I have to get my stuff from my room."

"Get in," ordered Greyson a second time. "This won't take long. Look, after we're done, I'll drive you to your class. But I have to talk to you first."

Greyson swept burger wrappers and dried-up fries from the passenger seat, and Chandler climbed in.

"What's your problem?" he asked.

"Look, I can't get into it now, but my timeline is changing. I had planned on us working together on some pretty cool shit. That's why I figured you should get familiar with Kabbalah. But we aren't going to have time for that now. I need to bring my work to the public much sooner than I'd intended."

"And this affects me how? Are you canceling my scholarship?"

"No. No, not at all. The opposite, actually. It means you won't have me bothering you anymore. You can just get on with your studies like all the other idiots at the college. In fact, I'll pay your entire financial obligations for all four years of your degree with a single transfer from my endowment to your college account. And I'll do it right away. That's providing I get your complete cooperation for the next few days, and I mean your complete fucking cooperation. Is that clear?"

"Doing what?"

"You have to find a dead guy for me. Just find him, and we're done."

"What dead guy?" Even before he asked, Chandler knew the answer. Bonnie had already told him. The cantor from Prague.

"Okay, so among the hundred fifty *Titanic* victims buried here in Halifax, I need you to find one grave, the grave of a cantor from Prague." Greyson dragged his briefcase from atop a bag of laundry in the back seat. He popped it open, rooted through envelopes and filthy tissues and pill containers until he found the file he required. "Here," he said as he handed the file to Chandler, "this contains everything we've been able to find out about this cantor. Pay particular attention to the fragments I found at the *Altneuschul* in Prague. They got me going on this hunt. I know the cantor sailed aboard the *Titanic*, I'm pretty certain he's buried here, and I'm positive he was transporting something, an amulet, from the *Altneuschul* to a synagogue in New York."

"Why do you think I can find him?"

"Stop playing coy with me. Because you can see the dead, right? In graveyards, beside their graves? I bet you could walk through the *Titanic* graveyard right now and find him."

Chris looked at Greyson for a moment, then muttered, "That's not how it works."

"I don't give a rat's ass how it works. Just get me that amulet, and we'll have nothing further to do with each other."

Just as he'd said to Bonnie the previous evening, Chris swore, "I'm not desecrating anyone's grave, not for any amount of money."

"Fine, then just identify the grave for me. I'll get permission to open the grave from the cemetery board or the province, or the Jewish community. That won't be your worry. You just have to tell me which grave the cantor is in and you'll get your cash. Clear?"

"Why do you want this amulet? It's because you think it has something to do with the golem legend. But you aren't actually thinking about making a golem, are you? Because that would really be nuts."

Greyson glared at Chandler. 'Don't you sneer at me,' he wanted to scream. But he didn't. As calmly as he could manage, he replied, "I'm not interested in making a golem. I just want the cantor's amulet to be the centerpiece of a presentation I'm preparing."

"What presentation?"

"I plan to uh, to exhibit all the work we've been doing in our lab, you know, with pharmaceuticals and holy words and ancient texts. But most important, I want to reveal to the world that the legend of the golem is grounded in facts. I'm going to display everything we've learned about Loew's recipe for making a golem, and the holy names he used to do so. And I want the amulet to be the crowning discovery among all our other artifacts."

"Where do you plan to make this presentation?"

'Anywhere I can crush heads and break limbs,' Greyson wanted to scream. But again, he struggled to control his temper. "Well, uh, I'm thinking, I mean I'm talking with the city's Jewish community about a special uh . . . seminar, uh in honor of some rabbi or other. It's a great opportunity. Anyway, that's not what's important. What matters is I need that amulet now! And I'll pay every penny of your degree to get it."

"So if I can identify this cantor's grave, you'll pay all my tuition and my room and board?"

"Right."

"And then we'll be done with each other?"

"Exactly. But you have to find the cantor so damned fast. I don't want to miss this opportunity. It will be great for the lab . . . and for the entire college."

"But what if I can't find him because he's not here, I mean because his body was never recovered?" Chris asked. "You have to know that's still the most likely outcome."

Greyson wanted to rip Chandler to pieces for that remark, but he gripped the steering wheel, gritted his teeth for a moment, and then said, "Okay, you convince me the cantor isn't here, and you still get your money, but you have to prove to me you've exhausted every possibility or you get shit."

"And what about Mallory? The Torajan demon you met the other evening?"

"Oh yeah, right. You wanted my help in laying her spirit to rest, right?"

"You said you knew something about Torajan religious ceremonies."

"Sure, right, okay, so then the faster you find the cantor's grave, the likelier I am to help you with your little demon problem."

"Okay, it's a deal. I'll begin right after class."

Greyson started the Porsche. Its radio blared, ". . . right outside Cavendish College in the early morning hours. Police have not yet released the identity of the injured woman pending notification of her family. Halifax Police Services is asking anyone who might have witnessed the accident to contact the Crime hotline as soon as possible."

"What's that about?" muttered Greyson.

****

Greyson's Lab

Ryan arrived on campus to find the place in turmoil. Cops were everywhere, and dozens of students were gathered on the sidewalk outside the college gate. They chatted amongst themselves, pointed at the police officers, shook their heads, or wept softly.

In Greyson's lab, the somber mood was deeper still.

"You're sure it was Bonnie?" Ashworth asked, his chair tilted back against the cement wall as he casually sipped a mug of tea and browsed through a stack of notes on his lap.

"Yes," replied Sheila, dabbing her eyes. "I saw paramedics place her backpack beside the victim on the gurney as they slid it into the ambulance. She never goes anywhere without that stupid Ghostbusters backpack."

"Bonnie's been hurt?" asked Ryan as he descended the steps into the cellar. "How? Is she okay? Have the cops said anything?"

"It was maybe a hit and run," replied Sheila. "That's what I heard one cop say, but then some other guy said it didn't look like a real hit and run, so I'm not sure."

"When did this happen?" asked Henry. "Like late last night?"

"That's what I don't get," muttered Jeffy, who had tears running down his cheeks. "Why would Bonnie be outside in the middle of the night?"

"Remember," said Ashworth looking up from his notes, "we asked her to cozy up to the Yank." He made deliberate eye contact with Jeffy, then Sheila, and said, "I bet Chandler knows what happened to Bonnie."

There was a heavy knock on the door, followed by a shout. "Halifax Police. Open up, please."

James climbed the steps and opened the door.

"I'm Sergeant Bain, and this is Constable Publicover. We're with the Halifax Police Services, and we'd like to speak with Professor Greyson. Is he here?"

"Nope," said James.

"Okay, well, it appears one of your classmates has been injured, and perhaps you lot might be able to help us figure out what happened."

"It's Bonnie, isn't it?" said Sheila. "I saw them putting her in the ambulance. Is she okay?"

"I can't confirm her identity, but no, she's not okay, and I'm sure you'd like to help us with our inquiries. So did any of you see her last evening, maybe when she went out, or when she came home?"

No one replied.

"I gotta tell you, what happened to the girl is really kinda weird," said Bain as he descended the stairs. "Like we found a couple of things that probably fell out of her backpack, but they were nowhere near her body. A prescription with her name on it beneath the college arch and a glittery comb on the opposite side of the road from where we found her. It's like she came into the college and then went back out to the street, dropping things as she went. Or maybe she was dragged back out to the street, and stuff just fell from her bag." Bain let the image sink. "So were any of you here last night?"

"None of us was here," muttered Ashworth.

"But that's not right, Michael, you were here," said Ryan. "I saw you getting your cot out before I left."

"You slept here?" asked Bain as he started across the chamber toward Ashworth.

"Okay, yeah, I did," Ashworth replied as he finally put down his notes and looked up at the cop. "Nothing unusual in that. I often sleep here when I have work to do."

"So did you see the girl last evening? Did she come in here?"

"No. Why would she? She lives in residence. She'd go there, wouldn't she?" Ashworth kept shuffling through the pages in his lap like he was searching for something.

"We've checked with the residence night porter," replied Sergeant Bain. "He says our victim signed out around 9 p.m. and never signed back in. So if she did return to the campus later in the evening, where did she go?"

"Why are you asking me?" Ashworth seemed agitated. "How would I know? We're not close. Maybe she went to meet some guy in one of the men's' bays." Ashworth looked around the chamber like he wanted backup. "Hey, wasn't she meeting Chandler last night? Yeah, sure, Chris Chandler, he might know something." With that, Ashworth's attention returned to his notes.

"And none of you is Chandler?"

"Nope, he's not here yet," replied Ryan.

"Okay," said Bain as he climbed back up the stairs. "When this Chandler does come in, tell him Detective Sergeant Bain wants to have a chat. He can call the Police Services. They'll put him right through to me." The police officers left.

Ryan couldn't understand why Ashworth's behavior had been so weird during the cops' visit. "You sure you never saw Bonnie last night, Michael? You were acting kinda weird while the cops were here."

Ashworth shifted in his seat and pulled at his shirt collar but didn't look up from his notes. "Just don't like cops, that's all."

"I have a bad feeling this Bonnie thing is just what the college needs to finally close us down," muttered Ryan. "You gotta think we're toast this time."

Now Ashworth looked up. In fact, he jumped to his feet and shouted, "No, don't say that. We can get through this. We just . . . we just have to stick together. Bonnie never came into the lab, and that's an end to it. Her getting hurt is nothing to do with us."

"You're an idiot if you believe that," said Ryan.

Just then Chandler entered the cellar. He immediately called out, "The radio said someone was hurt across the street. Who was it?"

"Bonnie," replied Ashworth. "But you probably knew that."

Chandler halted partway down the steps. "What does that mean?"

"You had a date with Bonnie last night, didn't you?"

"I was heading home alone when Bonnie just showed up. She said she was out for a walk but then she admitted you'd all asked her to find out about my meeting with Greyson."

"Anyway, the police were just here," said Ryan. "Michael told them you'd probably seen Bonnie last night, so they want to talk to you."

"We only walked as far as Camphill Cemetery. Then she took a cab home, so they can check with the cab company if they must. But did the cops say anything about her condition?"

"Only that she's really bad," Sheila replied.

"I'm going to the hospital," Chris muttered and bolted out of the door.

"That looked like a guilty conscience to me," said Ashworth loudly enough for everyone to hear.

****

The North End, Halifax

After dropping Chandler off at the college, Greyson drove to the North End and parked by *Big Eddy's Pawnsho*p. He had to get some cash, for smokes, for food, and for something to settle his nerves and stomach. The leather briefcase should get him a few dollars, and the Pentax camera might be worth a hundred or so. Maybe he'd even throw in the Rolex his mother had given him the day he received his Ph.D.

As Greyson climbed out of the car, three men emerged from the alley alongside *Big Eddy's*. They greeted him with broad smiles and shouts of "Speak of the devil!" and "Look what the tide washed in!"

"Fuck, how'd I miss them?" Greyson muttered under his breath as he locked the car.

The stocky fellow with the tattooed face and broken nose sauntered up to Greyson, his hands in his pants playing a vigorous game of pocket pool. "Hey Doc," he said, "we was just on our way uptown to see you. A little matter of your account, right?"

Greyson backed away slightly as he babbled, "Yeah sure, yeah, like that's uh, that's why . . . that's why I stopped . . . when I saw you. I uh . . . I wanted to pay an installment."

"Installment? You hear that fellas, the Doc thinks we run some kinda Christmas club or credit card service or something. Sorry Doc, we don't take no installments, right? You buy? You pay. Simple, right? Only you ain't paid in months, right?"

"Look, I just need a couple more weeks," said Greyson, "then I'll be able to pay the whole thing, I swear."

"With interest, right? You gotta realize what you owe is goin' up by the day, right?"

"Yeah, sure, the interest, I get it."

"There's a reason they say accounts is in arrears, right? Because if you don't pay, you gets a hot poker shoved up your ass. In da rear, right?" The three toughs howled with laughter.

"You know I have this big endowment fund," said Greyson. "I've paid you thousands in the past. I'm just having a little trouble at the moment with the bookkeeping. But when I get it sorted, I'll have lots of cash. I just need a bit more time . . . and—"

"And what?" asked the little guy as he shoved up against Greyson's chest.

"And a couple more items."

"Christ, what do you think we are?" Any semblance of humor vanished from the fellow's face.

"Please, please listen, babbled Greyson, "I always come to you because you can get stuff no one else can. You're the most reliable source of . . . of pharmaceuticals this side of Montreal, especially the exotic stuff. And that's what I need, something really, really exotic."

"Me, I do like a challenge, right?" the short guy said with a big smile at his buddies. "So what you lookin' for?"

"I need the strongest roofies you can find. I think they're called benzodiazepines. I understand they're extracted from plants in the nightshade family. I need something natural but as strong as you can get."

"So you want an anticholinergic alkaloid from the *Solanaceae* family."

The short guy's response caught Greyson off guard. "A what?"

"Like d-Tubocurarine. Some German bishop in the sixteen hundreds tried using an early version in his army's hand grenades to knock out the enemy. Anyway, this broad must be one big fucking bitch to need a roofie like that. It'll knock a horse out, right?"

"How do you know all that?" asked Greyson.

"You think I'm just some shithead, right? Just like I think you're a wasted, drug-fucked, human cesspool, right? Well, I was a pharmacist, asshole."

"Then why . . . ."

"Because I had a little disagreement with the licensing board over an old bugger's care. He thought his shingles warranted hours of my time. And I thought he deserved a skin moisturizer high in alpha-hydroxy acids for getting on my nerves so fuckin' much. It gave him one horrific allergic rash right on top of his shingles, right? The itching from the one together with the pain from the other practically drove the old bastard mad! I laughed so hard I nearly shat myself!"

His buddies roared with laughter.

"Christ," muttered Greyson.

"Anyway, turns out this line of work pays a shitload more than working behind some counter," the short guy continued. Then he poked Greyson hard in his chest and growled, "But the important lesson for you is, never cross your pharmacist. You never know what might be in your next medication."

The threat was all too obvious. Greyson coughed on his dry throat and asked, "So . . . you can get me this—?"

"D-Tubocurarine. Sure. And you're gonna get me a down payment, right? With that watch you're wearing. And it's so convenient we're outside my buddy *Big Eddy's Pawnshop*. That's where you were heading anyway, right? He'll give you a deal, and you'll pay me every fucking cent you get, right? Or you'll be seriously in da rears, motherfucker. Good, now go inside like a nice little boy."

****

Victoria General Hospital Emergency

The hours Al Bain had spent doing this, waiting outside the hospital's emergency entrance, smoking his lungs to crap, waiting to take a victim's statement, or interview a car crash victim, or for word on his partner's condition, or for the doctor's verdict on his wife's latest relapse?

Oh, Evie.

The ache never went away. According to their kids, her lung cancer was the fault of Bain's smoking. Of course, they were right, and they hadn't spoken a word to him since her passing. Christ, you'd think he could have stopped after that! But no. How he hated this place. It seemed like every patient taken through those doors was the victim of someone else's selfishness.

"Sergeant Bain?" someone called.

He looked around and spotted a nurse waving at him from the emergency entrance door.

"Coming," he called back as he butted his cigarette.

"Sergeant Bain, a young man is asking to see the patient, Bonnie Meredith. He came through the main entrance."

"Right, good, I'll talk to him."

"He's in the Admitting waiting room. Tall with long blond hair pulled back in a ponytail."

****

"Can I help you?" Bain asked as he approached the young man. The kid turned, and Bain was struck immediately by the icy blue eyes. Chandler. "Ah, Chris Chandler, I presume. Good to finally meet you."

The boy looked confused. "I'm sorry?" he said. "Do I know you?"

"I'm Bain," he replied, "Sergeant Bain with the Halifax Police. I've been hoping to talk to you."

"Oh yeah, a couple of people have said that. The first was Mr. Minhas."

"Right, about the guys that got beat up in the alley by his diner. And I also wanted to ask you about the girl who was beaten outside your college."

"Yeah, sure. But I wanted to see how my friend's doing first, and then I was going to call you."

"But you're here now, so let's talk, and while we're at it, let's also talk about the guy who got beat up in Camp Hill Burial Grounds a couple of nights ago and then about the vandalism at the *Titanic* Cemetery. Oh, and let's not forget the fire at your college some time back. They're all still cases on my duty sheet."

Chandler gave him a quizzical look, shook his head, and replied, "Sorry, Sergeant, but why would I know anything about those other cases?"

"Because for some reason, your name popped up in connection with almost all of them, even when you weren't actually in Halifax."

"Look, Sergeant, I can tell you what I saw outside the diner, and that's about it. But about the rest I know squat. And besides, I really would like to find out about my friend first."

"The Meredith girl."

"I didn't actually know her last name because we only just met, but please, can you tell me how she is?"

"Broken back, head injury, in surgery as we speak. Can't find any family. Looks very bad, I'm sorry to say."

"Oh, Christ." Chris turned away and ran a hand through his hair.

"You and she were close?"

"No, we only spoke once."

"Not what your college friends said. I got the impression you and she was out on a date last night. So what happened? Did she resist your advances? You get angry? Maybe you got a little physical? Maybe you fought?"

"No, nothing like that. I was walking home. She asked if she could accompany me. We walked as far as Camp Hill together. We had a little disagreement, so we said goodbye, and I thought she had gone home by cab. You can check with the cab companies."

"I have, and she did get a cab back to the college. But what was your disagreement about?"

The Chandler kid hesitated, shuffled his feet, shook his head like he wanted to get something off his chest.

Maybe a little prompting will get him started.

"Look, kid, I've done some checking on you. Complicated past you got. One minute you're just some high school kid, the next you're a statewide Jack the Ripper, then a hero, then the subject of a Governor's inquiry, then a hero for the second time, and now you're here. Seems like you've got more fans and more people out to kill you than . . . than Robin Hood. Look, I don't think you're a bad guy. Fact is, I know you're not. But you do know a lot more about all this shit than you're telling. So give me one thing. What did you and the girl quarrel about?"

The Chandler kid looked directly into Bain's eyes like he was trying to figure out, is this guy for real? And then out it all came.

"Okay, so she told me," began Chandler, "that Professor Greyson's, you know, his followers, that they raided the Jewish *Titanic* cemetery. Greyson's got a project going, and he needs something from a *Titanic* grave. That's all I'm prepared to tell you now because my whole future is at stake here. I don't think Greyson approved of what they did, but if

Greyson learns that I told you even that much, my college days would be over."

"Okay, but if Bonnie opened up to you about Greyson's project and the raid on the graveyard, then why did you and she fight?"

"Because I would never defile a grave, never, not for anything, and I consider anyone who would the worst kind of scum on the planet."

"Whoa, strong words." He'd clearly touched a nerve. Then things went really nuts.

"Yeah, maybe. But I've seen for myself the torment the departed suffer when their resting place is desecrated."

****

Greyson's Lab

After Chandler left for the hospital, the lab fell into a morose silence, each of the greylings wallowing in their own sorrow for Bonnie. Or so it seemed to Ashworth. He couldn't for the life of him understand their moping about. Bonnie had never been much help in their work. The one time she'd tried the salvi, she'd come apart. Besides, and way more important, the bitch deserved what she got for telling Chandler about their raid on the *Titanic* cemetery. What had she been thinking? Oh well, she wouldn't be doing much thinking now, not the way her brains had been leaking out of her skull when he dumped her in the road.

Anyway, enough about goddamned Bonnie. Now that Greyson was entirely consumed with his *Titanic* crap, Ashworth felt liberated to begin the article he'd been dying to write for months. An academic article had always been Ashworth's Plan B. If there was no saving Greyson from himself, then Michael was determined to reap what he could from the work he'd done on sacred language and hallucinogens. A scholarly article by an undergraduate was sure to get him noticed in the world of scholarship, maybe a place in a shit-hot graduate school somewhere, perhaps even a sizable scholarship. He'd actually been working on the article's outline for some time, but now he could really crank it out. Of course, he'd mention the other kids, but let's face it, he'd done all the work that really mattered. And besides—

"Oh Christ! Shit, shit, shit!" bellowed Ryan from the other side of the lab.

"What?" Sheila called. "What is it?"

"Look," said Ryan angrily as he got up off the floor. "It was sticking out from under the photometer." He was holding up a piece of blue plastic. "It's the right temple from Bonnie's glasses. And the rest of her glasses are stuck under the fridge."

"But she always wears her glasses," replied Sheila.

"Of course! Which means . . . .?" said Ryan like he was prompting her.

"Which means she came back here before she got hurt," interjected Jeffy.

"You think she broke her glasses here before she went out again?" asked James.

"Without her glasses, she couldn't go anywhere, never mind out in the dark," said Sheila.

"And besides, wouldn't she have picked up the pieces before leaving?" Henry piped in.

"So how did she break her glasses in the first place?" asked Jeffy.

"You're all missing the big question," shouted Ryan. And that's when he turned to Ashworth. "Bonnie obviously broke her glasses here after she came back. So why didn't you see her, Michael?"

Shit! Shit! Quick, think!

"I . . . I don't know. Maybe I'd fallen asleep or something."

Ryan clearly didn't believe him. "You didn't hear Bonnie break her glasses?"

"I don't know. Maybe she didn't want me to see her. Maybe she was creeping about with Chandler or something."

"Christ, Michael, give it up," Ryan shouted. "Tell the fucking truth. You know she came back. And when she wakes up, she'll tell the cops that."

"Not likely," muttered Ashworth.

"What do you mean by that?" asked Sheila.

Ashworth was angry now, being challenged in this way by a bunch of sentimental lightweights. "I mean, in the condition she's in, I doubt she'll be telling anybody anything. I doubt she'll even live."

"How . . . how can you know that?" gasped Sheila.

Shit. Gotta stay cool.

"I mean, you heard what that cop said."

"He never said she'd die!" shouted Jeffy.

"Jesus, Michael, what aren't you telling us?" asked Ryan as he advanced on Ashworth. The others were doing the same, gradually closing in on him. "She was here, wasn't she? And you saw her. And you know what happened. So tell us."

Ashworth's tone changed dramatically. He'd had it with these idiots. He was almost flippant. "I don't know why you're all making such a fuss. She was never really one of us, you know. I mean, she wasn't very bright, was she?"

Even Jeffy, at this point, was obviously getting pissed. "What the Christ are you saying?"

Why am I being defensive? What happened, happened, and it's probably for the best anyway!

"I mean, the bitch, she told Chandler we raided the cemetery. Can you believe it?" he shouted. "She fucking betrayed us."

"So what *did* you do?" Sheila asked.

"I never meant to. It wasn't my fault, not really. I mean, I got angry, and I threw a mug at her, that's all."

"And then what happened?" asked Ryan.

"Okay, so she was on the stairs, and when she turned away to dodge the mug, she tripped over her bookbag, and . . . and fell over the railing."

"Ahh! Christ. Oh my God," whispered Sheila.

Ryan was very close now. "What did you do then?"

"Well, I knew she, she wasn't going to get better, and I had to think about us, about our work. Because I knew what the college would say if anyone found her here. So I carried her outside. And I put her where I thought someone would find her. I only did it for us and . . . and for her."

"You mean you left her in the street to die," gasped Jeffy. There were tears streaming down his face.

"No! No, for someone to find her."

"And then you lied to everyone, including us," said Ryan.

And that's when Michael totally lost it. "That's right. I lied to all of you because none of you would have had the guts to do what I did. I did what had to be done. I fought for this place, for the work we're doing, because that's what leaders do. And if you can't see that, well then—"

"Well then, we can leave," shouted Ryan, and that's just what he did. He packed up his bookbag, grabbed his jacket and headed up the stairs, followed immediately by Jeffy and Sheila.

"Where are you going?" called Ashworth.

"Out of this sewer, you shit," Ryan shouted.

Their reaction made no sense. Why would they leave now? He'd done a good thing. He'd saved the lab. So why can't they see that?

"You really have no idea what you've done, do you?" said Ryan. "It's all over, Mikey. The college is going to close this place down, and it's probably time."

"No! No, it's not," shouted Ashworth. "Not while Greyson and I have work to do."

"Get real, for Christ's sake! Maybe we convinced ourselves we were doing something cool, but the truth is we were just screwing around with drugs and getting high. That's it. Nothing else. And now we're going to tell everyone on campus the truth about this place. So I suggest you pack up your shit and head for the hills because the mob will be storming this castle very soon, Dr. Frankenstein." And with that, Ryan, Sheila, and Jeffy left.

"Not true, not true," muttered Ashworth. "We're doing important— What are you staring at?" he screamed at Henry and James. "Aren't you going too?"

"No," replied Henry.

"Why the Hell not?"

"Because we owe Dr. Greyson a debt," said James.

"A debt? What kind of debt?"

Henry's tone was as cold as ice. "Doctor Greyson helped us get rid of our old man."

Then James spoke. "But if you're staying, Michael, then you won't be lying to Dr. Greyson or to us anymore," he said with a slight chuckle, "or we'll break you the way you broke Bonnie."

"Yeah, because we liked Bonnie, Michael," said Henry, "but we never liked you."

****

Gothall's Rooming House

After an afternoon class and an hour in the library reading about Prague's *Altneuschul*, Chris spent the evening helping Mr. Minhas empty grease pits and clean toilets before heading to bed. On the way upstairs, Sammy Brook intercepted him.

Taking Chris's arm, the old man said, "Come, come, I must ask you something." Chris followed reluctantly. Once in Sammy's room, the old man pushed Chris into his one upholstered chair and placed a plate of bread and smoked salmon on his knee. "I bought this today. It's very good. A treat, *mein Freund*."

"That's very nice of you, Mr. Brook, but—"

"I have to ask," Sammy interrupted, "Why are you studying Kabbalah? It's dangerous!"

"Well, it was a condition of my scholarship," replied Chris, "but it turns out my professor, the man who offered me the full scholarship, now only wants one thing from me. And if I do this one thing, he will immediately settle my entire account for the next four years."

"That's good, no?"

"He wants me to find a body."

"A body? What kind of body? A dead body?"

"Yes, dead. This Professor Greyson wants me to find the body of a cantor from Prague who was aboard the *Titanic*. Greyson believes the cantor's body was recovered from the sea, brought to Halifax, and buried here somewhere."

"Why does he want this cantor?"

"Because Greyson believes the cantor was carrying some sort of treasure to New York, a treasure which he believes is buried with the cantor."

"And he thinks you'll be able to find this cantor because you can see the dead?"

Chris nodded.

"What is this treasure?"

"An amulet that Greyson thinks once belonged to Rabbi Judah Loew."

Sammy straightened up. He clearly knew the name. "Ah, the Maharal of Prague. The Golem legend. Now I see. I hope you realize your professor is nuts. There never was a golem of Prague."

"No, I didn't think there was, but Greyson believes that finding something which actually belonged to Rabbi Loew will nevertheless be regarded as a major achievement."

"*Aber ja.* Rabbi Loew is very famous."

"Look, I appreciate your offer of help with Kabbalah, Mr. Brook, but . . . but—"

"But what?"

"Well, you said you learned Kabbalah from a Russian priest in the Mauthausen labor camp."

Sammy nodded.

"Why would a priest do that, for someone Jewish, I mean?"

"He . . . he liked my child. He taught her to read and write."

"You had a child with you in the camp?" Chris blanched, horrified. For a moment he couldn't speak, but then he managed to choke out the question he absolutely had to ask. "A child you took from someone?"

"No, no! She was my child, my daughter."

Chris could not imagine how a convicted murderer could have brought his own child into a labor camp. Sammy had to be lying, but he let the old man continue all the same.

"Every night, after my daughter fell asleep, the priest and me, we talked about everything, about life and God and guilt and punishment."

"So you said, Mr. Brook." Chris hesitated, not sure if he had the guts to proceed. What if he'd read the news clippings incorrectly? What if he was about to accuse an innocent old man of an unthinkable crime?

Even so, Chris pressed on. "From what I've read, Mr. Brook, you'd know a lot about guilt."

"What do you mean?" asked the old man. His face was hard, his eyes cold.

"I mean," said Chris, "you must know a lot about guilt . . . because you were a *kapo* for the Nazis, a guard for the *SS,* isn't that true?"

Brook said nothing, but then he suddenly lashed out, dropping his plate of smoked salmon to the floor. He grabbed Chris by the arm, dragged him to his door, and shoved him out into the hallway.

"*Geh, hear auf!* You know nothing," shouted the old man and slammed the door.

Chapter Ten

Thursday, September 17

Greyson's lab

An overnight gale had stripped the remaining autumn leaves from trees across the city. Now sodden from an early-morning rain, they clung to car windows, clogged gutters, and coated sidewalks in a treacherous brown slick.

Greyson arrived at the college shortly after nine, the earliest he'd appeared on campus in many months. He first stopped by the Humanities office to pick up his mail, something else he hadn't done in weeks. The three secretaries in the dean's office fell silent as he entered.

"What the hell are you gawking at?" he muttered as he crossed to his faculty post box and withdrew a large bundle of accumulated memos and letters.

The ladies shook their heads in disgust and returned to their work.

Greyson leafed through his stack of mail, tossing circulars and notices into a nearby trash can. But he paused when he came across one piece, a single, bright yellow sheet with the word Urgent in inch-high letters across its top. He unfolded the page and read,

This is to advise that on Tuesday, September 22nd, the Religious Studies laboratory in the cellar of the college chapel will be emptied and locked, and will remain so for the foreseeable future. All personal contents not cleared out of the laboratory before then will be hauled away and disposed of by the college's contracted haulage company. City police and college security staff will be on hand to oversee the closure.

"What the Hell?" Greyson shouted. He turned on the secretaries. "Is the dean in?"

"Yes, but she's on a phone call. You can make an ap—"

Greyson didn't let her finish. He stormed past the secretaries and hammered on the dean's door. An art historian, Dr. Angelica Marsdon was a tiny woman in her seventies, daughter of a prairie farmer, and as hard as the land that had shaped her.

"What do you think you're doing?" Greyson bellowed as he marched into her office.

In a voice as calm as cream, Dr. Marsdon said into the receiver, "Can I get back to you in a few minutes? A small matter has come up."

"You bitch, what does this mean?" bellowed Greyson. "You don't have the authority to close my lab!"

"It means we've got you, Dr. Greyson, we've got you at last," she replied. "Thanks to the testimony of your own admirers, we now have all the evidence we need to get rid of you once and for all, you goddamned fraud."

"What are you talking about?" What admirers was she referring to?

"I mean, your so-called greylings have reported in writing how that poor young woman found in the street yesterday was in fact brutalized in your lab. She was then dumped in the street like so much trash by one of your own minions."

Taken aback by the accusation, Greyson could only sputter, "But I don't know anything about that."

"Perhaps not," replied Dr. Marsdon, "but it makes no difference. It's one more instance of the ludicrous antics of your 'institute' and the last straw for the college governors and faculty senate. They met last evening in special session and nailed your hide to the barn door. So come Tuesday, you'll be history, Dr. Greyson."

"You . . . you can't."

"Oh yes we can. Next Monday morning, four days from now, the Provincial Government will hold a special press briefing to announce its new blueprint for postsecondary education, and at our chancellor's invitation, the government will conduct its briefing here at our college. After that, your position, your lab, and your endowment will be absorbed into the new divinity school, and *you* will be tossed to the curb. Now, if you please, will you get the fuck out of my office?" With a broad smile of satisfaction, Dr. Marsdon sat back and clasped hands in her lap.

****

Greyson left the Humanities office in a state of confusion. How had this all happened so quickly? It was bad enough his mother was demanding cash within weeks, but now the college and the province were threatening to move against him in a matter of days. Surely he still had legal options, didn't he? What about filing a stay of proceedings to buy time? But filed by whom? The faculty association? Probably not. His lawyers? No chance. His mother? Oh, shit, it was true. They had him. In the chill autumn air, as he crossed the quadrangle, Greyson's head cleared somewhat, and the answer came to him. Of course! He was, in fact, ready for this, ready to show the world what he'd accomplished. With the many extraordinary revelations he was about to make—about the Rabbi Loew, his golem, and his amulet—he was almost certain to grab all the headlines and upend the Government's announcement. He'd then be back on top of the academic world, and the province wouldn't dare move against him after that. But if by chance his revelations didn't do the trick, then he would take the most horrific revenge on the whole goddamned pack of them. And the press briefing would be the most perfect occasion to do that.

"So the traitors have cleared out, have they?" Greyson shouted as he returned to the lab. "Well, they went to the fucking Admin and told some story about a girl getting hurt here, and so now the Admin is planning to close us down next Tuesday."

He looked about at the three remaining greylings. Henry and James, of course they'd stay, and a good thing too since he knew he could trust them. But Ashworth? The weasel? Why was he still here? But he'd stayed, and Greyson was going to need all the help he could round up, so fuck it, he'd use the weasel.

"If we're going to save this lab," Greyson shouted, "we have a lot of work to do. The province is planning a big announcement on Monday, and we're going to crash their event with announcements of our own. But we'll have to be absolutely ready, so you three must do exactly what I tell you between now and then. Got it?"

The three hadn't moved since Greyson entered. But now they shook their heads vigorously. Ashworth even tried to speak.

"Uh, Professor Greyson, sir, uh, it was me who moved Bonnie after she got hurt."

"It was Bonnie that got hurt? Well, I'd offer Admin your ass if I thought it might save the lab, but the dean made it clear she blames me. So we're in this together, Ashworth, and if the cops come looking for you, then your only hope is to stick with me, right?"

"Right," replied Ashworth, more cowed than Greyson had ever before seen the weasel.

"Gentlemen, Armageddon is upon us. Henry and James, I have a list of assignments for you. We'll go over it in my office. But first, Ashworth, do you still have your notes on Rabbi Loew and his golem?"

"You told us to turn over our *Titanic* material to the American."

"To hell with the Titanic stuff. I need you to pull together every account you can find for activating a golem. You know, from Rabbi Loew's son, from Eleazar ben Judah ben Kalonymus, from the *Book of*

Creation, and from David Gans. I need you to summarize the key points for me."

"Okay, but that will take a while."

"You still don't get it, do you, Ashworth. Our time has run out! Either we rock the whole goddamned world on Monday, or we're out."

"Uh . . . all right."

"So you'll get me those rituals as fast as you can, or I swear, Henry and James will beat you to within an inch of your life." Henry and James looked at each other and chuckled.

At that moment, the door to the lab opened, and Captain Dahlman appeared.

"Who the hell are you?" shouted Greyson. "How'd you get in?"

Dahlman did not react to Greyson's anger. "The door was unlocked. My name is Dahlman, Captain Dahlman. The Admin office told me I might find a Christopher Chandler here."

"What do you want with Chandler?"

"We have a mutual friend and I'm hoping Chandler might help me find her." Dahlman remained at the top of the stairs.

"Seems like everyone wants Chandler to find someone," said Greyson with a sneer.

"I beg your pardon?"

"Chandler's not here," Greyson shouted. No way was this stranger going to interfere with Chandler's search for the cantor. "And besides, he's very busy."

"Any idea where I might find him?"

"In some rooming house down on Duke Street, but you can't bother him right now because he has something very important to do for me first."

"Well, forgive me, but I will see Chandler as soon as I can, and his work for you will simply have to wait." Captain Dahlman then left abruptly.

What the hell? "Fuck no!" Greyson bellowed after Dahlman. "Stay away from Chandler! You hear me? Stay away!"

****

Gothall's Rooming House

In the late afternoon, after his last class, Chris caught a bus to the city's North End and the *Fairview Lawn Cemetery*, site of 121 *Titanic* graves. In the last rays of a miserable day, Chris entered the grounds and was immediately assailed by overwhelming grief. Through the waning light and heavy mists, he glimpsed several mournful spirits hovering like clusters of green fireflies alongside their graves. The graves had not been desecrated but had more likely been misidentified. Without its occupant's name recorded correctly, no grave could provide proper sanctuary or grant its spirit eternal rest. Could one of the mournful spirits hovering amidst the deepening drear be Greyson's missing cantor? Chris couldn't bear to wander among the graves in his search; the grief of so many tortured souls was simply too depressing. He would need a far more precise target before he dared return.

As he got off the city bus a short distance up Duke Street from Gothall's Rooming House, Chris spotted Mr. Brook standing outside. He'd apparently been waiting there for some time, since his coat was drenched, and his wispy white hair was plastered to his scalp.

Head down, Chris ran through the drizzle to the doorway, said "Mr. Brook," and tried to get past the old man. He didn't want a scene. He just wanted to get out of the rain, but Sammy had other ideas.

"*Servus*, Mr. Chandler, sir. Please excuse me," Sammy said.

"Pardon?"

"I owe you an apology. You asked me about Mauthausen. I want to tell you about Mauthausen. Please. Let me buy you a burger or something so we can talk. Okay?"

They bought supper plates from Mr. Minhas and headed upstairs to Chris's room. Sammy returned to his own room briefly to get out of his wet things and then rejoined Chris. They ate in silence. Chris was unsure he wanted anything more to do with this criminal, while Sammy, for his part, appeared so nervous he was barely able to swallow.

"Please, you rest on your bed and don't look at me, okay?" Sammy proposed. "I will sit over there."

Chris did what he was told. Sammy sighed and began.

"I worked at the Mauthausen quarry for a very long time before Nazis arrived. I was the works foreman. But then I was sent to prison. I murdered my wife. Our daughter had just been born, and my wife, she . . . she was having a very bad time. She cried all the time, then got so angry, and then sad again. I was afraid for my daughter every day while I was at work. But then one day I came home from the quarry and my wife was with another man, and our baby was filthy and hungry and crying, so I . . . I got a shovel, and I killed them both. I was sent to prison but I wasn't executed because I killed only Jews.

"Then the Nazis came to Austria, and they took over Mauthausen. All the able-bodied Austrians were sent to fight. To work the quarries, the Nazis used slave laborers, Russians, Spanish, gypsies, and Jews. The work was hard. It killed many, but that was okay for the Nazis.

"Then the Nazis came to the prisons for guards to help the *SS* in their camps. They picked the hardest prisoners, the murderers first. But the day the Nazis came to my prison, my neighbors, Quakers who had adopted my baby daughter, they were visiting me. They'd been visiting every month since I was sent to prison. But that day, when an *SS* guy saw my daughter's dark hair and dark eyes, he guessed she was Jewish like me, since she wasn't blond like my neighbors. So the *SS* officer made me take my daughter with me onto the train. She was only small, a tiny little thing, not yet four.

"I was horrified when the train stopped at Mauthausen. And when the Director saw me, he recognized me. He knew I could make the quarry work well, so he made me his *kapo*. He gave me my own room in the barracks, let me hide my daughter, and even find another little girl to keep her company. Then I found an old Russian priest to watch the girls each day and teach them reading and arithmetic and tell them stories. In return, I had to manage all quarry workloads, all food distribution, all schedules. Every day, I took food from the poorest-performing barracks for my child. Every day I worked teams to death. Every day I ordered the weakest workers be given the most dangerous jobs in order to end their misery and save food and time. There were four hundred other children in Mauthausen. I took their clothes for my daughter. I ordered craftsmen to make her toys. I . . . I did everything for her. She was my only purpose. But I also made Mauthausen run very well. The Nazis were happy . . . and my daughter survived.

"Then one day word went round the camp that the British were coming and the war was about to end. I ran back to my room. The Russian priest had already killed the other little girl and he was choking my daughter. I pulled him off her and screamed, "Why?" Because, he said, when he was sure the girls would die, he did his best to make them happy. But once he realized they might survive, he couldn't let that happen because so many others had died for them to live."

"What did you do?"

"I strangled him."

For some time, Chris and Sammy sat in silence. Then Sammy continued.

"After the priest tried to kill my daughter, she was in shock. She couldn't speak for days. So when the British came, I slipped into the crowd of prisoners where I wasn't known. Few prisoners had ever actually seen me because I worked in the Director's office. I was eventually able to get papers and leave Austria. I came to Canada, learned a trade, and my daughter got better. But one day, when she was sixteen, on TV she saw a show about war criminals living in Canada, and they told a story about me. My daughter ran away to a friend's house. They hated me. Everybody hated me when they learned I'd been a *kapo*. My daughter's friend and her family took my daughter to Israel . . . and I haven't seen her since."

"Have you tried to explain to her what happened?" asked Chris in a voice barely above a whisper.

"Of course, but she says her life is cursed. She feels guilty for all the people I killed to save her. But why should she feel guilty? She did nothing wrong. She was just a child. A child cannot know guilt. A child just lives, believes the world is what it is and that she is the center of that world."

At this point in Sammy's story, tears were flowing down his cheeks like mountain streams.

"No, she says she will never forgive me for what I did. But *what* did I do? I saved my child. I know how I saved her was wrong. But to let my child die, that seemed so much more wrong. I know I will be punished. But what else could I have done? And so now, I think about good and evil every day of my life. Kabbalists, they say we have fallen away from *Ein Sof* and see only as our fallen world can see. But if we could see as *Ein Sof* sees, this would all make sense, and we would understand why *Ein Sof,* who created everything, created evil as well as good. But all I can see is that my evil saved my child and her hatred is my punishment.

"So now I just live until the time comes to pay for my sins. That won't be long now. But in the meantime, I do what I can. I know it makes no difference, since I have already done too much evil. But . . . I liked helping Mrs. Norris. I like Mr. Minhas. And, Mr. Chandler, if I can help you, please, I beg you, please let me try."

Chris sat for a moment and listened to the night sounds outside. Rain beat against his window. Cars splashed through the wet streets. A door slammed. Two dogs out for their evening walk with their masters snapped and growled at each other. The foghorn at the mouth of the harbor moaned to the mariners in its care. Dark and cold though the night might have seemed, it held no terror for most of its denizens. It is so easy to condemn others' choices when they were never yours to make.

Chris climbed off the bed, crossed the room to his bookbag, pulled out the file on the Prague cantor that Greyson had given him, and turned back to Sammy Brook. The old man's head had fallen forward. He sat weeping into his hands.

"Mr. Brook," said Chris, "I would be very grateful if you could have a look through this file for any issues of fact or translation that you might discover."

Chapter Eleven

Friday, September 18

Greyson's Lab

"You won't want to go outside, Michael," said Henry as he entered the lab carrying a bag of groceries. His brother James followed with a tray of coffees and a box of donuts.

Michael rolled off the common room couch, rubbed his eyes, and glanced at his watch. Just past 6 a.m. With all the work he'd had to do, he hadn't been able to get to sleep before 4.

"No police yet," continued Henry as he clumped down the stairs. "But Ryan and the others must have told people you caused Bonnie's accident because someone's made Wanted posters with your name on them. They're everywhere."

"You're kidding," Michael gasped. "For real?"

"Oh yeah, and somebody's also thrown garbage down our stairwell."

"Anyway," said James, "we got breakfast, so you won't need to face the mob just yet." He pulled sugar packets and creamers from his pockets, opened the box of donuts, and dumped pop tarts and cookies from the grocery bag. "Gonna need our energy. Got a lot to do today."

Loud coughing and belching preceded Greyson's emergence from his office. "Ah, boys, you're back," he said as he rubbed his stomach, and grimaced. "How'd your hunt go?"

"Good," said Henry. "We found this guy out past Lawrencetown Beach who slaughters horses, and makes glue from the hides. We bought a big pail of the stuff. Turns out he also had several sacks of lye, so we got them too."

"And then," said James, "just like it was meant to happen, we see this old horse trough in the long grass alongside the guy's lane. So we made him an offer, and now we got the tub you wanted."

"Well, that's outstanding," said Greyson, continuing to massage his gut. "Where is everything?"

"Back of our truck under a tarp."

"Good, we'll bring it in tonight. So what's left on your list?"

"We gotta get the clay, linen, linseed oil, and . . . ." Henry paused and looked over at Michael like he wasn't sure what could be said in front of him.

But Greyson clearly didn't care what was said. "And what?"

"The blood, sir."

"Yeah, we're kinda looking forward to that," said James with a grin.

"Get the other stuff today, but don't get the blood just yet. Not till I tell you. It's got to be fresh, so it should be the last thing we get before starting. Oh, and it's got to come from a transgressor, remember, not just from anyone."

"Sure, Dr. Greyson, and we know right where to find him." Henry then turned to Michael. "And perhaps you might like to help us?"

Michael couldn't believe what he was hearing. Why in Hell would Greyson need blood? Wasn't this all about making some big announcement of his discoveries about holy words and the Prague amulet? Besides, the prospect of going with Henry and James to hunt for blood? Christ, who were these two guys? He'd worked alongside them for two years and never had any sense of what monsters they might be. But under the circumstance, what else could he have said?

"Sure, I'll go. I'll do whatever."

"Now the ritual, Ashworth. How's that going?" asked Greyson.

"Uh, okay, good so far." He began rooting through the notes it had taken half the night to compile.

"Think I got everything. I looked at all the stuff you mentioned and we gotta do four things. Prepare for the ritual, form the creature, breathe life into it, and then animate it."

"So tell me what I don't already know."

"Okay, so purification is important. I looked at all the different ways to purify oneself, and it seems like washing will do the job. But I mean you've got to immerse yourself in what they call living water which I think means running water like a stream or a shower, just not a bath."

"I guess I'll have a shower," murmured Greyson. "Next?"

"And you should wear white."

"I've probably got a white shirt around here somewhere."

"And some accounts also say you shouldn't have . . . had sex for seven days before the ritual."

"Hmm," Greyson said as he counted on his fingers. "Okay, so we might have to bend the rules slightly on that one. So what's next?"

"Well, forming the body," continued Ashworth. "The accounts give all sorts of ways of doing this. Shaping a figure from mud on a riverbank, or scratching the shape of a man in sand, or spreading dust on the floor and writing in the dust the name of the thing you want to create. Stuff like that."

"Okay, skip that. I already have Judah Loew's own directions for making the creature."

"You do? I haven't seen—"

"Not your business, kid. So what's next?"

"Then there's breathing life into the body. Now that's where things get complicated. There's a whole range of options. At one end of the scale, there's Eleazar ben Judah, the rabbi from Worms. In his 12th century *Commentary on the Book of Creation*, he wrote that we have to permute—you know, like arrange—combinations of letters from the

Sefer Yetzirah with corresponding letters from the Hebrew alphabet. Then you have to combine all the letters in the Hebrew alphabet with every other letter to create the 221 gates, as he called them. And then you pair up every letter in the alphabet with the four letters from the four-letter name of God, *Yod He Vav He* or Yahweh. And finally, you have to pronounce each of the combinations with every possible vowel sound."

"Crap," muttered Henry.

"Jeez," said James.

Michael glanced up from his notes to discover the look of irritation on Greyson's face. "Okay, so that's probably too complicated."

"You think?" responded Greyson.

"But there's another version where we only have to combine the letters of the Hebrew alphabet with the name of the thing we wish to create. Trouble is, with all the meditating, breathing, and pronunciation techniques this version requires, it could take 36 hours or more to complete."

"Not going to happen," said Greyson. "Look, I told you to give us a ceremony we could actually do."

"Sorry, I was just trying to present the whole picture," Michael replied.

"Then a smaller picture, please," sneered Greyson.

"If you've already got Rabbi Judah Loew's approach, then you probably already know that he read from the Torah as the creature was being formed." Here Michael rooted through his notes and read aloud, "The Lord God formed a man—"

Greyson was obviously growing impatient. "Oh, for fuck sake, sure, right, from *Genesis*, I do know that."

"Then, according to Loew's son, he spoke the secret names of God over the Prague golem. He read the names aloud as he marched around the creature seven times."

"Short story, we absolutely must have Loew's amulet, or we're fucked," muttered Greyson. But then he broke into a broad smile and shouted, "Which we'll have very soon, of that I'm very sure."

"But, sir," Michael said hesitantly, "it is possible Loew's method for generating the sacred names might be really complex as well."

"We'll cross that bridge when we come to it," said Greyson dismissively. He was clearly not interested in hearing about any more complications.

"Okay, then finally, there's activating the body," continued Michael.

"Skip that. I know what to do," said Greyson abruptly. "So to sum up, we can do everything right here in the lab. Have a shower upstairs in the chaplain's washroom. Use Rabbi Loew's secret names of God. Animate the creature by reading the words from *Genesis*. And create the mud coating using Loew's formula."

"You have that too?" Michael asked, taken aback to hear Greyson already had so many of Rabbi Loew's secrets.

How long has Greyson known all this Loew stuff? We might have treated his Titanic *project totally different if he'd shared that information with us months ago.*

"I do indeed," replied Greyson with a broad smile. "That's why I kept telling you idiots, it's the *Titanic*, stupid, because I'd already discovered almost everything I needed to make history."

"But where? I thought we'd seen everything you found at the *Altneuschul*."

"In a monastery outside Prague I found a whole pile of crap written by Rabbi Loew."

"But that's great, really amazing. People will go nuts when you release Rabbi Loew's actual notes written in his own hand. And on top of that, you might even have the amulet with his secret names of God hidden inside. Hell, sir, you're gonna make headlines all over the world. No need for any golem crap, right sir?"

Greyson glared at Ashworth for a moment and then shouted, "We're way past headlines! Of course we need a golem, you idiot! Why the hell else would we be doing all this? I intend to create one motherfucker of a creature and if that's not enough to stop the college and the province in their tracks, then I will want our golem to rip guts out, and crush skulls, and pull the goddamned testicles off—"

Greyson fell silent, breathed deeply, and took a moment to pull himself together. But then he stuck his face right into Michael's and snarled, "Look, you little shit, we're not doing this to impress a bunch of know-nothing academics. And we're not starting with lifeless mud, either. We're starting with a soulless man. That was Loew's real secret. At the center of his golem he stuck some psycho, what he called a soulless man. But this soulless man was under Loew's control, and ours will be under ours, so long as we have the secret names of God. We'll march him into the press briefing for the whole world to see. But if we can't control the creature, well then, fuck it. We'll just let it do whatever the hell it wants, no matter how brutal that might be."

In that instant, Michael realized with horrifying clarity what Greyson's *Titanic* project was really all about. It had never been about making some kind of scholarly breakthrough. Greyson wasn't trying to buy forgiveness for all his scandals and embarrassments, or make up for all his wasted years. He had no intention of giving a lecture about the power of holy words or a poster presentation on his discovery of Rabbi Loew's amulet. No, the only thing Greyson cared about was revenge. Greyson's sole intention was to set loose on his enemies some kind of drug-crazed psychopath encased in mud. That was as far as Greyson's thinking ran, to bring about a bloody rampage of legendary proportions for all the world to witness. And Michael had cast his lot with this madman.

****

Gothall's Rooming House

"Coming," Chris muttered as he rolled out of bed. There followed another round of loud knocks on his door. "I said, I'm coming." His clock read 8 a.m., but after a torturous night, dreaming of starving laborers and burning bodies, of *SS* guards and skeletal children, his head was pleading for more sleep.

Chris opened the door and immediately stumbled backward. "Gillian," he exclaimed.

"Surprise!" Gillian replied, "Like my wig?" she asked as she whipped of her knitted cap. "It's the streetwalker look."

"I . . . I think you look stunning!" He moved back into his room and said, "Come in, come in." As she stepped through the doorway, he added, "God, I want to hold you!"

"So Mallory's still with us, huh?"

"I'm afraid so."

"And your room doesn't look like a bomb just went off, so I guess that means I haven't caught you with your new Canadian girlfriend."

"Sorry. You just missed her," replied Chris with a grin. But then he moved as close to Gillian as he dared and murmured, "You're a miracle."

"Yes, probably," she replied.

Chris teared up. "I'm sorry I wasn't there for you. I was so afraid."

"That I wouldn't pull through or that I'd come after you if I did?"

"No, of course not. No, I was afraid—"

"Oh, Chris, I'm just teasing. I know, or at least I think I know, why you ran away." Then she whispered, "You do still have the Magdalene charm, don't you?"

"Oh yes," he replied, but then backed away. "Wait," he said, "will it be okay if you get excit . . . I mean, after your surgery, can you . . . is it safe for you . . .?"

"I'm not some porcelain doll, you know. In fact, I'm a miracle of modern medicine, practically the bionic woman!"

"So you're sure the doctors would . . . ."

"Give me permission to make love? Oh, well, now you've certainly broken the mood," Gillian said, and turned her back to Chris.

"Gillian, you've got to understand. Part of the reason I ran away from the hospital was because I knew if I stayed, that sooner or later, you'd get hurt trying to help me. I swore I'd never again be the reason you suffered."

"All right, all right, enough of this," snapped Gillian. "I have an idea," she said as she pulled her knitted cap back on. "Why don't we go for a nice walk, talk things over, catch up, and afterward, once we're reacquainted, then maybe we'll both feel more like . . . getting reacquainted."

"That's brilliant," Chris replied. He quickly washed and dressed, and they headed outside.

****

It was a chilly autumn morning. Heavy gray clouds swam across the sky, gulls rose and tumbled on breezes rolling in from the open ocean, and tiny whitecaps raced across the dark waters of the harbor.

As they passed the diner's window, they spotted Jackie and Madelyn diving into heaping breakfasts inside.

Gillian explained how Jackie and Madelyn had tracked Chris down and engineered her escape from the hospital. Chris narrated their stroll along the Halifax waterfront, pointing out sites around the historic harbor: George's Island where Trotsky was said to have been held prisoner following his flight from the Russian Revolution; the Harbor Narrows, where the world's largest man-made blast occurred before the A-bomb leveled much of the city's North End in 1917; Hangman's Beach, where French corpses dangling from its gallows greeted British warships entering the harbor; and McNab's Island, where cholera victims had been quarantined and buried by the hundreds.

"It's an old city," Chris said as they sat down on a dockside bench behind the grand old *Nova Scotian Hotel*. "Lots of sorrowful stories."

"So what's your sorrowful story, Mr. Chandler? I mean, why did you come here?"

"I told you, I didn't want to ever put you in danger again."

"Okay, but was that the only reason? Why didn't you stay long enough to find out if I'd made it through surgery?"

"I guess I was a coward. I was terrified to know the outcome. If you lived, I'd want to stay with you, and then I'd almost certainly put you in danger all over again. And if you died, I'd have blamed myself and probably done something really stupid."

"You didn't leave because I'd become a burden to you?"

"Burden? No, never. You were never a burden. You always lifted me up, made everything possible."

"Okay, then get this straight, Christopher Chandler. In the future, I decide what's a danger to me, not you. I will decide what I do with my life. Don't you ever presume to make decisions for me. And what I've decided is that we have a mission. Our mission is to protect the dead together. *Together*, got it?"

"Got it." They both smiled broadly and resumed their stroll.

"But you still haven't told me why you came to Halifax?" Gillian asked.

"Well, I got this offer of a full scholarship from a religious studies professor here. Apparently, he'd read about what happened in Maine and concluded I was a Mortsafeman. I told him I'm not, but he thinks I have the skills of a Mortsafeman and my skills are what he needs to complete his research."

"But why did you need his scholarship? Nigel Harrow would have paid for your studies or maybe your parents, maybe even Bernard Monsegur? They all love you and would have done anything to help you."

"No, I couldn't ask others. I've been such a screwup until now, I can't ask anyone else to gamble on me until I prove I'm a good bet. And as for Mom and Dad, well, with the cost of Mom's care, I know Dad couldn't afford it. No, I have to do this myself. And the offer of a full scholarship seemed like the answer. I'd get a bachelor's degree and after that, examine my options. Law, business, maybe writing. So I came here. Trouble is, when I arrived, I discovered what a nutcase the professor who offered me the scholarship really is."

Chris explained how the college wanted to get rid of Professor Greyson and how he'd cooked up some crackpot scheme to resurrect his reputation by finding an amulet buried with a victim of the *Titanic* tragedy. Chris explained that Greyson had come to believe that a cantor from Prague had been carrying the amulet to New York when the ship sank and that he'd been buried in Halifax.

"And he wants you to find the grave of this cantor?" asked Gillian. "Does he want you to dig up the cantor as well?"

"I said I would never do that."

"So you find this cantor's grave and then what?"

"Once he knows where the cantor is, Greyson says he'll immediately transfer funds from his endowment account into my college account, and I'll be free of him."

"Then what?"

There it was, the sixty-four thousand dollar question. "Well, then I guess we'll figure that out together."

"All right, so let's go find this cantor," said Gillian.

"Okay, but maybe before we go cantor hunting, perhaps we should . . . ."

"Oh, have a little nap you mean?" asked Gillian. "What a lovely idea."

Jackie and Madelyn were still inside the diner chatting with Mr. and Mrs. Minhas when Chris and Gillian got back, but as soon as they saw Chris and Gillian, they raced outside.

"So? How's it going?" asked Madelyn in a squeaky adolescent fashion.

"Everything's fine," replied Gillian in an equally adolescent manner.

"Actually," said Chris, "Gillian is feeling a little weak after, you know, our walk. I think she could do with a short nap. Would that be okay?"

"Oh, of course," Jackie blurted out. "She must! She has to!"

"Actually, Mr. and Mrs. Minhas have just been telling us about the neighborhood," said Madelyn. Apparently, there's a mall up the street. Maybe we'll do a bit of shopping while Gillian naps."

"How about we meet in the little park by the harbor ferry terminal in, two hours?" Chris suggested.

With that, Jackie and Madelyn started up Duke Street and Chris and Gillian headed to his room.

****

The moment they were inside, Gillian began to undress.

"What, no poetry, no chocolates?" asked Chris with a smile.

"Look, mister, I've been remembering our first time and dreaming of our second for months. In fact, it was the last thing on my mind before I almost departed this earth, so if you know what's good for you, you'll get those clothes off lickety-split."

As her blouse fell to the floor, Chris gasped to see how thin she'd become. "Oh, Gillian," he whispered. "I'm so sorry."

"What? Other girls pay hundreds to lose this kind of weight. All I had to do was get my skull crushed, pass out on a beach, have ground-breaking surgery, and chase my boyfriend across international borders. But if that gets you going, how about this?" and she removed the wig.

Her scalp showed the first signs of a brush cut, and her right temple bore a wicked crescent-shaped scar that curved around her ear.

Chris smiled and replied, "Okay, so the Goth look. I can live with that," and he dropped his undershorts to the floor.

"Yes, it appears you can," purred Gillian, and wrapped her arms around him.

"Remember, you mustn't let go," Chris shouted as the room exploded.

Mallory burst from the swirling mass of smoke and flame like a white-hot projectile from a cannon barrel. She swept around the room, smashing the few sticks of furniture it contained, and then raced at the two lovers like the exploding boiler of an oncoming steam engine. But just as she was about to incinerate the couple, Mallory was suddenly thrown back across the room to crash into its far wall in an explosion of shattered lathe and plaster. Again she raced at the lovers, and again she was brushed aside like dust from old furniture. She howled and screamed and spun about the room, a crazed dervish of rage and pain, sweeping everything before her into a vortex of crackling sparks and cinders.

And all the while, at the very center of Mallory's maelstrom of hate, Chris and Gillian embraced and kissed and felt each other's passion mount. Chris whispered, "you are my miracle," to which Gillian replied, "And don't you forget it."

****

Halifax waterfront

The wind off the water was biting. Chris and Gillian found their friends huddled on a bench in the lee of a shuttered ticket booth advertising summertime boat tours of the harbor.

"The damp cuts right through you," shivered Madelyn.

"Glad you dumped the wig," said Jackie. "Feeling a little better?"

"Yes, much," replied Gillian as she ran her hand across her brush cut.

"Okay, well, Madelyn and I passed a bakery on our walk. It had some great-looking pastries in the window, and it even had a fireplace. So how about we get hot chocolates and cakes, and have a chat."

The three girls started for Duke Street arm in arm, with Chris trailing along behind and grinning like a child. As they were about to cross Lower Water Street, however, Sammy Brook came running down Duke Street shouting Chris's name.

"Mr. Chandler, it's great that I found you," said Sammy, panting heavily. He needed a minute to catch his breath. "Minhas said you'd gone this way."

"What is it?" Chris asked. "What's happened?"

Brook then realized Chris was in the company of others. "Oh, I'm so sorry. I wasn't aware you were with company. Am I interrupting?"

"It's all right, Mr. Brook, these are my friends from Maine. This is Gillian, my girlfriend, and these are her best friends, Madelyn and Jackie." Then to the girls, he said, "This is Mr Brook, Sammy Brook who lives below me and . . . and he trades in antiques."

"I'm so glad you have such lovely friends," Sammy replied as they all shook hands.

"What is it, Mr. Brook? Why were you looking for me?" Chris asked.

"Let me ask you first. Why do you suppose your professor wants this Prague treasure thing?"

"I told you, because anybody interested in Judaica will be blown away if he finds something that actually belonged to the Maharal of Prague."

"So not because he wants to make a golem?"

"A golem!" exclaimed Jackie. "You're trying to make a golem? Is that why you're in Halifax?"

"No, nobody's trying to make a golem. It's just some research project I was helping a prof with."

"And you're sure of this," asked Sammy, "that he's not planning on making a golem? Because if he is, then he . . . and you . . . might be in very great danger."

"Making a golem is an absurd idea. It's not possible." said Chris.

Sammy shook his head. "I'm not so sure."

Chris was taken aback by Sammy's response. "Are you saying you think that Rabbi Loew actually did make a golem?"

Again Sammy shook his head. "I'm not saying that, no. But somebody did. A boy, I heard many stories. If one is pure, one can make life. Our rabbi often said it and everybody in our community believed him."

"So you think Rabbi Loew made a living creature out of mud?"

"No, Rabbi Loew never do that," Sammy replied. "Only his son ever said Rabbi Loew made a golem, and he did that many years after his father had died. But during Rabbi Loew's lifetime, no one said the Maharal ever made a golem."

Chris was confused. "I don't get it, Sammy. I've seen the letter and the notes that Dr. Greyson found at the *Altneuschul*. The Prague rabbi clearly wrote to the 35th Street synagogue in 1912 to say that he was sending the synagogue's greatest treasure to them for safekeeping. If it wasn't the holiest names of God that Rabbi Loew had used to make a golem, then what else could the *Altneuschul's* treasure have been? They wouldn't have sent something in regular use like a Torah or menorah, or anything large enough to be noticed and stolen."

"But that's not what the Rabbi's letter says."

"I don't understand. I've read Greyson's translation of the letter. I know what the rabbi wrote," said Chris.

"That's the problem, the professor's translation. What your professor found at the *Altneuschul* was only part of a longer letter and the fragment doesn't make clear who is actually going to New York."

"But it says, the *Altneuschul's* cantor. The Prague rabbi wrote that *our* cantor will deliver treasure."

"No. The letter says the cantor from *their* synagogue, not *our* synagogue. See?" Sammy pulled the letter from the pocket of his threadbare peacoat, unfolded it, and pointed to the text. "Right there, see? בית הכנסת שלהם. It means *their* synagogue. If it said בית הכנסת שלנו, then it would mean *our* synagogue. Your professor, he missed the ה. It's the letter *He*. The professor did not notice the *He* because the letter got messed up in a fold of the paper."

"And that's serious? What do you think it means?"

"I think it means the treasure you're looking for is from a different synagogue. I think this other synagogue was sending its treasure to New York, and perhaps the guy from the other synagogue stopped in Prague before he set off for America to get help from the *Altneuschul*'s rabbi. After all, the *Altneuschul* was a very important synagogue."

"You're saying the cantor Greyson is looking for is not in fact the cantor from Prague?" Chris was rocked by this sudden twist in the story. "So all along Greyson's been looking for the wrong guy."

"*Aber ja!*"

"But then, where *was* this other cantor from?"

"I'm guessing maybe from another *shtetl* where the rabbi made a golem."

"You don't believe Rabbi Loew made a golem but you think someone else did?"

"There are many stories of holy men who made living creatures, like Rav Oshaia and Rav Hanina who made a calf each evening for their dinner."

"But a rabbi who made a monster to protect his congregation?"

"Well," replied Sammy very calmly, "I think that would be the rabbi of Chelm."

"Chelm?"

"It's in Poland. The Poles have always hated the Jews, so a rabbi there in 1570, Rabbi Eliyahu, he made a golem to frighten away enemies. Unlike the legendary Golem of Prague, there are many first-hand accounts of the Golem of Chelm. And perhaps, centuries later when the Russians tried to take over Poland in 1912, the rabbi in Chelm at that time feared his synagogue was in imminent danger and he had no choice but to send away his greatest treasure. And that could have been the most holy names of God Rabbi Eliyahu had used to animate his creature."

"So we're looking for the cantor from—Oh crap!" Chris exclaimed as the hairs on his arms bristled and the air about him crackled and sparked. "It's Mallory."

"Again?" asked Gillian. "Why?"

"I don't know," Chris shouted as he ran toward the docks. "But I gotta go." The others glanced at each other and raced after him.

They rounded the corner of a derelict warehouse just in time to see Mallory fall on Chris like a bolt of lightning. At the seaward end of a rotten pier, dust and debris engulfed Chris. Rusted spikes shot skyward from the split and twisted deck boards. They flew about for several seconds before being driven back into the decking like bullets from a machine gun. Rusted cables from around the wharf's pilings rose into the air, twisting, flicking, and lashing out like cobras in an Indian market. The oily water beneath the wharf swelled and bubbled. And Mallory screamed and growled, her mouth contorted by hate. She swirled about the dock in a roiling cloud of black smoke, her fiery eyes ringed with ash, her hair a tangle of flames. Then she withdrew into the smoke and fire, rose high above the wharf and the waves, and vanished.

"What was that?" muttered Sammy Brook.

"Mallory," Gillian, Madelyn, and Jackie all said.

Chris walked back to the women, brushing the dust from his clothes. "Something's got her very upset."

"I'm sorry to interrupt, but do you suppose we could get that hot chocolate now?" asked Madelyn. "I'm freezing."

They set off for the pastry shop, this time with Sammy along. Jackie had offered to treat him to a hot chocolate and then taken his arm for the hike up Duke Street. Once they were settled by the fireplace with their plate of pastries and mugs of hot chocolate, Sammy had a chance to say to Chris, "You . . . you have demon."

"Afraid so. Someone put a curse upon me," replied Chris.

"I assume you don't want this demon?"

"No," replied Chris and Gillian in unison.

"Who did this to you?"

"A man from Tana Toraja. That's a region on the island of—"

"I know, Sulawesi," said Sammy.

Somewhat surprised, Chris asked, "You know Toraja?"

"I've lived by this harbor for many years. Sometimes I eat at the Mission to Seamen and I meet crews from many ships. I have an acquaintance from Tana Toraja whose ship visits Halifax every three months. In fact he's here now, at the container pier by the harbor entrance."

Gillian's excitement was obvious. "You don't suppose he'd be familiar with Torajan rituals do you?"

"I could ask."

"That would be so amazing, Mr. Brook. We couldn't thank you enough," gushed Gillian.

"I'd be very happy to help you," replied Sammy with a broad smile. "Forgive me, but I haven't been able to say this to anyone for a very long time. You . . . you are a very lovely young lady."

Gillian blushed and lowered her gaze. "Even with a huge scar and no hair?"

"When you overcome suffering, you become even more beautiful," said Sammy. Gillian smiled and touched the old man's hand.

"Look, I don't mean to interrupt," Jackie said, "but what was all that stuff about our synagogue and their synagogue you guys were discussing earlier? I'm dying with curiosity. Are we on another adventure here?"

"No, just a project for one of my profs," replied Chris. "but I do have a class soon. Gillian, until I get back, maybe you and Sammy could explain about the cantor and the synagogue and the *Titanic*?"

"The *Titanic!*" exclaimed Jackie. "Really? *The* Titanic?"

****

Halifax waterfront

It hadn't taken Martin Dahlman long to locate Chris Chandler's rooming house. By midmorning, he was comfortably settled in a window booth of the bar across the street and nursing a repulsive local beer.

Then suddenly, there he was, the ex-boyfriend Chris Chandler whom he recognized from a newspaper photo the Bemishstock deputy had supplied. And Chandler was with a girl, a curious-looking bitch with a brush cut and a vicious scar around her right ear. "No accounting for taste," Dahlman muttered. He took a last sip of beer, threw cash on the table, and raced out of the bar in pursuit of the pair.

From behind a delivery van, he watched them meet two more girls in a small park by the harbor ferry terminal. A short while later, a very much older man joined them. They were engaged in an animated conversation when the most extraordinary thing happened. Chris Chandler suddenly galloped away and disappeared behind an abandoned warehouse. The others raced after him and Dahlman followed as well.

From the corner of the warehouse, Captain Dahlman got the first glimpse of his daughter Mallory in years, or rather of his deceased daughter's spirit in all its mad and vengeful beauty.

"She's returned," he whispered. "And I brought her back!" He couldn't help but grin as he watched her whirl about like a Valkyrie in a tumult of flashes and flames.

So what did this mean? For one thing, it meant that rat-faced Rudy hadn't completed Mallory's cleansing second death. For another, that Mallory's spirit was obviously fixated on Chandler. Dahlman had already figured out that his daughter died hating Chandler. The boy had to be going crazy with Mallory's bloodthirsty attacks so he was probably doing all he could to rid himself of Mallory's attachment. Which meant . . . that Chandler likely had some of Mallory's remains.

Mallory's remains! In the right hands they could be used to manipulate like a puppet the nightmare that his daughter had become. And of course, by parental right her remains belonged to him. And once they were returned to him, oh what fun he'd have then.

****

Freddy's Diner

"Martin? It's—"

Martin Koyman practically shouted into the phone. "Jackie! Where the hell are you? Everybody's been worried sick about you three!"

"We're fine. I'm calling from a diner here in Halifax."

"Halifax? Like in Canada? Why are you in Canada? Look, you've got to call Mrs. Willard. She's frantic. And Nigel Harrow, I think he's probably got the FBI out hunting for you all by now. What were you thinking, running off with Gillian like that? She's barely out of surgery. She could die!"

Jackie wasn't used to Martin berating her this way. Even as his intern, he'd always treated her more like a colleague than a student. He'd given her every opportunity to shine, promoted her accomplishments, given her bylines when he'd done as much of the work as she. And he was the one who'd demanded she be given her full-time position with the Bangor paper even before she graduated from journalism school. Martin Koyman was a friend and a mentor. No, he was more than that. He was her best friend and the father she'd never had. And she knew how deeply he cared for her, so his anger cut Jackie to the quick.

She began to weep. "I'm so sorry, Martin, I really am," she whimpered between sobs, "but I just had to help Gillian. I saw how brokenhearted she was to discover Chris Chandler had run away, and I really believed his absence might hinder her recovery."

"All right, all right, so stop that blubbering. I take it you've found Chris Chandler?"

"Yes, we have, and Gillian's fine and everything seems okay between her and Chris."

"Oh right, like that's all that really matters. Crap, you women!"

"Martin!" Jackie scolded and managed a small chuckle. "This is not a chick thing, no matter what you might think."

"Oh sure, like any male would have done the same thing. Smuggled a pal out of the hospital right after life-saving surgery. Driven across an international border on a road trip with his buddies in search of a girl who'd left him without explanation."

"Okay, so maybe this is a little romantic, and we will call Mrs. Willard to explain, but right now, I need your help."

"You're not in any trouble, are you? Chandler isn't battling some Canadian grave robbers, is he?"

"No, nothing like that," said Jackie, or at least she didn't think so, even if this business of a missing amulet and the *Titanic* did seem a little bizarre. "But Chris has to solve a puzzle for one of his classes and we're helping him."

"Chandler's in school up there?"

"Yes, college actually, and we're trying to identify a cantor."

"A cantor? Why would Chandler have to identify a cantor?"

"Too long to explain, but I just need you to tell me how I might find the name of a cantor at a synagogue in Poland in the sixteenth century."

"You're kidding."

"Martin, you're the only Jewish person I know, so I thought maybe—"

"And you're a Christian, so would you know how to find the name of a choirmaster in some cathedral in Poland in the sixteenth century?"

"Okay, so this is crazy, I know that, but if we could solve this puzzle, I think there just might be a really cool story in it."

"Oh, good. Just so we're not wasting our time, young lady." The sarcasm in Martin's voice was too obvious to miss.

"Please, Martin."

"Well, I can only think of one way we might possibly be able to do this. Some cantorial school somewhere might have a register of European cantors."

"You know of such a school?" asked Jackie.

"I grew up in New York. I recall the Jewish Theological Seminary there has a school of sacred music and a cantorial school. Dad loved to go to the graduation services. I suppose I could call their library and ask if they have records from the old country or if they know of another school which might."

"Martin, that would be great," said Jackie, and she promptly began sobbing again.

"Okay, okay, so what synagogue are we talking about?"

"Chelm, Poland in 1912."

"Chelm? Really?" replied Martin.

"Why? Do you know Chelm?"

"Anyone familiar with Jewish lore has heard stories about Chelm. Want to hear one?"

"If I must."

"You want to know how Chelm was created? The Lord sent an angel with a sack of foolish souls to be distributed across the entire world, but the angel tripped and spilled them all in the same place, Chelm."

"Not sure that's very funny."

"Oh, and my favorite. So word went around Chelm that the body of a young girl had been discovered. Village elders gathered in the *shul* to figure out how they would deal with the wave of accusations and violence against Jews that was sure to come. Suddenly someone rushed into the *shul* shouting, 'Great news! Great news! The dead girl was Jewish!' "

"That's terrible," exclaimed Jackie. "Anyway, you think maybe the theological seminary might know something about the synagogues in Chelm?"

"It's also a place where the rabbi was said to have made a golem. Wait, Chandler isn't mixed up with someone trying to make a golem, is he?"

"No, no, nothing like that. It's just a school assignment."

"Okay, I'll call the seminary and get back to you later."

"I love you, Martin," whispered Jackie.

"I know. How could you not?" replied Martin with a chuckle.

****

Greyson's Lab

Chris finished class at noon and headed across campus toward Greyson's lair.

Someone called after him, "You're the American, right?"

Chris stopped and looked back. "Excuse me?"

A kid in a letterman jacket and brush cut stepped away from his group of friends and took a few steps toward Chris.

"The guy in the school paper, that's you," he said. "Only I'd heard of you before, what you did in Maine. See, I'm from Orono, and I read all about that Bemishstock business back home and how you stopped that crazy doctor who was robbing graves. So when I read you were here, I was, like, holy shit."

"Well, we've all got to be somewhere," Chris muttered and continued on his way.

"Only," the kid shouted after Chris, "from the stories I read, it seemed like you were a good guy."

"Yeah?"

"Then I don't understand why you'd be helping this guy Greyson. Because everybody says his little buddies, they hurt that girl found in the street. So were you part of that?"

"I don't know what you're talking about."

"Because if you weren't, then you might want to put some distance between yourself and Greyson because come Tuesday, they're shutting his whole operation down. And then his followers are gonna have nothing to protect them . . . and you too, maybe."

Chris spun away and raced to the lab. He bounded down the steps and pounded on the door.

Closing Greyson down for good? So soon? Before my status at the college is resolved? I'll be totally screwed if Greyson is thrown out before he's settled my account.

Again Chris pounded on the door. This time, he heard a faint, "Yes?" from inside.

"It's Chris Chandler. I need to see Dr. Greyson."

The same voice shouted, "Dr. Greyson, it's Chandler. He needs to see you." The door opened just a crack, but Ashworth slipped out and closed the door behind him.

"Christ, Chandler," Ashworth whispered, "do you know what's going on here? Do you know why Greyson wants that amulet you're looking for?"

"For some kind of presentation," Chris said. "Why?" Ashworth's urgency was surprising. Previously, he'd always sounded weird, but this time he sounded totally unhinged.

"Oh shit, you don't know. You gotta stop helping him and get away now!"

Greyson opened the door. "Get away from what?" he asked.

"Nothing, sir," murmured Ashworth as he scurried back inside.

Greyson remained outside and closed the door behind himself. "Sorry, but you can't come in at the moment. We're doing some straightening up, and there's a lot of chemicals around that we haven't . . . anyway, so what have you got for me?"

"Okay, well, first, I think we've had a breakthrough. For one thing, I'm pretty sure why you haven't been able to find your cantor before now."

"Pretty sure? A fat lot of good that does me. I need to know where he is, not why we haven't found him," Greyson said.

"Okay," Chris replied, startled by Greyson's tone, given Chris's news. "We should know where he is by tomorrow."

"You better know, because I need that amulet by tomorrow night at the latest."

"Tomorrow night? Why tomorrow night?"

"Because I need to make a big announcement on Monday morning."

"Is that because they're shutting you down on Tuesday?" Chris had to know now, right this minute. Was this whole mess a lost cause? "And if that's true, then why should I bother finding your cantor's grave if on Tuesday you won't be able to do anything for me?"

Greyson glared, screamed, "Oh, for fuck sake!" and then shouted, "Come!" as he charged up the stairs and started across the quadrangle in the direction of Sinclair Hall.

Greyson was practically running now, with Chris trotting along behind.

"Where are we going?" Chris shouted.

"To pay your goddamned bill!"

They galloped up the stairs and into the admin building, marched down the hall, and entered the offices of Financial Services.

Greyson pounded on the service counter and announced, "I'm here to pay Christopher Chandler's student account in full," to the room full of finance clerks.

One older woman was bold enough to leave her desk and approach Greyson and Chris. "But Professor Greyson, you're too late," she explained. "Your endowment account has already been suspended."

"On whose authority?" Greyson shouted.

"Mine," announced a portly gentleman in a worsted suit. Chris was already familiar enough with college personnel to recognize the vice president of administration.

"Well, you had better unsuspend it," said Greyson, "because as you well know, you have no authority of any kind over the account, not yet anyway."

The vice president took some time to respond, then quietly admitted, "All right, so not yet, no."

Greyson smirked. "Furthermore, I'm here to make an immediate transfer from the endowment account to this student's account to cover all his tuition and living expenses for the next four years. I have the authority to make the transfer and Chandler complies with all the endowment's stipulations regarding my research requirements. He is my designated research assistant and you already have the paperwork to that effect. And he's fully registered at the college and attending all his classes. So with this," Greyson announced as he grabbed a blank check from the service counter and scribbled in all the necessary details, "I am exercising my authority . . . *my authority!* Got that?"

"But next week, Professor Greyson—" began the vice president, turning every shade of red, as he accepted Greyson's check.

"But next week nothing, sir," Greyson barked. "Next week, you will honor this check because, no matter what else transpires, the check has been written in accordance with all the provisions of my appointment in force on this date. So if you attempt to block the transfer, this young man will have every right to sue Cavendish College and you personally, and he will most assuredly win, correct?"

Again, the vice president conceded, "Yes."

"Well then, thank you for your service," said Greyson, "and let me suggest that you now stick the fucking check up your goddamned ass."

"Satisfied?" Greyson shouted as they raced back to the lab.

"Yes," Chris answered.

As Greyson fished the laboratory key from his pocket, he asked, "So will you now deliver the cantor's amulet to me?"

"I will deliver the cantor's location."

Greyson spun about and shrieked, "Don't play word games with me. I want that amulet, and if I say you get it, you get it. By tomorrow night! Or I will march right back to Financial Services Monday morning and rip up that check."

****

Gothall's Rooming House

Chris had no illusions about Greyson's theatrical gesture at the finance office. Come Monday, Greyson's check wouldn't be worth the paper it was written on. Getting Greyson to write it was a Pyrrhic victory and little more. Chances of Chris actually finding the Chelm

280

cantor in the *Titanic* cemetery were as remote as finding roses rooted in blue cheese. All the same, getting Greyson so worked up had been quite satisfying. By Tuesday, Greyson's days at Cavendish College would be over, and most likely, so would his own. A last stab at the bastard who'd lured him into this mess was some compensation, but not much. That said, Chris intended to honor his commitment and at least look for the cantor so he could say to Greyson in all honesty that the cantor and his amulet were categorically not in Halifax.

The trek across the city back to his room was as dreary as ever, but somehow not quite so depressing, nor did the rooming house seem quite so grim. As he stood with his hand on his doorknob, Chris realized why; because Gillian was back in his life. When he unlocked the door and stepped inside, however, he was disappointed to discover only Gillian's friend Madelyn in the room. His first thought was that something had happened to Gillian.

"Is Gillian okay?" he asked.

"And 'hi' to you," replied Madelyn, looking up from a book she was reading.

"Oh, sorry. Hi Madelyn. But where's Gillian? Is she all right?"

"She's fine. She and Jackie went down to the diner to get us some food. We were so hungry after tidying up your room. Boy, whatever you two were up to, you really ticked Mallory off," she said with a grin.

"This is amazing," Chris exclaimed as he registered just how tidy his room now was. All the dust and plaster and broken glass and splintered furniture had been swept away, and a few new pieces of furniture had been brought in to replace the pieces that Mallory had destroyed. Even the damaged wall was now covered with an armoire.

"Like everything?" Madelyn asked. "Your friend, Sammy, got deals on the mirror and the armoire, the armchair and the bedside table from a junk shop down the street. And he fixed your desk chair himself."

"Everything looks amazing. You guys must have worked all afternoon."

"No. Actually, we spent most of the afternoon at the city library. And you won't believe what we found out."

The door opened, and in came Gillian and Jackie carrying an array of paper bags. "Great, you're back," said Gillian as she placed the bags on the desk.

"What an afternoon we've had," said Jackie.

"Has Madelyn told you what we found?" asked Gillian as she handed Chris a burger and dove into one herself.

"Not yet, no."

"Well, your friend Sammy was probably right," said Jackie. "We're pretty sure your cantor originated in Chelm, not Prague."

As they ate, the girls ran through everything they'd discovered in the city library. It turned out that Chelm, from its founding, had had a Jewish community. Indeed, in the eighteenth century, Chelm had become predominantly Jewish and had remained so right up until 1912. The synagogue in Chelm, constructed in 1124, had been one of the oldest in Poland. It was the city's center of Jewish life for 800 years, until Nazi thugs blew it up in 1941 and plowed any evidence of its existence into the ground. But antisemitism hadn't arrived in Chelm with the Nazis.

Throughout Chelm's history, non-Jews had resented and harassed its embattled Jewish community. In 1570, the synagogue's rabbi, Rabbi Eliyahu ben Aharon Yehudah, out of desperation, was said to have created a golem to defend his congregation. Someone who'd actually witnessed the golem wrote an account some years later. It is the earliest known written account of any golem in Europe. He described how the rabbi made the creature out of mud and the blood of a transgressor and brought it to life using the most holy names of God. But at some point the golem injured a Jew or maybe even the rabbi himself, after which the rabbi destroyed the creature and hid the secret names of God he'd used to animate and control the creature. The names were believed to have been locked away in an amulet that the rabbi wore around his neck until he died.

The girls had also learned that the town of Chelm had been part of a Polish territory called the Kolm Eparchy, an ecclesiastical region caught between competing Russian, Polish, and Austrian interests. In the middle of the nineteenth century, the Russian Tsar had embarked on a policy of Russification of the territory. He ordered Russians, many of them in his own employ, to settle in Chelm. There, they were required to press for conversion of the local populace to the Russian Orthodox faith and to harass the local Jews. Hostility toward the Jewish community steadily intensified until Russia officially absorbed the region in 1912.

"What's really important," explained Gillian, "is that the Chelm rabbi in 1912 would have had good reason to send his synagogue's most treasured possessions out of the country, including perhaps Rabbi Eliyahu's amulet."

There was a knock on the door. "Mr. Chandler, is your friend Jackie with you? There's a phone call for her down in the diner."

Jackie dove for the door. "Thanks so much, Mr. Minhas," she said as she dashed past him and down the stairs. "Oh, and the burgers are great!"

"Oh, okay," Minhas replied, as he followed Jackie back down to the diner.

"That'll be Martin," explained Gillian.

"Martin? Martin Koyman?" Chris asked. "Jackie phoned Martin?"

"Yup. And he might have a lead on the cantor's name," replied Madelyn.

"Wow, you guys," Chris exclaimed.

Chris's door was still open when Sammy Brook appeared on the landing.

"Sammy, please come in," said Madelyn. "We asked Sammy to join us for dinner. Here," she said as she handed Sammy a bag. "Mr. Minhas said it's your regular. We added a bag of fries and some pie."

"Thank you. That's very nice of you."

"It's nothing after everything you did for us today," said Gillian.

"Chris, Sammy also has some very exciting news for you," said Madelyn. "Go on, Sammy."

"I found a Torajan priest. My friend! I know him as a ship's cook, but before that it turns out he was a priest. Can you believe it? And he can come tomorrow evening if that's okay. After that his ship is sailing."

Chris was stunned. "Does he know why I need him?"

"I explained about the demon and the curse, and the first thing he said was, 'an incomplete cleansing second death,' so I think he understands."

"Isn't he amazing!" Gillian exclaimed to Chris, and then hugged the old man and kissed his cheek.

"I'll go now," said Sammy who was very obviously blushing, "but thank you for dinner."

"No, please, stay," replied Gillian. "We have so much to tell Chris about Chelm. We may need your help."

"Okay, but I'll get chair from my room." He left and returned a few minutes later with two old kitchen chairs. "I'm fixing them to sell," he explained. "But they're okay to sit on."

Suddenly, from several floors below, they heard Jackie shouting, "Holy crap! Holy crap!" as she came galloping up the stairs.

"What is it?" everyone asked as she raced into the room.

"We have a name! The cantor's name was Dovid Rosenthal, and get this, he went missing in April of 1912!"

Chris's room exploded with laughter and clapping.

"I guess he was quite a wonderful singer," continued Jackie, "and it was said every lady in the congregation had a crush on him because he was also a looker, so when he disappeared, they thought he'd run off with some lady."

"The *Titanic* passenger list?" Gillian asked Chris. "You have the passenger list, don't you?"

Chris jumped off the bed, pulled Greyson's file from his bookbag, and spread its contents across the bedspread. "This is it," he said as he separated the sheets. Several pairs of eyes simultaneously scanned the list.

"No Rosenthal. Crap," Jackie muttered.

"Rosenblum, Rosenblatt, Rosewall, but no Rosenthal," Gillian said.

"Could he have been traveling under an alias?" Chris asked. "I mean, if he was worried about the amulet, or maybe he was trying to get a job, and nobody would hire a Jew?"

"Sammy, do you know what Rosenthal means?" Gillian asked.

"*Aber ja*. It means valley of roses."

"Okay, so any Rosevalleys or Redvalleys or Rosevales?" asked Chris.

"Nope, nothing," Gillian muttered.

"Wait!" Madelyn suddenly burst out. "That name, there. I know it. My grandparents came from Wales, and they only ever spoke Welsh to my parents, so I picked up a bunch of words."

"So?" Jackie asked.

"So, valley in Welsh is *cwm*, and rose is *rhosyn*."

"Okay?" replied Chris.

"Look there," Madelyn said as she pointed to a very curious-looking name.

Gillian struggled to pronounce *Anwylyd Cwmrhosyn*.

"You're telling us Cwmrhosyn means rose valley," Chris said to Madelyn. Then he turned to Sammy and asked, "So do you know what Dovid means?"

"I think like David, it means beloved. Was my father's name."

"Okay, Madelyn, the kicker! Do you know what Anwylyd means?" Chris asked. Everyone was on tenterhooks.

"Much loved!" Madelyn practically screamed.

"Amazing," exclaimed Chris. "The guy took a Welsh name!"

"I guess that might have helped explain away his Polish accent," Jackie mused, "and the Welsh do love to sing."

Chris continued to root through the *Titanic*'s lists of passengers and crew. "Anwylyd Cwmrhosyn is listed on the crew sheet as a tenor. He was hired in Southampton as a lounge singer for First Class passengers, and his stage name was Andy Simrose."

"Okay, so biggest question of all," Jackie said. "Was his body recovered?"

Everyone held their breath as Chris examined the mortuary list. "Oh hell, yes!" he exclaimed, and again the room filled with laughter and clapping.

"And look, there's a note beside his name," continued Chris. "He was one of the corpses the Halifax rabbi figured was Jewish, but the coroner overruled him because the body was wearing some kind of Saint Christopher medal."

"So is our guy buried with the rest of the *Titanic* victims in the Fairview Lawn Cemetery?" asked Jackie.

"No," replied Chris. "I guess because he was wearing a saint's medal, the coroner figured he must have been Catholic. He's buried in the Mount Olivet Catholic Cemetery along with the other seventeen bodies identified as Catholic."

"You don't think maybe this name stuff is just a coincidence?" asked Madelyn. "After all, he was wearing a Saint Christopher medal. Could anybody really mistake a Jewish amulet for a Saint Christopher medal?"

"Jews sometimes wear medals, Kabbalah medals," Sammy responded. "Many Jewish medals have Hebrew words, not pictures. But the picture might have been of an angel, a *mal'akh* that somebody mistook for your Saint Christoph. But a *mal'akh* is not for praying to or for luck. A *Mal'akh* is a messenger . . . so the medal could have been for concealing a message."

"Okay, so the medal might contain these holy names, but I still don't understand why would the cantor have needed a phony name," Jackie asked.

"Well, the Tsar's secret police were madly antisemitic," said Sammy. "They went so far as to concoct the infamous *Protocols of the Elders of Zion* in an attempt to frame the Jewish people for a fictional global conspiracy. Because the Tsar was determined to make Chelm Russian, maybe Cantor Rosenthal was afraid that he'd be followed by Russian agents when he left Chelm."

"And maybe he was," muttered Chris.

****

Freddy's Diner

Captain Dahlman topped his meal off with a delicious piece of apple pie.

"Wonderful fish and chips, some of the best I've had in years," he said to the slight Indian gentleman as he settled the bill.

"Thank you, sir."

"Uh, I noticed a young woman who came in a short while ago to use your phone," Dahlman said as he put away his billfold. "I think I know her."

"Jackie? She's a friend of one of our tenants."

"Jackie, that's right, I remember, from Maine," Dahlman said with a warm smile.

"Yes, from Maine," replied Minhas.

"I think she knew my daughter," Dahlman said.

"You're from Maine too, sir?"

"Hmm," Captain Dahlman replied, "I'll have to say hello if I see her again."

"You will, sir, if you dine with us again," said Minhas as he handed Dahlman his change. "She is visiting one of our tenants."

"Oh really? Then perhaps I will see her tomorrow."

"Should I mention that you'll be looking out for her?"

"No don't bother," said Dahlman. "I'm quite busy, and I'm not sure I'll have time to chat. But thank you anyway."

Oh, but I'll make time for a lot more than talk.

Chapter Twelve

Saturday, September 19

Gothall's Rooming House

Well past midnight, Chris and the girls all climbed into Jackie's Volkswagen Rabbit and set off in search of the Mount Olivet Cemetery. Turned out, it was located in a residential part of town and squeezed between a line of bungalows and a busy highway. The elongated cemetery afforded little cover from prying eyes and was quite brightly lit by the tall lamp standards alongside the thoroughfare. Since he had no intention of opening the cantor's grave, the seclusion of his burial plot was of little concern to Chris. Even so, in the damp and dark, Chris could make out the faint green outline of several specters weeping by the graves. Chris had no doubt the Jewish cantor interred as a Catholic under the name Anwylyd Cwmrhosyn would be among them. The girls dropped Chris back at the rooming house and returned to their hotel. He would love to have had Gillian remain with him, but the prospect of Mallory trashing his room a second time in twenty-four hours dissuaded him.

He'd awakened at sunup but remained in bed reviewing class notes and reading course material. With the cantor's location now known, the pressure was off. Chris had the luxury of doing nothing more than any typical college kid. Indeed, he even planned to do a little sightseeing with Gillian and her friends later that morning.

Just after ten, however, he heard a heavy pounding on the outside door of the rooming house. Someone then began bellowing from three stories below. "Chandler, are you in there? Chandler, get down here!"

Chris pushed his books aside, rolled from the bed, and stuck his head out the window. On the sidewalk below was a disheveled and obviously drunk Professor Greyson. "Chandler, get down here. I need to talk to you. It's urgent!" Then he muttered at a woman walking past, "What you staring at, bitch?"

Chris pulled on trousers and a coat, slipped on his running shoes, and bounded down the stairs, for fear the cops might arrive before he could silence Greyson.

He threw open the outer door and yelled, "Get in here before the police arrest you!"

Greyson stumbled into the tiny foyer, muttering, "What the shit do I care about the police?"

"Why are you here?"

"It's my mother," Greyson said and then burst into tears. He staggered backward and flopped against the bank of mailboxes. "The fucking woman is demanding two hundred thousand dollars on Monday! My own mother, can you believe it? And if she doesn't get it, she's sending cops to throw me out of my house. My own mother!"

"Why are you telling me this?"

Greyson's gaze went blank for the moment. "Oh, hell, that's not why I'm here!" he said as he hammered his head with his fist. The man was a lunatic. "I came because I have to know. Have you found the cantor?"

"Yes, I think we have," replied Chris.

"Oh, that's great, oh thank you! So now I have almost everything I need," gushed Greyson, giggling and rubbing his hands together. "But you must get it tonight. I have to have it tonight!"

"You already told me that, and I told you I'm not digging it up. You've got others to do that for you."

Greyson somehow managed to pull himself away from the wall and stand erect. His face hardened as he shouted, "No, you must get it!"

Chris tried to remain collected as he said, "That was never part of the deal. You asked me to find the cantor, and I have. There's no way I'm defiling anybody's grave."

Greyson stumbled forward and fell against Christopher, pinning him to the opposite wall. "The deal is what I say it is!" he bellowed. The man's clothes reeked of urine and perspiration, and his breath stank of drink and chips and coffee and desperation. Even his greasy hair smelled like rancid butter. Greyson stuck his face right in Chris's and whispered, "Until I get that amulet, you get squat."

Chris shoved the ruin of a man away. Greyson fell backward, struck the mailboxes again, and slid to the floor, where he wet himself.

Struggling to his feet, Greyson screamed, "I need that amulet! I need that amulet." Then he opened the door, stumbled outside, and shouted, "Tonight," as he headed for his car. "Call me when you have it."

Chris knew he should prevent Greyson from driving, but the man was such an appalling ruin that Chris couldn't stomach another second of his company. Instead, he spun about, let the door shut, and started up the stairs.

"You okay?" Sammy asked as Chris passed his door. "I heard the yelling."

"I expect everybody did." Chris paused on the landing. He was furious, as much with himself for getting involved with Greyson as he was with the treacherous ass. Chris needed several deep breaths to slow his racing heart.

"That was the professor who wants the cantor's medal?"

"Yes."

"If you give it to him, what will he give you?"

"Four years of college for free," answered Chris with a slight chuckle and a shake of his head as if to say, what an idiot I was for believing that was ever going to happen.

"And of course, college is what you want?"

Until that moment, Chris had never actually asked himself this one simple question. Did he want to attend college? In his heart of hearts could he truthfully say he desired this new course for his life?

"I . . . I think I do," he replied.

"And if no college? What then?"

Without college what would he do? Would he go back to Maine? There, Gillian would return to university, and he'd be the stupid drop-out boyfriend holding her back. It had been exciting to think they might one day have a life together, but only if he could pull his weight. And he couldn't ask anyone else to pay for his education even if some other college admitted him, which was highly unlikely given his past.

"I guess . . . I guess maybe I'd go out west and look for work."

What an utterly stupid answer that was. No skills, no qualifications except a stack of newspaper articles calling him everything from a murderer to defender of the dead. Yeah, sure, that was bound to get him a job.

"If you need the cantor's medal then we'll get it," said Sammy.

"I won't. I can't. I will not desecrate the cantor's grave."

"But it's not his grave, is it? Wrong name, wrong faith. His resting place has already been desecrated."

"Yes, I know, but . . . ." But what Sammy said was true; the cantor was almost certainly mourning over his remains buried as they were in a grave designated for a non-existent Welsh tenor.

"Well, then I'll get it for you," said Sammy. "I've already done too much evil in my life. What's a little more?"

Chris looked at the old man, this monster, this criminal, this sorrowful old sinner, and hugged him.

"But," said Sammy, "if you give the cantor's medal to this teacher, you won't help him do anything else. No rituals, no making a golem, nothing. If he tries to use the medallion somehow, you will leave immediately. It is very dangerous for someone to mispronounce the names of God. Your life will end. You may not believe what I'm saying, but I do. You hear me?"

"Yes, I hear you."

****

Greyson's Lab

Michael's throat burned with the acrid fumes rising from the bath of lye. He and the brothers had hauled bags of lye and the horse trough down into the cellar in the wee hours of the morning. Then they'd filled the caustic bath with buckets of water from the chapel washroom. Greyson had ordered that the bath be deep enough to completely immerse the victim and corrosive enough to remove all his flesh in fifteen minutes. Michael was seated on the common room couch, his mind a tumult, agonizing over how he'd got into this nightmare and how he might escape.

If he fled, some kid on campus would probably turn him in. The police were sure to charge him with assault or failing to render care to a badly injured Bonnie, if not for her attempted murder. And if the bitch died, then he was going to be in even worse trouble. And what defense would he have? None, because women always got the benefit of the doubt. Who was going to believe him if he tried to prove just how stupid and disloyal she'd been to her friends, how she'd brought the accident upon herself?

On the other hand, if he remained with Greyson, then he'd be implicated in whatever kind of blowup Greyson was planning. But if Greyson was successful in causing the disruption at the press briefing that he intended, then maybe the ensuing chaos might afford him an opportunity to get past the police and slip away into obscurity. Or if he did get swept up in the same police net as Greyson, then he might be able to plead ignorance of the professor's intentions. Maybe he could even claim he'd been one of Greyson's victims, that he'd been forcibly confined by the madman and his two henchmen. After all, the brothers had threatened him, hadn't they?

No, on reflection, running away now didn't seem like Michael's best course. His best shot at getting out of this mess was to do whatever Greyson told him to, and then, when the time came, to turn on Greyson and plead that he too had been the mad professor's victim.

"Open up, you idiots," Greyson shouted as he banged on the laboratory door. Michael galloped up the stairs and unlocked it. Greyson stumbled in just as several oranges splattered on the landing by his feet. "Bastards," Greyson yelled as he slammed the door.

The air in the cellar was pungent with lye, and the many other chemicals and liquids around the room awaiting Greyson's ritual of creation. Comfrey root, Lobelia, chalk, and linseed oil all gave off their distinctive stench. Greyson's own stink cut through them all, however. The man reeked like a walking corpse. Since he'd moved into his office, he'd neither bathed nor brushed his teeth. He'd slept in the same clothes for days, and in the past twenty-four hours, he'd vomited, urinated, and even soiled himself. All he'd consumed for days were pizzas and chips and several bottles of rye. He was swept up in a maelstrom of rage and self-pity. The only question was whether he'd be sane enough to execute his own scheme when the time came.

"He knows where the cantor is," Greyson bellowed, arms stretched upward in victory and fingers forming vees like Nixon departing the White House. "That bastard has figured out where the cantor is buried. We're gonna do this! We're gonna do this!" Greyson muttered as he started down the stairs. The man's balance was so precarious it was a miracle he made it to the bottom.

"So we've got to get organized. We've got to get everything ready."

"But you don't actually have the amulet yet," said Michael.

"Tonight! We're gonna get it tonight. We have to be ready. Henry, James? Now we need the blood and the mud. Ashworth, you gotta mix up the comfrey and the honey and chalk and shit. And me, I've got to get us a soulless man." And with that, Greyson fell to the floor in a dead faint.

The three stood over an insensible Greyson.

"What do we do now?" asked James.

"I guess we let him sleep. And when he wakes, we clean him up," said Henry. "Meantime, we do just what he said."

"Time to get the blood," James said with obvious glee. "Oh yeah!"

****

Laughlin's Pub across the street from Gothall's Rooming House

It had been a torturous day. To hang onto his window seat, Dahlman had had to buy more than one of the dreadful local beers. The bartender had attempted to make conversation, but he was an idiot, so Captain Dahlman discouraged him with a few subtle but cutting remarks. The dolt finally got the message and wandered away, muttering "goddamn Nazi" under his breath.

Midmorning, there'd been a brief but curious scene outside Chandler's building when some drunk pounded on the entrance door and demanded that Chandler come down. The two briefly disappeared inside the building, but then the drunk reappeared and drove away, narrowly missing two pedestrians and a parked truck as his car careened up Duke Street.

Shortly before lunch, the three girls arrived in the dark-haired girl's car, collected Chandler, and drove away. They returned late afternoon and didn't leave the building again until six, when they went to the diner for supper.

While they were eating, Captain Dahlman walked along the harbor front as far as the container pier, and got back to the bar just as it started to rain. This time, his window booth was occupied. First, he tried to shift the couple by saying he'd only been gone for a few minutes. When that didn't work, he asked the bartender to clear the couple out of his booth. He even offered the bartender a few dollars to do so. All he got for his efforts was a quick ejection from the premises.

In a steady drizzle, he watched the foursome finish their meal and return to the rooming house. Dahlman wandered up and down the length of Lower Water Street for an hour or more, sheltering from the rain as best he could and wondering what he was waiting for. And then it happened. Chandler and the old man came out of the building carrying a shovel and an old canvas kit bag, got into the girl's car, and drove away.

Two of the girls also departed the building and headed up Duke Street, leaving the bald girl alone, possibly with his daughter's bones. Dahlman couldn't believe his luck.

He splashed across the street and entered the diner.

"Ah, the gentleman from Maine," said the proprietor. "Oh my, sir, you are wet."

"Walked from my hotel. Stupid of me," Dahlman said as he shook the rain from his coat. "Got caught in this downpour."

"Can we get you some supper, sir?"

"Yes, but I was going to ask my daughter's friend from Maine if she'd care to join me."

"Actually, she and her friends just ate."

As if Dahlman didn't already know that. "Oh dear. Then I wonder if she and her friends would care to join me for dessert. Could I just nip up and invite her while my dinner is being prepared?"

Minhas took Dahlman's order, then led him out of the diner and unlocked the rooming house door. "They're on the fourth floor, sir."

****

From the landing outside Chandler's room, he could hear a young woman inside singing softly to herself. He drew a deep breath and kicked in the door. Its wood, dried to tinder with the years, splintered and flew in pieces across the room. Chandler's girlfriend, seated on the single bed, tried to rise, but Dahlman was upon her before her feet could touch the floor.

Dahlman's hand muffled her screams. "Shut up, or I'll open that wound of yours," he whispered. "Understand?" The girl fell silent, but her eyes were as big as pie plates. With his hand still pressed to her mouth, Dahlman said, "I don't want to hurt you. I've just come to collect something that belongs to me. If I remove my hand, will you be quiet?"

The girl nodded.

"All right." Dahlman removed his hand and climbed off the girl.

She wriggled as far away from him as the tiny bed allowed. "Who are you?" she whimpered.

"I'm Mallory Dahlman's father," he replied as he pulled a seat alongside the bed and sat down. "Your boyfriend killed my daughter. You can imagine that I'm not very happy about that." Then he smiled.

"Chris didn't kill Mallory. She killed herself," protested the girl.

Dahlman could hear the fear in the girl's voice, and it gave him a thrill. This was all so amusing.

"A technicality," he said with a slight chuckle. "Mallory wasn't very bright, I know. But the fact remains she wouldn't have died if it hadn't been for your boyfriend. And I will have my revenge. My dear daughter deserves it. But that's not why I'm here now. I'm here to collect my daughter's remains."

"I don't know what you're talking about," the girl replied.

"Ah, but I'm sure you do," the captain said in a soft, sweet, gentle voice. But then he suddenly leaped from his chair and whacked the girl across the side of the head with his closed fist. Her head flew to one side and smashed against the wall. Then she flopped down on the bed like a rag doll.

Standing over her, he bellowed, "Wake up! Wake up!" He grabbed her arms and hauled her into a sitting position. "You're going to tell me where my daughter's rema—"

The sudden crack across Dahlman's head sent him reeling away from the girl. His vision filled with stars and darkness. Dazed though he was, he still managed to spin around in an attempt to see who or what had struck him. But then his eyes filled with a burning spray, and he screamed. His hands flew to his face as the spray kept coming. In that moment, Dahlman's only instinct was to run.

Through the burning fog that filled his vision, he could just make out two figures between him and the door. With his arms flailing before him, Dahlman struck at anything and everything in his path. He managed to batter both figures aside as he stumbled from the room.

Out on the landing, he threw himself down the stairs, tumbling and tripping, crashing into the walls and cracking the old banister, until he collapsed on the foyer floor. He picked himself up, heaved the metal door open, and staggered out into the night.

The last thing Dahlman heard as he fled the building was a woman's voice screaming, "And don't come back, you bastard."

****

Mount Olivet Cemetery

In the rain and the dark, Chris drove Jackie's car slowly past the cemetery entrance. "Mount Olivet," read the imposing floodlit arch over a padlocked gate. Shortly thereafter, Sammy murmured, "There," as he pointed to a street ahead that exited the main road on the left. "It will take us to a dead-end lane adjacent to the cemetery."

Chris drove slowly through a neighborhood of older, smaller homes until they located the lane. He drove beyond the last house, turned the car around and parked alongside a scrub lot. The nearest lamp standard on the street was a good hundred yards away, so they sat in darkness. From their vantage point, they could see any activity on the street.

Judging by the number of beer cans at the curb, the empty land was a favorite party spot for neighborhood kids. But not tonight. The steady drizzle and plunging temperature had driven all but the homeless and the desperate indoors.

Chris and Sammy waited in silence. Peering through the willows and sumac that had overgrown the empty lot, they could just make out the cemetery's chain-link fence beyond, but it wasn't time yet to break into the cemetery. Instead, they watched cars arrive home, people disembark buses and dash through the rain to their front doors, dogs being walked by hunched-over owners, lights in windows turn on and off, and glowing televisions twinkle through the raindrops until one by one, each home on the street had fallen dark for the night.

Sammy unzipped the kit bag and pulled out knitted caps, heavy gloves, and cheap black plastic rain ponchos. They slipped on their gear and climbed out of the car. Chris grabbed the shovel from the back seat and asked, "Ready?"

"Ready," Sammy replied.

They hacked their way through the empty lot's tangled overgrowth then searched a hundred-foot stretch of the fence for any kind of gap or cut or collapse. They found none but did find a delve in the earth beneath a portion of the fence, which they managed to enlarge and then scramble through.

Sections of the cemetery were brightly lighted by lamp standards along the thoroughfare outside. Others sections, surrounded by overgrown rose bushes and an ancient stand of elms, were plunged in darkness. Chris and Sammy began their search in the shadows.

With tiny penlights the girls had purchased earlier in the day, they moved from one stone to another until Chris came upon the first of the *Titanic* graves. "Here," he whispered to Sammy several graves away. Shortly thereafter, he added, "Found him."

In the dark and the wet, they had to move carefully among the dead for fear of tripping over a marker, or sliding on a slab, or stumbling into a slumped grave. As Chris waited for Sammy, he stepped away from Anwylyd Cwmrhosyn's stone and squinted through the mist. Sure enough, Dovid Rosenthal appeared.

Threads of iridescent green, many tiny fragments, twisted and twirled in the heavy air like minnows in a brook, then drew together, coalescing to form first a torso, then legs, and finally the head of the tortured soul. He was kneeling by the grave of a man who'd never lived, face buried in his hands, body quivering with grief. Time and again, the threads of twinkling green drifted apart, then drew together once again like an image shifting in and out of focus.

"This is our guy?" whispered Sammy.

"Think so," replied Chris.

"I'll do this," Sammy said as he took the shovel from Chris.

"I . . . I can't let you."

"What choice do you have?" Sammy said as he plunged the shovel into the sodden earth. "Maybe someday, we'll put a proper stone on Dovid's grave, and then he can sleep."

Chris swore to himself he'd do just that when he had the chance.

Both men were sodden, shivering. Chris marveled at the strength of the old man as he lifted shovel after shovel of earth from the deepening pit.

"Will you have to expose the entire coffin?" Chris asked.

"There won't be a coffin. It will have rotted away long ago. But that's okay. We only need the guy's head."

As quickly as Sammy lifted mud from the pit, it filled with water. By now, the hole was almost waist-deep, and the water was up to Sammy's knees. Wearing sneakers, the only footwear the old man seemed to own, Chris couldn't imagine how cold he had to be.

Then up came a blade full of rotted wood, and in the next, a rusted hinge and strips of ragged cloth.

"We have him," Sammy murmured.

Suddenly, rising like a rounded white boulder above the surface of the muddy water, the crown of a skull appeared. Some of its hair was still attached, plastered to the head like seaweed to a rock at low tide.

"Dovid, dear God," muttered Chris. "I'm so deeply sorry."

"Now we find the amulet," Sammy said as he crouched down, his butt submerged in the dark water. He drove his hand down into the mud and began rooting about beneath the skull. With all Sammy's scrabbling and sifting, the skull did not move, still bound apparently to the cantor's spine by a few remaining lengths of cartilage. But the eye sockets from time to time appeared above the surface of the water like some nightmarish denizen emerging from its watery dominion in search of prey.

"Hey," someone shouted from beyond the rose bushes, someone out on the main road. Then a dog barked. "What are you guys doing over there at this time of night?"

Chris and Sammy froze, but then Sammy stood up and called back, "Funeral tomorrow. Grave has gotta be dug tonight. The weather sucks."

"Thought you guys used machines nowadays," said the passerby.

"Ground's too wet for a machine."

"Huh. And I thought I had it bad, walking my wife's damned dog on a night like this."

"Wives and dogs. Don't get me started," Sammy replied.

"Hah, too right! Well, hope your dig doesn't take too long. Have a good night."

"You too," Sammy replied and then returned to the noisome task of finding the amulet.

With both hands now, he sloshed about amid Rosenthal's remains, bringing up stones and bones and bits of clothing. He had to pause from time to time to shake the mud and water from his hands and breathe some warmth into them. He grimaced in pain as he flexed and stretched his fingers.

"The man is in his eighties," Chris murmured to himself.

At last, Sammy looked up from the pit and smiled. Then, triumphantly, he drew a muddy chain and a blackened disc from the dark pool and held them up for Chris to see. "I think we have it," he whispered as Chris accepted the prize from Sammy's frozen fingers.

"It's quite heavy," Chris said as Sammy climbed out of the pit. "Brass, I think." Then in the beams of their tiny penlights, Chris wiped some of the filth from the medallion, and they were able to glimpse the figure on its face.

"I think that's Gabriel," said Sammy. "He signifies the tribe of Judah. And on the other side? There, that's Michael, Uriel, and Raphael. They're archangels."

"So not Saint Christopher," said Chris."

Without answering, Sammy muttered, "We've got to go now." The old man was obviously shivering and clearly worse for the time he'd spent crouched in a pit of mud and death.

****

Gothall's Rooming House

"What the hell happened?" Chris gasped when he discovered the shattered door to his room and Gillian curled up in his bed holding a compress to her head. "Who did this?"

"I'm okay, just a little shaken up, that's all," Gillian replied, but then, as Sammy followed Chris into the room, she said, "Oh God, look at you!" The poor man was still shivering and a deathly grey.

Madelyn was seated on one side of Chris's small bed and Jackie on the other. "Here, Sammy, please sit," both girls said simultaneously.

"*Danke, Aber* I am filthy."

"Okay, then let's get you out of those wet things," Jackie said.

"I'll go to my room," Sammy muttered, his voice markedly weak as he started for the door.

"Jackie, could you go with him," Chris whispered. "He doesn't look so great. I'll go get cleaned up too, then you have to tell us what happened here."

"Okay, but Mr. Minhas will be up in a minute. He feels so badly about what happened. He's bringing a new door right away," explained Gillian.

"He feels bad?" Chris asked. "What does this have to do with him?" The anger in his voice was unmistakable.

"Don't get too upset. We'll explain everything once you've washed up," said Madelyn as she changed Gillian's cold compress.

"I'll kill him!" Chris snarled as the girls related their encounter with Captain Dahlman.

Gillian tried to reassure Chris. "I'm okay, really. The sutures are all good, no bleeding at all."

"But inside?" Chris asked. "How can we be sure?"

"I'd be having headaches. The compress is only to keep the swelling down."

Every nightmare Chris ever had now returned with a vengeance. "This is just what I was afraid of. Being around me is—"

Gillian snapped at him. "Being around you is my choice, so don't you dare tell me different."

"But if Dahlman's after Mallory's bones, he's certain to try again."

There was a ferocity in Gillian's look that both thrilled and intimidated Chris. "And we'll be ready for him," she said. "Besides, there's no way he's getting those bones, not after we've finally found a Torajan priest to free us from that wicked daughter of his."

"Okay, so most guys have ex-girlfriends," mused Madelyn, "but it must be so weird having one that barges in every time you're . . . you know . . . together."

Everybody had a good laugh at Madelyn's observation.

"Oh, we almost forgot! How about you guys?" Jackie asked. "You came back looking like drowned rats. How did you make out?"

Chris reached into his pocket and pulled out the medallion. The room filled with whoops and cheers, but after a moment, Jackie said quietly, "I thought it would be bigger."

"I did too," Chris admitted.

"Have you opened it yet?" Gillian asked.

"Trying to." Chris twisted and pried the medallion, scraped dirt from the seam between the two halves, even twisted it wrapped in a damp cloth, but the two parts wouldn't budge. Everyone else had a go, but all without success.

Just then, Mr. Minhas and the bartender from across the street arrived on the landing with a new door, or more correctly, a newish door. It still bore the word, "Exit" in flaking gold paint.

"We'll have this up in a jiffy," said Minhas, "but let me say, Mr. Chandler, how bad I feel for letting that man into the building. I'm such a fool. My friend Robert here, he recognized that man for what he was."

"You know Captain Dahlman?" Chris asked the bartender.

"No, but he'd been hanging around my bar for a couple of days, until I chucked him out. A real snotty sort."

"So Dahlman's been watching us for a while," observed Gillian.

"That's creepy," replied Madelyn.

"Creepy indeed," said Minhas, "but I promise it won't happen again. Anyway, we'll deal with the door and then leave you in peace."

"Mr. Minhas," asked Jackie, "would you have any idea how we might get the two halves of this medallion apart?"

She handed the medallion to Minhas, who turned it over in his hand several times.

"It's very old," he muttered.

"We think so too," explained Chris, "but we want to see inside to be sure."

"Is this what that guy was after?" Minhas asked.

"No. The medallion's for a school project," replied Chris.

"Well, I do have a trick. Boiling water and then ice. Once your door is up, I'll take care of that too."

A half hour later, Chris was back in his room with everyone staring at a scrap of vellum unfolded on his coverlet. The vellum was inscribed with columns of Hebrew letters.

"Is it some sort of code?" asked Gillian.

"No," replied Sammy. "I know what it is. It's *Shem HaMephorash*. It's the seventy-two secret names of God. You see, here are three verses from Genesis in Hebrew. Each verse has seventy-two letters. At first, the letters are written in blocks of three across the page from right to left. But then, like a swimmer in a pool, the direction of the letters turns back on itself and travels across the page from left to right, then back on itself again and then again and again, alternating left to right and right to left until all two hundred twenty-six letters are used up, And there you have the seventy-two names of God."

"Wait! You're telling us everybody already knows these so-called secret names?"

"No. Only rabbis knew *Shem HaMephorash*, and they only used it to cure illness or curse enemies," replied Sammy.

"But if only rabbis knew it, then how do you?" Jackie asked.

"A Russian monk, he told me. His Order believed that the *Shem HaMephorash* was a curse used to kill Christian children or make their cattle sick. It was one of their many sick accusations. In fact, Christian cabbalists had their own version of the *Shem HaMephorash*. They added Yah and El to the Hebrew combinations, and believed that in doing so, they'd derived the names of the seventy-two angels serving God. But in this version here, there are only the Hebrew names. See?"

"I don't get it," muttered Chris. "If so many people already knew this *Shem HaMephorash*, then why would the Chelm rabbi think he needed to conceal it?"

"That's the problem with trying to make a golem. Which secret names of God do you use? Use the wrong ones and the whole exercise could blow up in your face . . . literally. I'm guessing the Chelm rabbi figured out which formulation worked but he didn't want anyone else to know what formula he'd used," Sammy explained. "But now we know."

"And now I have to tell Greyson."

"Before you do, let me repeat," Sammy cautioned, sounding more like an impending storm than a friend, "once you give him the amulet, you must do nothing else. You hear me?" Sammy.

"Sammy's right," said Gillian. "You've done everything Greyson asked. So you're done with him. Right?"

"Of course. I do have to meet Greyson to turn over the amulet, but then, I promise I'll be done with him."

****

Abandoned Interprovincial Bus Terminal

The old interprovincial bus terminal had been shuttered for decades, but the lock on its toilet had been hacked away, and through bureaucratic oversight, its water had never been turned off. As a result, a string of makeshift shelters had sprouted like mold along its crumbling platforms, inside its derelict garage, and around the walls of its ruined waiting room. The corners of the waiting room were the most coveted campsites because they afforded the best view of one's neighbors. No one would be stupid enough to camp in the middle of the room because the shiftless bastards with whom one shared the space could raid one's treasures from any direction.

Henry and James knew the old terminal far too well. It was where they'd killed their dad. After his drinking had cost the family its farm, they'd lived in a cardboard shelter in the northwest corner of the waiting room for six years. Henry had been six and his brother five when they'd moved in. During their time in the terminal, their dad sank from drink to drugs, descended ever deeper into shambling madness, and paid his debts by renting out his children. Any act, any abuse, and any performance, for pennies. All hours of the day or night, the other human wreckage in the terminal might come scratching at their cardboard door, and away their father would send his boys, and off he'd crawl for drugs. This continued until one day, the boys discovered their abusers were, in fact, too devastated to defend themselves. Then the tide had turned.

The boys became the terrors of the terminal, beating their previous oppressors with lengths of rebar pulled from the crumbling walls, breaking limbs, cracking heads, and taking anything of any value. And once they'd amassed enough cash, they'd fled.

A decade later, they'd returned in search of their father and found him asleep in his own waste in an old tourist tent he'd pinched from someone's garbage. That he'd lived so long was extraordinary, but he wasn't to survive much longer.

Years earlier, Professor Greyson had delivered a lecture one afternoon at the provincial reformatory where the boys were being held on charges of assault and theft. "You've got to exorcise your own demons if you are ever to know peace," he'd said. From that moment on, the brothers knew the time would come when they'd take their father's life. The only question was how, and again Professor Greyson provided the answer.

Once released from Reform School, they'd contacted the professor and offered their assistance in any capacity he wished. Coincidentally, he'd had an unconscious young lady to dispose of, and they'd done the deed. After that, Greyson had somehow got them admitted to Cavendish College, and they'd gone on to help him out of several similar situations. One day, Greyson asked how he might reward them, and they'd asked him in turn how they might repay their dad. Greyson went to his cabinet of chemicals, found a jar of something, and told the brothers to force as much of the compound into their dad as they could. The more chemical he consumed, the more suffering he'd endure before he passed away. Their father had taken hours to die, screaming the whole time as his innards dissolved and his sons watched.

And so here they were again, back at the terminal, this time in search of blood. James pulled their truck up to the station platform.

"Shut them lights off," shouted several squatters from their make-shift shelters.

The brothers prowled through the hellish encampment in search of the perfect donor and found him squatting by a tiny fire burning in a juice can.

"Hello, Grandpa," said Henry. The old fellow was no relation, but the term of endearment was likely to befuddle the wizened sod.

"Fuck off," he replied.

"But Grandpa, we've come to take you out to dinner," said James.

"Dinner . . . like meatballs?"

"If that's what you want."

"Do I knows ya?" he asked as the brothers helped him into their truck.

"Of course," Henry replied, "we're Gertrude's boys." Henry chuckled to himself as he pulled the name out of the air.

"Oh, yeah, Gertrude," muttered the old man.

From *Mario's Napoli Food Truck* by the gates to the navy base, the old man ate a plateful of spaghetti and meatballs, drank a half bottle of rye the brothers provided, and fell into a stupor.

When he came to, the old man was bound by duct tape to a kitchen chair wedged in the mudflats by the city's sewage outflow. He had a needle with a long tube stuck in his arm, and his blood was flowing like piss from a barfly into a glass gallon jug labeled *Muscatel*. Good thing it flowed so well since the brothers had two jugs to fill.

"Don't worry about a thing, Grandpa, we're gonna replace all that blood with something much better. You just relax," said Henry. And so when the old man passed away with a full belly of meatballs and rye, he was probably feeling quite contented with his lot.

The boys then carried the old man and his chair to the edge of the incoming tide. On the count of three, they heaved both as far out into the advancing water as they could manage. Then they loaded the gallon jugs of blood into their truck and returned to the mudflats with buckets and a spade to fulfill their final task of the night.

Chapter Thirteen

Sunday, September 20

Halifax waterfront

In the hours before dawn, a fog smelling of rotten sea life rolled into the harbor with the tide and settled over the old city like a filthy blanket on a cart horse. Few lights burned in the buildings below the Citadel, and even fewer folk were about in its puddle-filled streets. But Chris Chandler and Sammy Brook were already up and out the rooming house door.

When Chris telephoned Greyson the previous evening to say he'd found the cantor's amulet, Greyson had insisted in slurred and garbled speech that Chris be in the ferry terminal parking lot at 5 a.m. to surrender the treasure.

Why in Heaven's name had Chris agreed? In fact, why did he keep doing whatever Greyson ordered? It tortured Chris to realize he'd even done the one thing he'd battled so many others to prevent. He'd desecrated a grave, and for what? A chance at a new life? How could he have ever imagined a new life might be possible for him? In a country that was not his, among people who hated him, in a college that wanted him gone? The whole idea of coming to Halifax had been a terrible mistake. It had to end. He had to cut his losses and get as far away from Greyson, Cavendish College, and this city as he could.

But then again, nowhere else had he been offered the chance at a free university education. If anyone had told him back in Bemishstock that he might one day be enrolled in college, he'd have said they were nuts. In the youth detention center, the notion would have seemed incomprehensible. And yet here he was, 24 hours away from a fully-funded university education, and all he had to do was deliver a ridiculous string of letters to a madman.

Chris had tried to dissuade Sammy Brook from accompanying him to the parking lot, but Sammy had insisted. He feared for Christopher because, as he put it, "That *goy* knows nothing of *gefar*. That's how we say menace or peril in Yiddish. In my life I have lived with menace every day. This guy Greyson, he is playing a dangerous game with the holy names. He is *gefar*."

They'd already been waiting for 20 minutes, huddled beneath a decorative cast-iron shelter alongside the ferry parking lot, when Sammy asked, "How long will we wait?" The old man was visibly shivering. Apparently, he had not yet recovered from his ordeal in the graveyard.

"I really wish you'd go back to your room, Sammy," said Chris. "You're going to get sick."

"No, I never get—" Sammy started to say when another voice broke into their conversation.

"You should have listened to the boy, old man," said someone behind them. "But it's too late now."

Chris and Sammy spun about as a figure approached down a narrow alley between two abandoned warehouses. In the heavy shadow between the buildings, Chris could only make out the man's silhouette, but he was clearly pointing a gun at Chris and Sammy.

"You have something that belongs to me, Mr. Chandler. Something close to my heart," said the stranger.

"Captain Dahlman," murmured Chris, the man who'd struck Gillian. Chris's face reddened with rage but he held his anger in check, for the moment anyway. "Mallory's remains," he said. "Sure. I'll be happy to give them to you after we've laid her spirit to rest. You do know her spirit is still among the living."

"Yes, I know, and no, I don't want her spirit laid to rest. I want her bones and her spirit returned to me just as they are."

"But it's your fault she's trapped here," said Chris. "Your son Rudy showed me the letters. You called her back from the dead."

"I was drunk. And Rudy was never my son."

Chris already knew from what Mallory had told him that her father was a perverted monster. Still, Chris would never have believed that any father could deny his daughter her final rest. "You *want* Mallory to remain a specter? Two years ago, you begged your wife to release Mallory's spirit by completing her second cleansing death."

"Again, drunk. My daughter wasn't much use to me alive, except as a means of torturing my wife. Then I saw her attack you and I realized how useful she could be dead. A vengeful demon at my disposal? I can't imagine why you'd want to let her rest. What an asset she could be."

"You've got it wrong. Her spirit won't take orders from anyone, not without this." Chris drew from his shirt the pendant Rose DuCalice had crafted from a sliver of the Magdalene's finger bone, the pendant that somehow bestowed a sphere of protection from Mallory's wrath.

"What is it?" Dahlman murmured as he stepped from the shadows. The captain was a wreck; his eyes were red and swollen, and his clothes were dripping wet. Judging by his condition, he'd spent the entire night outside in the rain, likely watching Chris's rooming house.

At that moment, as Chris saw Dahlman in all his pathetic misery, the realization swept over him just how much he loathed this man. Not only had Dahlman injured Gillian, but he was the root cause of every nightmare Chris had endured over the past two years. All the attacks, the battles, the prison, the abuse in the press, and the condemnation by an entire town—it all stemmed from this man. Dahlman had deliberately and systematically twisted his daughter into a hateful, selfish, cruel terror merely to torment his wife. And Mallory, in turn, had set Chris on a downward tumble that had brought him to this moment. He could not let it pass.

"See there," Chris said as he turned the pendant over in his hand and ran his fingertip across the delicate inscription, "its blessing is its power. It's the reason why I'm not harmed by her attacks."

Dahlman, his eyes glued to the pendant, moved closer still. And that's when Chris sprang.

Two strides and Chris had him, but just as he grasped Dahlman's arm, the gun fired. The bullet grazed Chris's head and the blow spun him about. But with all the fury he'd nursed since learning of Gillian's injury, he still managed to seize the revolver, tear it from the captain's grasp, and toss it away. Then he wrapped both arms around Dahlman and pulled him to his chest. They both tumbled to the asphalt with the force of Chris's attack. Dahlman's head struck the pavement with an audible crack. He lay stunned and breathless for a moment, giving Chris the chance to roll away, and that's when the air above Dahlman erupted.

Mallory's face, a portrait of vengeful madness, burst from a tunnel of fire. Amidst the whirlwind of flame and smoke, she thrashed about, flinging sparks in every direction and howling like a banshee. But then she glimpsed her father sprawled on the pavement and dipped down to within inches of his face. Her glare betrayed confusion and then, for just an instant, recognition, and with that, she took hold of her father. She hauled him up into the air and embraced him, first tenderly, then with ever greater force until his screams became nothing more than a blood-filled gurgle. Mallory released her embrace but then grasped Dahlman by the hair and hauled him even higher into the air before throwing him face-first down onto the asphalt. There she grasped his legs and dragged him a dozen feet across the cracked and crumbling ground, scraping away strips of flesh from his face. She then flipped him over and fell upon him like a pile driver. Breath filled with bloody sputum flew from his mouth.

In a curious twist, Mallory gave Chris a momentary look of confusion, even tenderness, as she lifted her father from the pavement and threw him like a rag doll at Chris's feet, like a macabre gift, an offering. She swept forward to stare into Chris's eyes. But she wasn't done with her father quite yet. She looked away from Chris and into her father's face. Dahlman stared back in utter terror. Mallory's hand emerged from the mass of flame which enveloped her to gently touch his cheek, but as her fingers burned like sticks of kindling, she grasped his entire face and roasted its shredded flesh. Finally she drew back, rose slowly into the sky, glanced once again at Chris, and disappeared.

An approaching rumble echoed down the empty streets and foretold Greyson's arrival. The old Porsche pulled into the parking lot, and Greyson climbed out. He looked a lot cleaner and more sober than the previous evening. The coming day, a mere brushstroke of gray across the horizon, had made its first appearance, and in its watery light, Greyson must have spotted the body sprawled at Chris's feet. Likely fearful for his amulet, he raced across the parking lot, shouting, "What's happened? You've still got it, right?"

"Yes," said Chris. But the adrenaline of Mallory's attack had waned, and the pain from his head wound swept over him. Blood flowed over his face like a theater curtain dropping at the end of a performance, and Chris sagged to the ground in a dead faint.

As Sammy knelt beside Chris, Greyson asked without a hint of genuine concern, "Is the kid dead?" He then stepped over Chris to have a look at Dahlman. "Hey, I think I know this guy. Kind of hard to be sure with his face fried like it is, but I think he came by the lab looking for Chandler. Christ, you guys really did a number on him."

"He's the demon's father, and she ripped him to pieces," Sammy replied.

"Oh yeah, that Torajan bitch," Greyson said as he poked and prodded the savaged Dahlman. "From the mess she's made of him, she must really hold a grudge."

Dahlman groaned. His eyes opened as pink foam trickled from the side of his mouth.

"Shit, he's still alive," Greyson said in amazement. Dahlman was obviously deep in shock. His eyes were empty and unresponsive.

"He's perfect," Greyson muttered to himself, "my soulless man," and then said aloud to Sammy, "Look, you've got to take care of Chandler, so let me look after this guy."

Chris's eyes opened, and he murmured, "What happened?" He tried to wipe the blood from his face, but it continued to flow. He felt nauseous and dizzy. He tried to get up all the same.

"Chandler, you're hurt bad," said Greyson. "That head wound is a real gusher. You need help. And we should all get out of here before the cops show up. So let me have the amulet, and we can leave."

Chris pulled the cantor's amulet from his pants pocket and passed it to Greyson. But then he sagged to his knees a second time.

As Greyson examined the medallion, Sammy said, "The medallion, it's very dangerous."

"Don't need any advice, old man," replied Greyson, pocketing the treasure. Then he dragged the unconscious Dahlman across the parking lot to his car, and stuffed him into the back seat. "Get Chandler patched up," he shouted back to Sammy. "And tell him to come to the lab tonight."

"He won't come," Sammy called back.

"Yes he will," snarled Greyson. "He'll do exactly what I tell him to or he gets nothing. Besides, he won't want to miss our performance.

We're going to make history. But I have to go. I've got to see my pharmacist."

Greyson slammed the car door and drove off, the rusted Porsche echoing like an old tractor as it rumbled away through the wakening streets.

****

Gothall's Rooming House

With the rising sun, the fog dissipated, but the heavy overcast remained.

From some boards on the wharf, Sammy fashioned a makeshift crutch to enable Chris to hobble back to the rooming house. By mid-morning, when the girls arrived, Chris had already cleaned and bandaged his wound. The bullet had sliced open his scalp but not damaged his skull. The wound bled like a water fountain, however, and Chris had to change his own dressing every half hour.

"You've got to use Rose's salve, please," Gillian pleaded. "You're losing far too much blood. Please, use the salve!"

Chris was propped up in bed with Gillian seated by his side. Madelyn and Jackie shared an armchair, and Sammy sat at Chris's desk. The remnants of their breakfast bagels were spread out before him.

"There's so little of the salve left. I'm saving it for a real emergency. I'm sure the bleeding will stop soon. I just need to rest."

"Why can't you go to hospital?" Sammy asked.

"Mallory," replied Jackie. "If anybody touches Chris, Mallory will tear them to pieces."

"Speaking of hospitals, after you gave Greyson the amulet," said Madelyn, "he took Captain Dahlman away?"

Chris nodded.

"I wonder how he explained Dahlman's injuries at the hospital."

"Probably said he found a stranger unconscious in a parking lot. That is the truth after all," replied Chris.

"Boy, I wish I'd hit him harder when I had the chance," said Jackie. "I only hope we've seen the last of him."

"And Greyson," said Gillian. "But you're done with him now, right? You've done everything he asked, so you'll be getting your scholarship, correct?"

"I'll know for sure Monday," Chris muttered as his eyes closed and his head inclined to the side.

"I expect it's the shock," whispered Jackie. "I think it's best if we let him sleep."

Sammy said softly, "Greyson isn't done with Chris. He wants Chris to go to his lab tonight, or Chris will get nothing."

"I'm not going," muttered Chris without opening his eyes.

"Good," said Sammy. "It would be far too dangerous to go."

"Dangerous? How?" asked Gillian.

Chris opened his eyes, took Gillian's hand, and said, "Sammy thinks Greyson is going to attempt a Kabbalistic ritual, and if it goes wrong, something bad might happen. But nothing will happen. Nothing can. Greyson's nuts, and his ritual is all nonsense."

"I'll go for you instead," said Sammy.

"Neither of you is going. Get that?" said Gillian very firmly.

"I think I'd better sleep," muttered Chris as his eyes closed once again.

"And I'll go to see my Torajan friend to find out when he'll be here," said Sammy as he left the room.

****

Greyson's Lab

Greyson was so excited he thought his heart might burst. Under way at last! Everything, absolutely everything he needed, was right here in the lab. The secret names of God, the drugs, the mud, the blood, and the soulless man! Nothing was going to stop him now. Admittedly, with his delicate stomach, he was finding the smells of the mud and the lye nauseating, and he might have to slip out at some point to get a breath of fresh air. But nothing else was going to prevent him from exacting the most exquisite revenge at the Education Minister's press briefing the following day. And after the spectacle Greyson had planned, his name would once again be on lips the world over. Never again would anyone ever doubt his genius.

With the three remaining greylings gathered round the common room table, he ran over the steps they'd follow in crafting their golem, the steps Rabbi Loew had laid out in his letter.

"Professor Greyson," asked Ashworth in that irksome wounded-toddler voice of his, "I don't understand why I had to review all the other descriptions of the golem ritual when you already knew how Rabbi Loew did it?"

"Because I wanted to make sure Loew's description wasn't too far off the other accounts. The fact is, I'm not certain the description I found among Loew's letters and notes was actually written by Loew. It might have been written by some other rabbi. That's what Chandler says anyway. But who the hell cares? Whoever wrote it had obviously made a golem. That's all that matters."

"Okay, but just one more question," said Ashworth.

Will this kid never stop?

"You said you ordered Chandler to join us? Why do we need him?"

Greyson gave Ashworth a look of condescension and replied with a question of his own. "If you had a pet python, you'd feed it live mice, right? Well, when we've finished our work, we'll have our python . . . and Chandler will be our mouse."

Judging by the smile on Ashworth's face, he found this response satisfactory.

"Now we begin," Greyson announced, his arms extended like a Pope blessing the crowds in St. Peter's Square. "Henry, James, lift our friend onto the table." The common room table had been cleared of cans, wrappers, and pizza boxes and given a quick wipe. "Then stir the bath to ensure the lye is fully dissolved while Ashworth and I prepare our soulless man for immersion."

They'd concealed Dahlman in a blanket and carried him into the lab while the college congregation in the chapel upstairs celebrated its first Sunday service of the new academic year. Still unconscious from Mallory's attack, Dahlman had been dumped on the cellar floor. There he'd been left to moan and shift about in agony for more than an hour while Greyson and his three assistants prepared for the ritual.

To purify themselves, they'd washed in a bucket of cold water and put on white shirts. "Good enough," Greyson had said, "if you consider how filthy anyone doing this in the fifteenth century would have been."

With Dahlman laid out on the table, Greyson ordered Ashworth to pry Dahlman's mouth open and jam a piece of wood between his teeth. Greyson then poured half the bottle of d-Tubocurarine his pharmacist had supplied down Dahlman's throat. Then Greyson removed the wood and held Dahlman's jaw shut. "You'll be thankful for this in a minute," he whispered into Dahlman's ear. "It'll take away your current pain and all the pain that's still to come."

Through the lab's stone ceiling, they could just make out the chapel choir singing Thomas Tallis's *Spem in Alium*. "Love this piece," murmured Greyson as he released Dahlman's chin. "So now we clean him up," Greyson said to Ashworth.

Together they pulled Dahlman's sodden clothes from his battered body. Ashworth gasped as Dahlman's bruises and lacerations emerged. "How'd he get this way?" he asked.

"You wouldn't believe me if I told you," Greyson replied.

With the same water in which they'd washed themselves, they wiped down Dahlman's body. Greyson then took a kitchen knife from a tray of cutlery nearby and drove it up to the hilt into Dahlman's leg. He displayed no reaction. "Good, good," muttered Greyson. "I think he's ready for the bath."

Henry and James, wearing heavy rubber gloves, lifted Dahlman from the table and lowered him into the bath of lye.

"No more than fifteen minutes," said Greyson.

Dahlman's flesh began to lift and shift as though living things were moving about beneath his skin. The liquid in the bath clouded as Dahlman's fatty tissue liquified. Whole chunks of dermis and epidermis detached from his body, first to float and then to sink down into the bath's increasingly horrid stew. The epidermis contains the body's tough connective tissue, hair follicles, and sweat glands. In contrast, the deeper subcutaneous tissue is composed of fat and fibrous material, and all were rapidly breaking down. Like rotten vegetables and putrid meat, the smell overwhelmed even the stink of the buckets of harbor mud.

As Dahlman's flesh fell away, his muscles, sinews, and tendons began to appear and then his organs.

"*Écorché,*" muttered Greyson.

"What?" Ashworth said.

"*Écorché*. It means a representation or a figure showing the body's musculature without skin. That's what we're seeing. That's what we want."

321

"Why isn't he screaming?" asked Henry. "You'd think he'd be screaming."

Greyson couldn't help but note the disappointment in Henry's question.

"Because we fed him enough drugs to knock out an elephant."

As the last chunks of skin came away from Dahlman's body, Henry and James prepared to lift him from the roiling soup of flesh and fat.

"Before you do that, we've got to remove the skin from the head as well. Here," Greyson said as he drew a roll of adhesive tape from his pocket, "use this to seal his eyes."

James tore off several strips and pressed them over Dahlman's eyelids.

"Good, now push him under," said Greyson. Dahlman's nose and ears, clumps of his hair and scalp, and both cheeks slithered off his face and sank into the repugnant soup. "Okay, let him rise. That's good," he muttered as Dahlman's lips peeled away. Then his teeth began falling out.

"Maybe we should have sealed his mouth," muttered Henry as he watched Dahlman's tongue float out of his mouth.

"As long as he can still draw breath, it doesn't matter that his tongue and teeth are gone. Right, so now you can remove him."

Henry and James lifted the monstrosity from the bath, being careful not to jostle any of Dahlman's organs from their proper position.

"Okay, now back onto the table. We have to rinse him and pat him dry but don't dislodge any tendons or veins or organs or muscle. Otherwise, the whole mess of him might slither to the floor, and we'd never get him back together."

As Greyson's three assistants rinsed and dried Dahlman, Greyson kneaded the mixture of comfrey root, lobelia, and honey that Ashworth had previously prepared.

"All right, now we have to work quickly. I'm going to apply this coating. It's like an artificial skin, and while I'm applying it, Ashworth, you read over and over again the passage that I copied out."

Ashworth droned away as Greyson layered on the artificial skin.

"The Lord God formed a man from the dust of the earth, and He blew into his nostrils the breath of life, and the man became a living being."

"I don't get it, sir," said Henry. "Why did we have to strip off the guy's old flesh if you just have to give him a new one?"

"This layer's like double-sided tape. It's so the final layer of mud and blood and clay will bind to the creature's muscles and move with him like his own skin, except the new flesh will not be under his control. It'll be under ours."

As Greyson cleared the artificial skin from Dahlman's nostrils, he heard air whistling through. "He's coming round," muttered Greyson. And when he wiped the comfrey mixture from Dahlman's sockets, sure enough, the eyes were filled with sheer terror, not to mention agony.

"A little uncomfortable, are we?" Greyson asked with a chuckle.

****

Gothall's Rooming House

Chris woke to the sound of Gillian's voice.

"I think he's running a fever. Don't you think he's running a fever?" she asked softly. "I really think he needs a tetanus shot and some antibiotics. Maybe I should run out and get some kind of antibiotic?"

Chris sensed Gillian's presence close by, seated on the bed alongside him, in fact. When he opened his eyes, Gillian was turned away from him, chatting quietly with her friends.

"Hi," he said, and Gillian spun round, concern written all over her face.

"Oh, you're back," she said with a tender smile.

"Was I asleep long?"

"Hours," Jackie replied. "Most of the day, in fact. We even had enough time to visit the *Titanic* graves while you were asleep."

"That place is so sad," added Madelyn.

"A doctor should see your wound," said Gillian. "You can't put it off. And the dressing has to be changed. It's been soaked with blood for hours, but we couldn't touch you."

He returned her look of concern with a tender smile of his own and said, "Okay, I'll change it," but then, as he glanced at Madelyn and Jackie, it suddenly struck him that Sammy wasn't present. "Where's Sammy?"

"He went looking for his Torajan friend just after you fell asleep, and he hasn't come back yet," replied Gillian.

"You don't suppose his friend has already sailed?" asked Madelyn.

There was a knock on the door. After Dahlman's attack, everyone was on high alert for trouble.

"Mr. Minhas?" Chris called out.

"No, it's Detective Sergeant Bain with the police. Minhas let me in the building. I need to speak with Chris Chandler."

Chris nodded at Jackie. She hopped out of the armchair and unlocked the door. "Sergeant Bain. Come in."

As soon as Bain saw Chris propped up in his bed with a blood-soaked dressing covering much of his scalp and several streaks of dried blood across his face, Bain blurted out, "What happened to you?"

"It's . . . it's nothing. I, uh, fell," replied Chris.

"Doesn't look like nothing. You need a tetanus shot?"

"I will," he replied with a smile in Gillian's direction. "What can I do for you, Sergeant?"

Madelyn surrendered Chris's desk chair to the police officer and moved to the far side of the room.

"Thanks," Bain said, as he slid the chair up to Chris's bed.

"Well, to start with, you can give me some straight answers. Look, as I told you before, I've checked you out. It seems you're some kind of hero to a lot of people. I gather you helped out an entire town in Vermont, so I don't understand why you can't help me."

"I want to."

"Okay, then, so fill in the blanks for me. I can't figure out what's been going on since you arrived. It's been like that movie *Ghostbusters*. Really weird stuff's happening everywhere."

Bain was obviously a good guy, tired maybe after decades of dealing with scum, bastards, dirtbags, and victims, but a good guy all the same. His timing couldn't have been worse, however. There was nothing Chris could say that wouldn't totally screw things up. Tell Bain about Greyson's antics, and he could kiss his scholarship goodbye. Tell Bain about Mallory and Captain Dahlman, and he'd be in the loony bin by dawn. Tell him about finding the amulet in the Catholic cemetery, and he'd be in jail by dark. What choice did he have but to stonewall?

"I'm not sure what you mean, Sergeant."

Bain practically exploded, his frustration and confusion on full display.

"Right before you get here, a college president bursts into flames, then the grave of some *Titanic* victim gets dug up by a bunch of Nazis, a guy gets beaten by a demon he claims. Then two guys almost get killed in an alley right beside this rooming house, and while they're too badly hurt to make much sense, they keep muttering about some whacked-out superman. Then a badly injured girl gets dumped in the street like garbage. Then another *Titanic* grave gets dug up. And just this morning, a couple of people who live in an apartment building near the ferry terminal report they seen some sort of flaming creature attack some homeless guys."

Chris attempted to interrupt Bain's tirade. "Sergeant, I'm sorry, but I don't see how I can be—" But Bain was not to be silenced.

"And on top of everything else, when the tide goes out this morning, we find an old man duct-taped to a chair and stuck in the mud. And get this. All his blood had been drained from him. What the hell is going on? None of these cases is normal. They're not your regular muggings or overdoses or vandalism crap. They've gotta be connected somehow. And I know you know more than you're letting on. I'm not saying you're guilty of anything, but you gotta know something because they're all so goddamned weird, and weird is what you do. Everybody said that. For Christ's sake, Chandler, some paper in Maine called you the defender of the dead! You gotta know something!"

Chris's heart almost froze. His eyes opened wide with fear. He shifted forward on the bed and blurted out, "Wait, what did you just say? Did you say that you found a guy drained of his blood?"

"Yeah, and I gotta tell you, it really shook me because I knew the guy," said Bain. For an instant, Bain's face tightened with grief. "Helpless old man, living rough ever since his wife died. Never hurt a fly."

What had the girls read about the Chelm rabbi? That he'd made his golem from mud and blood?

"Oh hell, Gillian," he whispered. "I think maybe Greyson is doing it."

"Who the hell is doing what?" Bain asked angrily.

At first, Chris hesitated, but then it just came out.

"Dr. Greyson, I really believed—or maybe I just wanted to believe—that he only intended to announce his discoveries. But now I think Sammy's right. Greyson plans to make a golem."

Bain looked utterly exasperated. "What are you talking about? What does any of this have to do with golans, for Christ's sake?"

"Golems," Chris corrected. "Professor Greyson is trying to make a golem. The idea comes from Jewish folklore. There's a famous story from the 16th century. This rabbi in Poland was believed to have made a monster from mud and blood to protect his people."

"And you think Greyson is trying to make his own monster?"

"Greyson got me to come to Halifax because he needed help in finding a lost medallion that he thought might contain a list of secret words, words the Polish rabbi used to bring his creature to life."

"And you found these words?"

"Yes."

"And you gave them to Greyson," Bain said as he slumped back in his chair. "So that's it?" he asked in apparent disgust. "An old man gets drained of blood, and you give some special words to Greyson, and from those two events, you figure he's making this mud monster?"

"That, and he's been experimenting with ancient texts and invoking demons for months, and he's going nuts over the college's plans to shut him down."

Even to Chris, the whole business sounded totally crazy. The incredulity on Bain's face was hard to miss. "Look, I don't for a moment believe Greyson will succeed in making a monster," said Chris. "But I do believe he's crazy enough to try, and if he is trying, then he needs blood, a lot of it. He might have killed the guy you found this morning, and he might also be planning to kill someone else."

"Like who?" asked Bain.

"Like a Captain Dahlman," replied Chris.

"I've heard that name."

Chris knew he'd already said too much; that was obvious from the look of irritation on Bain's face. But it was all going to come out anyway. Bain was going to have to hear everything, Chris was sick and tired of doing what he knew was wrong just for some stupid scholarship. He wasn't going to sit by and let Greyson do whatever his mad scheme required.

"We've got to stop him," Chris announced.

"Why?" Gillian asked. She looked incredulous. "It's Mallory's father. If anyone ever deserved to die . . . ."

"Look, I hate this too, all of it. It's bad enough we desecrated a grave for Greyson," said Chris.

"What?" exclaimed Bain. "You? It was you at Mount Olivet?"

Chris ignored him. "But I can't let Greyson murder Dahlman."

"For heaven's sake, Chris," said Gillian, "you let Mallory murder Balzer back in Bemishstock."

"Yes, but Balzer had killed his own son. And if anyone has a right to murder her father, it's Mallory. But Greyson doesn't have the right to do it, not for some crackpot scheme to create a golem."

"Who is this Mallory?" shouted Bain in utter confusion. "And she sure as hell doesn't have the right to murder anyone!" Bain jumped to his feet. "If I don't get some answers right now," he bellowed, "I'm gonna call in a truckload of cops and have the lot of you arrested!"

Sammy Brook walked through the door. "Hello," he said. "Is there a problem?"

"You were right," Chris said immediately. "Greyson's trying to make a golem. We have to go to his lab."

"You're not going anywhere," Gillian said angrily. "Aren't you listening to me?"

"Damn right, you're not going nowhere. No one is!" shouted Bain, pulling handcuffs from the pocket of his overcoat.

Again, Chris completely ignored him. "Gillian, please, we have to stop Greyson. The guy's nuts. Heaven knows how many people he plans to hurt."

Sammy tried to interject. "But Mr. Chandler, my Torajan friend, he's on his way here right now. He's sailing tonight. You have to see him now or you'll miss him."

"There, see?" said Gillian. "You can't go. This is your only chance, no our only chance, to break free from Mallory."

In that moment, Dahlman's words came back to Chris, 'how useful she might now be . . . a vengeful demon at my disposal . . . can't imagine why you'd want to let her rest. What an asset she could be.'

"Maybe I don't want to be free of her," Chris said very quietly, almost ashamed to admit what he was thinking. "Maybe she's like a blessing, a superpower. I could do a lot of good with her still around."

"For God's sake!" Bain shouted. "Who is this Mallory? Would somebody please tell me what's going on?"

Gillian appeared horrified by Chris's remark. "You don't really consider Mallory a superpower, do you? Even if she keeps us . . .?" Gillian was tearing up. "When you were sleeping, I thought you might have a fever, but I couldn't even touch you, never mind put a cool cloth on your forehead."

Chris was gutted by Gillian's reaction.

"I'll go to Greyson's lab," Sammy said. "Not you."

"No," Chris shouted. He was confused, bewildered. The right course was a mystery to him. But he couldn't let Sammy go in his place. "You said yourself, it's too dangerous."

"*Red' keinen Topfen!*" bellowed Sammy. "You're talking rubbish! You have beautiful girlfriend. You have chance to be free from your demon. And besides, you're far too weak to stop anybody."

"But I can't let you get hurt," Chris pleaded.

Sammy's tone changed abruptly. The quarryman, the convicted murderer, the vicious *kapo* re-emerged. Sammy rose to his full height of six foot four and marched over to Chris's bed. "*Das ist Wohnsinn!* That's crazy! You couldn't even stop an old man," he roared. Then he grabbed Chris by his shoulders and shouted in his face, "So shut up, little boy!"

Of course, Mallory struck. The room was suddenly ablaze with light and smoke; winds howled, sending books and clothes and toiletries flying in all directions. The girls dove for the floor as furniture spun and tumbled and splintered. Bain was thrown backward against the far wall where he slumped to the floor. Mallory then fell on Sammy, crushing him like an old car in a junkyard. He moaned in agony as the air was pressed from his chest.

Chris rolled from his bed and fell atop Sammy. There he struggled to pull the Magdalene pendant from over his head and to slip it over Sammy's.

In that instant, Mallory drew back, seemingly confused, but then she grasped Chris by the hair, dragged him from atop Sammy, and hauled him up into the air. There Chris dangled, his face directly before hers, his eyes pinched closed against the excruciating pain from his head wound. Blood flowed like water over Niagara Falls. For an instant, Mallory stared with unmitigated hatred at this boy whom she'd cursed with her dying breath. But then Chris opened his eyes and smiled at her, and in response, she howled maniacally, her cry a blend of pain and rage and confusion. She then dropped Chris like a sack of dirty laundry and vanished. Chris's head struck the desk chair as he fell, and he flopped unconscious on the floor alongside Sammy.

"What the hell was that?" muttered Bain as he struggled to his feet.

"*That* was Mallory," replied Jackie with dramatic emphasis.

"Chris, Chris," Gillian murmured over his unconscious body.

Sammy got to his knees and gave Chris a quick examination. "I think he's okay. See? He's coming round already."

Bain was shaking his head, muttering to himself, "Did I really just see a damned demon? Was that what's been beating people to a pulp? Setting people on fire? How the hell am I gonna arrest that? Oh, for fuck sake, and I gotta write this up! I'll be a laughingstock."

Gillian turned on Sammy. "Why did you do that?" she screamed. "I thought you were his friend!"

"Because he would have gone to Greyson's lab if I hadn't stopped him. He has to be here when my friend arrives to get rid of the demon." Sammy removed Chris's Magdalene pendant and returned it to Gillian, then he glanced at his watch and said, "It's 7:30 now. My friend is his ship's cook. He'll come as soon as he's finished serving dinner to his crewmates. He has to be back aboard ship by 2100 when his ship sails. Someone will have to be downstairs to let him in when he gets here, okay? So now I'm going to deal with Greyson."

"But why should *you* go to Greyson?" Gillian asked. "You don't need to get involved."

"No, but if I save Chris's scholarship, I'll have done a good thing, no? Besides, this is maybe a last chance for me." Sammy paused, turned away, and muttered softly, "Maybe it's the last chance I'll ever have to do one good thing in my life."

"What do you mean, last chance?" asked Gillian.

"I don't mean anything. I'm just getting sentimental. Besides, like Chris said, nothing's going to happen. How could it?"

"Hold on!" shouted Sergeant Bain, "if anybody's going after this Greyson guy, it's me."

"You're not going to stop me," growled Sammy.

"Okay, but I drive," replied Sergeant Bain.

****

Greyson's lab

The reek from the lye bath worsened by the moment as Dahlman's eight pounds of flesh broke down in the caustic soup and congealed into a gelatinous mass.

The chapel service upstairs had long since ended, and the voices of its congregants were but a memory. The only sounds in the cellar now were the occasional burp of gases escaping from the lye bath and the muffled screams and gurgled moans from beneath the creature's new skin of comfrey paste. Beyond the most obvious humanoid features— its arms and legs—the artificial flesh concealed every anatomical detail except for the creature's eye holes and nostrils. The new skin was achingly slow to dry. But the delay afforded Greyson long minutes of observing Dahlman's eyes as they darted here and there in frenzied agony or swam about in a sea of utter bewilderment. When he'd eventually become bored with gloating over Dahlman, Greyson retreated to his office for a nap, or so he claimed. The burning smell and then the thump of Greyson's unconscious body falling to the floor told a different story. The drugs would knock him out for hours.

From a list Greyson had provided, Henry spent the afternoon painting simple passages from the Torah—like *Hear O Israel, G-d is our L-rd, G-d is One*—onto strips of linen, and James in heaping his buckets of mud from the harbor flats into a large tin washbasin that the brothers had also scavenged from the Lawrencetown abattoir.

Michael passed the hours huddled at a small desk in the corner of the cellar as far away from the appalling smell of the lye bath as possible. He was making copies of the seventy-two names of God that Greyson had extracted from the cantor's amulet. Greyson said they'd need copies because he intended to press the original vellum into the creature's artificial skin.

None of the golem legends that Michael reviewed on Greyson's instructions had ever mentioned anything about inserting the names of God into the flesh of the creature. The words, *Adam* and *Truth*, yes, but never the names of God. So where the hell had these oddball directions actually come from? Greyson refused to show anyone Rabbi Loew's letter, which he claimed to have found in some old Czech monastery.

In Michael's estimation, Greyson was no longer able to tell the difference between reality and illusion. This supposed ritual might just as easily have been a figment of Greyson's drug-addled imaginings as the instructions of a long-dead rabbi. And it made Ashworth frantic to think he'd placed his fate in the hands of this maniac.

When eventually Greyson emerged from his office, his eyes were bloodshot and his movements halting and unsteady. He stumbled to the table where Dahlman lay and prodded him with a finger. "Okay, skin's good so just two more layers to go," he mumbled.

Michael loathed Greyson's utter lack of self-discipline. The bastard was royally screwing this up! They might actually have succeeded in fashioning a creature resembling a golem, or good enough to create a frenzy at the Government's press conference at least. But there was no chance this charade was going to work if Greyson kept sabotaging it with his erratic and self-destructive behavior. He was doing nothing right, not the purification, not the cleansing, not the animation ritual, nothing. They hadn't even purged Dahlman the way they should have, and now he stank from the shit trapped beneath his new skin.

What did the Raba bar Rav Huna say? *If the righteous desired it, they could, by living a life of absolute purity, be creators.* But who in their right mind was ever going to believe Greyson was pure enough to create a foot fungus, never mind a living creature?

When eventually Greyson emerged from his nap, he climbed on a chair and stood there wobbling like a drunk on a street corner. Then he cried out, "Last fucking steps!" and began giving orders like some two-bit Messiah. "Okay, so now we have to mix the ground chalk with the milk and the animal glue, then add the clay and the linseed oil. It's supposed to look like bread dough when we're done. We're gonna layer it thin-like all over the creature's body, and as it dries, it's supposed to bind to his new skin. It'll be like a rubbery suit that moves with the creature."

Greyson then shouted across the cellar. "Ashworth, you got those names of God ready yet? Or are you still fiddling your dick?"

That was when Michael snapped. He didn't immediately respond, but then he slowly stood up and said, "I just don't get it," shaking his head as he spoke.

"Can't hear you," Greyson shouted back.

Michael began calmly enough. "How could you ever have thought this was gonna work?" But then once he'd started, all his disappointment, humiliation, and fury came spewing out. "Don't you realize, if we walk into that press briefing tomorrow with a guy in a rubber suit the color of bread dough who stinks of shit, and you say you've found Rabbi Loew's letters and amulet and you've created a golem, the whole world is gonna know what a clown you really are? Everyone's gonna see you've finally and totally lost it!"

Michael was rolling now. It felt so good to be getting his feelings out once and for all. Greyson had to know what a huge disappointment he'd become. Someone had to tell him, and who better than Michael Ashworth?

"And if you think this doughboy is gonna frighten anybody," Michael continued, "never mind exact some kind of bloody revenge, you're out of your fucking mind! Everyone at the press briefing is going to laugh till they crap and then haul you away to the loony bin. Then Henry and James are gonna get charged with murdering some old drunk, and I'm gonna get arrested for injuring that bitch, Bonnie."

Greyson's face reddened. He responded slowly, clearly, like he'd suddenly become cold sober. "You've never believed in my work, have you?" His tone was icy, menacing, but Michael was oblivious to it.

As he started across the lab toward Greyson, his tone softened, and he seemed almost tearful as he spoke.

"That's just it, I did believe, once. I thought you were serious. It was so cool, exploring the power of holy language and all those ancient hallucinogens. We were doing real science. And even after you got caught up in your *Titanic* crap, we were at least able to carry on with our work." He looked at the brothers for some sign of their agreement. But he saw nothing in their faces except their usual indifference.

When Michael reached the table, he stopped directly in front of Greyson with his arms extended as if in supplication.

"Dr. Greyson, I really did believe, we all believed, that we were going to do something incredible."

At this point, Michael's pent-up anger got the better of him. "But then you had to totally screw things up! Same as always, with your girls and your drugs and your shortcuts and your goddamned American. So now, when we get one last chance to show off all that we've accomplished, you make an absolute shitfest of everything."

Michael was shouting now.

"It's always the same with you. You think you can screw around, mess up, and get away with it because you're so smart. Well, you're not. You're an idiot. You're not willing to do the work. Before the ritual, we were supposed to purge the subject, then purify ourselves and dress in a certain way, and we were supposed to pray. That's what every description ever written about creating a golem says. But not you! No, just do the minimum. That's your style. Just mix up all this clay and glue and crap. Where's the mystical power in that shit? Where's the mystic power in any of this? We're not doing anything extraordinary. We're just making a fucking Halloween costume!"

Michael hammered the table and screamed, "I needed this stunt to work! We all need it to work if we're going to avoid jail sentences. But how the hell can this golem trick work with you making such a hash of it?"

Shaking his head in utter disgust, Michael lowered his voice and muttered, "What an ass you are, sir," he said, his tone dripping with contempt.

With all that out of his system at last, Michael felt relieved, even proud, as he marched up to Greyson and poked him in his chest. "You have to know how much you've disappointed everyone who ever trusted you. Christ, even your mom can't stand you!"

A good six inches shorter than Greyson, Michael stood there, defiant, staring up into Greyson's eyes with a smirk on his face like he'd just won some kind of prizefight.

For the duration of Ashworth's tirade, Greyson had stayed stock-still, speechless, his face the russet color of dried blood. And he remained that way for several more seconds after Ashworth finally shut up.

Poor Ashworth never saw it coming.

Without a word, Greyson suddenly lunged forward, grasped Ashworth by his shirtfront, hauled him off the ground, and plunged him into the bath of lye.

Ashworth's shock at Greyson's attack was instantly swept away by the excruciating pain that enveloped him.

****

Greyson's Lab

Greyson merely stared as the rapidly liquifying Ashworth thrashed about in the noxious soup and screamed his guts out. At first, Greyson wasn't sure what he felt: horror at his own brutality or satisfaction at the demise of a defiant little worm? But then he knew. Oh yes, it was definitely the latter. Satisfaction, jubilant satisfaction! He grabbed a nearby broom and used it to push Ashworth beneath the bath's acrid surface and pin him there.

Ashworth's heaving and rolling about in the mire continued for several minutes, his arms occasionally surfacing to flail in the air as fingers fell off and flesh slipped away. When eventually Ashworth's face detached from his skull and rose to the surface of the bath like a rubber mask, Greyson withdrew what was left of the broom from the roiling fat and flesh. He then turned to the brothers and said, "We should get back to work."

****

The Streets of Halifax

As they drove through the rain-soaked streets, Bain turned off the police radio and asked the old man in the passenger seat, "I don't get it. You're a friend of this Chandler kid, and yet you attacked him."

"I haven't known him long," replied Sammy Brook.

"But you knew about his demon."

Sammy was deeply suspicious of this cop, of any cop. He'd helped guys with power before, and doing so had cost him everything. You can't trust a cop even when he says, 'Nice morning,' because he's probably asking something else, like, 'Were you here at sunrise when the murder took place?'

"Yes. I've seen the demon before," Sammy replied.

"This Mallory, she protects Chandler?" asked Bain.

"No, she hates him. But she hates his friends even more. If the demon sees someone touch Chris, she thinks the person is close to Chris, and she attacks."

"So you're saying Chandler can make this demon attack other people, which means these beatings we've been having are Chandler's work?"

"I know nothing about these beatings."

"And what about these grave robberies? Back at his room he said he was responsible."

"No," Sammy replied firmly. "You misunderstood. It was the professor's guys, they did it. And they painted the Nazi signs as well." Sammy wasn't going to mention the Mount Olivet Cemetery.

"So what do you think? Is this Chandler a good guy or a bad guy?" asked Bain. His question sounded genuine enough.

"He helped my friend, so I'm helping him."

"And Greyson. You really figure he's trying to make a mud creature?"

"He might try," replied Sammy. "But if he screws it up, terrible things could happen."

"So what should I charge Greyson with when we get there?"

"I don't know. You're the police, but I can tell you this. When we get there, I think it will be far worse than you can imagine."

Bain appeared genuinely shaken by Sammy's prediction. "And you. What do you plan to do?"

"I want this professor to agree that Chris has done everything he asked so Chris must receive his scholarship, or I will beat the shit out of the professor."

To describe Sammy as an old man was altogether misleading. Although he customarily stooped and was slow of foot, if he stood tall, he towered over most men, and even in his eighties, he was as thick as a tree and as hard as a dumpster.

"And I'll beat you as well if you try to stop me," the old man whispered.

Bain looked across at the old guy in the seat beside him. Even in the darkened car, the lights of the passing buildings glinted like ice in the old man's eyes. The eyes were fixed on Bain like the tips of two knife blades.

Bain pulled the police cruiser into the college quadrangle and parked. Almost 8 p.m. now. Most students had finished up in the dining hall or the library and had returned to their dorms for the night. The clouds had cleared, and the stars were out. A brisk wind off the land smelled fresh, free of the stink of the sea for a change, but it was also bitterly cold, a harbinger of the brutal winter months to come.

Bain pointed out the steps down to Greyson's lab and led the way across the quadrangle. But just as they stepped from the floodlit parking area into the heavy shadow surrounding the chapel, Sammy slammed his fist into the side of Bain's head. The cop fell to the grass like a carcass from a meat hook. Sammy grabbed Bain's arms and heaved him across the margin of lawn to a clump of tall shrubs. There he dragged Bain through the dense tangle of thorns and leafless branches to a narrow separation between shrubs and wall just large enough to accommodate the senseless policeman. "I'll come back for you," Sammy whispered. "You'll be safer here."

Sammy then descended the steps to Greyson's lair. The light over the stairwell had been smashed. Sammy hammered on the door and shouted, "Open up, please. I'm here for Chris Chandler."

****

Gothall's Rooming House

Jackie and Madelyn waited on the sidewalk for the Torajan priest and ushered him inside when he arrived. A tiny man, he couldn't have topped five feet on his tiptoes. Sammy and the Torajan must have made a curious pair when they walked side by side. All the same, Madelyn, who had to be half a foot taller than the Torajan, couldn't help whispering to Jackie, "He's sorta cute." The man was olive-skinned, with salt-and-pepper hair and a cleft chin like Kirk Douglas. He carried a leather bag over his shoulder, spoke perfect English, and addressed the two girls in the manner of an Oxford don.

"It's a pleasure to make the acquaintance of two such charming ladies," he said as they climbed to the fourth floor. He gasped, however, as they entered Chris's room. The room was still a shambles from Mallory's latest attack. Chris was spread out on the bed, barely conscious from the blow to his head, and still bleeding profusely from the gunshot wound across his scalp.

"It was Mallory," explained Jackie to the Torajan.

"Ah, Mallory. Our friend Sammy has told me a little about her."

"Forgive me," said Madelyn, "but you're not what we'd expected."

"What did you expect?"

"I . . . I'm not sure," Madelyn replied with a smile that hinted at a certain measure of curiosity concerning this exotic, handsome, and diminutive seafarer.

"I confess I've walked a curious course in my life. Religious studies in my village, a scholarship to Oxford, various teaching positions, then a very nasty falling out with my ex-wife and her powerful father, and my escape to the high seas. And so now I travel the world over and read and make interesting acquaintances like Sammy Brook. But I assure you, I know my Torajan lore."

"I didn't mean to grill you or anything," said Madelyn.

"That's perfectly all right. Of course, I'd like to have the opportunity to ask you about yourself some time. The next time I'm in Halifax perhaps?"

"Perhaps," replied Madelyn with a most uncharacteristic smile and coquettish tilt of her head.

"Sorry to interrupt you, Mr . . ." interjected Jackie.

"My name is Bunga Aru Maranda, but you can call me Aru."

"Gillian, who's this guy?" asked a groggy Chris.

"Sammy's friend. You remember. He's here to lay Mallory's spirit to rest."

"Where is Sammy?" Chris asked, looking around anxiously.

"He's gone," replied Gillian.

"Gone to stop Greyson? Oh Gillian, we have to go after him," muttered Chris as he tried to stand.

"We've been through this. You're staying here," commanded Gillian, her face stern, her resolve unwavering. "You will let Sammy handle Greyson. Oh and as for that nonsense earlier about keeping Mallory's spirit with us, I want to make this very clear. Commanding Mallory to do your bidding might have seemed like a superpower, but you're about to see the last of her. Never mind that she's a royal pain, you have no right to bind her to this realm when even she deserves her final rest."

The desperation on Chris's face ebbed away until he was almost smiling. Gillian was right. Mallory deserved to find Puya, the Land of Souls where the god Pong Lalondong judges the dead.

"Okay, Aru, we're in your hands," Chris said.

"All right, so can you tell me how Mallory came to be here?"

"Well, nearly two years ago, Mallory killed herself," said Chris. "Her father, who was in Sulawesi at the time, attempted a second cleansing death to free his daughter from the emotions which had driven her to take her own life. But the ritual was interrupted when her remains were stolen by a crazy guy who dismembered her corpse and tried to incinerate the pieces in a burn barrel."

"We saw her spirit escape from her remains in the fire," added Gillian.

"And I take it you are the object of her hatred," Aru asked Chris, "and she plagues you with her vengeful attacks?"

Chris nodded.

"Okay, so first things first. We have to lure her spirit back into her remains. Do we have any remains?"

"Yes," replied Gillian as she got down on her knees and pulled the battered suitcase from beneath Chris's bed. She lifted the case up onto the desk and opened it. First she removed Mallory's skull from the case, then several larger bones.

"We shall begin with music. I'd like you, young lady," he said to Madelyn with a smile, "to play this gong. Gongs are always to summon the dead. While you strike the gong every fifteen seconds, I'm going to play this one-stringed fiddle called a geso'-geso'. And if Mallory knows Torajan culture, she should be drawn to the music."

The undulating melody they played was both alien and haunting. Minutes passed but nothing happened.

"Okay, so now I'll sing a lullaby she's sure to know."

"*Suliram, Suliram, ram, ram*

"*Suliram yang manis*

    "*Aduhai indung seorang*

"*Bijaklah sana dipandang manis*

    "*Tinggilah tinggi si matahari*

"*Suliram, anaklah kerbau mati tertambat*

"*Suliram, sudah lamalah saya mencari*

"*Baru sekarang saya mendapat.*"[4]

Smoke and sparks suddenly filled the room, and from the swirling blaze Mallory's fiery, black-rimmed eyes emerged. She swam about the room, but not in a fury as was her customary manifestation. No, this time she glided about in a trance-like state, her incandescence rising and falling as if in time with the song, until gradually she was drawn toward the bones on the desk.

At first, she merely appeared curious but then angry as if she'd been netted by a force she could not resist. Mallory shrieked and spun about as she fought to break free from the pull of her bones. The skull and bones began to move, slowly at first but then violently, wildly, dancing on the desk like fat sputtering on a griddle. Suddenly the skull—soiled, with clumps of flesh and filthy hair still plastered to the crown, with one desiccated eye like a dried raisin still nested in its socket, and with the jawbone still dangling by a single leathery tendon—became so much more. Translucent flesh enveloped the skull like the morning mist on a mountainside, eyes appeared in the bony sockets, and blood-red lips blossomed across the dangling jaw.

"Mallory," Chris murmured.

As if trying to see its environs, Mallory's head tilted first toward the singer and then toward Chris. And then it screamed, screamed as if all the world's agony had suddenly descended upon it.

"It's the torment," Aru shouted over Mallory's cries. "She's reliving the anger she knew at the time of her death and the pain she now feels at being trapped in her dismembered corpse. But we can't weaken!"

He reached inside his bag, pulled out several sheets of paper, and passed them around.

"Our task is to bring her peace, to wipe away her hatred and pain. You must read these prayers along with me. Do your best with the pronunciation, but you must not hesitate. You must read continuously. We Torajans pray like a waterfall, in a rush, without hesitation, so that our prayers fall upon the ears of our gods like the roaring plunge pool at the bottom of a cataract."

"Couldn't we read them in English?" Jackie asked.

"All prayers, irrespective of language, flow to the one unknowable Creator, just as all rivers flow to the one great ocean that covers the whole world. But when you buy tickets to a Mozart concert, you expect to hear Mozart, and when the Creator listens to Torajans, she expects to hear Torajan."

So they prayed without the slightest idea of what they were saying except in the belief their words would sweep away Mallory's anger and calm her anguish. And sure enough, as the minutes passed, her skull ceased its frantic rattling about, and her ghostly eyes slowly closed.

"Now we must ask the gods to take her from this life once again," whispered Aru as he signaled them to turn to the second sheet of prayer.

As their prayers droned on, the ghostly veil about Mallory's bones began to fade. In a final flourish, Mallory's diaphanous presence rose from her skull like perfume from a night garden to float about the room and absorb one last draught of this life. However, when Mallory appeared to sense Chris's presence, she suddenly descended upon him. He instinctively shrank back in terror. But Mallory abruptly halted directly before Chris's face. There she stared at him, first with curiosity as if seeing him for the very first time, and then with a hint of a smile. And with that, she vanished.

"Did she . . . did she just forgive me?" whispered Chris.

"Now, we must pray for Mallory's guidance to Puya, the Land of Souls." Their prayers continued until Aru signaled them to stop and announced, "Her pain has been wiped away, and your torture is ended, my friend."

Chris and Gillian looked at one another, at first in amazement, then relief, and finally, joy. They gently caressed each other's cheeks, and kissed with a tenderness and calm that Mallory's presence had never before afforded them. Jackie and Madelyn hooted and clapped.

"I guess we won't be needing this any longer," Gillian whispered as she held up the Magdalene pendant.

"Sammy gave it to you?" Concern etched Chris's face. "I hope he's okay."

"I know what you're thinking," Gillian said as she wiped the blood from Chris's face and adjusted the dressing on his scalp. "Okay," she said with a smile, "so now you can go save your friend."

"I'll drive!" shouted Jackie.

"But remember, you no longer have Mallory to defend you," Gillian shouted as Chris and Jackie raced down the stairs.

****

Greyson chuckled at the sight of Dahlman's eyes following him as he paced around the table.

"Still in there, eh?" he muttered. "Ah, but the best is yet to come."

What satisfaction it gave Greyson to realize he'd executed every step of Rabbi Loew's directions with complete success. The creature lived, the new skin adhered to its *écorché* perfectly, and the linen had been fully embedded in the artificial skin. So now they were about to embark on the last two steps, the coat of mud and blood and the creature's animation. The only negative in an otherwise gratifying day was the appalling stench in the lab. Greyson's eyes burned with the acrid fumes from the lye bath, his stomach roiled from the creature's stink of shit, and his head spun with the noisome odor of the harbor mud. If he didn't get some fresh air soon, he was sure to lose his dinner—well, the whisky, amphetamines, cold coffee, and apple he'd consumed in place of dinner.

Across the lab, Henry and James were mixing the creature's final covering, the blend of harbor mud, linseed oil, and blood. Greyson watched with admiration as James poured quart after quart of blood from the two muscatel jugs, and Henry, up to his elbows, kneaded the mixture into a shiny, maroon-colored mass having the consistency of warm tar. How prescient he'd been to help the brothers murder their father.

"Mix is ready, Dr. Greyson," Henry called.

"Okay, so roll it on over," he replied.

Henry wiped off his hands and arms while James pushed the wheelbarrow across the lab and parked it alongside the creature.

"We'll do the front first," said Greyson, "let the coating set, and then roll him over to complete the back. All right, so make it a nice even depth everywhere. Let's begin."

But at that moment, someone hammered on the cellar door and shouted, "Open up, please. I'm here for Chris Chandler."

"Sounds like that old man, Chandler's friend," Greyson said to James. "Let him in, but then don't just lock the door. Secure it somehow."

As the door opened, the intruder at first lurched backward, probably from the stench, but then took a deep breath, and stepped inside.

"What are you doing here? Where's Chandler?" called Greyson as he applied the first handful of mud and blood to the creature.

"He—oh!" As the old man opened his mouth to speak, he almost gagged at the smell. "Chandler's . . . Chandler's gunshot wound is serious," he barely managed to choke out.

"The poor dear," Greyson replied with an unmistakable sneer in his voice.

"But I've come to say that you must give him the scholarship you promised. He's done everything you asked." Descending the stairs, the old man must have caught sight of Ashworth's remains in the lye, but he neither flinched nor looked away.

"What's your name?"

"Sammy. No, I'm Samuel Bruchner."

"Bruchner, all right," Greyson replied, "I will reward Chandler, but the fact is, we're not quite finished yet and I need him for one last job."

"He's not going to do any more jobs for you. He can't."

"Relax, it's not that hard. In fact, you're probably better suited to the job anyway. You're Jewish, is that right?"

"Yes."

"Perfect, and if you do the job in Chandler's place, then he'll get his scholarship, and I will make no further demands."

"What is this job?"

"When we're done with this final coating," replied Greyson, "someone has to read the names of God over our creature, the names I suspect you helped Chandler locate. Is that right? To animate our creature someone has to read the most holy names very carefully and precisely, and I suspect that person should be able to pronounce Hebrew letters better than me."

"Where are the names?"

Greyson pointed across the cellar. "On the desk over there."

The old man crossed the lab, located one of the copies Ashworth had made, and began reading.

"Professor," he called out, "do you expect me to read the three letters in each combination together" —like the four consonants are read as Yahweh, or should I read the letters individually?"

"Since the actual names of God are never to be spoken, I think it best that you read the three consonants in each combination individually. Besides, that way I'll know if you miss any. Now get on with it, You have half an hour to practice."

Greyson couldn't help but wonder how an old Jew from Europe had got mixed up with a kid from Maine. Why did Bruchner care about Chandler, and why was he helping the kid? Then again, what did it matter?

"Bruchner, I don't think I need tell you that mistakes are forbidden," shouted Greyson. "I'll be following along, so don't screw up, got it? My boys here will make you pay dearly for any mistakes you make."

Greyson returned to the task of covering his creature with the malodorous concoction of blood and mud. Time ticked by as the coating, the color of rotten rhubarb, spread across the creature's mass and then slowly cured to a jelly-like consistency. Greyson couldn't resist poking the creature from time to time to test the coating and antagonize the demented brute inside.

After another pharmaceutical snack, Greyson announced, "All right, I think it's time for the grand finale. We're going to animate our friend. Bruchner, get over here."

With the four of them gathered around the creature, Greyson gave instruction for the final phase. "Bruchner, I want you to walk around the table seven times reciting the names of God. And mind you, any mistake might screw up the ritual and damage our creature. So don't you dare mess up God's names, or we'll mess you up something fucking awful."

He drew from his pocket a folded piece of yellowed paper. "Recognize this, old man? It's the original list from Loew's amulet," he said. "As you are walking, I will press it into our creature's chest, and once we're both done, we shall witness history. So let's begin."

The old man was just about to start his march when someone pounded on the cellar door.

"Professor Greyson, it's Chris Chandler. You've got to let me in, please."

"You lied to me," Greyson snarled at Bruchner. "You said Chandler was too sick to come."

Sammy shouted to Chris, "Go away, Chris, get away from here. Go now!"

"Shut the hell up," Greyson bellowed. "James, let the kid in. He deserves to see this. I want him to be a witness."

James raced up the stairs and unfastened the wire bindings he'd used to secure the door. It flew open, and there stood Chris Chandler along with some girl and Bain, the cop. The three gasped and stumbled backward as the stink from the cellar enveloped them.

"Dr. Greyson," said James, 'it's not just Chandler. It's that cop and some girl."

"Does the cop have a search warrant?"

"No warrant," Bain started to say, "but—"

"Then just him," snapped James as he yanked Chris inside and slammed the door.

349

"You fool!" Sammy shouted at Chris. "I said to go. This is going to be hell!"

****

Greyson's lab

The scene and the stench were far worse than Chris could ever have imagined. A tub filled with a congealed mass of fat and flesh, a humanoid shape partially covered in maroon muck, and a stink to drive a dog mad.

Over Bain's incessant pounding on the cellar door, Greyson, his hands up to the elbows in the blood-colored mess, shouted, "Welcome, young Chandler. Ignore the old man. He's just a bit squeamish. But you're just in time to witness history."

Sammy stumbled to the foot of the stairs. "Please go, please," he cried to Chandler. "Tell the others to go too."

"Shut the fuck up, old man," said Greyson. "Nobody is leaving. Bruchner, you've got a job to do, unless that is, you want Chandler to take over."

"No, I'll do it," muttered Sammy as he turned back to the table.

"Chandler, down here. And James, bar the door again and then watch Chandler. If he tries anything, don't hesitate to crack him over the head with a hammer."

Chris was appalled to see a tangle of bones protruding from the tub of congealed fat. A skull, carried to the surface by a bubble of gases, bobbed there for a moment, and then sank once again into the human stew.

Worse still, as he approached the monstrosity over which Greyson labored, Chris was horrified to realize the creature's lidless eyes were following him.

Greyson handed a copy of the names of God to Henry and said, "I need you to follow along with Bruchner as he reads the Hebrew letters so we can be sure he's saying them in the proper order. Got it? Good."

Sammy grasped Chris's arm and pushed him to one side. He then began the ritual march and a droning intonation of the holiest names of God.

Hobbling around the table, he read, "Vah Hey Vah, Yud Lamed Yud, Samech Yud Tet, Ayin Lamed Mem, Mem Hey Shin, Lamed Lamed Hey, Aleph Kaf Aleph, Kaf Hey Tav, Hey Zahin Yud . . . ." From time to time, he glanced toward Chris as if attempting to convey a signal or a message, but Chris had no clue what Sammy was trying to say.

****

Greyson's lab

It was all coming together. Greyson was almost breathless with excitement. Soon, very soon, he'd turn his creature loose on Chandler and Bruchner, and what an excellent test that would be.

Greyson bent over Dahlman's chest, pressed the folded vellum deep beneath the surface of the coating, then touched the creature's arm . . . and it stirred. "It's working, it's working," he whispered. "Keep going!" he shouted to Bruchner.

"Aleph Lamed Daled," the old man intoned, "Lamed Aleph Vav, Hey Hey Ayin,"

"It's . . . the creature is trying to sit up!" Greyson shrieked with joy. "Keep going, don't stop!"

Upstairs, the pounding on the cellar door continued without pause. Bain was now threatening to have his officers blast their way in.

"Yud Zahin Lamed, Mavet Lamed Hey, Hey Resh Yud, Hey Kuf Mem—"

"It's up! It's sitting up! Now raise your arm," Greyson shouted in the creature's face, and its arm began to rise. "It's obeying my commands. Keep reading, damn you! Don't stop for anything."

"Lamed Aleph Vav," Bruchner resumed, "Kaf Lamed Yud, Lamed Vav Vav, Pey Hey Lamed."

The creature's movements were stiff and slow but deliberate. "Good, good," Greyson muttered, "now put your feet on the floor, that's great."

"Nun Lamed Kaf, Yud Yud Yud, Mem Vav Tav, Chet Hey Vav, Nun Tav Hey."

"Professor," said Henry nervously. "Professor?"

"Good, now can you stand?" said Greyson, then, "What?" he bellowed at Henry.

There were more sirens outside now. "I'm authorized to make an armed entry," shouted Sergeant Bain through a bullhorn.

"Go," Bruchner cried out to Sergeant Bain. "Get away. It's too late!" Then he screamed at Chris as well, "You have to go too!"

"What's too late?" asked a furious Greyson. "What do you mean?"

"Professor," Henry shouted this time, "I think maybe the old man said one of the names wrong, or maybe he just read the wrong line."

Greyson suddenly lost all interest in Bain and the chaos outside. "What? What did he say, Henry?" Then he screamed at Bruchner, "What did you say?"

"He said something like *Mavet* or *Mamet*," answered Henry, "when he should have said Mem Lamed Hey. It's number 23, see?"

Greyson snatched the list of names from Henry, crumpled it, and threw it in Samuel Bruchner's face. "*Mavet*? You said, *Mavet*?"

"Maybe I just heard wrong," muttered Henry.

"Oh no, you didn't hear wrong. No, he didn't hear wrong, did he, Bruchner, you bastard!" Greyson shrieked at Sammy.

"What's it mean?" asked James.

"It means death," replied the old man.

Greyson raised his hand to strike Bruchner, screaming as he did, "If you've harmed my creature, you goddamned—"

Chris raced to block Greyson's swing but then stopped, aghast at the monstrosity closing upon the maddened professor.

Greyson spun about at the raucous shrieks and grunts behind him. The creature, that just moments ago had been slouched over the edge of the common room table, was now lurching about and desperately striking its forearm against its facemask of mud and blood. The mask shattered. Pieces large and small fell to the floor. And then came the fire.

****

At first, the flicker of scarlet from the creature's nostrils looked like a nosebleed. But the truth was far more horrifying. As the mud and the blood, the clay and the animal glue fell away from the creature's mouth, it screamed, "I'm burning!" And like a burst of fire from a blast furnace, flames exploded from the creature's eyeholes, nostrils, and mouth. The creature staggered like a drunkard as its artificial skin first bubbled and then spat and splattered like grease in a frying pan.

Chris tried to grab Sammy's arm and drag him up the stairs, but the old man pulled away and ran to the opposite side of the cellar.

"Come with me, Sammy, please," Chris shouted, but the old man shook his head and pressed his back to the far wall.

Beneath its disintegrating skin, Dahlman's fleshless figure was already engulfed in a white-hot inferno. And yet, he remained standing, screaming and pleading for release. "It will not let me die," he cried.

"The fire, it will not let me die! Please, I beg of you! Kill me! Kill me, please!"

But no one was listening. When at last the creature's monstrous blanket of liquifying gore exploded, blobs of the burning fat and glue flew in all directions, clinging to and igniting everything they struck. Furniture, lab equipment, clothing, and of course flesh, it all went up in flames.

James took a hit directly to the face. His screams were cut short as his mouth and throat were consumed by the liquid fire. He ran about blindly, hands to his face, frantically attempting to wipe away the burning material. But all James managed to do was ignite his hands and arms and everything else over which he stumbled.

Henry was not struck, and could only watch, aghast, as his brother was engulfed. But then, from behind, a different horror was about to take him. He'd been standing in front of the metal locker containing the lab's collection of illuminated manuscripts. The locker suddenly began to rock, its doors shook, and its metal sides bent outward. When the doors flew off, a throng of creatures straight from their illuminators' drug-crazed imaginations swirled around Henry in a demonic whirlwind. Last to appear was Lilith, who'd died at the stake a thousand years earlier and who, in her incarnation as a fury in a monk's nightmare, still burned. She clearly knew the agony of incineration and smiled with such pleasure as she took Henry in her embrace.

A blob of Dahlman's burning flesh struck Greyson's arm. Flames immediately engulfed it to the shoulder, but Greyson seemed oblivious to the sizzle and crackle of his flesh as he clambered about in a vain attempt to avoid Dahlman, the shambling human torch, pursuing him. As Greyson did, he stumbled against the bath of lye. It tipped, the contents sloshed back and forth, and when Dahlman too fell against the tub, it toppled over entirely.

Ancient Romans were the first to discover that a torch dipped in sulfur and lime could not be extinguished in water, and that was precisely what the bath of lye contained. The fluid ignited as it flooded across the cellar floor, setting ablaze everything that was not already in flames.

The wave of burning fluid washed around Chris's legs like an incoming tide around pilings, but there was no pain, no fire, no damage. Instead, an iridescent glow like cut crystal in candlelight rose around Chris and drove away all hellfire. Chris grasped his Magdalene pendant and mouthed a silent thank you.

From the upturned bath, another flaming horror arose. Michael Ashworth was back, or what was left of him. Like a figure crafted from charred kindling, Ashworth's skeleton teetered toward Greyson. Greyson's legs were now on fire up to his thighs, and both arms to the shoulders, but when he glanced up and saw the blazing stick figure approaching, he started for the stairs. Greyson screamed at the top of his lungs, "Break down the door! Christ, break down the door!" But no one, whether inside or out, could have heard his cries over the roar of the inferno.

Bain's hammering on the door had ended when its iron straps and hinges began to glow from the intense heat inside.

****

At the top of the stairs, Greyson struggled to remove the wire that James had used to secure the door. But the flames engulfing his hands obscured the wire's many twists and knots. In one last desperate search for help, he spun about and surveyed his lab.

Fire everywhere. Its tongues now lapped at the cellar ceiling some twenty feet above the concrete floor. Through the blaze and the whirlwind of smoke and flaming debris, he spotted Chandler, borne through the fire unscathed inside a shimmering crystalline globe, and evidently pursuing the teetering figure of Michael Ashworth. Chandler carried a fire ax he'd pulled from a bracket on the wall. Greyson watched as Ashworth appeared to realize Chandler was hunting him and the burning stick figure toppled to his knees. There he pleaded with Chandler, but for what? For release, because that was precisely what Chandler delivered.

Chandler raised the fire axe high over his head, and with one mighty blow, cleaved the skeletal Ashworth in two. The weasel immediately fell to pieces like a tower of kindling undone by the first lick of flame. Was this Chandler's new mission then, to mete out mercy to the undeserving? Should Greyson beg for Chandler's mercy? Never! No fucking way!

On the far side of the cellar, Greyson spotted Bruchner standing motionless, witnessing what his damnable mispronunciation had accomplished. Was the bastard actually smiling?

Greyson's back to the cellar door was roasting against its iron straps like steak on a grill. He was oblivious, however, mesmerized instead by the sea of fire creeping up the stairs toward him. Suddenly, at the bottom of the steps, there appeared a dark void, an emptiness like a hole in the ocean. It grew wider as he watched, from mere inches to several feet, like a portal to elsewhere. Wherever that might be, it would be away from this inferno, and so Greyson descended toward the darkness.

At the edge of the void, he paused. In the inky black within, he glimpsed figures moving to and fro. They appeared to be marching along a circular pathway bordered on either side by deep trenches. 'Enter,' he sensed a presence calling to him. 'After all, what choice do you have?' And so Greyson stepped into the void. Only then did he realize the figures marching about in the shadows were utterly devastated.

Many lacerated themselves as they walked. Some carried their heads in their arms, while others disemboweled themselves and had their hands tangled in their entrails. Several had even been hacked in half so their legs now dragged their torsos along the endless path.

"Welcome to *Malebolge**," the voice whispered to Greyson and then laughed.

* Dante's Eighth Circle of Hell reserved for fraudsters like counterfeiters, hypocrites, grafters, seducers, and sorcerers.

****

Greyson's lab

As the fires of Hell incinerated Greyson and every other hideous thing he'd spawned, the sight of Chris Chandler moving untouched amid the flames gave Sammy a final moment of satisfaction. For once in his benighted life, he'd served the right cause. But then he lost sight of Chris behind the wall of fire.

Tongues of flame consuming the cellar seemed to writhe and dip and rise again like so many desperate specters pleading for escape and begging for mercy. Sammy knew them all, all the ghosts from his past, the ones whom he'd starved, and beaten, and worked to death. He heard their cries, saw their faces, each one at first hopeful, then fearful, and finally resigned to their fate. Sammy would never be forgiven, he knew that with utter certainty. He never could be. Covering his face, he sobbed and fell to his knees as the fiery contents of the bath of lye finally reached his side of the cellar. Without regard for the fiery pool, Sammy slumped to the floor and curled up amid the flames like a child settling into its crib.

The tiny creature nestled inside Samuel's coat whimpered with the biting cold. He drew the child closer still and resolved to steal someone's blanket the first chance he got. "Forgive me, little one, I will never let you be cold again," he whispered to his tiny daughter, and then they both slept.

****

Greyson's lab

Chris watched as if from inside a bell jar as the world around him was consumed by flames. He'd tried to reach Sammy, but after the old man misspoke the names of God, he'd fled across the cellar seemingly to witness the destruction of Greyson and his creature from afar. At some point, amid the flames and chaos, Chris lost sight of Sammy altogether.

The fire licked at Chris's limbs but left no mark. The heat was unquestionably merciless but he felt no hint of it. The Magdalene's pendant bore Chris through the flames like sunlight through stained glass. He saw the brothers reduced to tar. He'd dispatched Ashworth's fiery skeleton with one blow from an axe and then watched as his bones twisted, shattered, and crumbled to ash. He'd also tried to end Dahlman's agony with a similar swing of his axe but to no effect. As Dahlman wailed interminably, what remained of his artificial flesh and muscles and tendons roasted and spattered like the crackling on a pork roast until there was nothing left of him but charred bones and oily gristle.

As for Greyson, Chris had screamed at him to remain at the top of the steps until Chris could reach him. For some reason, however, Greyson had ignored Chris. Instead, he'd descended the steps directly into the most intense area of the blaze where the chemicals and electrical equipment had been stored. But then, as Greyson reached the bottom of the steps, he'd somehow continued descending as if the very jaws of Hell had opened beneath him.

Was there nothing Chris could have done, no one he might have saved from the inferno? Defender of the dead, be damned. Could he not, just once, have saved the living? Could he not at least have saved Samuel Bruchner?

Across the cellar, as the conflagration grew as bright as the sun, Chris caught a final glimpse of Sammy. Chris clambered over piles of burning debris, through clouds of black smoke and orange flame, and past crackling pieces of spattering flesh to reach the old man. But he was too late. Curled up against the wall, Samuel was already burning like a pile of autumn leaves. And yet, in spite of the blaze that consumed him, Sammy slept like a child in his mother's arms. On his face the old man wore what Chris could only imagine was a smile of contentment.

Chapter Fourteen

After the Conflagration
Halifax, Nova Scotia

The Chapel Conflagration, as the press dubbed it, killed six people: three students and three other adults, one of whom remained unidentified. The Fire Marshal determined that a faulty gas line was responsible for the explosion and very likely for an earlier fire in the office of the college president. In neither case, however, could the Fire Marshal identify the source of ignition. For some time, stories circulated to the effect that the cellar had been a bomb-making lab, a drugs lab, and even a den for the black arts. But the wheel of events ground on, and the press lost interest in the story. Thereafter, the rumors evaporated, until that is, Michael Ashworth's parents from Connecticut sued Cavendish College over the death of their son.

Although Ashworth's parents admitted they hadn't seen their son in three years or even known he'd moved to Canada to attend university, they sued for millions in compensation for the loss of their beloved child's affections. In depositions, they suggested all manner of sinister methods—brainwashing, pedophilia, and satanic rituals—that Cavendish College might have employed to steal their son's love. Their press interviews rekindled speculation concerning the presence of a suspected war criminal and an unidentified man at the scene of the fire. The college was eventually forced to settle out of court to stem the tidal wave of bad press. Legal wrangling and the associated costs delayed renovations on the chapel cellar. In time, however, it reemerged as a student health center bearing the name *Ashworth Clinic* and a brass plaque honoring the three students who'd lost their lives.

Sergeant Bain spent three days in the Victoria General Hospital recovering from burns and a head injury he'd sustained in his heroic but unsuccessful effort to save the victims of the Chapel Conflagration. In the days leading up to the Coroner's inquest, Bain had agonized over what he'd say. In the end, he concluded there was nothing to be gained from testifying about demons and golems.

After settling on a story with Rashid Minhas and Chris Chandler, Bain testified that he'd followed Sammy Brook to Cavendish College at Minhas's request after the old man had some kind of run-in at the diner with Professor Greyson. Bain explained that Greyson's lab was already on fire when he got to the college. He couldn't explain how he'd been struck in the head, but likely by flying debris. Bain also testified that Chris Chandler, whose reputation by the time of the inquest had already been widely reported in the press, was nowhere near when Greyson's lab caught fire. Of course, Bain said nothing about Chris's miraculous emergence from the inferno, but he would never in a million years be able to put the image out of his mind.

Bain had in fact stumbled out of the shrubbery just as Jackie and Chris arrived at the college. Thereafter, with all the bellowing and pounding on the cellar door, and then the smoke and the bullhorn, many students quickly gathered in the quadrangle to witness the horrifying blaze. Bain instructed Jackie to keep everyone away from the cellar steps. The intense heat and the nightmarish screams from behind the cellar door made that task a simple one. But as time passed and the screams from the cellar faded, the crowd pressed forward. Then, just as the fire engines pulled into the quad and parked between the crowd and the steps, the cellar door blew off its hinges.

White-hot flames, cinders and smoke erupted from the cellar and flew up the steps like a volcano. The on-lookers once again fell back and covered their faces against the blinding flash and the blast of burning debris, everyone, that is, except Sergeant Bain. Bain momentarily turned away as the door disintegrated but then he immediately turned back to watch in horror as Chris emerged from the inferno. Enveloped in a whirlwind of fire, Chris climbed the cellar stairs as if in a dream. He calmly opened the iron gate, which glowed crimson with the heat, and walked to Bain's side. There he murmured, "They're gone, all of them. I couldn't save anyone," and then fell unconscious to the ground.

In the months following the Conflagration, Sergeant Bain underwent a spiritual awakening of sorts, quit smoking, and patched up relations with his children. He then took early retirement and joined a group of senior citizens building schools in Kenya.

Freddy Gothall finally surrendered to his cancer. He bequeathed his building and seafront home, as his will stated, *to the most tolerant and honorable man I have ever known, Rashid Minhas*. Mr. and Mrs. Minhas promptly decided to renovate the entire ground floor of the building into an upscale restaurant and the rooming house above into spacious condominiums. Should Chris choose to return to Cavendish College, Minhas said he would offer him and Gillian a heavily discounted family rate, especially if *Dolly Minhas's Fine Indian Dining* catered their wedding.

The morning after the fire, Gillian's mother insisted she be flown by helicopter ambulance at the Harrow family's expense back to the Bangor Hospital for an urgent examination by the surgeons who'd performed her operation. Their tests found nothing, and so, to satisfy her mother, she consented to talk about her reasons for running away. Gillian had expected the chat to be difficult, but it wasn't, because she was unequivocal in saying she couldn't have remained in Bangor a moment longer without Chris. With that, talk turned to her mother's upcoming nuptials. Then everyone, including Chris, flew off to New York City for a wonderful week of wedding celebrations.

Following the Harrow-Willard wedding, Chris returned to Halifax to complete his school year. The college had agreed to honor Greyson's check, and Chris confessed to a particular fascination for the old seaport. "After all," he said, "it's not so bad when you get used to Atlantic weather and the smell of the sea."

Gillian, too, applied for a transfer to Cavendish College. She feared it might be heartbreaking to say goodbye to her friends back in Maine, but what choice did she have? She and Chris were talking seriously about formalizing their commitment to one another. And besides, as it turned out, her friends were also considering extended stays in Halifax.

Jackie was contemplating a return to Nova Scotia to research her first attempt at a novel, a thriller about the *Titanic* and a young heroine carrying an ancient amulet. Martin Koyman, a recent Pulitzer Prize winner for his investigative articles on the devastating AIDS epidemic, hinted to Jackie that he might follow her to Nova Scotia if only "to make sure she eats properly."

Madelyn, who'd become a diligent pen pal of Aru Maranda, the Torajan priest, was exploring the possibility of enrolling in Nova Scotia's Merchant Marine Training Institute. How her tune had changed since she'd repeatedly bemoaned the bone-chilling gales of the North Atlantic.

One last task remained. Although Chris and Gillian had submitted all the documentation they'd collected to the Board of Trustees overseeing Halifax's *Titanic* graves, the Board had not yet rendered its decision on renaming Cantor Dovid Rosenthal's grave.

****

A month after the Chapel Conflagration, and just days apart, two letters arrived in Halifax.

The first letter was addressed to Sergeant Bain.

Tirza Bruchner had written to thank him for conveying the news of her father's death and for his brief but moving description of her father's unselfish act of heroism that had saved Bain's life. She concluded her letter by saying she hoped to visit his grave someday. Sergeant Bain hadn't mentioned that Rashid Minhas had taken possession of Sammy's remains and buried them on Freddy Gothall's—now Minhas's—windswept oceanfront property. Sammy's resting place high above the relentless waves was marked with a stone that read, *Samuel Bruchner. Even Diamonds Must Be Broken to Become Gems. How You Glistened at the End, Dear Friend.*

Two months after receiving her letter, Bain got a telegram from Tirza Bruchner. Enroute to a conference in Boston in two weeks, she planned to make a brief stopover in Halifax to visit her father's grave. Together with Chris, Gillian, Minhas, Jackie, Madelyn, and Martin Koyman, Bain hastily arranged a service of remembrance in time for Tirza Bruchner's visit.

When Tirza Bruchner arrived, Sergeant Bain picked her up at the airport and drove her to Sammy's place of rest where everyone had assembled. "Your father's friends," Bain explained. The service began with a recitation of *Psalm 23*, then *El Malei Rachamim*, a prayer of rest and compassion for Sammy's soul, and finally the Mourner's Kaddish. Then Martin Koyman spoke. He did not conceal Sammy's dark past but closed with his own message.

"I am currently engaged in telling the stories of hundreds of young men dying of AIDS who have been reviled and condemned merely for having loved whom they chose. Public indifference to their plight has been appalling. It is evil, and my anger was eating me alive. How could

I ever find the peace of mind to do my job? But then I read somewhere that to forgive is neither to forget nor to condone. It is neither weakness nor a free pass for the evildoer. Rather, to forgive is to liberate oneself from the self-inflicted punishment of simply surviving. It is to set aside one's pain and allow oneself to recall brief moments of glory and courage amid the grim. And then to move on with the work of finding justice."

Tirza Bruchner was moved to tears by the brief service and concluded her visit to her father's graveside with a blessing of her own. "I shall pray for the papa who held me, fed me, sang to me, and kept me from the cold. I shall not forget the terrible price so many others paid for my life. But I shall no longer relinquish the memory of my father's own tenderness and sacrifice."

There was one other joyous outcome to Sammy's memorial. Following the service, Chris and Gillian's mother took a walk along the cliffs together. Mrs. Harrow unburdened herself of all the anger and resentment she'd harbored toward Chris for her daughter's injuries and unconventional decisions. And Chris promised his unwavering support for whatever life choices Gillian made from that day forward. Their walk ended in hugs and kisses, and tears.

The second letter to arrive in Halifax after the Conflagration was addressed to Chris Chandler.

> *Order of the Knights of Callixtus—The Mortsafemen*
> *1181 Ilchester Place,*
> *London W14*
> *Sir,*
> *Your exploits have come to the attention of our Order. Let me begin by saying how impressed are my brethren and I. Few know how devastating for the dead it is to have their places of rest defiled. Clearly, you do. The public record attests to your*

boundless determination to save our lost loved ones from the unending pain of a desecrated grave.

For this reason, the elders of the Order of the Knights of Callixtus—the Mortsafemen—have asked me as Marshal General of our Order to invite you to join us in our centuries-long struggle against the defilers of the dead. If you accept this invitation to join us, we ask that you present yourself at a service of investiture and dedication in Rome on the 14th of May, 1988. Our annual conclave and investitures take place at our Mother Church, the Church of Santa Maria in Traste-vere, where our patron Saint's relics reside. There we shall instruct you in the work of our Order and the duties of its knights. We shall also detail your remuneration, which I am confident you will find generous, and the first assignment you shall undertake on our behalf.

Yours in faith and consolation,
Adrian Anthony Morningfrost, Viscount
Marshal General
Order of the Knights of Callixtus

****

Crystal Crescent Beach, February, 1988

After a twenty-minute drive down a rutted sandy track, they pulled their car into a gravel clearing and parked by a weather-beaten picnic table. Deep into the darkest days of winter now, Chris and Gillian had taken a Sunday off from their studies for a drive in the country. On such a bitter, blustery winter's day, not surprisingly, theirs was the only car in the parking area. From beyond the curtain of trees that surrounded the clearing they could hear the pounding surf. Even in the woods they felt the sting of the icy salt spray tossed high in the air by the crashing waves.

Chris and Gillian followed a path through the woods and emerged from the trees onto the rocks and sand of Crystal Crescent Beach. The wide sand margin between seagrass and waves stretched half a mile into the distance, forming the enormous half-moon bay. Seaweed marked the line of the morning tide. Jumbles of boulders and broken stones divided the bay into three separate areas. The grey-green waves crashing ashore had deposited ice floes the size of mattresses along the entire length of the great crescent.

Chris and Gillian fastened their coats up to the collars, pulled on woolen caps and mitts against the biting gale, and set off. There was not another soul on the beach at that hour. Gillian strode out onto the sand and marched away. "Keep up," she shouted over the howling wind and the surf, "gotta keep warm."

Was it really just two years since they'd first met? They'd waited together for the school bus at the top of Willard Lane, not speaking for the first month, not until that fateful night when Gillian suddenly emerged from the darkness near the Willard Family Cemetery. Two years ago, Chris had been depressed, purposeless, lonely, and lost. Even he had considered himself a wacko. And then along came Gillian.

Like a plastic model kit, he'd been all bits and pieces until Gillian put him together, giving him purpose and direction. And so here they were—after so many battles, friends lost and won, ghastly discoveries, horrible injuries, and extraordinary triumphs—beginning a new life together.

Chris's days of defending the dead were behind him. He still wore the Magdalene amulet given him by Rose DuCalice, but no longer had a vengeful demon to fight his battles. The letter from the Knights of Callixtus had made him feel like a fraud. How could they ever have believed he possessed the qualities of a true Mortsafeman? And why would he want to become a Mortsafeman anyway? For weeks after the Conflagration, Chris had beaten himself up over his failure to save anyone from the blaze. Saving the living seemed like a far higher calling than defending the dead.

No, Chris was resolved to become a normal guy in a normal relationship with a normal future before him.

He remembered Felicity Holcomb telling him to embrace all the love that came his way, and Rose DuCalice saying it wasn't how many years you lived that mattered but how much love with which you filled those years. So now Chris was going to act upon their advice.

Gillian had climbed into the dunes and tall seagrass above the beach. "Up here," she called out. "Come see."

She'd come upon a tiny cemetery almost lost to the seagrass and sand. Surrounded by a rusting and partially toppled wrought-iron fence, the enclosure contained six gravestones. Each leaning to one side or another, the rude stone memorials were to four girls and two boys, all children of the same family. They'd been much beloved . . . or so read their inscriptions. More than a century ago they'd sailed to the new world in the hope of better days. Yet here they lay, their markers barely legible, all memory of them erased by years of salt spray and sand.

"You have to wonder whether they'd have been better off if they'd never come here," Gillian murmured. "Their graves might at least be tended."

"But their rest hasn't been disturbed," Chris replied.

"No spirits mourning by their graves?"

"Nope," said Chris.

"But you *can* still see spirits, right?" asked Gillian.

"Sure. Why?" asked Chris.

"I mean, Mallory is gone, but you still have your amulet, and you can still see spirits."

"What are you getting at?" asked Chris.

"Nothing. Forget it. Come, sit by me," Gillian said as she dropped down onto the sand.

Snuggled against each other, they sat with their backs to the cemetery fence, as the biting wind carried icy spray over the dunes and the afternoon shadows lengthened.

"How could any parents bury their children in sand?" murmured Gillian.

"I don't suppose the sand was here when the kids died. This was probably the end of their fields, but with the years the beach has been creeping inland."

"The parents aren't in there," said Gillian. "Just the children."

"Maybe the parents moved away after they lost their kids. Or maybe there was no one left to bury them when their kids were gone."

Okay, so now's the time . . . .

"Speaking of parents," said Chris.

What a ludicrous segue.

"When my parents visit in May," he continued, "can we tell them we're getting married?"

Gillian shifted away from Chris, and turned to look him directly in the eye. "Wait, are you asking me to marry you?"

"Yes."

"Well, of course," Gillian shouted, "I wondered for weeks when you'd get around to asking." Then she threw herself against Chris and pressed her lips to his.

"Sorry," whispered Chris between kisses, "no ring yet, though."

"That's okay," replied Gillian with a grin. "You're good for it, and I know where you live."

Suddenly a whirlwind of sand rose into the air, seagrass whipped about and was almost torn from the dunes, and the wrought-iron fence twisted and rattled, sending flakes of rust and fractured iron in all directions. The air crackled and hissed with sparks and bolts of electricity, and deafening shrieks resounded the length of the sandy crescent.

Then through a torrent of smoke and fire, Mallory appeared, her face swathed in whirling flames, eyes smoldering like embers, and her expression, malicious, menacing, murderous! Then away she flew, up into the sky like a rocket, out over the sea, and down to within inches of the rolling waves.

"How can she be here?" cried Gillian. "She's supposed to be in Puya!"

"Maybe she couldn't find it," Chris bellowed in reply.

"Or she didn't want to," Gillian called back.

"She's not attacking us. Why isn't she attacking us?"

"Maybe Aru's cleansing death ritual did work," replied Gillian, "just not his guidance to Puya."

"What does this mean?" Chris wondered aloud.

"For one thing it seems she doesn't hate us anymore."

Mallory swept down to within inches of the two lovers, leered, bared her teeth, and then screamed before shooting away, darting over the sand and waves like a goldfinch over a meadow.

"But if she isn't here to torment us, then why *is* she here?" Chris asked.

"Perhaps she enjoyed ripping people to pieces," muttered Gillian. "Maybe you've got your superpower back."

Swathed in a starburst of white-hot fire and roiling smoke, Mallory dove and rose over the beach like an avenging angel, shrieking with apparent pleasure to once again be free to soar and torment among the living. As she swooped and turned, she left a fiery trail across the sky like a child's sparkler waved in the dark.

"That invitation from the Knights of Callixtus?" said Gillian. "Maybe you should reconsider."

"Why? I thought we wanted a more normal life. It was you who insisted we lay Mallory's spirit to rest."

"Sure," replied Gillian, "when she kept us apart. But now? Besides, let's face it, with everything we've seen and done, were we ever going to be content with normal lives?"

They watched Mallory rise into the sapphire sky, explode like a ship's flare, and then vanish. The sun was closing in on the horizon, gulls turned and tumbled in the strengthening wind, and the incoming tide marched steadily up the sand.

"I'm getting cold," said Gillian. "We'd better go soon, don't you think?"

Chris, who'd been deep in thought since Mallory's disappearance, took Gillian's mittened hands in his and whispered, "If I do go to Rome, will you go with me?"

"No, my love," Gillian replied with a tender smile. "I'll stay here to plan our wedding. And you'll return with that attractive compensation package the letter mentioned . . . and a ring." She chuckled and kissed his cheek.

Perhaps it was the approaching night, or maybe the ice-filled gale, but in that moment Chris shuddered as if someone had just walked across his grave.

References

[1] Sefer Yetzirah, Warsaw 1884, translated by Isidor Kalisch. New York, 1877

[2] The Jews' College (London) translation of the Babylonian Talmud (1935-1952) under the editorship of Rabbi Dr. Isidore Epstein

[3] There is no formally accepted spelling of Kabbalah. For this story, I chose to use the most common form, *Kabbalah,* to refer to the ancient and esoteric method, discipline, and school of Jewish thought, and Cabbalah to refer to its Christian corruption. The term Ktav Kabbala means license or permit to perform the duties of a *shochet*.

[4] *Soleram*, Wikipedia *Soleram* or *Suliram* is a traditional song of the Riau people. There are many variations in the lyrics found in Indonesia and Malaysia. Several artists have recorded the song including western artists like The Weavers, Pete Seeger and Miriam Makeba.

> *Suliram, Suliram, ram, ram*
> *Suliram, who is so sweet*
> *Oh, whose child is this*
> *So right to look so sweet*
> *High, oh, high is the Sun*
> *Suliram, the tethered calf of the buffalo has died*
> *Suliram, long have I sought for you*
> *But it's only now that I have you*

About the Author

Ivan Blake was born in England and immigrated with his family to Canada when he was five. He did his graduate studies at the University of Chicago and taught in universities for fifteen years before joining the Canadian Public Service. He served the Government of Canada for twenty years and then went on to lecture and advise governments all over the world. He now travels and writes solely for pleasure, and delights in reading, wines and his grandchildren.

Coming Soon!

IVAN BLAKE'S

READERS' FAVORITE AWARD-WINNING
EARTHEDGE

"An epic fantasy tale of war and adventure that is humorous, at times heartbreaking ... [with] robust characters, deft plotting, and beautiful prose.... Earthedge sets the bar when it comes to a blend of alternate history and fantasy." —*Readers' Favorite*

Earthedge is set in England in the 1960s, but an England in which Edward 8th never abdicated, electricity has not replaced steam, the Realm has waged three recent wars with the USA, and all scholarship must be approved by the all-powerful Royal and Ancient Academy of Knowledge. The Chancellor of the Academy, Lord Edmund of Muckyheath, harbours a dark secret, however, a secret which all his predecessors have concealed for five hundred years. It's a secret which if revealed will utterly destroy the Academy's credibility, and a secret which an upstart school teacher is determined to now tell the world. If the Chancellor doesn't kill him first, that is. What follows is a rollicking tale of exploration, young love, and war, involving stone boats, gum Arabic shooters, airships, and automata.

**For more information
visit: www.SpeakingVolumes.us**

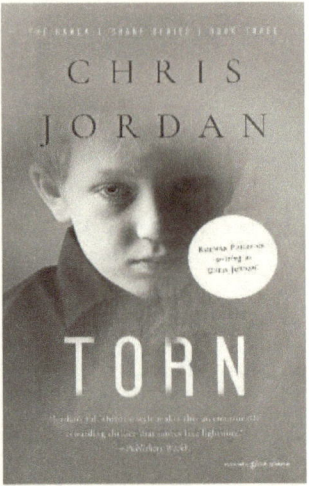
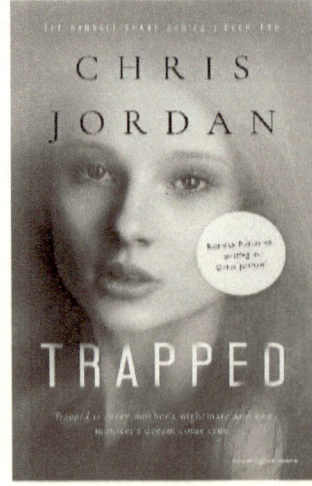
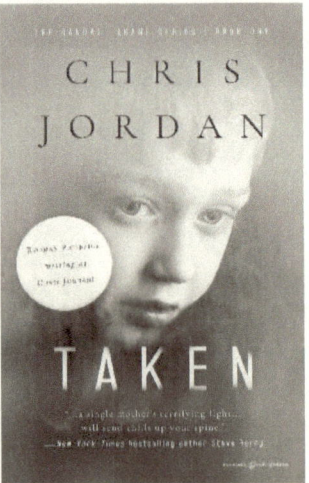

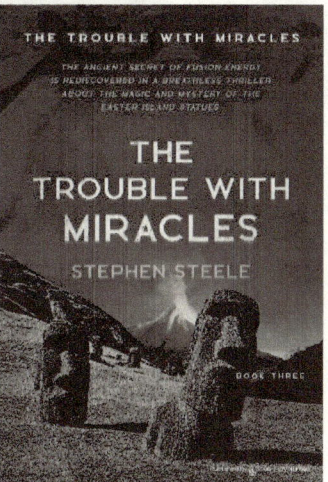

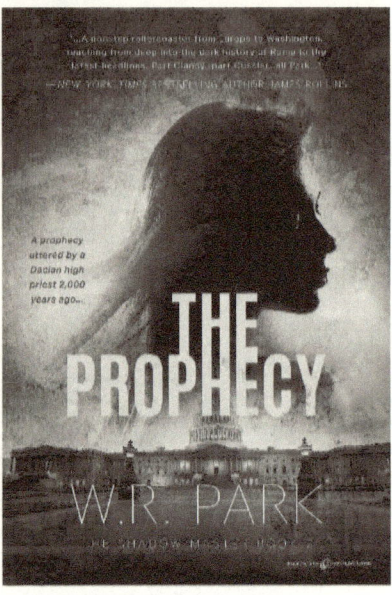